HELLBOUNCE

———————————————

THE ARC CHRONICLES BOOK 1

MATTHEW W. HARRILL

For the family Harrill:
Tricia, Ben, Scotty, Sammy, and Jess

THE ARC CHRONICLES

PROLOGUE

Madden Scott jammed his foot on the brake pedal of the stolen Chevrolet Malibu, causing the car to skid to a halt.

"I'm right. You're wrong. Get used to it."

Several white Toyotas blew past the end of the alleyway, their blue lights flashing and filled with Montego Bay constables, oblivious to the fact their prey had, for the moment, eluded them.

He took a moment to gaze up, through the pouring rain, at the building in front of him, the air conditioning only just enough to clear the moisture from the windshield. White. Colonial. Classic Jamaican Imperial architecture. He let the wheels find their grip on the dirt track.

"See? Where are we?"

"Canterbury," came the reply from Turell, the gang leader and mastermind behind their failed robbery on the local branch of the bank of Nova Scotia. Despite their argument, he kept his eyes trained on the road. "Let's go, man. They gonna notice we not there any minute now, man."

With voices of assent from the other two gang members,

Joseph and Delon, Madden took a breath to steady his nerves, and eased the car back out onto the road. His heart thumped hard in his chest, the sound thudding in his ears. Sweat made his palms slick and he squeezed the steering wheel to regain control. He edged the car back out, fearing pursuit. The wide road allowed a good view, dense woodland on one side in stark contrast to the dwellings of the rich and shameless on the other. Madden gunned the throttle, and the car lurched into action, back down towards the center of Montego Bay.

In the passenger seat, next to Madden, Turell turned to keep a watch out the rear window, his rancid breath causing Madden to turn his head away from the stale after-effects of a jerked-chicken feast.

Turell caught sight of his brother. "Damn, Jo. You got hit."

"I'll live. Bullet went right through. Babylon can't aim right." Joseph cradled his arm as Delon tied a makeshift bandage tight, blood seeping through the material almost as soon as it was complete.

Madden concentrated on driving. "So where to? You will have to tell me at some point, or we will run out of road."

"You concentrate on the driving, buccra," Turell used the Jamaican term for 'White Man' in such a way Madden was left with no illusion this was going to end well, "and I will tell you where to go. We are on Upper King Street. Head for Gloucester Avenue; let's blend in with the crowds."

Madden did as instructed, intending to blend with the busy traffic in downtown Montego Bay. Driving with purpose, but not too fast to be singled out, he considered the choices he had made to find himself in this position. He was not without regret.

Madden was a loner by nature, flitting from place to place, not really caring how he was received, using charm to wheedle jobs and women alike, his good looks and shoulder-length brown hair a natural attraction. He had developed a taste for fast cars, and in recent years, had come to settle in Jamaica, the laid-back lifestyle suiting him. His love of the underground street-racing scene had earned him the nickname 'Mad One', a play on words on his own name. And with time, he had come to know Turell Banks. Small courier jobs had become bigger and more illegal. Now he had reached the point that he was a getaway driver, albeit a reluctant one, in a robbery. He had to see this through to the end. Turell was not a man one said no to.

The rain beat down, and Madden opened the window of the Chevrolet for a better view, as the moisture inside threatened to render the air conditioning redundant. Water sprayed in, adding to the sweat on his hands. Taking a couple of back streets, he avoided the highway that had been the scene of the chase.

"Man I'm hungry," Joseph complained. "Mad One, there's a KFC up ahead. I'm bruk-pocket. Go get me."

"Yu mussi born back a cow," Turell admonished his brother. "No food till we make it safe."

Madden stopped the car in traffic, attempting to appear nonchalant. They were in the busiest part of town now, near the beaches. Even in this mild tropical storm the streets were busy. He had no choice but to move slowly. As he did so, he spied the blue-and-whites of more Jamaican police. One officer saw him, and raised a walkie-talkie to his lips.

Turell warned, "Them seen us! Drive!"

Several police cars converged toward their spot, sirens

blaring. Madden had no choice but to floor it. The car lurched forward, beaches and stunning ocean to the left, with police in pursuit. People jumped out of the way, but they were a blur as Madden focussed on the road, becoming one with the car. "We are on Gloucester," he shouted above the noise of the engine, and the ricochet of bullets on the road as their pursuers tried to take out the tires, "but the road is blocked up past the Coral Cliff Hotel and that's only a kilometre off. So if you have a plan, tell me now."

Turell just stared ahead, his wits deserting him.

"Damnit Turell, where? The Coral Cliff? Burger King? The sea? Where?"

"Tru dem barrier." Turell answered.

"What?"

Turell brandished the glock he had taken from his police victim. "You drive, tru dem barrier, or I kill you myself, Iree?"

Madden shook his head and concentrated. Behind them, several police cars were jostling for position, each trying to get around him. He held the line of the road and the beaches flashed past all too quickly. The so-called 'Hip Strip', known for its restaurants and bars disappeared in moments.

The road veered away from the coast for a moment. "You had better be right about this," Madden growled.

As the road swung back to the coast, Madden saw flashing lights ahead. By the Margaritaville restaurant, perched right on the edge of the water, several police cars blocked the road. A small army of police waited behind, guns already raised. Waves burst over the rocks, blurring with the slate-grey sky. Madden aimed for the small gap between the middle two cars, preferring the attempt to a bullet to the head. About ten metres out, a boat was moored;

white with a pale-blue underbelly, it rolled with the waves churned up by the storm. In a moment of clarity, Madden saw one officer raise his gun, take aim, and fire.

The bullet smashed a hole in the windshield, whistling past Madden's ear. In the rear-view mirror, Madden saw red mist and gore all over the back window.

"Joseph!" Screamed Turell, "Joseph, No!" Turell tried to climb to the back seat to comfort his already-dead brother as more shots were fired. The front left tire exploded.

The car swerved, skidding on the wet surface, and jumped as it hit the curb. The momentum lifted the car up over the all-too-small sea wall and out through the spume over the cerulean water.

"Hold on!" Madden shouted, and threw his head forward, protecting his neck with his arms.

Screams from passengers rang in his ears. The car flipped upside down as it flew through the air, and Madden felt the air blast in through the now-smashed windshield. There was a crunch as the car landed atop the boat, and then an instant of heat and darkness.

Madden found himself adrift in the water, a couple of feet from the surface, and propelled himself up with sure strokes. Unsure how he got there, he floated for a moment to get his bearings. He ached, but it was more of a tingle, and not the pain of someone recently in a car wreck. Just metres away, he could see the mangled mess of car and boat, on fire in places and mostly submerged, a small oil slick being whipped up by the waves.

He swam away, using the momentum of the waves to push him toward the shore where he climbed the rocks, and sat shivering against the sea wall. Behind him, the lights of the police vehicles flashed blue, magnified by the addition of his pursuers. Police approached, and stood beside him.

"Man, ain't nobody gettin' outta dat alive," one said to his fellows. "There's four bodies to be pulled out. Them say it's Turell, his brother, cousin and them white boy driver. Let's go grab a brew and wait."

The police stared for a moment, and moved off, seeking the refuge of the Margaritaville. Madden sat there confused, staring at his shaking hands. Something swelled beneath the skin. Madden closed his eyes and took a deep breath. When he opened them, his hands were normal again. The police were chatting in the distance. They hadn't even noticed him.

CHAPTER ONE

The ABC logo flashed up on the television set, white letters on a blue circle. The logo glinted for a moment and disappeared.

"Welcome back to ABC news with Jeanette Gibson," blared the strong male voiceover. The screen showed an elegant woman approaching her middle years with the confidence of a consummate professional, along with the knowledge she was fronting one of the biggest media outlets in the world.

It never failed to impress Eva Ross, who had wished for a career in media as a child, but through happenstance and a natural aptitude for the human mind, had studied hard to become a psychotherapist. She tried to work out the depths of the human psyche, specifically in those who lacked morals. Her career path had led far from her home of Sioux City, Iowa. She had studied at several universities, gaining accreditation that had eventually led her to the Worcester State Hospital in Massachusetts, a post she had held for two years now.

"In other news," Jeanette Gibson announced with a

look of mock severity on her face, "there has been a wave of amnesia attacks in Marblehead, a small town in Essex County, Massachusetts. The coastal community has been plagued by sailors who, dressed as eighteenth-century smugglers, seem unable to remember their names or how, in fact, they even arrived at the town."

The screen cut to footage of a group of men with wide trousers, flared sleeves, all bearing the three-pointed Tricorn hats of the era in brown and black.

"Those affected are undergoing treatment in a local hospital, but lacking any credible proof, police suspect it to be either a local hoax, or as one officer put it: 'Something in the water'".

Eva let her mind wander, no longer paying any attention to the police officer the reporter was interviewing, trying to sound grave and sincere about such a light-hearted topic.

On her break between counselling sessions, she relaxed by watching the world outside, wishing she was there. It was late autumn, a hazy afternoon that showed yellow leaves clinging stubbornly, in an all too common attempt to deny the onset of winter, to the grove of American Linden that grew around the hospital. It was a lovely time of year, and for a moment, Eva could forget exactly where she was and why.

"And finally, the strange case of a convenience store clerk who was held hostage while the kidnappers ate everything in sight."

Eva flicked the television off, and tied her shoulder-length brown hair back with one of several hair bands she habitually kept on her right wrist. Donning her red sweater, Eva set off for her office. Tradition held they should all wear the white coats so typical of their profession, but only her boss stuck to it, and despite his apparent officiousness, never insisted on anybody else doing the same. It reminded the convicted criminals with which they dealt too much of where they were.

On her way through the corridors of the rotting clock tower that was basically all that remained of the old hospital, Eva mulled over the questions she was going to ask her current patient. A clever man, highly intelligent and, in no small way, devious, Harold Fronhouse presented a challenge. Unlocking his mind was a gradual process. She was so preoccupied with her plan of attack she jumped when a hand touched her shoulder.

She turned to see the grinning young face of Jenny Slater, all blonde curly locks and movie star visage. "I'm sorry, Jenny, I didn't hear you."

"I shouted loud enough, four or five times," the grad student replied in a husky voice that belied her relative youth. "I'm joining you today. I was told you are interviewing."

"Oh, you are?" Eva gave her a sly look and began to walk on, amused by Jenny's attempt to include herself. "What you mean is you were nosing over my schedule trying to see whether what I was doing today would help advance your studies."

Jenny had the credit to look embarrassed, a slow flush creeping into her cheeks. "Well yes, there is that. But Doctor Homes has given me permission to sit in today."

Eva stopped and turned, putting her hand on the wall, the whitewash chalky under her hand.

"He doesn't have the right."

"Well that's what he told me. He said I had to find you and sit in on the Fronhouse interview. He said it would be a good case to study an extreme case of borderline personality disorder."

"There is more to it than the Wikipedia definition of borderline personality disorder you know," Eva warned. "We used to call them 'psychopaths' and this one is as bad as they come."

They passed through secure doors to the interview rooms. Fading light bulbs gave the corridor a sinister feel.

"Are you certain you wish to do this?" Eva asked, placing her hand on the younger woman's shoulder. There was an eagerness in Jenny's eyes that screamed innocence and a lack of caution.

"Yes. I started this, and now I need to be responsible for my decisions. Even if I don't like what I am getting into."

"You get immune to it after a while."

"If you look at them as animals, I am sure you do."

"Save the psychoanalysis for the patient, Jenny. You can tell me later just how you convinced Gideon to approve this."

Outside the room, a guard waited. "Dr Ross," he said by way of a perfunctory greeting, "our boy is acting up today. You sure you want her in there with you?"

Eva turned to observe Jenny, who still didn't look right, and could feel the guard's eyes on her. She dismissed the puerile male stirrings. "You are fine, aren't you, Jenny?"

"Yes... yes. I am fine."

The guard shrugged meaty shoulders as if he didn't care either way. "Don't say I didn't warn you."

. . .

He led them into a white room, bare of all furnishings except two seats and a small table. Sterile luminous light gave the room a pale eerie glow, but it was the other occupant of the room that drew the eye.

Harold Fronhouse was a short man, not far over five feet in height. He sat secured in a straightjacket, and strapped to a wheelchair. He wore no mask. As Eva and Jenny entered the room, he watched, unblinking. As Jenny sat down, he gazed at her with the eyes of a predator. "Nice."

Eva glanced at Jenny, who watched Harold the way a small child watched a stranger, not taking her eyes off him. She was uncomfortable.

"Harold. How are you today?"

"Hungry," came the reply, although Fronhouse still had not taken his eyes off Jenny. This was going bad quickly.

"Well I see from your records you don't appear to have had much problem with your meals."

Fronhouse eyed Jenny up and down once more, and then turned his head to Eva. "Unsatisfied." His eyes widened slightly and he fidgeted.

"Nothing changes then," agreed Eva, motioning Jenny to take notes, more to give her something to do than for the need. "Harold likes to play games," Eva lectured. "One-word answers can go on for days if he feels like it. It's a shame. He is such a conversationalist. But I know what you love to talk about, don't I?" Eva spoke as she would to a pet.

In response, Fronhouse grinned, the vacuous smile of one not in possession of all their mental faculties. "The bomb."

Eva leaned forward, a conspirator to his cause. "Yes the bomb. Why don't you tell us the story of the bomb?"

Fronhouse trembled with excitement, and looked at Eva as if seeking to please a master. "I was young, not more than a child. We lived in a farmhouse in the hills. My parents used to have parties. The sorts of parties where you put your car keys in a jar and the wife left with whoever owned the keys she pulled out. They loved that sort of thing. It gave them excitement.

Over time, my mother pulled the same keys repeatedly. My father grew suspicious." Fronhouse cackled to himself at some perceived vision.

"He took me with him once and showed me my mother and her lover through a window in the house. He was behind her. They were naked. She was moaning." Fronhouse again watched Jenny as he said this, evidently gauging the impact of his words. Jenny had dropped her pad and pen in her lap, just staring.

Fronhouse, restless now, fidgeted more. "My father took me home and told me he was going to make my mother pay for this, and he wanted my help. We built a bomb, and fitted it under her car." He turned his head to one side and growled: "Yes, I can feel it, too."

"What can you feel, Harold?"

Fronhouse smiled, a cold, calculating mask. "When she shifted into fourth gear, the bomb blew, and the car was incinerated. There was nothing left. As for the man, my father cut his throat. We cooked him and I ate his face. GET THESE SHACKLES OFF ME. HE IS CLOSE!"

"Who? Harold, who is close?"

"I can't tell you. The mere thought of it would send you into madness, a despair of such black depths you would end yourself in moments." Fronhouse shook his head, and his eyes focussed once more. "I have shared myself, with you. Now you can share yourself with me. An eye for an eye, Dr Ross."

Jenny was clearly shaken. The experience was nearly

too much for her. "No, I don't think so. That is enough for today." Eva went to pick up her notes and leave the room.

"No. It is not." Fronhouse's voice was commanding. "Your brat wants to taste a little more, to see into my brain. Am I not right?"

Despite everything, Jenny answered. "That is correct. I want to know what makes you tick."

"You want to know why I do the things I do. Pain. I am in pain."

Eva put her hand to her forehead, rubbing her eyebrows. "Aren't we all?"

"I will share my pain with you, little bird, when you tell me about how your father abused you as a child. I can see it in your eyes, read it in every fiber of your being. You are broken, and you seek redemption through understanding, knowing there was something that drove him to it, and not just his own small-minded cruelty."

Eva had warned her, and despite everything, Fronhouse had her. Jenny had put her hand to her mouth, and wordless sounds came out. Pain beyond description welled from every pore. He had hit right on the mark.

"This ends now."

"No!" Jenny contradicted her. "He is right. There is always a reason."

"Jenny, you do not have to do this."

"Oh but she *needs* to, to find out who she really is." Fronhouse continued, and his face grew angry. "My skin, it tingles. I can end this all now. Let me out!" In an instant, his demeanour changed back to the intelligent, cold mask of a killer. "How to describe what I am? Bound but not gagged. Never gagged. How to describe you? Slut. You drove him to it. You encouraged him, and you loved it."

Jenny fled, throwing the door open, her feet echoing off the stone of the hallway as she ran.

Fronhouse grinned, satisfied. "Well wasn't that fun?"

Ignoring him, Eva looked to the guard. "What is his medical condition?"

"Fine, last time we checked." He implied that next time, Harold Fronhouse might not be in such a good condition.

"See he stays that way."

It was meant to be comforting to the patient, since Eva was a firm believer that while many patients needed a strict regimen, those not in authority far too often took it upon themselves to impose revenge.

Fronhouse screamed at her, a wordless expression of rage and anguish; the impotent struggle against his bonds not deterring him at all. "I need to get free! He is near!"

"Who, Harold? Who is near?" Eva stepped closer.

"One weaker than I am. I can prey on him. The pain. It is everywhere. I can feast and then I am free." He howled at the walls once more. "Master, I can do it. Unbind me!"

"Who is your master, Harold? Tell me. Who are you seeking?"

Fronhouse twisted yet more, wriggling beneath the straightjacket, his legs taut against the straps. His narrow eyes focussed on her.

"You think anything you do matters? You think this matters? Release me, and it will be over quickly. Leave me here, and another will do my job. But others will make it last forever."

"What others?"

"To describe what they do would drive the sanity from your being. We flee. You would do best to run and hide, though they will find you. They find everyone." With that, the fight in him evaporated, and Harold Fronhouse sat motionless, looking through her.

Eva recognised this particular state of catatonia. "We won't get anything more from him, now. Take him back to his room."

The guard wheeled Fronhouse out, and Eva stared at the walls without noticing, her heart thudding in her chest. She screwed her hands into fists, her nails digging painfully into her palms. She had almost reached him. The words of Harold Fronhouse still echoed from the walls. "Others will make it last forever... I can feast and then I am free... He is near..." The phrases left her uncomfortable and nervous.

CHAPTER TWO

Outside, Jenny stood waiting as Eva closed the door. Her face was a mask of horror, pain mixed with the re-emergence of memories that had been repressed for far too long.

"Jenny, I am so sorry." Eva enfolded her in a hug, feeling the warmth of tears on her chest as Jenny's shoulders trembled with each sob.

At length, Jenny calmed down and stood back, taking the tissue Eva offered to dry her face.

"Satisfied now?"

"Dr Ross, I didn't mean to undermine you in there. I just wanted the chance."

"Yes, you did," Eva replied with genuine amusement. "I am afraid you are a little too much like I was once for your own good. You will learn."

"You still don't think it was a good idea?"

"No, as a matter of fact, I don't, but I promised you we would abide by Dr Homes' decision, and that is exactly what we did. It is your decision whether the end justified the means."

Eva handed Jenny a file and started down the corridor.

"Take a look on the way and consider carefully what I said to you earlier about BPDs."

As Eva walked, she could sense Jenny trying to keep up, and falling farther behind as she became engrossed in the notes. The silence became oppressive. As they descended to the first floor where the more dangerous patients were housed, Eva looked back to find Jenny had stopped, her face drained of colour. "Do you see now what you were dealing with?"

"He... He actually did this? Ate a man's face? While he was still alive?"

"Yes, and he was shot and wounded as he tried to escape. The victim is still receiving treatment in Miami, six months after it happened. Harold was transferred here within a month of being detained for evaluation. Dr Homes recommended an extended term given his particular characteristics."

"Which are what?"

"He has an uncanny ability to get inside your head. He is extremely intelligent. If you are not careful, you end up feeling like you are the interviewee and not the interviewer. He can get right under your skin. The point is he knew exactly what he was doing when he started to feed on that homeless man, much as he had a plan of attack the moment you stepped through that door. I want you to consider everything you witnessed in that room, not as the victim of his cruel abuse, but as a future Doctor of Psychology. Put away emotion, and look at what was said, the stimuli for each of his responses. You might have been an innocent in that room, but you damned well came near to unlocking him. I'll expect a report in the morning, but for now, I have questions of my own that need answering.

Go on home. My next conversation may not be for your ears."

Jenny turned toward the exit. "Eva, thank you."

Eva smiled at her, and resumed walking.

The long white, sterile corridors glowed eerily under the lights did nothing to put Eva at ease. The air conditioning whined in the background, straining as it sought to keep the old building at a reasonable temperature. Eva sometimes imagined there were voices whispering behind that noise.

Reaching the top floor of the hospital via narrow stairs crowded with faded paintings of Worcester in its infancy on the walls, Eva avoided the temptation to seek refuge in her own office, instead knocking on the door of her colleague and mentor, Dr Gideon Homes.

Dr Homes was considered pre-eminent in the field of compulsive mental disorders, and over the time she had known him, he had molded her in his image. A once rash and outspoken young grad student had become a thoughtful, introspective doctor under his tutelage. *That is what Jenny hopes I will do for her*. Eva thought as a voice called, "Come in".

Eva opened the door and entered the room. Gideon Homes turned in his chair from a bank of screens that piped feed from all over the hospital directly to his office. Bespectacled, and with a shock of iron-grey hair, her mentor, friend, and colleague greeted her with a smile. Standing up, he towered over her, at several inches over six feet, and, with a frame one could only call 'brawny', he cut an imposing figure.

"Quite a session, don't you think?" he observed. "What do you make of it?"

Eva shook her head. "Ravings of a paranoid delusional.

It could be the key to his present state, or it could mean nothing at all. You know these cases as well as I do. Better in fact." Eva shuffled her notes and sat opposite him, the ancient leather of her seat creaking in protest. "What should not have happened there is Jenny. You should not have given her permission to attend. Harold saw right through her, and toyed with her like a damaged hare given to a pack of wolf cubs. The poor girl could be scarred for life. How dare you presume to treat one of our own staff like that? What were you thinking?"

"The girl learned a valuable life lesson," Gideon countered, the smirk on his face betraying his amusement. "Never run before you can walk. I don't think we will see her attempt that again, not until she is much more mature. Wanting and having are two different things altogether do you not think?"

"Jenny thought an interview with such a deranged mind would be good for her, much like children dream of petting animals at a zoo. Did you give her that impression?"

Gideon responded by picking up an apple and crunching into it, waving the fruit around in the air with his left hand as he mulled the idea over.

"Interesting," Gideon replied as he leaned back on his desk, "that you describe them as such. They have minds, and at some point in their lives have had the capacity to make rational choices, yet you label them with a common denominator. They are in here against their will, and we view them without any necessary attachment, yet this is not the zoo you claim to think it is."

Moving to lock a cabinet he nearly always kept shut, Gideon continued, "No I think this is more the result of a ploy for you to keep our little fledgling safe, Dr Ross. It sounded like a great idea to me. There are times when we should act with caution and others when we should go with instinct. If this bird believes it is time to fly, who are we to clip her wings?"

"But Harold Fronhouse...'

'Is unstable, impulsive, has, in the past, shown cannibalistic tendencies, and you don't know from one second to the next what mood he will be in. Yes, he is an interesting 'animal'."

The way Gideon used her words against her was not lost on Eva.

"He is also bound in a straightjacket, and has guards with him at all times. If he needs sedating, we have Thorazine. If you fear what he might say to her, please remember you were similar in age when I first spotted you, and you were already deep into a thesis on stress-related paranoia and had interviewed several inmates at Cedar Junction. That is a maximum security facility, not unlike this."

Eva stared at Gideon, aghast a man she had trusted to guide her so many times in the past had acted with such recklessness.

"Are you saying that this was all part of an experiment? Just so you could sit up here and observe from afar, the dismantling of a young mind? You could have ended that young woman's career in there."

"And you could have made it your triumph. Consider it a lesson for you and her both. As you rightly said, you nearly unlocked the mind of one seriously beyond redemption."

His tone infuriated her. "That is not just wrong, it is unethical. What happened to you, Gideon? You never treated me this way when I was a student. I am going to my office, and then home. I have had enough of this for one day.

If this is your current approach to medicine, I don't expect much in the way of results. Not if you don't have any staff. I'll see you in the morning."

Gideon had already turned back to his research, and Eva had been taught very early on that was his method of dismissal. Never before had it been used on her.

CHAPTER THREE

Still fuming, Eva made short work of depositing her documents and leaving the hospital. Her mood was tempered somewhat by the gorgeous afternoon, but she still appeared stained. She turned once, glaring at the clock tower, a monolith thrust amongst a sea of greenery, turned, and walked off.

Her house was only a half-hour stroll from the hospital, so most days Eva walked. Prudence kept her to the roads that snaked through the bio research park, but feeling belligerent, Eva took a straight line through the remains of the woodland that had once formed a great forest over much of Worcester.

The grove of American Linden towered over Eva as leaves crunched underfoot, the thinning canopy a riot of bright yellow. In the breeze, small nuts, disturbed by the motion from their casings, dropped to the ground. Chipmunks scampered around in a frenzy amidst the fallen leaves collecting the treasure, twittering warnings at her as she passed. She had not been in the woods long, on the path that led to one of the many parking lots, before Eva sensed she was not alone. Turning slowly, she saw a figure sitting on a bench, facing away from her. The figure was hunched, shoulders shaking. Anger broke like a wave against a cliff of compassion, and Eva walked over to a sobbing Jenny.

Sitting beside Jenny, Eva put her arms around the girl, but Jenny pushed her away.

"I don't deserve comfort. I've done terrible things."

"Would it help to talk about it?"

Jenny wiped her face with the sleeve of her hoodie. "No, not particularly. You warned me. I was not ready. He was right. There are some things that are unforgiveable."

"You mean your father? You cannot be held responsible for the acts of others, if that is what happened."

"Well, he was right. I am a slut. If I am allowed to dwell in this kingdom of self-loathing, it is because it is a realm of my own making. He raped me as a child, but I think I wanted him to, even though he was my own father. The memories are beyond horrific, now I consider them as an adult. Can we leave here?"

"Certainly. Where do you live?"

"Wells Street, though I spend more time with my boyfriend a couple of blocks away."

"I'll walk with you, if that's okay. You live two streets down, and I'd rather make sure you got home than wake up to hear someone else has jumped in front of a car on Belmont."

Jenny shrugged and set off. The girl did not want to talk, and, after the recent revelations, that was understandable. Eva walked alongside in silence, enjoying the late afternoon air despite everything that had happened. They passed the huge white bulk of the research center, looming above the trees like some huge squatting spider. Every time Eva saw the building, she got the chills. There was something unwholesome about the place, something sterile and unnatural. She did not know what went on in there, but had heard stories about vivisection and worse. It was what kept her on the roads rather than taking this more direct route.

At length they reached Belmont Street, the main road that bisected Worcester, and waited to cross the six lanes of traffic.

"Steady now," Eva warned. "No dramatic gestures."

This brought a laugh from Jenny. "You know what I just figured? Be very careful when a trained psychologist asks you if you are okay."

"True, but we don't always ask for professional reasons. I'm concerned for you, personally, not professionally."

A further guffaw from Jenny coincided with the lights changing, and then they walked across. The arterial traffic faded into the background very quickly as they walked down a very quiet Plantation Street, and then Jenny made a turn.

"This is me. Thank you for walking with me. I'm afraid I am not much of a conversationalist on days like this."

Eva looked past her up the road. "Your father..."

"Is dead. I pushed him down some stairs and something inside him broke. I sat with him and watched him die as he tried to call for help. It's not something I am proud of, but he got what he deserved. The police only saw a dead fat man with his small daughter. It is certainly not something you are going to get me to admit in front of anyone else. Come to think of it, I may be leaving anyway."

"Don't make a hasty decision," Eva warned. "You could have a good career ahead of you."

"My time is limited." Jenny countered. "That much will become obvious soon enough. Thanks for the company."

Leaving her standing at the end of the road, Jenny trudged off without looking back. Amused at the impulsive tendencies of youth, Eva smiled and headed home.

Northboro Street was a typical example of the affluent Worcester suburbs. The houses were large, and, for the most part, spread far enough apart to give decent privacy. Eva did not see it this way. It instilled in her a sense of isolation. There was no community spirit, and everybody kept to themselves, with furtive glances or twitches of a curtain being the only methods of communication. The gardens were all huge, and the gnarled trees betrayed evidence of the ancient woodland that had been invaded by the city.

Since Eva wasn't feeling particularly sociable, today she was glad of the quiet nature of the place. Strolling down the road, she paid scant attention to the other houses, instead concentrating on her own.

About halfway down the road, on the left, loomed a white house with green roof; her husband's utility truck parked out front across the path. The house was shrouded by birch trees on one side, and giant spruces to the rear, leaving it gloomy even in the afternoon sun. In the silence outside, Eva could sense something was amiss. An insistent banging was coming from within her house, and it appeared several of the windows had been boarded up.

Worried, Eva walked round the side of the house and entered the utility room. "Brian?"

The banging stopped. There was no movement, just silence. Eva looked around, seeking some cause of this odd behaviour. Nothing was amiss in the kitchen, aside from a smattering of unwashed dishes. However, there was nothing unusual with that. The house stood empty for most of the day. Eva was at the hospital, and Brian was the manager of a local sporting goods store.

Their lifestyle suited them. Eva had fallen for Brian at school, where he played football. Despite his marked intellectual inferiority, and his tendency during the early years to embark on a series of affairs, they had remained together. Many times Eva had asked herself 'Am I attracted to bad boys?' and could not see beyond the simple answer that she was. They answered a call in her. They were everything she was not: rugged, primal, dependent. Brian had dropped out of the College of the Holy Cross, where he had been awarded a football scholarship, in order to work at Modell's, where his athletic prowess had earned him status, and the aforementioned female interest.

Still, he had provided for her, and while she had studied, he worked. When a nervous proposal of marriage had come along, Eva felt obliged to say yes, even though deep down she knew she could have done better. "Sometimes you just accept what life deals out," her father used to say, implying she would never amount to anything.

"Brian?" Eva called again. Still nothing. Moving from the kitchen, she glanced in the study. Nothing, but the windows were indeed boarded up. The living room, bedecked with antique fireplace looked like it, too, was set to be a refuge from an external assault, wooden slats nailed haphazardly across the window panes.

Eva climbed the stairs. Afternoon became twilight in the reduced light. In silence, she put her hand to her mouth as she saw one of the walls had nearly been completely torn down to provide wood for the windows. With a slowly mounting sense of dread, Eva checked the rooms. Still nothing. The windows were all boarded in the same untidy fashion, but of her husband, there was no sign. Curtains had been torn asunder in their bedroom in haste. Nails strewn across the floor suggested this was the latest site of her husband's mysterious activity, but he was nowhere to be seen.

"Brian. Where are you? Why are you doing this? Come out and we can talk." Eva stood in silence, trying to gauge any sound of movement.

The banging resumed, as loud as if it were next to her, and she realised the reason was the laundry chute to the basement. Unintelligible mutterings accompanied the noise.

Not waiting for her husband to move again, Eva flew down the stairs, two at a time, and screamed.

CHAPTER FOUR

BRIAN ROSS, A BALDING MAN WITH A BARREL CHEST and a raptor's gaze, stood in the hallway blocking her exit. In one hand, he held a well-worn hammer, gripped like a club. He grinned, but it was not a grin of amusement.

"Brian, what are you doing?" Eva searched her husband's face, but it was as if there was nothing familiar between them. He recognized her, but his expression was one of someone who coveted a prize.

"I know what you are thinking," he began, "and you aren't going to do it. We have been together for too long for you to leave now."

"Brian, what are you talking about? Leave? Why would I want to leave?"

Her answer confused him "I... I know you think you are better than I am. You always have all the answers. You are always right. I know you have been thinking about going. I see the cases packed."

"Cases? What cases? Brian, you are making no sense."

"I see the cases packed," Brian insisted. "I won't let you go."

Years of experience told Eva there was something very wrong here. Her husband had always been jealous of her intellect, but she thought he had accepted her for what she was, and their differences were not a barrier to a relationship. He seemed to be coming unhinged, and she was alone in this boarded-up house with him. And he had a potential weapon in his hand.

"Brian, why don't you put the hammer down, and we can talk. It's clear something or someone has upset you."

In response, he threw the hammer past her head, where it embedded itself in the wall. Now his hands were fists. "Yes, why don't we do that?" His reply dripped sarcasm. "Why don't I take a seat, and you can make a lovely cup of tea for us both while I wait." He stalked off into the living room.

Eva took a deep breath and tried to remain calm. "I won't be long."

"Take all the time you want," came the reply. "You aren't going anywhere."

Realizing her peril, Eva went straight to the rack of knives hanging from the kitchen wall. All gone. In fact, any implement that could be used as a weapon had been removed. There were only teaspoons left in the drawer. Trying to make as little noise as possible, Eva tried the door that led out the back of the house. It was bolted, and nails had been driven into the door through the door frame. Gently shaking the door, she found it would not budge.

"I told you that you are going nowhere," came her husband's voice from right behind her, and Eva jumped as he gripped her shoulder hard. "You won't leave me again. Not now."

"Brian... you are hurting me. Why are you doing this?"

"I came to the realization when I was talking to a

customer at work," he began. "You pity me. You think I'm pond scum. You always have. You leave in the morning, without even saying goodbye. I might as well just be another houseguest to you. You have been looking for a way out for years. Even before we got this place. Well, I don't want to lose you and now I'm not going to."

"And how is boarding the house up going to accomplish anything meaningful?"

Brian shoved her hard into the table, knocking the air form her lungs. "Well, you are in here aren't you? You can't get out, can you? Who's not so clever now?"

There was a knock at the front door. Brian paused in his assault, pulled out a silver snub-nosed revolver and pointed it at her. With his free hand, he put his finger to his lips. "I am going to answer that, and you are not going to make a sound."

Eva was trapped. She sat against the table, rubbing her forehead with one hand. Floorboards creaked as Brian moved down the hall to open the door. Eva dared not move. Brian's anger could be ferocious and misdirected. She took slow breaths, trying to keep a rational mind.

In the hallway, Eva heard a young woman speaking to Brian. She edged closer, seeking to gain a glimpse of whoever it was. As she peered past the doorframe, things suddenly became very clear.

"Dan, you have to let me in. We have to talk."

"I'm sorry, Jennifer. There are many alterations being made. It would be dangerous for you to come in here. Let me come out and we can go for a walk."

"No, I don't have time. Look Dan, I'm going to lay it out straight for you. I'm late."

"Late for what?" The enormity of the statement hit Eva

worse than the table had, but the words were lost on Brian, who was trying too hard to put on a false front.

"My period. I did a test and... well... see for yourself." The young woman handed something to Brian, and as he reached out to take it, Eva could see 'Jennifer' was, in fact, Jenny. Eva covered her mouth with her hand, but could not prevent the tears coming. Her stomach contracted, and she thought she would vomit at any moment. She placed her other hand over her own womb. This girl had achieved something Eva thought was never going to happen in her own lifetime. Her grief blended with anger, and suddenly, Eva didn't see a potential captor, not even a patient. She saw something she loathed.

Brian waved the pregnancy test around. "What is it? A thermometer?"

"Dan, it says I'm pregnant. Look, we need to talk about this. I have a job at the hospital. I am going to have to give this up if I don't get rid of the baby."

"No... No you won't do that. Life is precious. Look, go on over to Chuck's, the cafe on Vineland, and I'll meet you there in about ten minutes. There's something I have to take care of first."

The way Brian said 'something' sounded like 'someone' to Eva. She moved back to the kitchen table, her fury consuming her.

Brian came back in, the effort of his facade still showing on his face. "So you heard all that, I guess?"

Eva was so mad; she had trouble forming the words. "Yes, *Dan*. Everything is clear now. I can see why Jenny wants to leave. I can see why you want me boarded up in here. I can see I should never have trusted you after the last time you had an affair."

The warning signs had all been there. Her husband was

cracking up, but Eva was too mad to care. Whereas the affairs had been meaningless and forgivable in the past, now she saw them in a different light. Before, he might have been endearing, now he disgusted her.

In response, Brian picked up a potted plant, and smashed it against the wall, obliterating it and showering the floor with dirt. He wasn't ready to assault her directly, yet. "This is all your fault," he shouted.

"Really? How so?"

Brian stalked round the kitchen, pointing at her. "You pushed me away. For years, you have. No loving, no comfort. Always your smug superior glances. The sex was always bad."

"What sex?"

"Exactly!" The roar stopped her in her tracks. "I am a man. What do you expect me to do? Sit around and wait for you to be in the mood? I have needs, too!"

"Clearly," Eva observed. "Brian, you have to understand we are in a relationship. There is more to a long-term relationship than just having sex. There is commitment, for one."

"Don't you start to analyse me, woman. I am not one of your patients. I have had affairs, more than you ever knew about. I never stopped."

He wasn't listening, and any remaining sympathy was rapidly draining out of her. "And now you have got exactly what you wanted. A child on the way. Responsibility."

"And I have you to care for it, to bring up my child as the mother you should have been. Get used to these boarded windows, Eva. You aren't going anywhere." Brian pulled out his gun and pointed it in her direction, his arm steady. "If you even think about breaking out, I will use this to make sure you can never leave. We have both watched 'Misery'."

"You won't have any child as soon as Jenny's parents find out she is pregnant," Eva taunted. "You had best go get your prize, if you intend to keep her."

The comment appeared to disrupt any thoughts Brian was having of torture, and his arm wavered. He looked towards the front door. "You wait there. Right there. If I hear any creaking floorboards as I leave, you can bet the first thing I do when I return is make good on that promise." Brian backed out of the room, hungry eyes watching her the whole time.

Eva remained still, although inside she was seething and terrified. It was best not to give him any excuse to stay. The door slammed and the locks clicked as Brian bolted her prison. Eva counted to sixty, praying his attention span only left him waiting outside that long, and crept to the window.

Brian was halfway down the street, with the occasional glance back. There was no way he could see her moving now.

Not waiting a moment longer, Eva dashed upstairs to the room she had shared with her husband, threw open the cupboards and drawers, and began to stuff clothing into a suitcase.

Being of fastidious nature, Eva had all of her clothes sorted and organised. It did not take long. Throwing toiletries on top, Eva paused as she looked at a small statuette Brian had given her on their first wedding anniversary. Tempted to keep it as a memento of better times, Eva remembered what she was doing and why, picked up the statuette and pocketed it. Money would not be a problem. She was the main breadwinner and they had no joint accounts, a fact that had riled her husband immensely over the years. A picture of her parents and her as a child topped the bag off and she was done.

Eva began by trying the slats nailed in their bedroom. She had to give Brian his due; the nails were embedded deep in the frame, driven there with force derived from rage. Her husband was becoming a very dangerous creature. Bag on shoulder, Eva worked her way methodically around the house, aware Brian could return at any moment. Everything was firm, on the ground level, too.

Flummoxed, Eva rested against the heavy front door. Then a thought hit her. "He was in the basement," she said to the empty house. Not wasting a second, Eva charged down the hall and prayed as she tried the door to the basement. It was unlocked. Heart hammering in her chest, Eva flicked on the lights and descended.

The basement was a scene of chaos. Everything Brian had taken from her was down here. Normally this room was Brian's domain, his man cave, and showed evidence of his habitation. Beer cans lined one wall. Unmarked DVD's, the contents of which Eva shuddered to consider, surrounded the television and video. Cutlery was strewn on the floor, and the doors up the steps to the garden... were secured by only one fastened wooden plank.

Excitement overcame fear. Eva pulled out the statuette, using it to work the nails loose. It was an onerous task, and the nails were reluctant to give up their hold on the doors. Eva persisted, and was rewarded when one end of the plank worked loose. Reinvigorated, Eva jammed the head of the statuette under the wood and heaved.

The wood sprang free, and the statuette flew from her hand, smashing the screen of the television. Not waiting to enjoy the triumph, Eva pushed one of the doors open with great care, hoping Brian hadn't returned.

All was silent outside. The sky had greyed somewhat as afternoon approached evening. This only served to make the atmosphere more oppressive. He could be anywhere. Eva closed the door for the sake of appearances, and set off through the woods at the back of her garden. The coverage was good, but Eva stuck to the shadows nonetheless. Not wasting time on hiding her tracks or doubling back, Eva headed straight through into the garden of the house beyond the woods.

At the road, she stopped and looked left. The cafe was down this road. Eva wanted to see if Brian was still there. A shout in the distance made her jump, and Eva ran across and into the garden opposite, unmindful of the occupants.

Two more gardens and Eva found herself almost on Plantation Street. Brian wouldn't catch her now. Eva paused and tried to gather her thoughts. Her phone buzzed; it was a message from Gideon. Her first thought was to call him, and escape this situation, but his recent behaviour impeded on her thoughts. Eva wasn't ready to talk to Gideon just yet.

A bus pulled up, and Eva realised she stood at a bus stop. Confused at her lack of movement, the driver leaned over and called, "You gettin' on, Lady? I gotta schedule ta keep!"

Eva glanced both ways down Plantation Street, fearful her husband may yet approach. "Where does this bus go?"

"It's the number fifteen, lady. Straight to the city center and bus depot."

Eva handed the driver a ten-dollar bill and refused the change. "Keep it," she said. "Buy a beer after your shift."

Sitting down about halfway along the bus, Eva clutched

her bag on her lap, and, bent over, started to cry. Brian's betrayal racked her body to the very core. The bus turned down Vineland Street, and Eva forced herself to watch. The cafe flashed past. It was empty. Her stomach tightened and her legs tensed.

"He wasn't there," Eva concluded, causing a couple of old ladies further down the bus to perk up and turn around. "He knows."

CHAPTER FIVE

THE BUS PULLED UP OUTSIDE THE DCU CONVENTION center and Eva decided to get off the bus. "A word of advice if this is your first time in town," he said as she stepped down, causing her to pause. "Be careful if you are in a hotel round here. I've been round here a lot over the years, and delegates come in two types. Those here for work, and those here for play. You stay safe, and keep to the first type."

"I'm not planning on any type right now," she answered, flashing a grateful smile, "but thanks for the advice."

With a wave, Eva stepped down and crossed the road to the nearest hotel, the Hilton Garden Inn. Still nervous about her husband, Eva checked in under an assumed name and booked a room for the foreseeable future, paying a premium in cash, but unmindful of the cost. She had money to spare. Taking the elevator to the fifth floor, Eva let herself in and bolted the door of her room shut.

Letting her bag drop to the floor, Eva curled up on the bed, and wept. Great sobs racked her chest, and she gave into the despair and let it all out. Never had she felt so alone.

Perhaps an hour later, after a brief sleep, Eva felt a little better. The rage mixed with grief and sense of betrayal had left her feeling rather whimsical. Taking a shower, Eva luxuriated in the heat, using the experience to wash away her fears and emerge clear-headed once more. A weight had been lifted from her shoulders; Eva felt free for the first time in years. There was no way Brian would contact the police, not to have them come looking at the house. He had little imagination, so he wouldn't even know where to begin looking.

As if the thought was a trigger, her phone buzzed into life. It was Gideon. Eva answered and held the phone to her ear. "Gideon?"

"Is everything alright Eva? Your husband just left the hospital. He came looking for you, saying you hadn't returned home."

The feeling of dread sprang anew. "What did you tell him?"

"That I haven't seen you since you left."

"Nothing else?"

There was a slight pause. "No Eva, nothing else. Any professional disagreements we might have stay at work. They aren't the business of 'significant others'. For what it's worth, and bearing in mind what transpired, I now believe you were right to suggest prudence. You are a good judge of character."

"Thank you, Gideon. I am fine. I don't believe I can say the same for my marriage. Just make sure Brian doesn't come anywhere near me."

"You have my word. Where are you staying?"

The question caught Eva off guard. She wasn't ready to

divulge her whereabouts just yet. "I am safe. I'm in a hotel. I'll see you in the morning. Thanks for the concern, I appreciate it."

Not giving Gideon a chance to pry further, Eva ended the call, and for good measure switched her phone off. Brian would only plague her. "What to do with you." She said to her reflection in the bedroom mirror. On a whim, she tied her hair back, swapped her sweater for a jacket, and went out for a drink.

The hotel bar proved a little spacious and somewhat impersonal, full of delegates from the local trade convention. They were intent either on securing business deals or a bed with other individuals for the night. With the bus driver's words weighing on her mind, it was easy to see who was who.

The game didn't last long, and soon Eva found herself leaning on the reception desk, looking at a map of the city.

"Help you, miss?" came a voice from her right. One of the concierges, a large black man bearing the name 'Vinnie' regarded her.

"Maybe. I was trying to figure out if there was a decent bar somewhere other than here. Something cozy."

"Oh that's easy, miss." Vinnie beamed. "Try Moynagh's up on Exchange Street. Place is homely as you wouldn't believe. Hasn't changed in decades. Down Commercial Street, first right, and it's up the hill on the left."

Eva flashed the man a grateful smile, and made for the exit, the thought of some old-fashioned comfort dispersing any worries about her husband.

· · ·

Outside, the afternoon had given way to the slate sky of dusk. As Eva crossed the busy road in front of the hotel, she considered how her life had changed so radically in the space of a few hours. Her professional, dispassionate observations made her shake her head in disbelief. At the same time, she very quickly came to accept that if there was ever just a time to move on; this was such a time. What did she have in the house she was willing to lose? The contents were Brian, through and through.

Eva mulled this over as she passed the monstrosity of the convention center, its delegates scurrying in and out like bees in a hive, before turning up Exchange Street. She did not have far to look. Moynagh's sat, nestled on the corner, amongst the much larger buildings. Indeed, it looked as homely as the concierge had implied. Eva wasted no time in getting out of sight of strangers.

Inside the bar, infused by the warmth of the place, Eva began to relax. A crowd of perhaps thirty people, of all ages, gathered round the bar, avidly watching a television. The bar was old wood panelling, evidently once part of a bowling alley. A framed liquor licence hung above the bar, proclaiming the establishment had been there since the days of prohibition. The rest of the bar was old, dark wood, and the atmosphere reached out to her.

Eva moved around the edge of the crowd trying to get a glimpse of what was so enthralling. Suddenly, as one, they threw up their hands and let out a groan, some of them ripping up paper and throwing it to the ground.

"Here now," called the bartender, a bearded man who appeared to be in his early thirties, "make sure you pick that up!" He regarded Eva, who stood at the fringe of the crowd. "Help you, miss?"

"What was all that about?" Eva asked.

"Keno, it is sort of a lottery on the television. They like to play it in here. Always have. To be honest, I thought everyone played it. Are you not from around here?" The barman began to eye her suspiciously. Clearly, he was cautious towards outsiders.

"Yeah, I live over near the bio-med center. I don't get to watch a lot because of my job."

"And that is?"

Eva leaned forward on the stool she had chosen to occupy, putting her elbows on the bar. "Doctor."

Upon hearing she was local, the barman appeared to relax. "Get you a drink?"

"Sure, what's good?"

The barman indicated several taps. "Ales, from the motherland. Guinness, if that's your thing. Several Irish whiskies. Most of this lot only drink Jameson's. Not a lot of calls for anything else in this place. The only new drink we have introduced in the last ten years is the 'Passion Plunge'".

Eva could not help the grin that spread across her face at hearing the name. "Sounds perfect. What's in it?"

"Sour mix, orange juice, ice, dash of soda and of course a double shot of Irish whiskey. I made it in honor of the charity event we always send a team to." He indicated news clippings behind the bar; a team of people were diving into the ocean to raise money for the Paralympics.

"Absolutely. I think I will have one of those. And add the change to the charity jar." Eva handed over a fifty-dollar note, welcomed and warmed by the atmosphere and the barman's affable nature.

"Thanks! You should come join us."

"I think I'll be just fine keeping my feet dry, especially, if your event is in February."

The barman moved off to make her drink. The crowd had dispersed into smaller groups around the room once the Keno had finished. A young couple and a slightly disinterested blonde woman occupied seats further down the bar, but otherwise, Eva was alone. Hearing the sound of the evening news coming on, she found her attention drawn to the screen at the end of the bar.

Moving down a couple of seats, toward the television, Eva took her drink, and absently nodded thanks to the barman. Her attention was already focused on Jeanette Gibson on the screen.

"Thank you for your kind response to the coverage of the mysterious events reported earlier today. This station has decided to continue the coverage as more details emerge." Jeanette shuffled some papers and Eva took a sip of her delicious Passion Plunge. She nodded her appreciation at the barman, who winked back at her, before he resumed his conversation with the blonde. The bar door opened, some people entered while others left. Eva noted a dark-haired man, well-muscled, and a salacious gaze which settled on her. Eva turned back to the television; she had had enough of such men for one day.

"Tonight's top story is one that has been reported on widely in Jamaica: that of the missing driver." The screen shifted to scenes of Jamaica, kids playing cricket on dirt roads, old dreadlocked men smoking, the red, gold, and green of the Rastafarian movement displayed on clothes and flags everywhere.

"Six months ago, what started off as a standard attempted bank robbery in the area of Montego Bay, Jamaica, has become one of the biggest mysteries the island has ever seen." A map appeared on the screen, a red line detailing the route. It reminded Eva of the red line in the *Indiana Jones* movies when they tracked the adventurer's movements whenever he was on board a plane.

"The high speed chase was seen by hundreds of passers-by, involved most of the Montego Bay police force, and ended when the getaway car landed in the ocean." A montage of scenes followed, showing a column of squad cars behind an unmarked vehicle, obviously filmed from a helicopter. The car attempted to avoid a roadblock, hit the curb, flipped and dove into the sea. Eva winced as she watched it do so.

"As it transpired, underwater rescue specialists were on hand in case such an event occurred. Within a minute or so of crashing, the police apprehended the perpetrators. All of them, except the driver. All of the doors were shut. Windows adjacent to the driver were shattered, but local police were on scene. In short, there was nowhere for him to go. Yet, he has simply vanished."

"What makes this case even stranger is that none of the other occupants of the car can remember what he looked like, or if he was even there."

The scene cut to a police interview showing a swarthy Jamaican, one arm in a sling. The name 'Turell Banks' appeared on a banner at the bottom of the screen.

"Man, I tellin' you, me dunno!" The man was clearly agitated, confused. "We had us a wheel man. Him just up and gone. No name, no face. Him vanish like a ghost."

"The other members of the gang have offered similar explanations. They all know they had a driver, but they were all unable to provide the police with a description. Polygraph tests on all three men indicated each man was convinced he was telling the truth. Whoever the mystery driver is, he has kept his identity well hidden. Jamaican police were satisfied with one outcome, however; the apprehension of a local underground drug lord."

Again, the scene shifted to the man from the previous interview, a particularly evil-looking man, in an orange jumpsuit, his face a mixture of rage and confusion.

"As a result of Bank's capture, our mysterious gang member became a hero in the eyes of the authorities through his choice of escape route, although many admit confusion when it comes to an explanation of his disappearance. One thing is certain; the legend of the disappearing driver is sure to grow. Coming up next: a man in Georgia claims to have seen a demon walking on the streets. More, after these important messages."

The screen flicked to an advertisement and Eva lost interest. Above the growing hubbub, she heard a voice speaking to her. She had been so engrossed in the newscast she had been unaware the seat next to her had been taken, Eva said, "Excuse me?"

A strong voice, full of confidence replied. "I said: it's all a load of Hoodoo. African magic. They say the Jamaicans have been practicing it for generations. Many believe the man was removed from the car by magic."

Eva turned to look at the source of the outlandish statement. Her breath caught in her throat, and for a moment, she was sure her heart was going to stop.

CHAPTER SIX

Eyes of the deepest blue regarded her from beneath a mop of brown locks, dishevelled and pushed back from his tanned face. Eva had no reason to, but she found herself memorizing every detail. His slim body, with wide shoulders, was dressed in suit trousers and a pressed shirt, his collar unbuttoned. He was tall, but sitting down, she was not sure just how tall he was. His smile was calm, confident. Eva stared a moment longer, then became painfully aware he was doing the same, since she had not yet responded.

"Hoodoo? Don't you mean Voodoo?"

His smile broadened. Eva watched his lips, sensuous and inviting. "No, there is a difference. Voodoo is the religion. Hoodoo is the magic. It's like comparing a belief in God to spoon bending, for lack of a better term."

"You seem to be an expert on the subject."

He shrugged, his shirt pulling taut as he did so. "I have lived in the West Indies on and off. It's hard not to immerse yourself in the culture when you are around it every day." He held her gaze, smiling, as he signalled to the barman. "Whiskey please, and whatever the lady is having."

The barman left the blonde to the mercy of the hawk-faced man, who stared at Eva, unblinking, even as Eva watched him speak to the blonde. Eva leaned back. She noted *her* stranger's eyes drop to her chest as she did so, and it warmed her. The hawk down the bar had not taken his eyes off the newcomer. He was not watching Eva any more, but his rival. The barman frowned, and reluctantly came to serve them. "Another Passion Plunge?"

"Please."

In moments, the barman had made the drinks, and served the glasses. Eva barely noticed. "So what are you doing here?"

"I am just passing through; staying at a hotel nearby and thought I'd visit the oldest bar in Worcester. What's your story?"

Eva was tempted to tell the man her entire recent history. "Just an after work drink," she said, instead.

"A Passion Plunge, eh? Why would such a beautiful woman be drinking such a drink? Oh, where are my manners? You don't even know who I am. My name is Madden Scott."

Madden Scott. The name sent a shiver of pleasure down her spine.

"Madden Scott." Eva repeated the name, savoring how the syllables rolled off her tongue. For some reason the bar had just gotten warmer.

"And you, mysterious woman, do you have a name?"

Eva blushed. She didn't know whether it was the unusual heat of the bar or the whispered, husky tone of his voice. "Eva. My name is Eva."

"Just Eva?"

"Tonight, it is just Eva; let's leave it at that."

"A beautiful name it is. It is taken from a Hebrew word meaning 'mother of life'."

The knowledge, the insight this man had, ignited a stirring within her. It was a feeling Eva had never felt with Brian more than once. Without conscious thought, she found herself removing her jacket. Madden stood up from his bar stool, took the coat from her, and turned to place it on the back of her barstool. There was an air of mystery about him that held Eva within its grasp.

As he returned to his seat, Eva glanced around the bar. Couples were sitting closer than she remembered seeing when she had come in. Strangers were touching, unabashed, and intimate. Eva shook her head. These were people that, until mere moments ago, had been playing Keno on the television.

"Thank you," he said before she could question her sanity any further.

He smiled, causing her to shiver with excitement.

"What were we talking about, before I took your coat?"

"You were telling me your name. I am sorry; I could have sworn you told me."

He reached over and circled the back of her hand with one finger. That simple touch caused an ache of longing within her. "My name is Madden Scott, Eva."

"Madden Scott." Eva savored the words rolling off her tongue, and, for some reason, had a sense of déjà vu. "You... you didn't tell me your name before?"

"You never asked," Madden purred.

"But I told you mine?"

"Indeed. Long day?"

Eva laughed. "Yes, you could say that. This bar, is it usually like this?"

It made her feel a little self-conscious. She toyed with

the buttons on her blouse, suddenly wishing there weren't quite so many. The hawk-eyed man was still watching Madden, but unconsciously played with the blonde as he did so, his hands moving around her, seemingly of their own volition. It was hard for Eva to concentrate, but she felt something was going on, something not normal.

"I hadn't noticed." Madden replied, drawing Eva's attention back to him once more. The rich timbre of his voice made her want to melt into his arms. In response, she felt a slight throb between her legs. Blood was flowing, in a way Brian had never managed to make her feel, and she knew she wanted this man. It was hard to concentrate; there was a sensual air in the bar. She could hear clothes rustling as they fell to the floor. Somewhere nearby, a woman gasped in pleasure.

"Is it such a sin for people to enjoy themselves?" Madden asked, trailing his hand through her hair and down the side of her neck.

"It is one of the seven deadly sins," Eva replied, each word faltering as her body began succumbing to the over-whelming atmosphere.

"And... each... sin... has a demon," Madden said as he kissed her neck, "In the Bible, Asmodeus is Lust. He might be with us in spirit, now."

Eva moaned. His kisses felt so good. She was scarcely aware of her surroundings and the others that shared the bar with her. She wanted to give in, to open herself to him right then *and* there. Eva ran her hands through Madden's hair, pulled him to her, and kissed him deeply, relishing the feeling, as their tongues touched.

Then years of psychological conditioning took over. "Wait. This is wrong." Her sudden change confused

Madden. Before he could protest, she continued, "No, not here. This is wrong. We have to get out of here."

Fighting the feelings of lust radiating through her body, Eva pulled herself together long enough to grab her jacket, drag Madden away from the bar, and out into the darkness. Still caught up in the moment, he followed.

The hawk-eyed man watched them cross the room while he toyed with the woman he had chosen in his dance of lust. He realized he had become caught up in the moment, and regretted his momentary lapse of concentration. From across the room, a woman alone smiled at him, oblivious to the carnal riot going on around her.

"You never could concentrate on the task at hand, Asmodeus," she purred.

He smiled, and continued administering kisses to the blonde. In between kisses, his teeth grew to needle points, and, with a fierce bite, he ripped her throat out. She dropped to the floor, too overcome by lust to have even registered her peril. Nobody in the room noticed.

"All in good time, Belphegor. All in good time."

Eva, with Madden alongside, walked down the hill towards the convention center. She stopped, turned to him, and said, "What happened just then?"

"I have no idea," he replied, seemingly disconcerted by what had happened. By the look on his face, still a little in the moment, he grinned. "Fun though."

Eva smiled in return. She was still attracted to the man, but self-control had overpowered the lust that infused her.

"Fun, but looked at in the cold light of day, somewhat unnerving."

Straightening her clothes, wrapping her arms around herself, she trudged on. "I feel dirty. I want to go back to my hotel, and go to bed."

"Nightcap?" Madden offered.

This made Eva laugh. "It's barely eight o clock. Not quite time for a nightcap."

"Drink, then," he countered. "Things started off so well. Before it all got weird, they did, at any rate. Just imagine what may still be going on in that bar right now."

Eva shuddered. "It's probably harder to imagine something that 'isn't' going on in that bar. I really do need that drink." Saying nothing more, Eva picked up the pace, Madden right beside her.

Moving with a purpose, they made it to the hotel in minutes. Looking pretty much the same as when Eva left earlier, she noticed a few more businessmen had gravitated to the lobby. Eva marched straight to the bar and signalled the bartender.

"Do you know how to make a Passion Plunge?"

"Sure," he replied. "You take a nice cold shower. What we got is what you can see here, ma'am."

Ignoring his rudeness, Eva peered past him to look at what was on the shelf. "Double Jameson's, straight up."

"And for you, sir?"

"The same."

Madden noticed the abrupt nature of the man and bristled at the comments directed to her, and Eva approved. Chivalry was rare in the modern world. Before he could demonstrate his chivalry further, Eva paid the tab. Nothing more was said and the bartender moved off.

Eva raised her glass and Madden touched his glass to hers. "Cheers," she said, and downed the drink in one swallow. The warmth made her insides glow in response.

Madden sipped his whiskey, placing the glass on the bar. "You should have let me say something to him."

"Don't think I didn't appreciate what you wanted to do. It is just the nature of the place. This hotel is across from a huge convention center; that guy is probably very busy and used to being spoken to with such impatience."

"Sounds like you know this sort of place fairly well."

Eva laughed. "Me? No, not at all. I work in a hospital that is more akin to a prison, and I spend my days consumed with working. My nights are... were... taken up with a husband. However, my life is all such a mess that I do not know what I will find when I go back. If I ever go back. Suffice it to say, this is the first night out I have had in years. I am sure it hasn't been since I was a grad student, probably."

"What happened, to your husband, I mean?"

Uncertain of how much to tell him, given the fact that Brian was out there, somewhere close, Eva delayed her answer by ordering another whiskey.

"He has had indiscretions, shall we say. He just decided to make a point of them a little too often."

"And you had enough?"

Eva toyed with the now refilled glass, swirling the amber liquid as she considered her words. "I guess I had had enough a long time ago, and was kidding myself. He was simply the wrong man for me, and despite forgiveness on a number of occasions, he continued to throw his inferiority complex back at me as if I was offering some sort of challenge."

"Ultimately a challenge doomed to failure."

"Well yes, since you put it that way. But what do you care? You are just trying to talk yourself into a place to sleep for the night."

Madden had the grace to blush, but he did not back down. "Is it working?"

It was Eva's turn to blush. She was not used to a lot of alcohol, and this much whiskey was going straight to her head. "I haven't decided yet, as presumptuous as you are. What makes you think a bit of whiskey and soft words are going to lead you down that path?"

"I think if you didn't want my company, we would not even be here now. I think you are upset by this so-called husband, unnerved by the bar, and deserve, if not happiness, then certainly a distraction."

"And I think there is more to you than you let on, Madden Scott." She knew she had made her decision. She was not going to lie down for others any more. She was going to reach out and take what Eva deserved. "I think you are right. Will you join me?"

Madden stood and offered her his hand. "I don't have anywhere I would rather be, at this moment in time."

"Oh yes you do. You would rather be upstairs, with me." Eva leaned into him and he kissed her. There was none of the frenzied lust from before, but the warmth of his lips and the touch of his hand as it trailed down her back warmed her nonetheless. Without another word, Eva took his hand, and confident she was going to finally doing something just for herself, led him to the elevator. Inside, Madden kissed her, oblivious of any other occupants. When the bell chimed for their floor, she could barely pull herself from his embrace. The feelings had returned, but this time they were aches of longing. Something special was going to happen to her, and Eva could not wait to grasp it. She pulled Madden through the doorway, into her room, and, as the door slammed behind them, two people were already in the throes of passion.

Soon, two bodies lay replete, exhausted, amidst a ruffled duvet and crumpled sheets. A person walked down the hallway outside, smiling. It was a smile of satisfaction and genuine amusement at how easy mortals were to manipulate. The smile spread across his face, wrinkling the corners of hawk-like eyes.

He entered the elevator where a woman confronted him, her eyebrows arched in query. "Well?"

"Success," he purred. "As I said, all in good time, Belphegor. You plant a seed and it cannot help but grow. Now, it is your turn."

CHAPTER SEVEN

EVA'S EYES OPENED TO A NEW WORLD, AND INSTANTLY she regretted it. Her head was fuzzy, mouth dry, and eyes gritty from drinking late. The sun blazed across white sheets at the foot of the bed, dazzling her. It was too much. She clamped her eyes shut once more, determined to begin this day anew.

As she tried to gather her thoughts, she felt a movement behind her, and an arm snaked around her waist. Eva realized she was naked. She had not slept naked in years. Unsure as to whether she was in peril, Eva turned in the stranger's embrace and came face to face with a somewhat familiar man.

His eyes still shut; he pulled her closer. "Morning, gorgeous. You weren't kidding when you said you wanted something for yourself." He shifted to kiss her, and Eva backed off, placing her hand on his chest.

"I think we did enough of that last night, Madden." The name was difficult to recall which unnerved her. She had a good memory.

"In my book you can never have too much of a good thing," came his cheeky reply.

"If you have a good thing too often, you lose the taste for it, I find," countered Eva.

This brought Madden fully awake. He lay there studying her. After their intimate night together, she felt no self-consciousness at all "Did you get what you wanted?"

Eva stretched. There was a dull ache in her loins, but it was an ache of satisfaction. "Most definitely. But it ends there."

"It doesn't have to, you know."

Eva smiled in spite of herself. There was an addictive appeal to Madden and she found herself wanting to be drawn in once more. It was clear in the morning light how she had been beguiled by his charm, but it did not bother her in the least. He was an attractive man and she had gotten what she needed.

"It does for now, Madden. I know you to be honorable, and you will back off. Whatever else, I am still a married woman. Even if I don't love my husband, there are customs to be observed."

"Come away with me," he pleaded. "I can take you to Jamaica; show you the whole West Indies. We can sit on a tropical beach drinking rum and coconut while the melon traders hawk their wares in the distance."

"Sounds nice, but I can't. I would love to drop it all, but I have responsibilities. I have patients who rely on me, investigations I need to complete. What's the time?"

Madden leaned over to check the clock. "About half past nine."

"Christ! I'm late!" Forgetting her lack of clothes, Eva jumped out of bed, grabbing whatever she could. With an armful of clothing Eva turned back to find Madden admiring her.

"You look good like that. Nice bum."

In a moment of sheer rebelliousness, Eva dropped her clothes and stood, hands on hips, staring back at him. "Just a reminder of the night for you. I'll put my number on this note. Thank you for last night, Madden. I had a great time. It's probably best if you aren't here when I get out of the shower."

He climbed out of bed, as naked as she was. "I could scrub your back."

"Tempting, but no." Eva brushed his lips with her own. "You leave your number and I may call you when all the unpleasantness is over." Refusing to look him over once more, Eva bolted for the bathroom, and locked the door.

It was all Eva could do to keep the door shut, but she knew she was taking the sensible course of action. Brian was still out there, and would be all the more dangerous because she had escaped his prison. After one night of freedom, Eva knew she had to take control of her life.

"Small steps," she said aloud, and turned the shower on. 'Small Steps' was a book her boss had had published. It was what had carried him to prominence in his field of psychotherapy. Eva had read it as a student and become a devotee of Gideon Homes overnight. The book preached a simple approach to the understanding and treatment of mental patients, specifically looking for minor improvements regularly rather than the big cure. Eva took this approach with everything. As she luxuriated in the hot water, she realised her first small step was last night's encounter with... the name evaded her again. The second step was this shower, then going to work, eventually leading to the final confrontation with her husband and leaving him behind her.

But what was his name? As Eva thought to call out and ask, she heard the hotel door slam shut, and her stomach tightened. Eva tried to picture the man in her mind, but there was nothing. She began to panic. The ache in her loins, which she had thought was a pleasant reminder of last night's encounter now only served to indicate she had sex and nothing more. She had used no protection.

"Oh my God. No protection!" Eva cried to the room. The uncaring spatter of water on the shower cubicle was the only answer. Eva turned the shower off, grabbed a towel and wrapped herself in it. As the possible implications of the night before hit her, Eva lost control. Sliding down the wall of the bathroom, Eva collapsed in a heap and sobbed. She had been date-raped. That had to be the only answer.

She remained, numb with shock, for a good five minutes or so before her logical mind began to reassert itself.

"I must have been given something," Eva said to nobody, "but what?" She began to tick off drugs on her fingers. "Zolpidem. Benzodiazepine. GHB. They are most likely. Zolpidem doesn't last very long though, and Benzodiazepine is so powerful a sedative I wouldn't be up now doing this. It has to be GHB. It is. It must be. It is tasteless in strong alcohol."

The realization of this made Eva's stomach clench, and she vomited into the toilet. She remained this way for a good half hour, waves of guilt racking her body and sending her stomach into spasms. Finally, utterly wasted, and unable to now recall a single moment of the previous night's encounter, Eva stumbled out of the bathroom and to the bed.

Sitting, she reached for the notepad provided by the hotel. Looking at it in the sunlight, she could see her own number engraved in the sheet, in her own handwriting, but Eva, for the life of her, could not remember writing it down. Whoever had been here had taken it. She grabbed her handbag, fearing robbery. Inside everything was as it should have been. Whoever had drugged her must have only been interested in the sex.

Eva switched her cell on, and it blared into life with a barrage of message-received alerts. Reading down them, Eva went cold. They were mostly from Brian. Whatever had happened last night, her memory was crystal clear regarding the afternoon before. The messages were mostly apologies, but there was an undertone that chilled her.

The office messages were more perfunctory. Enquiries as to her well being from Gideon. Given she had nobody else to call, and her job was important, Eva settled on phoning him. The other end of the line clicked into life.

"Homes."

"Gideon. It's Eva."

"Eva? What's happened? Are you all right? Where are you?"

Trying not to break down, Eva bit on the knuckles of her free hand. The fear of what had been done to her without her knowledge grew into outright panic. "Gideon, I think I have been raped."

There was silence for a moment. "You think?"

"Yes. I think. No. I know. Gideon, someone has given me GHB and raped me and I can't remember!"

"GHB? Eva, are you sure?"

The uncertainty in Gideon's voice sent her into a fresh outburst of tears. "It has to be. I went out, and I must have had a lot to drink. A cocktail maybe, I don't know."

"And you think GHB why?"

"Because diazepine and Zolpidem are too short term, and I would know them. We have used GHB with the patients, but only in drinks that are strong so it is masked. Plus, it lasts longer."

"Are you injured?"

"No... no. Nothing other than the usual after effects of such an encounter. There is another problem though. I don't think any protection was used. The bed is a mess. Gideon. I'm married. What if I end up having a child?"

"Worry about that later. First things first you need to call 911. We need to make sure you are safe. Eva, I have to ask. Is this to do with Brian?"

"No. Yes... Oh, I don't know. It is and it isn't. Could Brian have done this? Not a chance. He doesn't think that quickly."

"So I have noticed," came the sardonic reply. "Call the police. I will be at the station as soon as I can."

"No, that won't be necessary." Eva asserted, still, despite his concern for her, a little reluctant because of the previous day's argument. "Look, I'll speak to you later on, Gideon. Thank you for your concern."

Not waiting for a reply, Eva switched her cell off, and reached for the phone beside the bed. Dialling in the numbers, becoming numb with shock, Eva spoke the words mechanically: "Police, please. I think I have been raped."

CHAPTER EIGHT

DRESSED, EVA SAT ON THE EDGE OF HER BED, oblivious now to what had happened the night before, the only thought in her head being she had been so careless and stupid. She had given her details, and the faceless woman on the other end of the line had asked her to remain where she was. They would send somebody to bring her in.

In the back of her head, Eva's logical mind informed her the central office for Worcester was only a couple of minutes drive away, up the road that passed the hotel. It was no more walking distance than the bar she may or may not have visited.

After what seemed an agonising amount of time, Eva's hearing registered footsteps outside her room. A short loud knock made her jump.

"Miss Ross? This is the Worcester Police Department. May we come in?"

Wary now, with paranoia threatening to overcome her, Eva approached the door with caution. "How do I know you are who you say you are?"

"Put the door on the latch and open it, ma'am," said a female voice.

Eva did as she was told and through the crack in the doorway, she could see a short blonde woman dressed in a tight grey suit, holding up her WPD shield. Working with mentally ill prisoners, Eva had seen her fair share of police ID, and as reluctant as she was, she opened the door to them, letting it swing ajar as she turned away.

Doing so caused her to look once more at the bed, the scene of the attack. She let out a whimper and almost fell to the floor, but the woman caught her, deflecting her into one of the chairs.

"Mrs Ross, I am Detective Tina Svinsky, and this is Detective Mike Caruso."

The words barely registered. Eva looked past the woman to find a white-haired man of below average height wearing a blue suit that appeared three sizes too big. He nodded, unspeaking, and resumed scanning the room.

"I called as quickly as I could," said Eva by way of an explanation.

"No judgement," Svinsky replied, holding her hands up in a suggestion of innocence. "You are the victim in this, but it would probably be better if we got you out of here. Would you like us to escort you home?"

"No! Absolutely not!" The vehemence in her own voice surprised Eva as much as it did the detectives, and caused a look between the two. "Well we can always do this at the station. It is quite close and you will be safe there. Are you up to that?"

"I... Yes. Why not?"

Svinsky nodded at her partner. "You ok to hold the fort?"

Pulling out a pair of what looked to Eva like surgical

gloves, he replied, "Sure. Crime scene unit is en route so I'll just poke around until they get here."

Eva was led through the corridors into the elevator. Her mind was still a mess, trying to recall any image or sensation of who or what assaulted her the night before. When they reached the lobby, it was clear the arrival of the police had already drawn some attention, and Eva noticed strange and sometimes hostile looks from many there who had presumed she was the cause and was being arrested. The bartender from the night before had a smug look on his face, but even he said nothing. Perhaps they remained silent upon seeing the terror that shone through on her face, she wondered.

Detective Svinsky did her the courtesy of making a show of no cuffs. This calmed any potential outbursts. A criminal would be in cuffs, everybody knew that.

A car waited outside the lobby, and Eva was ushered into the front passenger seat, instead of the caged rear of the vehicle. This was enough for most, and the congregation in the lobby looked again to the elevator and stairs, seeking a new target for their growing wrath.

Detective Svinsky took her place behind the wheel, and drove off with no further comment. They moved out onto the road, and no more than a minute later, the police station came into view. Svinsky chuckled.

The noise was enough to break Eva out of her mood. "What?"

"Well it certainly beats walking."

"I guess."

Svinsky glanced at her. "Look Eva, we will do our damndest to find out what happened to you, but you must remember time is a great healer. Things will get better. It's hard to consider how that is the case right now, so all I want you to do is concentrate on anything that happened last night or this morning. Chin up, girl. I usually find corpses, not live victims. You are at least alive, so that puts this as a rosy day."

"It certainly doesn't feel like it," countered Eva.

The detective pulled up to the front of the building and signalled a colleague to take the car. Eva felt the numbness of shock, the detachment, as if she were looking through someone else's eyes. Through sheer reflex she moved into the building, barely noticing the yellowed corridors, the out of date seventies wood panelling of a building still stuck forty years in the past.

She was shown into a room that belied this impression. Large bay windows opened on to a small garden, fenced off from the outside world. The sun shone through the foliage, highlighting the autumn leaves. Eva sat on a sofa that smelled new, surrounded by pale pink walls. The room felt false, meant to offer comfort, but its ultimately sterile nature could not be disguised. The garden reminded her of the fact everything would soon end one way or another.

"Would you like tea? Coffee?" Eva thought she recognized the voice asking the question.

She turned to find a face from the past, looking her over with concern. "I know you... Miss Grouse?"

"Just call me Brenda, dear. It has been a long time since the library in high school. I can see you have been in the wars; otherwise you would not be here. What can I get you?"

"Tea, please."

"Sugar? It will help calm your nerves."

"That would be nice."

As Brenda poured, Detective Svinsky returned. Through the door, Eva could see Detective Caruso, a concerned look in his face.

"We just need to go through a few basic details with you, Eva, if you feel up to it?"

Eva sipped her tea; the sweet liquid tasted good. "I don't mind. I don't remember much but I will help where I can."

"Okay, then. Well, we have your name and address, and from that, we can see you are married to Brian Ross, of the same address. Would you like us to contact your husband for you?"

The fear began to return. He was still out there. "No. No, I don't want him involved." Eva glanced at the detective to see a look of concern on her face, mixed with a steady gaze of observation. It was a look she had no doubt she used many times. Empathy and study.

"That is fine. This is a delicate time. Do you have any next of kin you would us to contact, instead. Someone to offer you support?"

"No, nobody nearby. My family moved to Wyoming and I haven't spoken to my parents in years."

"So that makes your husband your only next of kin."

Eva shuddered. "No!"

Again, the look of suspicion. "Eva, was it your husband that did this to you?"

Even the simple questions left Eva feeling confused. "I don't know. I have no memory of who did this to me. I was drugged. Somebody must have used GHB on me. Look, by now I am sure you know I am a psychotherapist at Worcester State Hospital. I am fully trained and versed in drugs used in the treatment of patients. I wrote a thesis on the subject for God's sake. Gamma-hydroxybutyrate has effects similar to alcohol, and I can guarantee there's not a person in this station who does not know what alcohol does to you in great quantities."

"We will need to take a blood sample then to confirm this." Detective Caruso had slipped in unannounced.

"You aren't allowed in here." Svinsky protested.

"That's red-tape protocol bullshit and you know it, Tina. Look we need to get this sorted as quickly as possible to ensure the drug doesn't dissipate in her system. Mrs. Ross, if you don't mind, I would like to have one of my colleagues test your blood for drugs, GHB or otherwise."

"Please do, if that is what it takes to convince you all." Eva held out her arm. "Go right ahead."

Caruso ushered in a blonde woman wearing a white coat with a crime scene kit. The woman looked at her for a moment. "Dear Gods, Eva. It's Julie. Julie Bilous."

"Julie Bilous? You were in my postgrad course in Boston."

Detective Caruso rolled his eyes. "It seems everyone from your past is ending up in the same room. Let's get on with this."

Eva allowed herself to be ministered to by her old colleague. She had her hand cleaned and finger pricked by the police doctor.

"It's not Brian up to his old tricks again is it?" Julie said in a conspiratorial whisper, seemingly unaware Detective Svinsky was right next to them.

Eva remained quiet, but the tension in her body was clear for anybody to observe.

"Are you absolutely sure there is nothing else you wish to tell me, Ms. Ross?" Svinsky asked. "We don't appreciate having our time wasted by domestic disputes if there is no apparent victim."

"I am not wasting your time." Eva persisted. "It's just... Well my husband hasn't been the most faithful of people in the past." Eva refrained from further comment, aware there was a small crowd growing in the room.

Finished, Julie smiled at Eva and left, followed closely by Caruso who now appeared to get the hint.

"Would you care to elaborate?" asked Svinsky.

"Ever since high school, my husband has had an inferiority complex. He knew he didn't equal me intellectually, so he sought other ways to prove to himself that he was a man. I was just very forgiving. He proved himself many times. It wasn't him. Whatever happened here was far too clever for Brian. He can't plan that far ahead. At least not most of the time."

"Are you saying this time could have been different?"

"No. What I am saying is I was leaving him. If you go to my house, you will find it is boarded up. That was done for a reason since he tried to keep me a prisoner. I was staying at the hotel because I escaped and I have had enough."

Svinsky was writing all this down on a pad, and without looking up, asked, "Could you tell me about last night, then?"

This frustrated Eva. "I have to tell you the same thing over and over, it seems. I left the hotel. I walked past the exhibition center, and turned up a street. I went in a bar for a drink, but I don't recall the name. From that point until this morning when I stepped into the shower, it is all a blur. I remember nothing. I will tell you one thing though. It was not my husband. I just don't know who it was."

"Well, first things first, I think we should wait for the blood work to come back to see what you might have been given."

"Detective, I know procedure in this state. Shouldn't you be conducting a rape kit? My clothes for example might hold evidence." Eva held up her hands. "My fingernails and what's under them?"

Svinsky smiled. "Sweetie, you have been watching too much CSI. We have a backlog of rape kits filling up a room somewhere in here. If we were to process that, it would be months if not years before we got to you. Besides, you admitted your memory returned in the shower. Any chance of something on the outside of your body giving us a clue has long since gone. I think it best you just wait here until the results come back. There is enough tea to swim in, and cookies aplenty. I will be back presently."

Svinsky left the room, flicking through her notepad. The door slammed shut as if it were a prison cell. "They don't believe me," Eva said aloud.

Time passed. It could have been minutes, but to Eva every moment felt like hours. If she was not racking her brains about the night before, she was worrying about where her husband could be, and about Jenny, the poor girl who was his latest conquest. What kept her going was the steady supply of sugar-enriched tea and the occasional bouts of self-righteousness where Eva remembered that for Jenny to have been at her house meant she had consented. Unlike her experience, that was not rape.

Understanding the psychological damage that could be done to a rape victim made her feel a little better. She could use that to bolster herself against the symptoms that usually affected a victim. She would not be beaten by it. The most unnerving fact was that somehow it did not feel like rape. Humans were predisposed to be afraid of the unknown, and it was the unknown that frightened her more than the act.

At length, Eva could see bodies gathering down the corridor beyond the door. The two detectives were arguing with two others, with occasional glances in her direction. Eventually, Detective Caruso broke free of the argument and opened the door, the others in his wake. All four of them entered the room.

"Mrs. Ross, I am going to be as blunt about this as possible. Your blood results show no abnormalities whatsoever. In fact, they show barely any trace of alcohol. The levels indicate you had nothing more than a few drinks, for what is left in your system. Yet you maintain you are the victim of date rape. The evidence does not stack up in your favour."

Eva was lost. "Well how can this be? How come I cannot remember anything about last night if I wasn't drugged? Do you now think I am making all of this up?"

Detective Caruso was clearly beginning to lose patience. He threw the test result file onto the table in front of her. "Read it yourself. You are a doctor. It reads as clear as day that you were under no influence. Mrs. Ross, are you absolutely certain you aren't the guilty party here? Are you sure this wasn't just a one night stand and now you are crying rape? Are you sure this isn't just a call for attention?"

"Mike, that is too far," argued Detective Svinsky. "You cannot make such an accusation based on one set of evidence like that. We don't even have the DNA profiles back from the room yet."

"And what do you think are the chances there is only one profile located in the room?" accused Caruso. "If it were up to me, you would be arrested for wasting police time, Dr Ross."

"Well, it is lucky it is not up to you, Mike." Detective Svinsky purposefully put herself between the other Detective and Eva, blocking her view of the man. Off to one side, the two lab technicians, by their faces, clearly believing themselves to be the cause of the uncomfortable situation, appeared to want to bolt for it. "What do you want to do, Eva? Remain here in safety to see this out, or find somewhere else to stay?"

"I would like to return to my room at the hotel, please."

"Not possible. That's an alleged crime scene. We can see about getting you another room, though."

"No. Thank you, Detective Svinsky, but I need to be in my original room. I need to try and figure out what happened."

Detective Caruso butted in, saying, "It is a crime scene, one way or another, until proven otherwise."

"But how can it be a crime scene if you don't think there has been any crime?"

CHAPTER NINE

Not wishing for any fuss, Eva slipped in a side entrance once the police had dropped her back at the hotel. Having only just called him, Eva was nonetheless unsurprised to find Gideon waiting in the lobby with Susan McFey, one of the other doctors from Worcester State.

Susan got up and embraced Eva. "You poor thing, are you all right?"

"Aside from an apparent case of retrograde amnesia, I don't appear to be too bad. Crazy probably, according to the cops. They don't appear to believe me at the moment. But physically, I'm fine."

Gideon held back, remaining in his seat. Eva smiled a thank you to him. They both understood a woman who recently cried rape would not be seen in public embracing another man the day after.

"You can take as much time off as you need, Eva. The hospital isn't going anywhere."

Eva accepted a glass of whiskey from Gideon and eyed it cautiously. "Oh for God's sake, if I start looking at every glass of liquor like it's full of poison, I'll end up exactly the same as any other victim." With that, she downed it.

"Better?"

Eva smiled. "Much. But no more. That's what got me into this in the first place."

"I'll leave you two alone." Gideon rose and put his coat on. "Eva, I'm glad to see you are all right, but the hospital needs me, at least. You just get in touch when you want to come in."

Gideon left without another word. Susan leaned forward.

"Want to talk about it?

"I wish I could, Sue, but I can't remember. I have no memory of last night past leaving this lobby and heading to a bar. Moynagh's I think it was. Beyond that, the first thing I can remember is getting out of the shower."

"And you are sure it was rape? Drugged rape?"

Eva reached up to rub her forehead, squeezing the skin between thumb and forefinger. "I don't know. I was sure it was at first. What else could it be? The funny thing is while my mind, through being screwed with, still screams rape, my body doesn't. It doesn't feel forced. If anything, it feels as though I enjoyed it."

"Well, do you want to take a walk up to that bar and see if we can find anything out?"

"No, the police are doing that. Honestly, all I want to do is go up to my room and lie down. Take a bit of rest."

"Well at the least let me see you safely upstairs."

Eva stood and embraced her friend. "No, I'm fine. You go on back to the hospital. They need you there."

· · ·

Eva left her colleague in the lobby and made her way to her room. Despite the warning of the police, Eva had purposefully not returned her room key and checked the floor was empty before she unlocked the door and squeezed between the crime scene tape into her room.

The bedclothes had been completely stripped, and it was evident the room had been thoroughly picked over. Closing the door, Eva sat on the bare mattress, trying to puzzle out any clue about what had happened to her. There was nothing. Her memories ended at the bar the night before, and began again in the shower, as cleanly as if a surgeon had removed them with a scalpel. And whoever it was had her cell number.

Eva reached for her phone. The barrage of messages from Brian had grown desperate, promises mixed with threats. He wouldn't stand a chance if the cops saw them. There was nothing else. The phone rang as Eva was gazing into space, and she jumped.

"Mrs. Ross? This is Detective Svinsky."

"That was quick. Do you have anything for me?"

A pause. "There have been some... developments." The voice was cautious, not telling the whole story. "Look, are you available to come back in? Say in about three hours?"

"Sure, if you need me. I can't add anything to what I said earlier though."

"Perhaps we can, Mrs. Ross. I will see you later; will you need a car."

"No thanks. I'll be fine."

The phone clicked off with no more wasted words. Eva lay back on the bed, determined to get at least a couple of hours of rest before the next ordeal.

· · ·

Three hours later, Eva walked along the sidewalk between the hotel and the police headquarters. Refreshed and clean, she at least felt equal to the task of being grilled once more. As before, she was ushered into the 'victim room' as she had come to call it, and was asked to wait.

After a short while, Svinsky and Caruso entered the room, document-packed folders in their hands.

"Thank you for coming back, Mrs. Ross," began Detective Svinsky. "There have been some developments in your case."

"So quickly?"

"It happens sometimes. We can get lucky, or as things stand, much less so."

"What do you mean?"

Svinsky looked to her colleague and Detective Caruso continued. "We have taken DNA samples from the room you were so quick to reoccupy. It seems the two of you had quite the night together. The samples were all over the room."

"If you say so. Go on, Detective."

Caruso shuffled through the folder in front of him. "Well, that is where the trail goes cold. We have access to the CODIS database, which has the DNA of most anybody that's committed a serious crime, and when we run the sample, the search stalls."

"You mean it can't find the DNA of whoever did this?"

"No, Mrs. Ross. The search freezes. It is almost as if the system itself doesn't want to find the target."

"Like it is forgetting what it is doing."

"Yes, you could look at it that way. That is the least of our problems, though. We have been to the bars around the area, the most prominent being Moynagh's on the corner of Waldo and Exchange street. The owner remembers you.

He said you ordered a..." Caruso flicked through his notes. "Passion Plunge. Do you remember this?"

"No, Detective Caruso. I can't remember a thing about last night. Nothing has changed from earlier."

"Well, would it interest you to know this is now another crime scene? A large blood stain was found on the floor. There is no evidence of a struggle, nor is there any sign of a body. Now, we have you accusing a mystery assailant of rape, and what appears to be a murder, happening within blocks of each other, and you have been in both places on the same night. Do you have any opinion on that?"

"Sounds like a dreadful coincidence to me."

Caruso gave her a look that made it abundantly clear he didn't believe her. "Mrs. Ross, I do not believe in coincidence. Nor luck, fate or any other deterministic concept. I believe in facts and logic. The facts here are firstly you were in this bar at some point yesterday evening, and there is a large blood stain no more than a day old in the same establishment. Later that night, you and an, a yet unidentified male, had sex in the Hilton Garden Inn. You claim you were raped, and yet there was no sign of anything other than two people enjoying themselves. Extensively. Logic dictates from these facts there is no suggestion you were raped at all, and yet, you claim that you were."

The very idea the detective was trying to turn this around on her made Eva want to reach out and slap him. As she opened her mouth to retort, Detective Svinsky, who had clearly sensed the same thing, stepped in.

"I think what my colleague is getting at, Mrs. Ross, is that despite all the facts we have here," she emphasised the word 'facts' with no attempt at hiding the glare for Detective Caruso, "we are waiting on your memory to return."

"And what about the DNA? You have this record of the

man in my room, yet you don't seem to be able to use it to identify him."

"We will keep trying to reference the database, Mrs. Ross," said a calmer Detective Caruso. "As futile as it is, you are still the key to all of this. All we can ask is you don't leave the city until this is concluded."

"I will be staying at the Hilton until further notice, in that same room. Unless you are in the habit of arresting victims, which it appears you to want do; that is where you will find me."

"Good to know. Just one more thing if I may, Dr Ross?"

"Sure."

"Have you ever come across the term 'Prosopamnesia'?"

Eva thought for a second. "Yes, I brushed over it in one of my courses. It is the inability to recognise or remember faces. It is extremely rare, having been diagnosed in only two cases. I don't remember who they were, though."

Caruso gave her a level stare. "That is not funny."

"It wasn't meant to be. It is a very serious condition and no, I am not suffering from it. You may as well allege I have Asperger's or Parkinson's disease for all this is going to help you."

Eva rose to leave and, without looking back, headed for the door. She heard a murmured 'thank you' from behind her as she let the door close in her wake.

Outside the station, it was all Eva could do not to scream aloud. The frustration that had been simmering all day was close to boiling over. Clenching her hands, she closed her eyes and took several deep breaths. It was early evening again, only twenty-four hours since she had left her husband and his makeshift prison behind her. What had stopped her from telling the police all about Brian she did not know. Perhaps deep down, she still felt a glimmer of loyalty towards a man that had shown her none. That very thought made her feel guilty. He had treated her like dirt and she was still worrying over him.

The street was crowded. It looked to Eva like a gathering of one of those 'flash mobs' that were currently all the rage. She half expected everybody to break into a mass dance, but the passersby kept on moving. Eva realized in the detached reality of the hospital, being so close to home, she had never realized just how busy the center of the city would be. She had never had any cause to come in before, with out of town shopping malls and giant grocery stores practically on her doorstep. The effect was somewhat unnerving.

Seeking a place of refuge, Eva spied a restaurant with a sign reading 'Club Maxine'. Feeling a sudden near-overwhelming need for food, she ducked out of the pedestrian traffic and into the restaurant. It was a high-class establishment, but Eva was too hungry to care. The only other occupants were a blonde woman in one corner near a grand piano, and a bored-looking waiter.

The waiter ambled over. "Help you, miss?"

"Do you have anything quick to eat?"

"Bunch of bar snacks, some fries, maybe a few things cooked up early for the evenin'. Any of that sound good to you?"

"It all sounds great. I'm starving."

"Okay, miss. I'll get right on it. Beer for you while you wait?"

The previous night's events left a sour taste in her mouth when it came to alcohol. Whatever else had happened, she had definitely drunk more than she had in years. "No, thank you. I would like a soda, please."

The waiter nodded and moved off to see to the order. Eva found herself a seat at a table near the large window that looked out onto the sidewalk, and the rushing public. She felt a little safer behind the protection of the glass.

The room was warm, and Eva found herself drooping while waiting for the food. She jumped awake when the waiter placed her soda at her side.

"Won't be long, miss. Food's almost done."

"Thank you."

The jump had made Eva a little more alert, and she surveyed the premises while she waited. The blonde lazed around on a sofa, an untouched glass of champagne at her side. Something about the woman tugged at Eva's memory. She felt as though she had seen the woman before, but she couldn't place her.

Feeling emboldened by her recent encounter with the detectives, Eva started to approach the woman when a shadow fell across her from the other side of the glass. The blonde woman was now looking at her, no, past her, at whatever was blocking the light, a strange smile of satisfaction on her face.

Not interested, Eva began to rise, and there was a tap on the glass. Eva turned, and her stomach tightened. There was no avoiding it, no escaping this particular threat. On the other side of the glass loomed her husband.

CHAPTER TEN

Brian Ross stared through the glass at her, his wide eyes bulging, his whole body speaking of potential menace. For an instant, panic overwhelmed Eva, she had no idea what to do, but soon her reasoning reasserted itself and she saw an unorthodox solution.

Leaving the table, and a somewhat baffled waiter behind her, Eva exited the restaurant and came face to face with him.

"What do you want?"

Brian's expression did not alter. "What have you told them?"

This was something new. The menace Eva could feel was tinged with panic. "Told who?"

"The cops," he growled.

Insistent he would not get the better of her any more, Eva put on her most nonchalant face and started ticking facts off using her fingers, every fiber of her being screaming 'run'.

"Well, first I told them I was once devoted to you no matter what. Then, I told them how you have had the proclivity to screw anything without a dick, despite that devotion. Finally, I told them how I have had enough of you, Brian."

His eyes turned calculating. "You told them nothing more?"

"No, nothing more. However, before you think you can take me back there, to raise your little hell spawn, remember we are within sight of the Worcester police precinct. If I scream, a dozen cops will jump you, maybe more. We are done, Brian. There is nothing you can say to change anything."

"But I am sorry, Eva. I know now I have done wrong, that I have sinned. I have changed since you left. I want to make amends."

Eva couldn't help but bark out a laugh. It didn't seem to make any difference to the masses, who appeared oblivious to the argument in their midst.

"You? You have changed? In the course of one day? Brian, you haven't changed in a decade or more. You are still the jock who thinks the world is at his feet. Time to wake up, superstar. You are going to be a father. I wonder if this is the first of your conquests you have managed to knock up. Quite frankly, I'm amazed you even knew the right spot to find. I can only thank God it is not with me."

Brian had not heard a word she had said by all accounts. He leaned forward and enfolded her in a hug. Eva remained motionless, aware of the rage he could summon in an instant. It was all she could do to not give in. The close touch of her husband had won her over in the past, too many times to count. This time he had gone too far. Eva was burning her bridges. She had the courage not to respond to him, remaining with her hands at her sides, giving him no sign of any acquiescence. It had the expected effect.

Standing back, his eyes full of tears, Eva watched as Brian's muscles bunched. "You are my wife! You will obey me! You are my...!"

Something tugged at Eva's hand. She looked away from her husband to find a small girl of perhaps six or seven years old looking up at her, eyes wide, face framed by a mop of curly blonde hair. She was terrified.

"I can't find my mommy."

Ignoring Brian, Eva knelt down and enfolded the girl in her arms. "Oh, you poor thing. Were you walking along here with her?"

Brian ripped the girl from her arms and shoved her away.

"You will listen to me now!"

"Brian! What in the hell do you think you're doing?"

The girl had fallen onto the path and blood ran down her leg from a cut on the knee. Somehow, Eva felt the mood of the crowd change; although they still bustled past, the crowd felt more directed towards them. She reached down to help the, now crying, child to her feet.

"Let me see to that." Eva took out a tissue and mopped up the blood. "Brian, you are going to be a father. I suggest you start acting like one and stop bullying every innocent that gets in your way. There, that's better," she said to the child.

Eva had finished mopping the blood, and held the tissue to the girl's knee, stemming the flow. In truth, it was not a big cut, but to every child it was alarming. The girl had quietened, and Eva wiped the tears from her face.

"Now where did you last see your mommy?"

The girl looked around, blanching when she saw Brian still glaring. "I... I don't know."

Eva hugged her tight. "It will be all right."

"What a mom," said Brian sarcastically. "Get up, Eva; you are coming home with me."

"Sorry Brian, those days have passed. You are on your own now. If I was parent to this child, and saw what you did, I would have had you arrested for assault."

"No, it's fine," said a voice. "I'm sure it was just an accident."

The voice belonged to the blonde woman from the restaurant, who now stood in the doorway. Eva had another flash of recognition. She had seen her somewhere before today, but the location eluded her.

"There you are," she said to the girl. "I told you not to wander off."

The girl had calmed the moment the woman spoke to her. In fact, her face was strangely expressionless. There was no relief or emotional outburst associated with a child finding their parent.

"I'm fine, now," said the girl. "This is my mommy." The voice was flat, chilling Eva. It made her want to leave. Something was wrong. Terribly wrong.

"Are you sure you are fine?"

"She is well," the woman assured her. "She gets overcome sometimes when she gets lost. Thank you so much for pointing her in the right direction. You will make a wonderful mother one day."

Full of petulance, she left him with a parting shot. "If you think you will get anywhere near any child after that, Brian, you had better think again. I am going straight to the police and tell them everything. You won't abuse Jenny and her child. I'll make sure of that.

As for us, I regret the day I first laid eyes on you. I am no longer your wife. I am your nothing, you ill-tempered little boy." Not giving Brian an opportunity to reply, Eva turned and walked away through the crowd. She wanted to run. A strange musty smell had begun to permeate the area and it scared her.

"EVA!" Brian yelled from behind her.

She stopped and turned. He was perhaps a hundred yards or so back, the crowd had bunched around him.

"If thou hast done foolishly in lifting up thyself, or if thou hast thought evil, lay thine hand upon thy mouth. What benefit did you reap at that time from the things you are now ashamed of? Those things result in death!"

Brian was quoting the Bible? Before Eva could respond, the smiling woman lifted the girl into the air, and passed her to him. The feeling of hunger magnified a hundredfold, and the crowd began to growl, unutterable sounds that could not be recognised as human. There was an eager anticipation in the air, as if an abomination was about to be unfettered.

As one, the mob surged at Brian, and both he and the girl disappeared from view. Eva couldn't see what was going on, but the mob piled into the space where Brian had stood, baying and scrapping.

Eva felt compelled to join them, but something inside her fought the feeling, preventing her from moving. She stood, immobile, as others ran past her to dive in.

Above it all, there was a piercing wail, tortured and desperate, extinguished almost as soon as it began. It wasn't Brian they were after. He wasn't protecting the child. He was slaughtering her! Then a flash of red sprayed up from the seething mass, and Eva began to scream.

She was a frozen nexus in the midst of chaos, powerless as more and more people dove in to the space where blood and gore were splattered over an unbelievable distance. She had her chance to remove the girl from this; Eva screamed as the horror of what she could have prevented permeated her to the very core.

Everybody ignored her, desperate in their hunger to attack the remains. Eva couldn't help but watch the carnage unfold. The sounds of gristly clicking as joints were dismembered and bones snapped made her want to throw up and she could not stop screaming.

At one point, a shredded arm was thrown aloft only for the mob to jump up and grab it. There was no rage, just a desperation to feed. And all the while, the blonde woman watched her from beside the shop, a satisfied smirk on her face.

Eva realised now where she had seen the face. Memories began to trickle back from the night before.

"You were in the bar," Eva whispered in horror.

It was impossible she could have been heard amidst the yelps and growls of the humans turned animal, yet the woman turned to address her, and Eva heard every word of the triumphant whisper.

"Be not among winebibbers; among riotous eaters of flesh: for the drunkard and the glutton shall come to poverty: and drowsiness shall clothe a man with rags. We shall meet again, you and I. Your little man can't hide forever."

She spread her arms as if having accomplished a task, and Eva looked at the mob, now milling around, some chewing, many licking blood from each other or from the sidewalk. The hunger compulsion dissipated in an instant, and people started to realise what they had been doing.

There were several different reactions. Some screamed. Many threw up. A few just stood where they found themselves, blood on their clothes and faces, blank in shock. One old woman sat down, and held herself, beginning to rock, her mind gone and her face covered in cuts. Many panicked and ran in random directions, seeking to escape the scene of carnage.

Of the girl, mercifully nothing remained that could identify her. Eva had expected a corpse of sorts, but as she watched from a distance, it was evident there was nothing more than a few shards of bone. The mob had done its job with murderous efficiency.

Eva had hoped for a moment Brian was one of the few that lay at the middle of the melee, unconscious, but that was only wishful thinking.

Brian rose, facing away from her, and slowly turned. He lurched a step as he did so; clearly, some damage had been done to him. His face caused Eva to retch. He was covered with gore from his head down; his jeans were soaked in blood. Unidentifiable parts of flesh from his victim still clung to his shirt, as if desperate to cling to the life that so recently filled them. His eyes were blank and, to Eva's horror, he clung to what appeared to be the top half of a skull, gore dripping from within, and the surface licked clean.

Finishing chewing, he looked himself over, as if not quite sure what had happened, and began to laugh. A slight chuckle to begin with, flowering into a cackle that spoke volumes about his sanity.

Those around him, roused from their stupor by his noise, began to do the same. Brian regarded the skull fragment and threw it aside.

Then two things happened at once. In the midst of his insanity, Brian noticed her standing there and police sirens beginning to wail from the nearby precinct. Those people left milling around came to their senses and began to run. Of the blonde woman, there was no sign.

In the distance, the flashing lights showed this had been noticed on a grand scale. After her recent interview, and contrary to the duty of care she felt as a doctor, Eva did not want to be seen around this. She began to back away, keeping her eyes on her husband.

Brian seemingly came to his senses as she did so. There was no remorse on his face. No shock at what had happened to him. "Eva! EVA!" He began to pursue her, zombie-like, his leg hampered by an injury apparently gained in the feast.

Eva turned and ran.

CHAPTER ELEVEN

Eva ran until her lungs felt as though they would burst. The occasional glance over her shoulder showed Brian in pursuit, albeit hampered by his injured leg. He was fitter than she was and had retained much of the athletic prowess from his youth. Fortunately for Eva, the hotel was not far away, not more than a few hundred yards. The mad dash and ominous pursuit made it feel like several miles.

Eva hurtled into the lobby to be met by the concierge, with whom she nearly collided.

He smiled, catching her as she was about to collapse. "Whoa there, miss. Plenty of rooms left yet."

"There's a man following me." Eva began to panic as she realised how little time she had. "He knows I came in here. I need to hide."

In the distance, the wail of police sirens grew as more cars converged on the horrific scene up the road.

"Is there anything I can do?" The concierge seemed genuinely concerned.

"Yes, let me hide. I have a room, but I just need to get

away from him for now. You will know him when you see him. He is covered in blood."

"I have the perfect place. Quick. Up those stairs and there's a large sofa behind the pillar. Catch your breath there."

Not wasting another moment, Eva dashed up the central lobby stairs and found the indicated sofa. Sure enough, it was situated behind a pillar at least a yard across, and afforded her a good view of the lower lobby whilst retaining anonymity.

She was not a moment too late, for as she sat on the sofa, Eva heard the heavy footfall of someone entering the lobby. She backed into the seat, trying to make herself as small as possible despite the protection from view.

"I am sorry, sir," she heard the concierge announce, "but while we might not have the tightest clothing regulations in Worcester, you certainly can't be seen in here dressed like that. Is everything all right, sir?"

Eva stole a peek at the scene. Brian was peering round the ground floor, the concierge bravely blocking his way, as he was a good foot shorter than Brian was.

"Eva! I know you are here. I saw you run in. Answer me! Eva!"

She ducked back behind the pillar, suddenly afraid a yard or so of concrete would not be enough if Brian grew a brain and overpowered the concierge.

"Sir, you can't behave like this here," the concierge insisted.

"Get out of my way, bellboy." The sound of a body hitting the floor indicated Brian had lost his fragile patience. "Eva! I know you are here. There is nowhere to run. There's no place on earth I won't find you. You think this is your choice to make? You are wrong. It is my choice. Mine and mine alone. If you walk out on me, I will track you down. Hell will freeze over before I let you go!"

Eva stayed silent, terrified. It seemed the monster had finally been unleashed from within him. Tears rolled down her face. She closed her eyes and prayed under her breath he would leave.

As if in answer, the sound of several large men thudding across the lobby was followed shortly by a roar of rage from Brian, and the sound of a struggle. The sound of flesh meeting flesh ricocheted up the stairs, causing her to wince. It seemed Brian had been quickly overtaken, and he began to yell again.

"Eva! I will find you! I will find you!"

Silence descended on the lobby as Brian was bundled out. Eva rose from her hiding place, hesitant, but determined to ensure he had gone. There was a police car outside, and someone struggling violently was being bundled in the back.

As the car drove off, Eva descended the stairs. The concierge sat on a nearby seat, a bar towel pressed to his face.

"He hits hard, that one. You would be Eva, I take it?"

"I am. Look, I can't thank you enough for that. You didn't have to get in his face. It was brave."

The concierge stood, massaging his jaw. "He must have been a foot taller than me. I don't care. He wound me up, and he was covered head to toe in blood. What on earth was he doing out there?"

"I'm not sure exactly what it was." Eva admitted, not really ready to trust her own recollection and still too scared to think rationally. "That was my soon to be ex-husband."

"Don't blame you, miss. He doesn't seem like a keeper."

Eva laughed. "So true. So very true. Look, here's something for your trouble, to say thanks." She folded up a hundred and placed it in his hand, folding his fingers over the top. "Before you protest, this was a team effort, yes? Buy your colleagues a drink when the day ends."

The three porters who had since come back in stood there grinning.

"Far too good for him," the concierge said.

"If you only knew." Eva replied, and left them to clean up.

The levity didn't last long. Eva couldn't put the memory of the little girl's face out of her mind, no matter what she tried. In desperation, Eva took the one remaining avenue she had. Pulling her phone out, she called Gideon.

"Eva?" He said by way of greeting.

"Sorry for bothering you, Gideon. Could you come and get me?"

"What's happened?"

"I... I'm not sure. I just need to get out of here. Can you pull the car around back? I don't want anyone to see me going."

"I'll be right there. Stay where you are. I'll call you when I arrive." The line went dead.

Eva took the intervening time to pack up her belongings into her travel case. In truth, it did not take very long. She sat on the couch, trying to make sense of everything that had happened. A mob for no reason slaughtered an innocent child. Her husband quoted the bible. Strangers disappeared.

"Why? Why me?" Eva asked the empty room.

In response, her cell rang.

"On my way," she said without pause and made her way to the service stairs at the back of the hotel.

Outside, Gideon waited in his silver Chrysler, the engine still running. Trying to maintain her composure, Eva put her case on the back seat and climbed in the front, hugging Gideon as she did so.

"So what happened?" He asked as he pulled out of the car park.

Eva explained as best she could the recent events, omitting nothing. Gideon remained silent the entire time. If his lack of response to her fantastic story surprised her, she put it down to his concentrating on the road. That and the fact Gideon clearly had his analytical face on. No emotion. That was Gideon all over.

Her recounting took the entire journey. Only once did Gideon interrupt her, asking if she was certain she saw the girl ripped to pieces.

"Gideon, I know what I saw," she replied. "That crowd moved as if possessed."

"Interesting. Well, here we are. What do you want to do now?"

"Could I sit in your office? I don't want to be alone at the moment, and there aren't many people left I can trust."

A smile touched the corners of Gideon's mouth. His mouth only. "Of course. Mi casa es su casa. I'll just go ahead and tidy things up."

Gideon hurried off ahead, leaving Eva by the car. He had taken the keys so she couldn't lock up. She took her travel case from the back seat and followed after Gideon.

· · ·

When Eva reached Gideon's office, she could hear the frantic tidying beyond the door. He was certainly in a hurry to clear something. She pushed the door open to catch him slamming shut the doors to a large cabinet. He locked the cabinet, rattling the doors to make sure they was secure and turned to her, his face still expressionless.

"There. All tidy. Please, won't you come in?" He rubbed his arm, and for a moment, Eva saw a bead of blood as if he had been injecting himself. Gideon pulled his sleeves down and Eva saw no more.

Eva sat down on the large comfy sofa, where they had had so many discussions over the years. "Thank you Gideon. Thank you for being there for me."

"Don't even think about it, Eva. The question is what are you going to do next?"

Eva leaned back into the sofa, luxuriating in the comfort. "Well to be honest, I don't have many choices. Home is alien to me, and a death trap waiting to happen. I can't remain at the hotel since that is where the police will come for me, and they will no doubt have come to the conclusion I am responsible for the gluttony as well as the rape."

"Why do you say that?"

"The Detective. Mike Caruso. He has been nothing but hostile. His partner seems a bit more inclined to look at things objectively, but he has been on my back from the moment we met. If they find out I was anywhere near this, he will have me clapped in irons before I can blink."

"Doesn't leave you a lot of choice."

"I was considering bedding down on the couch in my office."

"In the midst of a nest of psychopaths? You're brave."

Eva smiled. "We used to say they had borderline

personality disorder," she said, recalling a conversation with Jenny just the other day. So much had changed since then.

"We still do," Gideon answered. "Look, I have patients to see. Stay here if you like, but I might lock you in. Security and all that."

"You might want to lock your car while you are at it," Eva advised.

Irritation crossed Gideon's face, as if it were something he just did not want to deal with right now.

"Just call my cell if you want out." Not giving her a chance to answer, Gideon hopped to his feet, and was through the door in an instant. As he locked it, he gave her a look that spoke volumes. She was trapped.

Eva leaned back, momentarily confused. What did Gideon mean by that? Peeking through the high window on the door, she checked the corridor was clear. On this floor, it ran half the length of the building, and Gideon was nowhere to be seen.

Looking round the room, Eva noticed Gideon had left his computer on. She had surely caught him at a bad time. Intrigued, Eva flicked the switch to the monitor, which flickered into life and displayed a file network.

Curiosity overrode caution and Eva sat at the desk and started clicking the mouse, opening folders. What she saw left her bewildered. A list of all current residents of the hospital, and from what she could see all past patients, as well.

Eva selected files at random, and every patient had been requested by Gideon, not recommended by the state, as was proper procedure. It appeared he was gathering patients of a specific type, and long before Eva had come to work at the hospital.

Older files suggested they had been gathering patients

for decades. Since computers hadn't existed back in the 70's, these files must have been recreated to gather all the data in one location. Eva wondered if there was a paper versions somewhere.

"Maybe that's what you were doing," Eva said aloud to the empty room.

She switched off the computer and approached the cabinet. Remembering happier times with Brian, Eva pulled a hairpin from her head. Brian had once boasted he could pick a lock, and to prove it to her, had shown her how to do it.

The cabinet, more a full-sized metal wardrobe, was imposing and heavy, but the lock was plain, and easily susceptible to one that knew the tricks. In moments, Eva had sprung the lock and the doors swung laboriously open.

What she saw inside confused and then horrified her. On nearly half of the shelves sat vial upon vial of drugs and blood. There was a syringe in a dish along with a half-filled vial.

Careful not to touch it, she examined the label. It read in small neat letters: *Gamma-hydroxybutyrate. HB 239-A. Subject: GH.*

Gideon was mixing his blood with a known date rape drug? Eva was chilled to the bone at the idea of him doing so, but what concerned her most was this was the exact drug she was convinced she had been given. But what was HB 239-A?

There were documents on a shelf higher up, and Eva grabbed a box file. Gideon might return at any time, and this would end her career, yet it seemed too important not to look.

Inside the file was a series of resumes. The top document was headed 'Gideon Homes' and yet the photo attached was that of another man. There were another four or five resumes attached. They were names Eva recognised as past heads of the hospital. But why would Gideon have somebody else's face attached to his?

Behind these documents were a series of newspaper clippings that someone very meticulously had sealed in plastic. Each clipping referred to the hospital, and Eva put her hand to her mouth in shock when she realized Gideon appeared on all of the photos. Exactly as he was now. One photo was labelled '1965'. That was impossible.

Still farther back, Eva found script writing quite unlike anything she had seen before. It may have been a language; she was not sure. Convinced it was a very bad idea to remain where she was, Eva, on a whim, stowed the documents, along with a folder listed 'Requested Transfers', in her bag.

There appeared to be nothing else in the cupboard, but Eva ran her hands along the back just to be sure. It would be obvious to Gideon that she had been there, so she may as well be thorough. Her sleeve caught on the shelf edge, and as she tugged it free, there was a click and the reek of carrion washed over her. The back of the cupboard slid away to reveal a dark opening.

CHAPTER TWELVE

Eva fought the impulse to retch. The hole was high enough for a man to walk through. A tall man. It was bricked and faded blue paint covered the sides. This had been in place for a very long time.

Trying to ignore the stench, Eva entered. Every fiber of her being screamed caution, but her natural curiosity won the battle. A hallway of not more than a dozen steps led to a room lit with candles at the end. Eva tried to picture where in the hospital this hidden passageway might show up, but there was nothing obvious. Gideon kept his office up here for good reason, it seemed.

The hallway opened into a large square room, thrown mostly into shadow in the early evening. A small window in the far corner provided what daylight was left, the rest coming from two half-burned church candles placed at either end of a raised platform. The flames rose straight, with not a hint of a flicker.

Eva approached the platform, her eyes drawn to a stone tablet in the middle. It was carved with icons, seemingly the same icons she had found in the back of the file in Gideon's office. She found herself entranced by them, her eyes following each glyph in order, trying to find where each ended. The tablet felt menacing, a brooding energy just willing her to release it, if only she knew the way.

Eva shook her head. She had no idea how long she had been standing there looking at the tablet, but as she became more aware of her surroundings, there was a sense of frustration and anger in the room. It was as if she had almost found the answer to unlock the tablet.

On the middle of the platform lay several documents. By their wrapping and smell of preservative, she could tell they were ancient. Eva picked them up and stowed them with the rest of the information from the office in her bag.

There were more documents, writings on lined paper and maps. These Eva also pocketed. She was about to turn away when she caught sight of a piece of paper folded and wedged almost beyond sight between the platform and the tablet. She retrieved it and carefully unfolded the note, reading aloud by candlelight.

"To whoever finds this, know I am being held against my will. He came in the dark, and trapped me here. I have been forced against my will to research the tablet. I am so close to unlocking the ethereal power contained within, but I dare not reveal this to him. I fear the consequences would be too dreadful for me to consider and remain sane. Judging by my cellmates, he means to assume my identity. Yet, at this time, there are two altars free. One for me, and one for another. If you are reading this, you may be the last. I fear he needs six bodies to open the portal. Get out. For God's sake, flee if you are able. My Ellie-May, my Jessica. You are in my thoughts always. Gideon Homes."

It was only as her eyes adjusted to the light that Eva beheld the full horror of her surroundings. Six columns rose from the floor, three to each side of her. Upon five of the six columns lay a body.

Fighting panic, Eva leaned over to examine the nearest remains. The skin was tight around the bones and as tough as shoe leather. This body had lain here for a long time.

The other bodies were in varying states of decay, some clothed, some not. The most recent, and the source of the strongest stench, lay sprawled on the column next to the empty one, as if just thrown there. There was a lab coat folded up under the head.

Trying to avoid looking at the rotting face, Eva pulled the coat out. A faded brass badge was pinned to the front; the words 'Ide' and 'Home' were still visible.

"Ide and Home," Eva mused aloud. "Gideon Homes. Oh. My. God."

She stepped back, straining in the eerie glow of the candles, to seek more detail from the grizzly scene in front of her. There were name plates attached to the end of each column.

"George Grouse, Donald Buckland, Reginald Harley, Colin Andrews, Gideon Homes... all past heads of the hospital. Evan Ross. Evan?" Eva stared in confusion. "Evan? He means for me to...? Oh no..."

The danger loomed large, and fear filled Eva. She ran from the room, through the hallway, and out into Gideon's office.

The door was still locked. He, whoever he was, had not returned. Taking deep breaths to steady her nerves, Eva replaced the sliding door, and arranged the cabinet as best she could. There was no way of locking the cabinet, but Eva hoped that she could at least get out of the room. That way, at least she had a chance of getting out of the building.

Down the hallway was movement. Eva saw him strolling back towards her. Something was not right. Eva looked around. Her bag was done up, albeit looking slightly bulkier than it had before. He was halfway up the hallway. The cupboard doors were shut. Two thirds of the way up. The computer!

Eva had no time to shut all the files down, so she closed as many as she could and turned off the monitor, praying he wouldn't look. She sat down, trying to look disinterested, but inwardly terrified. Turning towards the door, Eva jumped as he gazed in. The look on his face was one of a predator.

Unlocking the door, the man known as Gideon let himself in.

"You all right?"

"Long day. I'm exhausted. You know when, despite racking your brains, you can never find a good enough explanation? Today has been like that for me from start to finish. Thanks for the haven here. I'm fine now. If it's ok with you I'll go make a cuppa and hole up in my office for the night."

He watched her steadily, as if weighing whether to believe her or not. "Okay. You may go. Just don't leave the building. You never know where Brian might end up."

Eva flashed him what she hoped was a convincing brave smile. "Out there is the last place I want to be. Nobody I can trust."

"You can always trust me," Gideon said, smiling and, for an instant, Eva almost believed him.

"Goodnight, Gideon." Eva picked up her bag and left

him alone. She pulled the door close. He had already dismissed her from his mind, and had turned to his computer. He had left the key in the lock, and she turned it as quietly as possible. Only his back was in view. It would not be long. Eva walked down the hallway, and when the door rattled, she ran as fast as her feet would carry her.

"Two flights of stairs, five security doors, one security station, and out." Eva reminded herself as she ran. The sterile lighting made this part of the building look sickly. Eva took the first set of stairs two at a time, thanking fortune she had worn sneakers instead of heels.

She burst through the door onto the first floor and ran towards the security doors. Leaning against them to catch her breath, Eva flashed her security card at the electronic lock.

Nothing happened.

Eva tried it again. Still nothing.

"It won't work, Eva," whispered the fake Gideon from all around her.

Eva screamed in fright. The lights flickered, and went dark.

"You locked me in this room, but answer me this: Which of us feels the more trapped? Which of us feels the more alone?"

Eva looked about her for a means of escape. The only exit was a chute used for bedding and went to the laundry in the basement. Unlikely she could get out from there, especially since the chute went down vertically for two stories. She had not known about Gideon's master control; her only recollection was of a system at the security office by the reception. Perhaps if she could reach it she could override his access.

There was a more immediate concern. She was trapped in a hallway and the patient's cells were only one locked door away.

As if to bait her, Gideon's voice echoed through the hall.

"You have seen my secrets. I cannot allow you to leave. Come. Put back what you have stolen and take your place alongside your predecessors. If you like, consider it a promotion. I have only ever used the heads of the hospital."

"Come back? You're a goddamn lunatic," Eva said to herself as much as the walls around her, hoping to find an element of bravery.

"Lunatic am I?" Gideon's reply caught her by surprise. He could hear her. "Tell me Eva, would you like some company? I am positive there are plenty of gentlemen nearby who would love to make your acquaintance without the restriction of a strait jacket."

At this, the patients, who could hear what was being said as clear as she could, started hammering on their cell doors, screaming obscenities and making it abundantly clear what they would do given that chance. It was like the hooting of excited hyenas.

"You monster!" Eva screamed at the security camera.

"Monster is it? You are clearly frightened. That is good. Animals can sense fright. Some feed off it."

With no warning, a klaxon sounded. Eva looked for a method of escape. The klaxon was only used when there was a problem with the doors. Either side of her, one door away, patients burst out of their cells. Initially they began to fight each other. These were men without conscience, without limit. It did not take long for their attention to focus on her, and then the hunt was on.

As a net of raving humanity closed on Eva, the taunting voice floated above. "Who said I needed you alive?"

That decided it for Eva. Better to take her chances with the unknown rather than face the prospect of imminent and probably fatal violence. As the inmates fumbled at the door, she thrust her bag into the laundry chute and jumped in after it.

Screams of frustration followed her down, but Eva concentrated on the darkness below. Metal flashed by and in moments Eva hit a curve in the chute and bounced out onto a huge pile of soiled sheets. What was on some of them did not bear thinking about, but Eva offered a silent prayer for the fact washing day was yet to arrive that week.

In the gloom of one smoky yellow light, Eva located her bag. It had survived as well as she had, with no more than a bump or two. Not waiting for the inevitable, Eva picked it up and opened the door.

The hallway beyond was dark, and empty. Eva had only been down here once or twice. The basement was mostly storage, and by all accounts had avoided becoming part of the imposter's surveillance network. Trying to slow her breathing, Eva forced herself to calm down. She only had moments left.

Feeling her way, she moved through the darkness, encountering door handles, but nothing more. At one point, she stumbled as she rounded a corner and her hand met nothing but air. It turned out to be an open doorway.

A flicker of light met her from the other end of the hallway as somebody descended the stairs. Eva dodged into the room, and using her hands attempted to find a place to hide. There were large drums in the room, stacked two high and placed haphazardly around. Eva moved between the open door and the nearest set of drums, and waited.

Not long after, whispered voices intruded the silence.

"She could be in any of these rooms."

"The boss said to look in the laundry. She couldn't have survived that fall."

"What about these other rooms?"

"Leave them. They are full of, how can I put it... ex-guests of this facility, stored against God only knows what future. His orders. Best not argue. Not if you want to live."

Eva had a terrifying vision of what was in the drums around her, and as soon as what sounded like two of the orderlies had passed round the corner, Eva moved from her hiding place, and up the corridor towards the stairs and freedom.

All around, Eva could hear feet rushing about, and the feral noises of fighting. As she pushed the door open and stepped into reception, expecting to be confronted by the massed population of the hospital, she was surprised to find it empty.

Not wasting time, Eva crossed the room and pushed the main door. Nothing happened. She tried again, rattling the door. It was locked.

A ghostly chuckle echoed through reception. "So close, Eva. So very close. You had your chance, and now you will be brought before me."

Two of the patients appeared around the end of the hallway leading into the hospital. One eyed her with greed, drooling as he shuffled towards her. The other had a metal bedpost in his hand, blood dripping from the end.

Growing desperate, Eva began to beat at the door,

trying to force it open. Keeping her eyes on the two patients, one of which she realised with horror was none other than Harold Fronhouse; Eva screamed and punched at the glass, bloodying her hands.

They stalked her, eyes unblinking. Eva sank to the floor, still beating at the glass, but with less effort as she came to the numbing realisation she had lost. She would never escape this place. She curled up and sobbed.

The patients now stood over her, the stink of unwashed bodies and unclean breath mingled with a dusty aroma, the same distinct smell from earlier in the day.

"He promises me a prize," Fronhouse purred. "He promises me you."

"Harold... you don't have to do this." Eva pleaded without looking up.

"Oh, but I do," he purred. "When I die, the master has promised me I will return. I will be a god. In the meantime, Dr Ross, I have you to feed on, to make me immortal."

Hands grabbed for her, and she fought them off. One last desperate act of defiance. Then as it seemed Eva was about to be dragged to her fate, the imposter's voice screamed over the loudspeaker.

"It's him! Forget the woman! Get him instead!"

Eva looked up to see a man hurtling towards the door, and threw herself to one side. The door crashed open behind her and the man jumped past, grabbing the drooling patient and pulling him away from her.

"Get out!" the stranger yelled, while wrestling with the Drooler and Fronhouse.

Numb with fear, Eva found it hard to move.

Fronhouse however had evidently recognised the danger. "Get away from her," he hissed. "She is mine." With menacing swings of his bedpost, he advanced on the stranger, who swung the arm of the drooler at him in defence.

"Eva. Dr Eva Ross. Get out of here now!"

There was something familiar about the man. Eva began to move, reaching for her bag.

The stranger had positioned himself between her and Fronhouse, protecting her from the wild swings of the gore-covered bedpost. Fronhouse was getting more agitated by the moment. "No!" He screamed and aimed a wild blow at her rescuer, who ducked.

The bedpost crushed the side of the drooler's head, caving it in. The weapon stuck. Fronhouse refused to relinquish his hold on his only advantage and went down with them, crumpling in a heap as the stranger landed a solid blow to the face.

"Eva? Eva! It's Madden." He held her by the shoulders, as if he had somehow done this before.

"I'm sorry, I don't know you."

"Be that as it may, I know you. Do you want to get out of here?"

Eva came to her senses. There was a car, engine running, just outside the entrance. "Hell yes, I do."

Down the hallway, more patients came running. "I think now would be a great time. Good luck, Gideon," Eva said to the security camera above the reception desk. "Looks like you miss out on number six."

The howls of defeat from the speaker followed them out of the hospital. Eva and her rescuer jumped in the car and he slammed his foot on the gas, leaving their pursuers behind. Eva looked up at Gideon's office. In the near dark of the evening, she saw him there, highlighted by the lights attached to the building. His face appeared strangely elongated.

He disappeared in a moment. Eva looked around the car and began to chuckle.

"What is it?" The stranger asked.

"Irony," Eva replied. "You've stolen Gideon's car."

CHAPTER THIRTEEN

Eva rolled over, twisting her legs in the duvet. The bed was so cozy; she didn't want to admit to waking. And yet, something nagged at her. She had arrived here with a man. He had known her yet she could not remember him.

She sat up, brushing dark hair out of her face. Who was he? The room was empty, and Eva started to get the feeling she would never know. It was a feeling much akin to her experience a couple of days ago.

Eva was just on the verge of panicking when there was a knock at the door.

"Room service," a friendly voice called, and in he walked. "They don't serve breakfast on the weekends, so you have to fend for yourself. Still, the kitchen is pretty well stocked."

Eva's confusion was washed away in an aroma that had her stomach in knots. Fresh coffee mingled with toast, eggs and bacon, the acid tang of orange juice. Eva realised she was starving.

"Thank you for this... Martin?"

"Madden. Madden Scott." The name was said with an air of patience, as if he were used to having to do this.

"And I know you?"

"You could say you did. We did quite a bit of 'knowing' a couple of nights back.

Then it struck Eva. "The bar. You were there."

"I was. Quite the atmosphere that night. Hard thing to forget."

Forgetting her state of undress, Eva began to tuck in to the food. "So what was last night? Round two?"

Madden looked hurt, as if his sense of chivalry had been called into question. "We drove here. You slept most of the way. I've never seen someone so exhausted. When we arrived, I let you get comfortable then I slept on the couch."

Eva couldn't help but look over to the couch, where dishevelled cushions and a rumpled blanket betrayed evidence of the truth.

"Where is 'here'?"

"Bristol, Connecticut. Just the other side of Hartford."

"Almost a hundred miles away..." Trying to cover her lack of trust with a change of subject, added, "why don't you turn the TV on then come have some of this?"

Madden did as he was bidden, and perched on the edge of the bed, helping himself to toast.

The television came alive with a buzzer announcing someone had just failed to win ten thousand dollars in some nonsensical quiz. The show ended and the ABC logo flashed up, with the familiar face of Jeanette Gibson.

"Good morning and welcome to a special news report from world news. Our hot topic: the only subject worth talking about. Cannibalism. Murder. Lust. Strange events erupt in Worcester, Massachusetts."

The screen cut away to show some strangely familiar

places. The bar, the convention center, the police station. All were covered in the report. Eva looked away when the camera panned up the road where the girl had died."

"You have been busy," Madden commented.

"I didn't have a lot of choice in the matter. There's something sinister going on out there."

Eva was about to elaborate when a picture of her flashed up.

"And in related news, police are searching for the whereabouts of this woman. Eva Ross, a psychotherapist at Worcester State Asylum, is believed, by some, to be connected to these unusual events. Police would like anyone with information the whereabouts of Dr Ross to contact them."

Brian Ross appeared on the screen, looking quite upset. In the background, an unconscious Gideon was being loaded into an ambulance.

"She was always quiet, aloof," Brian said in tones that led the viewer to believe he was traumatized. "She was obsessive with her work. She had all the windows barred because she said we were going to be attacked. She was paranoid, obsessive. She scared me."

This caused Eva to laugh. "People won't believe this crap."

"You would be surprised what people will believe. To some, these unusual events are almost a religion. The human mind is easily convinced. It sees what it wants to see."

The news report concluded at the hospital. "And with the escape of all high-risk inmates from the asylum, police have asked the general public to exercise caution when approaching strangers. Some say Eva Ross is connected to this event, too, along with the injuries caused to key members of staff."

Eva was dumbstruck. "It's all one huge lie."

Madden was watching the apparent tragedy unfolding on screen with distaste. "I'm amazed you ever married a man like that. Not to worry for the moment. They won't find us here. They will be looking locally."

Eva eyed him with suspicion. "How do you know they will?"

"Because they don't remember me. The same way you don't. Look, before you ask, no, I don't know what's going on. I have always had a knack for remaining anonymous. I never considered it any great use, but recently it has been a boon."

"To get women into bed?"

Eva jumped when Madden dumped his breakfast on the tray and rose from the bed. "I came looking for you because I thought you might be in trouble. When we met the other night, I pursued you, yes. I'll admit to that. However, it was not all one sided. There was something strange going on in that bar, and we were a part of it. When we went back to your room that was all you. You gave me your number, and I called. It was always switched off. In the end, I thought about coming to where you worked. It seems I found you just in time."

Eva couldn't bring herself to look at him. "I'm sorry. I don't mean to accuse. I'm just on the defensive after days of this. When there was no trace of you, the cops treated me like a suspect. It looks like my disappearance has only heightened belief."

"So what do you want to do?"

"First off, more food. Then a shower. Then try to figure a way out of this mess."

· · ·

Feeling clean always helped. Eva always looked at the day in a much more positive light after a soak in the shower. She returned to the bedroom to find Madden poring through the documents she had stolen.

"I don't recall saying you could go through my stuff."

Madden grinned. "Your stuff. Yeah right. So have you come to any conclusions?"

"Well going back home would be a fool's errand. If those inmates have been released, they are looking for me, but they can't get very far on foot. What's got me interested is they were after you, too. Whoever that was, running the hospital told them to forget me and get you. Like I was bait."

"What's an Iuvart?"

The question caught her off guard. "An Iuvart? I have no idea. Why do you ask?"

Madden waved some of the documents in her direction. "There are a lot of references to something called an Iuvart. Also, lists of patients, locations, transfer requests."

Eva looked at what Madden was holding. "Strange. These are requests by Gideon Homes to have patients from all over transferred to Worcester. Normally the requests come to us from other hospitals, not the reverse. For this to happen must mean he knew about them in advance."

The documents were all marked 'Project Iuvart'. "I have no idea what that word refers to. What else is there?"

Madden reached for the documents Eva had taken from the chamber. "We have these maps. A furnace somewhere. A tomb near a river. All very cryptic with absolutely no names whatsoever. Also this text. It must be some ancient language, Hebrew or some sort. It's nothing I can read at any rate. Maybe it's related to this."

Madden reached for the ancient-looking documents

Eva had hidden under everything else. As he touched them, he hissed and pulled his hand back out of the bag.

"What the hell?" He reached for the documents once more, with much the same result. "What have you got in there? A taser?"

"No, though the thought has occurred to me on more than one occasion. It's just some ancient book my boss kept on an altar next to the corpses."

The offhand manner in which Eva said this had the desired effect. Madden stopped worrying about his hand and gawked at her. Eva reached in and withdrew the book. On an impulse, she touched the book to the back of his hand, expecting a spark. None came, but Madden yelped in pain, and the contact left an angry red welt on his skin.

"Interesting. Maybe it's poison."

"If that's the case, how come you are fine?"

Eva winked at him. "Maybe it's *man* poison."

Madden laughed. "Well, whatever it is, you can be sure I won't be touching it again."

Eva opened the book. The same ancient script filled the cracked pages. Careful not to disturb it more than she already had, she closed the book and wrapped a cloth around the leather cover.

"That's not going to help us. Best keep it safe."

Madden was reading the transfer manifests. "Are you planning to go back to Worcester?"

Eva sighed, "I don't see how I can."

"Well since you are the prime suspect for everything that's happened, and we have all this information, why don't we try using it. Might lead somewhere. If nothing else it might help convince the cops you aren't mad."

"With all I have seen over the past couple of days, I'm

not entirely convinced I'm not. At any rate, I'm not going back, and I am certainly not letting you out of my sight."

"Oh?" Madden leaned towards her, and she felt a familiar warmth towards him. "Made an impression, did I?"

"You are far too interesting a specimen to let wander through this world without study. Plus, you have your uses."

Madden looked crestfallen. "Well I'm glad to help."

"Plus, I have all these repressed memories of you. I want to see if having you close by helps me remember our night together. Now, where's closest to us in these documents?"

Madden shuffled through the papers. "We have a transfer manifest from Allentown State Hospital here. It seems there were several patients your boss was more than eager to get his hands on."

Eva pondered this for a moment. "Allentown... Allentown, Pennsylvania? Let me have a look at the document."

Madden handed it to her. "Just as I thought," she said. "This is a few years old. Allentown State shut down. This document seems to be a demand from Gideon for just about any patient going. It's a good place to start."

"Please excuse my naiveté, but how is a closed hospital a good place to start?"

Eva placed her hand on his arm. "Because only a few miles away is Lehigh Valley Hospital, and in there works an old friend of mine. He might be able to help us."

Madden looked dubious at the prospect of another man's help. "And you trust him?"

"I have no reason not to. He is preeminent in his field of study; a very respected man." Eva began to pack the documents away. "If you don't want to come, I would understand."

"What was all this about studying me?"

"I can't force you against your will, Madden. Allentown it is. To be honest, the further away we get from whatever it is that's killed the real Gideon Homes the better."

CHAPTER FOURTEEN

Packing did not take long, for the previous evening had been mostly about sleep. Eva felt a sense of disappointment upon leaving the hotel. It was a great Tudor mansion, surrounded by gardens patrolled by semi-naked trees.

"Shame we couldn't stay here longer."

Madden paused to look back at the building. "Yes I guess it is kind of quaint. I've never really paid attention to the surroundings as I mostly seem to arrive and leave in the dark."

Eva chose not to pursue what it was that led Madden to keep such unusual hours, instead getting into the car. As Madden climbed in, a thought struck Eva.

"We need to lose this car."

"You sure? A nice comfy Chrysler like this? All the bells and whistles."

"And belonging to the one man who wants the both of us captured by all accounts. If they aren't out all ready, how long do you think it will be before the police are out looking for it? How do we know this thing doesn't have lojack?"

Madden brought the engine to life, slipping the car into gear and pulling out onto the driveway. "I guess we will just have to take our chances. There's no point worrying about it."

"That's easy for you to say. You have everyone forget you because you are a conman or a spy. You aren't being accused of murder, not to mention a whole page of other offences."

"I am neither of those, Eva. What I am is concerned for you. If it means that much, we can get another car. There's a place down near Westport with some people who may remember me."

The morning traffic was slow because of an autumn fog that had rolled in off the Long Island Sound. Nevertheless, they were soon on the interstate heading south. Madden chose the scenic route, taking them along route 95. The fog was thicker here, and there was only the occasional glimpse of water. The fog made Eva withdrawn, and despite his repeated attempts, Madden could not engage her in conversation.

It must have only been an hour after they started when Madden turned off the interstate. As they did so, the wail of sirens approached from the other direction.

"Whatever happens, stay calm," he advised. "Maybe I can talk us out of it."

Convinced by the noise that her fate was sealed, Eva remained silent, her fingers gripping the seat so tightly she was sure she would pierce the material.

Lights flashed in the gloom, and three fire trucks roared past. Eva began to laugh.

Madden exhaled a deep breath. "Close."

"How far to go?"

"Hard to tell in this murk. Normally you can see the houses from the interstate. Westport isn't big though, and the house is by the sea. Not more than a mile or so."

They passed a large sign reading 'Mill Cove Historical District' and entered an area of Woodland. Amidst the trees and fog, Eva could see large colonial style houses.

"Looks like you have taken us back in time."

"Yeah, they pride themselves on looking old here. The older the better."

A mansion Eva could only think to describe as immense loomed out of the fog. Madden parked the car next to several others.

"Here we are then. Time for a change of carriage."

Looking at the other cars, Eva said, "You aren't going to just steal one are you?"

"No need. Come with me." Madden led her into the house through the nearest door. The house inside echoed the look of the exterior. They walked through to a large living room that overlooked the bay. In the distance, Eva imagined one could see Long Island from here, but the fog hid everything.

"This is gorgeous. I love these furnishings. They look like they had been stolen from the civil war."

"I'm glad you approve," said a voice from the hallway behind them.

Madden turned, a broad smile on his face. "Cath!"

A woman, who appeared in her sixties, an impish grin contradicting the maturity of iron-grey hair, reached forward and embraced him.

"Madden, you young pup. I didn't expect to see you

back so soon. I thought you were headed north and staying there."

Madden turned to Eva. "This is Cathy Knott, an old friend. Cathy this is..."

"Eva Ross. Dr Eva Ross according to the news." The smiling face became solemn. "You appear to be in a lot of trouble, my dear. Madden, you were right to bring her to me."

"I thought it best," he agreed.

Eva began to back away. "What is this? Madden, I trusted you."

Before Madden could explain, Cathy interrupted him. "And right you should do so, my girl. He has his faults, to be sure, but trusting him is no bad thing. What he means is I am a person not without resource. Anyway, I think the police have their hands full at the moment. Come and see."

Cathy turned and led them into the room from which she had emerged, where a small table and several sofas surrounded a small black and white television. The news report showed a raging fire consuming the better part of a large building. The camera zoomed out to show large gardens and familiar trees before focussing on the news reporter.

"My god," Eva pointed at the screen. We were just there."

"Not more than an hour or so ago." Madden confirmed to answer Cathy's questioning look.

"Well it seems peril is snapping at your heels," Cathy observed.

"Cath, when are you going to get a decent television."

Cathy gave Madden a smack on the arm. "Cheeky bleeder. I have one in the conference room. Large screen.

Companies use it for projecting when they hire the place. I have always said this house is too big for just little old me."

"You mean you like to show it off," Madden said, and skipped out of the way of another well-aimed smack.

They went back to the large room, made somewhat dim as the fog closed in. Madden plugged in the enormous screen and set about finding the news report.

"Don't you find this all a bit eerie?" Eva asked, waving her hand in the direction of the shore.

"Oh no, dear," Cathy replied. "Well, not any more. When my Ted died seven years back, the fog used to scare me. I was alone. I was Jamie Lee Curtis, and the fog held all sorts of terrors for me."

Eva smiled at the movie reference. It was exactly what she had been thinking. "No zombies out there then. No pirate ship and golden cross."

Cathy gave her a knowing look. "Who knows what dangers lurk hereabouts."

Eva turned to watch Madden fiddling with the remote. It was always funny to watch a man in dire straits with something so basic.

"How long have you known him?"

"Madden? Why all of his life. His father was an assistant to my Benjamin while he ran the state."

The statement hit Eva like an anvil. "Your husband was Benjamin Baker? The Governor?"

"Yes, God rest his soul. I still miss him, even now. Do you mind if we change the subject?"

"I'm sorry."

Cathy's smile was still there, though now it was tinged

with sadness. "It is fine. You were asking about Madden, dear?"

"Yes. In the time you have known him have you ever lost memories of him, things you should remember?"

"I can't say I have, dear. Did you want to know more about him?"

Eva was about to answer in the affirmative when Madden shouted across the room, "Got it!"

The color screen blinked to life, showing the hotel. A reporter was in the foreground.

"Chimney Crest Manor, a mock-Tudor hotel which dates back to the nineteenth century has been ablaze for the past two hours. Despite the damp conditions, and the presence of seven fire crews, the fire is still raging out of control. Police have not yet ascertained the cause, though several victims have been pulled from the fire. Be advised some of these pictures may not be suitable for younger children."

The camera switched to a handheld, shaking as the cameraman jostled through paramedics. Peeking through a screen, the cameraman revealed several men in bandages.

"It's funny, your comment about the civil war," Madden said. "Look at what they are wearing. That's army uniform."

"Looks like period costume," observed Eva.

Cathy stared at the screen a moment longer. "We have a lot of those societies in this area. That's Navy. Smuggling and privateering was very common on and around Long Island Sound in the seventeenth and eighteenth centuries. Judging by the tailoring, I would say seventeenth; the sash round the middle, the dark blue jacket with all those brass buttons. Even if they were ruffians to a man they at least had a uniform and a sense of style."

"Look," Eva said as she pointed to one side of the screen. "Something is happening to one of them."

The view was partially blocked, but ice crystals were forming on the screen around another of the patients. Through the opaque material, something writhed before becoming still. At that moment, the cameraman was bundled out of the medical area, but not before a paramedic pulled back the screen to reveal an empty bed.

"As you can see, this hotel has been host to some very unusual events," the reporter continued. "Police arrived very quickly, and efforts are being made even at this early stage to ascertain the identity of those responsible."

Eva's stomach clenched as the camera panned round to reveal several police, and amongst them, Mike Caruso, Gideon Homes and Brian. The camera flicked to an impromptu press conference Caruso was leading.

"We believe this event to be linked to a number of such occurrences across the northeast, through Connecticut and up into Massachusetts. It is important you contact us should you or anybody you know suffer episodes of sudden amnesia. We believe the couple responsible for these events are using drugs to render people uncontrollable while they commit these atrocities."

As Caruso spoke, Brian and Gideon exchanged knowing looks.

"What are they doing there?" Eva asked.

"More importantly, what are they doing there together?" Madden added.

"You know them?" Cathy asked.

"You could say that. The tall guy, I thought was my boss, the muscled one is my husband, and the cop with the oversized trousers is convinced I am responsible for every bizarre event occurring in North East America. I could explain it to you, but with the last couple of days I have had, you would have to take a lot on faith, and I don't want you to have to lie for me."

"Oh I think you wouldn't be here if everything was fine," Cathy countered. "Why don't the two of you explain to me just what has been happening."

Eva did as asked, and covered the last few days in as much detail as she could remember. Cathy sat and listened, nothing on her face giving away whether she believed a single word that was spoken. As Eva covered her references to Madden and the amnesia, Cathy glanced at him with sympathy in her eyes. Eva noticed this but kept her thoughts to herself.

Cathy became much more intense, questioning every facet of Eva's story when it came to the hidden room in Gideon's office. She handled the ancient book with reverence, and not a small amount of awe, though she tried to hide it well.

Upon conclusion of her description of Madden's reaction to the book, and their current course of action, Cathy bridged her fingers, her elbows on the arms of her chair, and remained silent for a long time.

Eventually she came to some sort of conclusion, as if weighing all the information was a long and bitter battle.

"Here is what I am going to do for you. First off, I will ensure that car of yours never sees sunlight again. Lojack or not, consider it done. Second, I will replace it with one of my own, plates from another state, something nice and nondescript. You can choose. There are several out there and I don't mind which. Third, how are you set for cash?"

"I have a couple of hundred," Eva replied with a shrug. "In truth I am afraid to use my cards in case they track me."

"Wise girl," Cathy approved. "My Benjamin would have liked you."

Cathy reached into a drawer and removed an envelope. She handed this to Eva. Inside was a wad of hundreds, still sealed around the middle.

"Oh Cathy, I couldn't."

"Yes, you damn well could, my dear. You are going to need it. I have a feeling you are going to be a long time on the road, and I have no idea where you will end up. Also in the envelope is a Federal Reserve credit note, allowing you to draw more money from any bank should you wish to."

"You shouldn't do this, Cath." Madden cautioned her.

"Young man, I do not believe, with your track record, you are one to lecture me on what I should and should not do with my money. This young woman has become enmeshed in your life with no apparent say in the matter. The least you can do is support her.

Go to Allentown. It may be you find the answers you seek there. You say you know one of the staff? Well that is as good a place as any to start. But go now. Don't let them find you."

Cathy hurried them to the cars, and in no time at all Madden and Eva were safely under way in a black Toyota bearing federal plates. Nobody would stop them. She stood for a while, watching the fog billow through the trees as the sound of the car receded into the distance.

When the morning was still once more, Cathy returned to her home and picked a phone from a hidden closet in her private room. She pressed one button – a speed dial. After several rings, a nondescript male voice answered.

"They are out there. Now it is up to you."

. . .

Hanging up, Cathy selected her favourite jacket, and after closing the doors, walked on to the beach. Standing on the shore, she never felt alone. She had been used to being watched all of her life; such was the life of a Governor's wife. It was not long until the fog began to reek of malevolence, as if it wanted to rip her to pieces then and there. Her husband was with her, as always.

"Don't worry, Ben. It's been a long time coming, I'll be home soon."

Cathy sensed the two figures approaching. Closing her eyes, she felt one either side of her. This was her fate.

"They are gone, you know. Beyond your reach. I have seen to that."

Desire rose within her. She had expected this, had expected one of them. But when the hunger to consume joined with it, her fear multiplied. The hunger was for the water, the infinite mass in front and below her. It began to overpower her.

"They are never beyond our reach," said a man's voice.

Cathy turned to confront him. But for the soulless eyes, he might have been attractive, with his broad shoulders and dark hair.

"Asmodeus." Cathy dismissed him with a sniff. "I expected more."

"She has balls," the pretty young blonde at his side commented. "Get on with it."

"So you are what passes for Belphegor?" Cathy laughed. "Hell is doomed." The look that passed between the two was one of fear, not triumph.

"Perhaps, that has yet to be determined. We are here.

Others will come. But for now we are going to watch you walk into your grave, your watery tomb."

The desire for the water surged within her. Cathy had strength enough to crush the cyanide capsule in her mouth. Release would be quick as her body failed her. "I think not."

Her victory was short. Asmodeus chuckled, a deep rumble that shook through the spasms of pain. "You are no angel. I sense the sin in you. You will pass into my realm, and when we unlock the secret, I will drag you back screaming into this world and then you shall know real pain. In the meantime, I will make your fugitives my playthings."

Cathy dropped to the sand. As darkness crept in and overwhelmed her vision, the last thing she saw was a couple disappearing into the mist.

CHAPTER FIFTEEN

THE FOGGY CONDITIONS AND DENSE TRAFFIC IN THE greater New York area made for slow roads. Allentown was little over a hundred miles from Westport, but it was not until nearly midday that Eva saw Lehigh Valley Hospital, dominating the skyline next to the interstate.

"Where are we likely to find your friend?" Madden asked. "That is one huge building."

"Simple. We park the car and we follow the signs. It is a hospital after all. People need to know where they are going."

Thus began a good two hours of futile searching. Despite Eva's confidence, the psychiatric unit was squirreled away in one of the older buildings at the core of the complex. It wasn't until mid-afternoon that they reached their destination.

"Dr Mohammed El-Rafi," Madden read off the name plate. "That him? Doesn't sound very American."

"I never said he was from America. He is naturalized, but he was born in Egypt. What he is though, is brilliant."

Eva knocked on the door.

From the other side a voice yelled, "Not now, I'm studying."

Eva laughed. "Fat chance of that. You couldn't sit still long enough to read a single chapter of text."

A whoop answered her from the other side of the door and in moments, it was thrown open. A slight-built man beamed a grin at them. "Evie! C'mere! Give us a squeeze."

"Hey, Mo. How have you been?" Eva managed to croak as the air was squeezed out of her.

"Bored. Patients are so uninteresting when you have interviewed dozens and all they talk about is how they love killing. Don't you find the same thing?"

"Not lately. Remember Fronhouse?"

"The face eater? Man, I would have loved to have that one. What an interesting creature."

"He tried to kill me."

"Really? Fascinating!"

"Fascinating wouldn't be the word I would choose to use," Madden said drolly.

Having been concentrating on her, now her old colleague finally began to register Madden's presence. He looked Madden over cautiously and then turned to her.

"Friend, or foe?"

"Friend. Definitely friend." Eva replied, knowing any answer lacking in conviction would clam her old friend up. He did not trust strangers. "Madden Scott, Dr Mohammed El-Rafi."

The two shook hands, and after a brief eye contact, Mo turned to her.

"So what's up, gorgeous? Finally left that brute and

come to make an honest man of me? Or is this one taking his place?" Mo looked Madden over. "Definitely something different about you."

"Yes, and no."

The answer seemed to catch Mo by surprise. "What to what?"

"Yes I have left Brian, but no I have not come to you looking for a replacement."

"Shame. Could have been fun." He turned to Madden and clapped him on the shoulder. "Congrats, pal. She's a fox. A real one-in-a-million type."

Madden seemed ready to correct him, but having experienced his sense of honour Eva could see this going sour so she interrupted.

"You and your assumptions. I swear that's how you get your awards."

"I'll have you know that's exactly right!" Mo replied with mock self-importance. "If you aren't here to make me your lover, then you must be after information. But of what kind? Given you work for that monster Homes, and he is widely known for getting what he wants, I will bet my liver you are after information, something he couldn't get, or something that escaped him. I will *assume* therefore you are after information regarding patients released into the community, patients he wanted but could not get."

"Madden, hand it to him," Eva asked.

Madden handed over the transfer request and Mo bellowed in triumph. "Don't you just want to marry me!" He turned and flicked on his computer.

"Humble," Madden muttered under his breath.

"You have no idea," Eva replied.

"Right then," Mo concluded after a few moments.

"They are beyond your reach. They can't be transferred anywhere."

"We guessed," Madden said wryly.

'No, infant, what I mean is they have been released. They were, as you are probably aware, guests of the old Allentown State hospital. When they shut it down due to our blessed Government's need to save a few bucks, they kept minimal records of most of the patients since they were already at least partially rehabilitated. The worst ones it seems your Dr Homes got a hold of, but most escaped his clutches."

"Damn it." Eva was going to use some of her patients more colourful language, but Mo continued.

"There is one I have been keeping tabs on. He doesn't take much effort since he's only just down the road. Within walking distance."

"Oh? Do tell."

Mo turned about, getting his bearings. "Go out of the main gate, turn right. Take the first left and walk about a mile. There's a museum down there about native America culture. His name is Janus Lohnes and he works there, doing menial chores and the like. He's friendly enough, if a little quiet."

"And he was in the psycho ward?" Madden scoffed, earning a look of disgust from Mo.

"Don't tar everybody with the same brush, imbecile. He has Asperger's syndrome. His mind approaches that of a genius, but he has his issues. Not everybody from the old hospital was a felon."

"Then why is his name on the list?"

Mo considered this. "Honestly, no idea. He didn't seem to be Gideon's typical brand of poison. Now since you kids have your direction, is there anything else?"

"Mo, have you been watching the news?"

Mo laughed, long and hard. "Evie darling, when have I ever had time for speculative fiction? I have far too much to deal with here."

"Do me a favour. Watch ABC when you get a chance. Oh one other thing, have you heard of something called Iuvart?"

"Can't say I have. Sounds familiar. Biblical reference perhaps, though you know I never went in for any of that."

"Well it was worth a shot." Eva got up and hugged Mo again. "It was good to see you, old friend. Don't be a stranger. If for any reason you think of something, call me."

"Count on it," he replied. "Good luck with her, pretty man," he said to Madden, shaking his hand. "Don't lose her, or I'll snap her up in an instant." The way he said the first bit was as serious as Eva had ever heard him.

Madden gave Mo a look that said as plain as day, he would not.

"Interesting chap," said Madden as they walked through the parking lot.

"I don't know if he is wasted here or not." Eva opened the driver's door and got in. "My turn to drive. I'm not walking there. I want a means of escape after what's happened recently."

"Shame." Madden looked up at the iron-grey sky, threatening rain. "And it's such a lovely day, too."

As Mo had predicted, the museum was only moments away. Madden gave her a look that said 'I told you so' but Eva chose to ignore it. The Museum of Indian Culture was what appeared to be a converted farm. Eva parked out front next to a blue pick-up that had seen better days, its panels corrupted with rust.

"Just us, then," Madden observed. "Maybe it's closed."

"Well I have nowhere better to be right now. Let's go have a look."

They approached the farmhouse along the carefully manicured path from the parking lot. A sign that read 'Open seven days a week' fluttered in the wind. Eva gave Madden a silent look questioning that fact.

The door to the museum had been left ajar, a permanent invitation or a desperate plea. Eva could not decide which. There was nobody about inside, but Eva found herself soon lost in examining the various carvings and artefacts. A wealth of furs hung from one wall, and Eva luxuriated in running her hand along the surface.

"Help you?" said a voice behind her, and Eva turned to find a young woman of native-American heritage regarding her.

"Hi, yes, I'm sure you can. We have come from the hospital. A friend of mine, Dr Mohammed Rafi, said someone here used to be a patient at the old Allentown psychiatric ward. I was hoping to speak to him. Janus Lohnes?"

Upon mention of his name, the young lady broke into a smile. It was clear she was fond of him. "Sure. Janus is out back, mucking out the stables. Just go back out the way you came and follow the house round to the right. I'd show you but I'm not really supposed to leave the room. Cash till and all, not that we have anything to put in it."

Eva felt a pang of sympathy for the girl. Tourism was a fickle beast. "Thank you. Is he well?"

"I think so," the girl replied. "Maybe a little stranger of late. Quieter."

"I'll see if I can be of any help," Eva decided aloud, and beckoned Madden along with her.

As directed, Eva followed the exterior of the house. The late afternoon was quiet, but for the distant sounds of somebody working. Wanting to observe for a moment before speaking to him, Eva put her finger to her lips and shot Madden a warning glance, who nodded in return.

As they got closer, the noises became clearer.

"That is not the sound of working," Madden whispered. "That's a fight."

Not waiting for her, Madden charged ahead, skidding to a stop when he saw what was going on. It took a moment more for Eva to reach him, and she could see why he was staring.

A small, balding man in a checked shirt and jeans was attempting to wrestle a spade away from a character that appeared dressed for a period-drama. Long coat, high collar, white cravat and mutton-chop sideburns spoke of someone highborn, but the naked rage that consumed the man belied that impression entirely. There was also about him a sense of agony, as if it pained him to be there.

Eva beheld the struggle, until the combatants became aware of the audience. The small man's eyes widened as he looked at Madden, and his opponent roared with glee.

"I am strong. You are weak!" He yelled in an accent that left no other conclusion than he was German, and moved towards them.

No, Eva corrected herself. Towards Madden. It seemed

as if nobody had noticed she was even there. Something was drawing this strange figure to him.

Quick as a flash, the small man picked up the spade and brought it around, smashing the German's legs out from under him. This brought a roar of rage, but the man's eyes never left Madden. One leg smashed, he crawled towards them.

"Let's get out of here," she urged Madden.

"No!" Came the abrupt reply.

Ignoring them both, the man who must have been Janus stepped to one side and smashed the flat of the spade as hard as he could on the head of the crawling man.

Still he came towards Madden. The back of his head was crushed, splinters of bone sticking out at all angles. He began to utter a gurgling laugh.

"Sie haben keine Ahnung, was mich erwartet. Für Dämonen ist die Hölle ewig, und schon bald wird sie auch Sie holen. You can come with me now, hell beast."

"What?" Madden answered. "What do you mean?"

Before the abomination before them could answer, his conqueror reversed the spade, plunging the narrow wooden handle through the body of the fallen, pinning him to the ground.

As if finally realising his impending doom, the German looked up and began to scream; a thin wail, accompanied by a hiss. The air grew cold. Eva tugged at Madden, who remained immobile.

"Madden, get back. We have to get away."

His eyes refocusing, Madden came to and looked at her, and then down at the screaming cadaver. "What? Yes. Out of here."

He began to back away from the gurgling mess staked in front of him. As he did so, the air chilled around them.

"Madden," Eva yanked on his arm, trying to hurry him along. He was entranced again, his eyes focussed on a point beyond the German.

Ice crystals started to form on the posts of the doorway, shooting rapidly up the wood until the whole structure stood frozen. They did not stop, swarming across the beams above them, and across the floor under their very feet.

"Look!" Madden screamed, and Eva followed his gaze. Where Madden had been pointing, a hole had opened in the air. From within emitted a sickly white glow.

"Get out!" Eva screamed, and bowled into Madden, throwing him backwards through the doorway.

They both stood and watched the horror unfold. From the hole swarmed several tentacles, each the thickness of a man's arm. The tentacles reached hungrily for the fallen German, whose voice changed from a wail to a full-blown shriek as they found him, worming their way into his body, writhing under his skin.

The air around Eva began to move, sucked into the portal which was now at least a yard across. The tentacles flexed and pulled the German aloft. His eyes had filmed over, becoming a translucent blue. The sickly glow intensified.

"Die Hölle ist ewig," said a hollow voice that came from the mouth of the creature, and the tentacles pulled him through the portal. In an instant, the portal collapsed and the light winked out.

CHAPTER SIXTEEN

"WHAT... WHAT DID WE JUST SEE?" EVA ASKED rhetorically, trying to make sense of it all.

"The same thing that was just off camera on that news report," was Madden's answer. "Sometimes it's scarier to not see it all."

"And sometimes quite the reverse." Eva walked back into the barn. Inside was a scene from deepest winter. Frost clung to everything, even Janus, who stood immobile in the center of the room, his hands at his side.

"Janus? You are Janus Lohnes aren't you?"

He remained where he was, unmoving, his eyes averted.

Madden walked towards him, reaching out to shake him. Janus reacted with violence, pulling Madden past him and into an arm lock, forcing the bigger man to the floor.

"What are you?" He demanded.

"I'm just... trying to... help," Madden said through gritted teeth.

"Leave me alone!" Janus pushed Madden to the ground and ran off.

Madden made to rise and give chase. "Madden, don't,"

Eva warned him. "It's not his fault. He's autistic. Sometimes they don't like eye contact, or to even be spoken to. It has to be all on their terms. They are just wired that way."

"And yet he's capable of fighting and defeating whatever that was? And what was all that German? And why did he call me 'Demon'? And why did that other guy recognise me?"

Eva could see Madden was bordering on hysterical. His eyes were wide, and despite the cold, his face was dripping sweat. It was as if something wanted to burst from him. She put her arms round him, attempting to calm him. She found it was not an unpleasant experience.

"Let's deal with one thing at a time. First off, you need to calm down. We aren't going to accomplish anything with you acting like a madman."

Madden drew a series of deep breaths. "They used to call me 'Mad One', making fun of my name."

"Who did?"

Madden smiled and shook his head. "It's not important. Maybe I'll tell you some other time. So the language, what was it he said at the end there? Die Hölle ist ewig?"

"Sounds close enough. We will have to do a bit of digging though if we want an answer. I don't speak German."

"It means 'Hell is eternal'," said a voice from by the edge of the house. The girl from the museum rounded the corner and approached them, looking past into the barn. "What happened there?"

"We aren't entirely sure," Madden replied, "but I would suggest two things. First, you don't go in there as it might be unsafe, and second it seems your Janus has a bit of 'Fight Club' in him.

She smiled. "He's always been strong, if a bit elusive.

Was that all the German you needed? My grandfather was German, and insisted we all learn the language."

Eva repeated everything she could remember of the period figure's speech.

The girl frowned as she tried to work it out. "It means something like 'For demons, hell is eternal. You have no chance to escape; it will claim you all,' or something to that effect."

The translation had a chilling effect on Eva, and by his face, Madden too. Their conversation progressed no further as the sound of an engine starting disturbed the now tranquil setting.

Madden started running. "That's our car!"

Eva ran after him as fast as she could, but by the time she reached the parking lot, all she could see was a trail of dust leading away west.

"It was him," Madden panted. "Everything was in that car."

Eva patted her bag and winked. "Not everything."

"I am so sorry," the girl said between breaths as she caught them up. "He has his moments, but he's never done anything like that before."

"We should get a car and go after him. We could still catch him."

"To what end?"

Madden turned to face her, frustration showing on his face. Her question had thrown him.

"He is autistic. He is not like any of the patients we ever had. If anything, he is actually a genuine case. Why Gideon wanted him is the biggest mystery."

"That truck belongs to Janus," the girl offered. "Maybe you could use that if all else fails. Sometimes he goes off, but never for more than a couple of hours. He lives here in one of the guest bedrooms as part of his release from the hospital. If you want to stay and wait for him that would be fine. My name is Charlie. I live with my mom, Carla here. There are plenty of guest rooms, and I'm sure Mom would welcome the company, especially with Dad upstate."

Inside, Eva celebrated a victory for Charlie. Two 'helpless' women would appeal to Madden's sense of chivalry.

"Your dad lives here also?" He asked.

"He does. He's away on Lenape council business." Charlie turned to address Eva. "The mall is still open. If you want I could drive you there and we could get some clothes." She turned to Madden and grinned. "You sir, would look great in some of the traditional Lenape clothing we have on sale in the museum shop."

Both Eva and Charlie burst out laughing.

Several hours later and darkness surrounded the museum. There was no street lighting so the nearest light was the eerie glow in the sky from the nearby hospital. Janus had not returned, and any headlights that came towards the museum continued east, dashing any hopes of his return.

Eva and Madden sat at a table with Charlie and Carla, enjoying a hearty meal, but both looking out of the window where they knew the road to be.

"I don't know what to say, honestly." Carla remonstrated. "And you say he fled after you found him in the barn?"

"Yes, that's right. Dr Rafi is an old colleague of mine, and we have been looking into ex patients of the old hospital." Eva purposefully left out all mention of the ice and the bizarre portal incident. It would have just scared her. A knowing glance from her daughter said this was the right path to take.

"Well if he doesn't return by morning, please take his truck. That is the least I can do for you. We bought it for him. It is well maintained, if a little aged."

"Charlie here mentioned Janus has a room with you. Do you mind if we take a look?"

Carla inclined her head in assent at Madden's request. "If you think it will help. His room is actually in between the two I have set aside for the pair of you. Follow me."

Just down the hall from the kitchen, there was a row of doors. It appeared guests were a common occurrence. Charlie unlocked one, flicked the light switch and ushered them in.

The room stank. Unwashed clothes were dropped randomly on the floor, and the bed appeared more like a nest, more clothes and rubbish intertwined with bed sheets.

"I'm so sorry," Carla apologized. "If I had known it was like this, I would have never let you in, or at least tidied it first."

"It's no bother," Eva assured her. "Best we see the room for ourselves as it is. That way we won't miss anything."

Eva and Madden searched the room with Charlie's help while Carla looked in from the hallway, fretting and encouraging them to leave so she could tidy. The whole room was a random mess of junk. Eva began to suspect there was nothing of value in there.

"I think we should leave it," she finally decided. "He genuinely is what he seems to be. There's just too much evidence to think anything else. He is probably a dead end in terms of the answers we seek."

"Or so it would seem," Madden replied as he worked his way beneath a loose floorboard under the bed. Sitting up, he brandished a plastic envelope marked 'secret' on the front. "Pay dirt."

Opening the envelope, Eva sifted through yet more obtuse documentation. What appeared to be a chart of solar eclipses, maps of a desert, were put to one side.

"This appears interesting," she said. "It's by Dr Rafi. 'Study of unstable people in places of supernatural convergence'." Eva flicked through the pages of the study. "It mentions Janus by name in several places."

Eva read a bit more, and then shut the document. "Got it."

"Got what?" Madden asked, left dangling with anticipation at her lack of an answer.

"We had mention before of a furnace. This study reveals Mo was taking patients to reported hauntings to study their reactions."

"The doctor did take Janus away for a few days not too long back," Carla admitted.

"Any idea of where they went?" asked Eva.

"No, but Janus was very different when he returned; as if his illness had been compounded."

Eva turned to Madden. "Sloss Furnaces in Birmingham, Alabama. It's one of the reputed most haunted places in America. And we are on the way."

A map in the study showed several locations dotted across a map of the United States. Eva showed this to them.

"That has to be the better part of a thousand miles away." Madden moaned.

"You got anything better to do?" Eva asked, declining to mention the ongoing investigations and point out the fact that three very deadly individuals were tracking them. Madden understood this all too well.

"We are going to need an early start then," he decided, walking out of the room muttering.

In stark contrast to Janus's room, Eva's own was very well tended and comfortable. At some point in the night, Eva found herself slipping into Madden's room, and in the early hours. The life-changing love affair was rekindled. A while later, exhausted but satisfied, Eva crept back to her own room and slept peacefully until dawn.

As Eva woke and dressed, she realised that unlike the night in the hotel, she remembered every detail of the man she had spent the night with. It gave her reassurance.

In the kitchen, Eva slid up to Madden and kissed him. "I know you, Madden Scott," she breathed. "Looks like your powers only work on strangers."

"You sure you want to do this?" He asked. "That's one hell of a drive."

"And yet it feels right." Using all the willpower she could muster to turn away from him, Eva took the keys from the table, read the note of farewell from Charlie and replaced it, with a hefty sum of money underneath for good measure.

"They need it," she said when Madden whistled in awe at her action. "Besides, we can get more."

Outside Eva approached the truck with intense trepidation. It looked like it wouldn't make it out of the city, let alone to a city several states away.

"Hunk of junk," Madden said, reinforcing this belief. He picked at some of the rust. "Hey, this isn't rust at all. This is painted on."

They climbed in, stowing their replacement gear. Eva slipped the key in and tried the engine. It roared into life with none of the expected protest. "This is well maintained," she observed, "and it has a full tank."

"More than meets the eye," agreed Madden.

They set off at a conservative pace, sticking to the speed limit like glue. In the dark, Eva felt isolated, despite Madden at her side. Eva had a feeling Gideon and her husband were not very far behind. Even so, their truck was alone.

They made good time despite the traffic thickening in the morning, stopping for breakfast just outside the city of Harrisburg. After, it was slower going, but they pulled off the interstate and stopped for lunch in a small town called Stephenson at a restaurant called 'Chick-fil-a'; it was there Madden leaned over to whisper in Eva's ear.

"You see that blue sedan that's pulled up outside?"

Eva could see the car, a beaten up blue seventies Lincoln across the park. The drivers had not exited the vehicle. "I see it. What of it?"

"I don't mean to alarm you, but it's been tailing us since Hagerstown, so about thirty or so miles. They pulled off when we did."

"Coincidence?"

Madden shook his head. "I don't believe in it. Since we

are not alone any more, why don't we have some fun with them?"

Before Eva could warn him off, he had turned to a couple in the next booth. "Excuse me, but are you a cop?"

The man, a large, well-muscled chap wearing security uniform regarded them. "Next best thing. Security guard. Name's Will Cleveland. This here is Emily. Can I help you at all?"

"Sure can," Madden grinned. "See those guys out there in the blue Lincoln? They are trailing us, something about her being an ex of one of them. They won't leave us alone. Think if we slip out the back you can delay them?"

Will winked and a vicious grin spread across his face. "You give me a minute, and then make your exit."

Emily rolled her eyes. "If he wasn't bad enough before, now he will have this to boast about."

"We really appreciate it," said Eva, and slipped Emily a hundred-dollar note.

Her eyes widened. "You don't have to do that."

"You have a son, don't you? Buy him something nice." Eva left the dumbstruck young lady and pulled Madden to his feet. "Time to go."

"How do you know she has a son?" Madden asked as they left by the exit the other side of the restaurant from where Will Cleveland was now in a fully-fledged argument with two middle-aged men stood by the Lincoln.

"Psychologist," Eva replied with a mysterious smile. "You aren't the only one with secrets. "Besides, they will forget all this won't they?"

"If history is anything to judge by, they will have forgotten me and everything associated with me within five minutes." Madden said no more and left Eva where she stood as he went for the truck.

In moments, he was at the wheel, exuding calm in direct proportion to the panic Eva felt, and eased the truck out of the parking lot and around the restaurant.

Eva got in, and closed her eyes. "Slowly, then floor it."

Madden did as told, and soon they were flying down the interstate, the well-tended engine of the truck barely above a purr.

For about a half hour Eva felt a sense of hope, but then she spied a familiar blue car in the wing mirror. "They are back."

Madden slammed his hands on the wheel. "Crap. Any bright ideas?"

"We can't escape on the interstate. How about we get off at the next town and lose them in the hills?"

"How about we do something more immediate?"

Before Eva could answer, Madden slammed on the brakes, causing the truck to shudder as it tried to stop. The Lincoln crashed into the back of the truck, crumpling its hood. Madden floored the gas pedal, leaving a multi-car pile-up in their wake. "That should do it."

Two more cars veered around the mess and plunged after them. "Maybe not!"

Eva turned in her seat. "Jesus, will this never end?"

The chase was on. To Eva's eye, Madden became a different person, focussed on driving. It was clear he had done this before. He weaved and dodged, using traffic around them to shield their escape from the pursuers.

"Where are we?"

Eva looked at a map she had found under the seat.

"Woodstock. There are roads up into the forest from here. We could lose them that way."

"Let's try it." Madden swerved the truck off the interstate at the very last moment, but failed to lose the cars. At the junction, another blocked their way. "Look out!" He yelled as he sideswiped the car.

Twice they tried to get off the main road that hugged the foothills of the Appalachians to their left, and twice they were denied.

A sense of oppression began to fill Eva's head. "They are herding us."

"Maybe, but they won't have us until we are stopped, and in this beast I don't plan on stopping."

They tore through the town of Edinburg, Madden almost tipping the truck over as traffic forced him to turn left up into the mountains. A sign that read 'George Washington National Park' flashed by as they began to climb. The power of the truck began to tell, and slowly the cars pursuing them dropped off. Turns in the road distanced them yet farther, and the gloom perpetuated by giant trees helped hide them from view.

At length, Madden began to ease back on the gas. Eva stopped clutching the seatbelt and forced herself to be calm.

"So where are we now?"

Eva consulted the map. "I have no idea. We are in the middle of the forest with bears and coyotes and God alone knows what else around us."

"And several cars full of very mean-spirited individuals. Don't forget them."

Eva gave him a look that spoke volumes about what she thought of that comment. "I would say if we keep on this road and bear left where we can, we will come down out of the mountains near a town called Luray. But don't hold your breath."

Lights flashed in front of them. Madden never had a chance to answer as suddenly the trucks tires exploded and the truck began to spin.

"Stinger!" Madden yelled. "Hold on!"

Eva braced herself as the spinning truck headed towards dense woodland. It seemed there were people everywhere.

"I'm sorry," Madden said. There was a crunch, the splintering of glass, and, as blackness enveloped Eva, she felt gravity fall away as her body began to tumble.

CHAPTER SEVENTEEN

Eva could not see. She opened her eyes but everything remained dark, not a speck of light. Instinct made her panic. The loss of one of the primary senses could overwhelm most at first, so instead of reacting to her body's plight, she closed her eyes again and forced herself to consider her situation.

By wriggling around, Eva concluded she still had use of her limbs, albeit in a limited capacity. Various aches all over her body showed she had survived the crash more or less intact, though she could still not place where she was. A lot of rustling indicated the presence of leaves, and the earthy scent meant she hadn't hit her head so hard she had lost her sense of smell. She decided to try her voice, wary it could bring the wrong sort of attention, but too desperate to really care.

"Hello? Can anybody hear me? Help. Help me!"

Knowing she could be stuck here for days, Eva gave up on shouting and instead decided to try and wriggle free. It was slow going, and all Eva really accomplished was to get her bottom wedged against what she perceived to be her route of exit.

Eva became aware of footsteps outside of the 'cave' she must have been in. While she was desperate to escape, something warned her to silence.

Nevertheless, she yelped when a hand grabbed her thigh, running all the way down her leg to the ankle. Another hand then did the same thing down the other side.

The hands grabbed her just above each knee and tugged hard. For a moment, her bottom caught again, and then she slid free, sliding a few feet down the slope.

The reason for her lack of sight became very clear. It was nearly dark. That, coupled with the dense foliage and the fact the now-wrecked truck was resting on its crushed roof answered all her questions. Except one. The figure by the truck.

He made no move towards her, remaining where he had pulled her out. In the gloom, she spied a familiar checked shirt.

"Janus?"

He shifted uneasily. Eva approached him with caution, but also relief. "Janus, are you ok? What are you doing here?"

Janus' only response was to say, "You can walk."

Eva realised now he hadn't been groping her, but had been checking for injuries. "Yes. I can walk. I'm a bit bruised, but I'll live."

Taking that as some sort of affirmation, Janus turned and began to walk away.

"Wait. Janus, wait! I have some things I need from the car."

Janus continued to walk. "They have him."

"Madden?"

"They have him," he repeated, and rounded the truck.

Forgetting anything of material value, Eva hurried as best she could after Janus. She was pleasantly surprised to find the black sedan parked just down the track. Even more so, when she saw Janus had evidently salvaged everything from the truck.

Letting Janus drive, Eva sat in the back getting whatever rest she could.

"Is it far?"

Janus declined to reply, but after only one bend in the road, he parked up next to a trail, threw the keys to Eva and grabbed the shovel he was evidently fond of. He waited for her to exit the car, which she duly locked.

A sign at the end of the trail read 'Duncan Hollow Loop', which Eva had to squint to read.

"We are going to get him back," Janus said, as Eva straightened, her back aching.

"Yes. We are," Eva agreed, causing the small man to smile. "You don't appear to have a problem in the dark. Why don't you lead on? I'll try to keep up."

Janus crept down the track, never moving beyond a pace away from Eva, who even at a crawl was having trouble keeping up as muscles cooled and stiffened.

In the distance, there was light. Somebody must have had a roaring bonfire going. Janus turned to her and nodded as if agreeing with her assessment of the situation. He put his finger to his lips. She nodded

In the dark, mist filled the gaps between the trees, the mist enraged with an orange glow from the distant fire. The track opened out to a wide expanse of farmland, dominated by a large house. On the other side of the house, the fire raged, its flames visible above the roof of the house.

Janus pulled Eva into the woodland as they began to circle the farmstead. "They have rock from Duncan Knob. They have made an altar. It was said in ages past, the Devil appeared, that he could bring minions forth at will. He was defeated here, they say, by an ancient tribe. Before they sent the Devil back to hell, they cast a spell over him to remove knowledge of the way back. But some already knew the way back, and they prepared for His coming. One would come to open the door for others, willingly or not. He would be the least of equals, and his blood on the sacred rock would open a door that could never be closed."

"And you think Madden is that man." Eva leaned on the tree trunk. "You think Madden is... a demon?"

Janus did not answer her. Instead, he looked out of the woods towards the fire. Nearby, several figures surrounded a stone block, working with frantic haste to secure an unconscious figure in a macabre parody of Christ on the cross. It was Madden.

"We are all sinners," Janus whispered. "They are all demons. We are all demons. It is just a matter of time."

"We need to get him off there. They are going to kill him."

One hand on his shovel, Janus reached the other around her, pulling her slowly back with a strength that brooked no argument. "Watch."

One of the men, his features distorted by the flames, approached the altar and bowed. "Dyaa hoo-ah in tocholin Nag Hamaddi," he bellowed aloud.

Janus hissed.

Whatever that meant, Eva had no idea, but Madden's lack of an answer enraged him. He reached up and bashed

Madden's head against the altar. "Dyaa hoo-ah in tocholin Nag Hamaddi!"

Madden uttered something unintelligible and his captor pulled out a gun, whipping the butt across Madden's forehead. He hung limp, and the man with the gun walked around ranting at his cohorts, who formed a semicircle and knelt, chanting.

Eva turned to whisper to Janus, only to find he was gone. Looking around in the dark proved futile, but the answer to his whereabouts came quickly as roars erupted across the clearing.

Janus had appeared amidst the chanting mass and was wielding his shovel like a scythe with terrific strength. Bodies toppled and limbs flew in every direction, but none of them could touch Janus, who kept them all at arm's length with his whirling 'blade'.

Those who had not been touched, egged on by their leader, massed for an attack. Janus retreated, drawing them away from the altar. He was doing this on purpose!

Eva ran as fast as her battered body would allow her and used the bulk of the building as cover. Edging round, she was surprised to see all the bodies were incapacitated, but none had yet died. Then she saw Madden. He was conscious, if barely, and chained to the rock altar.

Eva ran to him and yanked at the chains. They were padlocked and no amount of yanking at them would make any difference. Spying some loose bits of rock, Eva began to bash away at the locks with a sizeable chunk. With a little effort, the lock popped open.

Wiping her forehead, Eva noticed the silence around her. But for the moans of the fallen, the clearing was empty. Janus had drawn the rest off into the woods and there the killing had begun in earnest. Even with the light of the fire behind her, Eva could see the bursts of white as whatever had claimed the loser in Allentown claimed those dispatched by Janus's ferocity. The air began to chill, and Eva registered a new threat. If whatever was claiming the victims came near, it might take Madden.

Renewing her attack on the remaining padlock, she was rewarded by not only the lock breaking, but also Madden waking fully. He struggled against the chains and Eva helped remove them. As soon as he was clear, he grabbed Eva and kissed her soundly.

Memories came flooding back. The entire night they had spent together erupted in her mind. Instinctively she slapped Madden's face as hard as she could.

"You knew! You knew exactly what you were doing that night. How could you?"

Holding his face where she had hit him, Madden glared at her. "I was not the only one who knew. What were you doing walking into a bar by a convention center on your own? Looking for a conference? Everybody knows what it is like around there. Booze, sex, and no guilt, no questions asked."

"I didn't know."

"And yet you were there for that very same reason, for a night you could forget. Besides, after what we have seen, do you think it was all up to me? I am no saint, but a child being eaten alive? Portals springing open in mid air and dragging people out of existence? You cannot hope to lie that at my feet. How can you, knowing that, blame me for the bar? You have seen what happens to people around me. They forget, and yet you are remembering. How are you so different?"

"If we get out of this, you are going to tell me all about yourself, Madden Scott. I want to know everything. There are a lot of miles to Birmingham and you are going to fill them with your story."

At the edge of the clearing Janus appeared, shovel over his shoulder. He was covered in blood, and by the way he was walking, none of it was his own.

"What's his story?" asked Madden.

"I have no idea. Just don't pick a fight with him."

Ignoring them both, Janus examined the fallen in the clearing. One spat at him, and then said something that clearly was not complementary. Janus reacted by bringing his shovel round in an arc and severing the head. He then dispatched the rest of the fallen.

"Move him back," Janus instructed.

Eva took Madden's hand and pulled him out of the way to the shelter of the house.

"Come to me." Janus held his free hand up.

Without knowing why, Eva returned to him. As before, the air grew cold, frost crystals spreading across the ground. The inert bodies began to wail in a language that sounded both ancient and alien. The roaring bonfire became muted, the ice threatening to stifle its energy.

Portals popped into existence, one for each of the defeated. Hungry tentacles reached for the bodies, bearing them aloft. Where limbs had been severed, they started to thrash as if reanimated. The cold was numbing, stinging her eyes as Eva tried to peer through the nearest portal. Just bright white light beyond, no hint of anything else.

The fire had faded in the cold, the heat sucked out of the very air into the portals. One by one, the portals winked out of existence, until was just one left. The tentacles grabbed the ringleader, but then paused, and began to stretch towards Madden.

He refused to move initially, until they neared the

house, feeling their way along the ground. Four yards...three...two.

"Run!" Eva screamed, and Madden jumped to one side and safety.

As he did so, Janus stepped to the portal and swung his shovel, cutting through the largest of the tentacles. It fell to the ground, writhing like the tail of a lizard. A roar of pain mixed with anger burst through the portal, and the remaining tentacles whipped back into the portal, which then went out.

The clearing was still. The fire had been smothered by the cold so much so, only embers remained, a mute reminder of the ferocity that had so recently assailed them. The tentacle, upon losing contact with its place of origin, had ceased moving, and collapsed into a rotten mess, black ichor oozing from decomposing skin. In moments, a burn on the ground was all that remained.

Madden joined them in the clearing, scuffing the burn marks of the tentacle as he did so. "I don't get it," he said as he stared at the ground. "Why was it going for me? I'm not dead."

Eva turned to Janus, who was now cross-legged on the ground with his shovel resting across his knees. She knelt on the cold, dead earth in front of him. "Well something is definitely up. I don't know what your story is, but you are much more than you seem."

"Nice of you to say so," Madden quipped.

Eva stood back up to face him. "You both are. You saw what happened here. Let me give you a little perspective. We stood in the middle of these portals that should not exist, from which come limitless tentacles that take what

Janus presumes to be demons and sucks them into what, for a lack of a better term, can be called 'Hell'. They do not touch us, not even when Janus severs one, and yet they sense you, and reach for you. You were captured to be sacrificed. Janus tells me a story about a portal to Hell opening with a sacrifice; that sacrifice seemingly being you. Figures out of history recognise you. You affect those around you in a more subtle, but nonetheless profound way. That just does not happen. And no matter in what car we travel, they always find us."

In the distance, in the darkness of the woods, an intelligible human voice emits a bellow of unbridled rage. From other locations, some closer, some farther away, others answered. They were still not alone in this valley.

Janus stood, hefted his shovel and began to walk back up the path. "Can we go?" He asked, without stopping.

Eva remained standing, staring at Madden. The revelation was momentous. "But we had sex," he wondered. "What if..?"

"What if I am pregnant? We shall have to deal with that in time. There are more pressing issues right now. Let's get back to the car and get out of here first, if there is any place we can hide."

Madden's face had dropped as he evidently came to the same conclusion she had, but Eva needed to say it.

"Madden, I think you must have died at some point. I think you are a demon."

CHAPTER EIGHTEEN

Janus scuttled up the path, Madden between him and Eva. They began to stretch ahead, and Madden turned to wait.

"No. Don't." Eva waved them on. "Get the car started. I'll be right behind you."

They disappeared for a moment around a bend, and for once, Eva felt none of the confusion that had so far accompanied Madden's every exit. The spell had truly been broken.

The voices were growing less distant, and more frenzied as it became evident their prey was eluding them. It didn't take Eva long to reach the car. The engine was purring, Madden at the wheel.

Eva breathed a sigh of relief. She had been worried Janus would insist, but in the presence of others, he was happy to be subservient. Climbing in she said, "Go. They aren't happy, whoever they are, and I have a feeling they would finish the job if they get hold of you again."

Madden pulled out onto the road, heading west back

towards the interstate. Eva stole a look at Janus in the back. He was fast asleep amidst their now-doubled baggage.

"He looks cozy."

"Fell asleep the moment he climbed in. Right after I made him remove his blood-stained rags and put on one of my shirts."

"You had time?"

"He seemed eager to be off, so I just told him we would go nowhere if he didn't."

Trees rushed by in the stygian light of the fog, the car's high beams cutting like scythes through the night. The dark outside their sphere of travel was absolute, corrupted by no man-made device.

"Okay, time to talk," Eva decided. "What are you, when and where did you come back and how did you do it?"

Madden stared into the night for a moment. "My name is Satan. I have come from the darkness beneath to bring you all to my domain, where every moment you exist will bring you ten lifetimes of torment." He turned to offer one of his disarming grins.

Eva stared back, waiting for a decent answer.

"Oh come on, Eva. Lighten up."

"I will lighten up when you answer my questions."

"I don't know the answers. For all I know, I have always been the same old me. I grew up in a household where my parents spent their lives pandering to the every whim of the Governor. If I ever did anything wrong, things had a habit of correcting themselves without me having to do a lot. Otherwise if word got out, it would ultimately be reflected on the Governor, and we couldn't have that, oh no. I used to have my own personal clean-up squad. I just got used to not having to ever look back."

"But you were in Jamaica. Surely the Governor of Connecticut's influence didn't extend that far?"

Madden remained quiet for a minute or two. "There were things I did in Jamaica that I am not proud of, nor will I try to justify them. Suffice it to say, I was involved with the underworld there. I drove for gangs on robberies. I was quite in demand. I can drive. Well. It is a gift."

"And nothing unusual happened there?"

"Define unusual. I was lucky to escape all manner of crashes and police incidents."

"Well how about any incident where you crashed and died, or were shot and killed?"

With reluctance, as if he did not want to admit it even to himself, Madden began to talk, this time with none of his usual evasiveness. His eyes gazed off into the darkness as he relived it.

"They had robbed a bank, or at least had attempted to. It had all gone wrong, and we were on the run. If I think about it now, I reckon we were set up. There were cops everywhere, in every place to make it impossible to escape." He shook his head and laughed. "They had really done their homework."

"And you crashed?"

"At first. They shot out one of the front tires and the car spun and flipped over a wall and into the sea. I was driving very fast, so we ended up quite a way out in the water, crashing upside down on somebody's boat. Nobody escaped the car. Nobody survived."

"Well if you are normal, if you are no demon, then you surely did?"

Madden glanced sideways at her. "Or I never had an explanation until now. You got internet on your phone? Do a search on 'Margaritaville car boat death'. There's only ever been one crash like that there."

Eva concentrated on the small screen on her phone as she searched. An article popped up with a small picture of a bar and some police. "Three bodies were pulled from the wreckage. Three Jamaicans. No mention of a Caucasian male."

"And yet there I was, sitting on the sea wall next to cops who totally ignored me."

"Did you feel different?"

"I felt wet. I felt cold, and I ached, but is that unusual? Come to think of it, I ached for a very long time afterwards, but I just accepted it and I got used to it."

"You ache now?"

Madden laughed. "Damn right I ache! I was just bashed up in a car, dragged who knows where, chained to a massive lump of rock and pistol-whipped. I have felt better. But as for the other, it is no more than a tingle on my skin, a sensitivity."

"That gets worse when you come into contact with an ancient artifact, something that might be Holy."

"What. You mean that old book?"

Eva held up her phone where Madden could see it as he drove. The words 'Nag Hamaddi' headed a paragraph of text about lost books, and ancient holy scriptures.

"When you were chained, your captor was yelling something at you in what sounded like Arabic. The only words I could pick out were those. And I have a book here that burns you on contact. Want to bet anything it's not connected?"

"And my skin tingles every moment I'm awake, and people forget me after they have met me, at least when they haven't had fantastic sex with me."

Eva smiled, but no more conversation was forthcoming. Her only thought now was of the following summer, and if she would be blessed or cursed.

Not too long after the road, they were following opened out onto a highway.

"Go right," Eva instructed.

"You don't think they want us to go that way?"

"What choice do we have? New Market is down there, and we need gas and food. Besides, somebody needs to reorganise this mess, even if Janus is comfy back there."

"This isn't going to be easy if they know where I am."

"Have you been chased ever since the accident?"

Madden pulled off the road into a large Exxon gas station. "No, come to think of it, until recently I always made my own way. But what about those that chased us? What about the reaction from Janus when we found him?"

Eva unclipped her seatbelt. "Let's say for the sake of argument they can sense you close up, but on a broader scale they have a feeling, a rough sense of direction. Perhaps they are being guided by someone else."

"Or something," Madden called as Eva slammed the door and waved him to wait where he was.

Gas didn't take long, and Eva made sure the notes she used were well crumpled. In moments, she was back in the car. "Time for food."

At this, Janus perked up. "Custard!"

Both Madden and Eva looked at Janus. He was staring expectantly out of the window of the car.

"Random," Madden observed.

"I was thinking of something a bit more substantial," Added Eva.

They drove along the highway for a few minutes, until out of the trees shone a beacon of joy, a reminder to Eva that even though there was so much wrong with the world, something so simple could bring happiness.

The sign read 'Pack's Frozen Custard', and upon seeing it, Janus leaned forward with expectation.

"Well it looks pleasant enough," Eva said. "Since Janus is responsible for us both being here, I don't see why we can't treat him."

Madden nodded and pulled the car over, though his face showed he was less than enthusiastic about the idea.

"What? Don't demons like ice cream?"

Madden clenched his jaw and parked the car.

Inside, Eva found herself sat with Madden and an excited Janus as they consumed, in silence, a late-night helping of frozen custard in various forms. Given their recent experience, this all seemed somewhat surreal.

Behind the counter, a bored-looking teenager watched them; evidently hoping they wanted no more and he could shut up shop and be off to more exciting entertainment.

Enjoying the silence, Eva let her gaze wander. They were outside, the car just behind them. Distant street lights highlighted the fog that rolled down from the mountains behind them. There was a distinct chill in the air, and Eva pulled her jacket tighter about her shoulders.

Madden, a quizzical look on his face, looked up from their table. "Eva, we aren't alone."

She rubbed her forehead with one hand. "Isn't this ever going to end? How do you know?"

"This recognition of others. I think it works both ways. There are several of them. They are full of... pride. They are here for a reason." He stared at Eva, confusion mixed with comprehension on his face. "How do I know all this? Do they know the same of me? Am I giving everything away?"

The lights of the cabin faded, blinked once and then everything went dark.

"They can't have caught up with us. Not already."

Eva turned in the blackness to where Madden had spoken. "What if they were already here?"

"Yes, young lady what if? Perchance what if that very thing?" The voice came from near the road. "Why it does seem we were prepared to apprehend any that might cross our tracks this very eve. But the pinch of the game will not come until we at least get to see your faces."

"You might have thought of that before you took the power offline," Eva shouted to the night.

"Oho, I like this one," said a voice from the other direction. "Pray she is as comely as she is peevish. I like to teach the pretty ones their lessons, even if they speak strangely and out of turn to their betters."

"Darkness is our ally," said a third. "Is it not yours?"

"If you have a flashlight, you may light it," said a deep voice from closer to them, unnervingly close.

"The car," Eva whispered to Madden. "High beams." To the darkness she shouted, "We won't be a moment."

Madden squeezed her hand and slipped into the darkness. Shouts of alarm came from around them as he brought the engine to life, becoming screams of panic as he shifted the car into reverse and floored the gas. Eva counted two thumps as the car tore across the asphalt, a third as Madden brought the car around with the lights still off.

He returned the car to its original position, albeit turned the other way. Out in front three portals popped into existence, tentacles grasping and tearing, and the light from within casting a sickly pallor over the restaurant. All too soon, their demon assailants had been spirited away and darkness smothered them once more.

It was then Madden turned the car lights on. In the high beams, the parking lot showed one more inert body, and a fifth figure struggling against something.

"Janus?" Eva called.

"Show him," Janus called back as he fought to keep his grip. "Show him his fate."

Eva understood the implication. Too many of them had tried to take Madden from her for her to care. Deliberately she walked up to the struggling captive, and then to the car. Taking Janus's shovel from the trunk, she raised it aloft, and then drove it through the unconscious man's neck.

The portal burst into being directly above the dead man, as if whatever was there on the other side, had been waiting for it. Tentacles plunged into the corpse, and one grabbed the head, which began to emit a low moaning noise.

Janus held their final assailant close enough for the tentacles to swerve unerringly in their direction. His captive struggled but could not break his hold.

"Is this what you wish?" Eva asked. "Eternal damnation? This is your future, like it or not. You are damned. You have come back from a place that should not exist. You do not belong here. You belong in there, wherever there is."

Janus moved forward a step, attracting the attention of a free tentacle. It snaked towards them, and their captive began to shriek, writhing helpless in Janus's iron grip. Janus waited long enough for the tentacle to brush the leg of the struggling man, if man he was, and yanked him out of the way. Eva struck at the tentacle, and it whipped back through the portal, which winked out leaving them alone in the darkness.

"I can't move my leg," said the captive over his shoulder to Janus. "You have hobbled me, sir."

Madden got out of the car and joined them, causing the injured man to hiss at him. "Yeah, whatever pal. I get a lot of that. So what are we doing with him?"

"Janus, let him go please," Eva asked.

Janus complied, and their captive collapsed to the ground moaning.

"I guess there is truth there. Don't get anywhere near the tentacles, Madden. Janus, bind him and let's put him in the car and get out of here. I have had enough of forests and darkness and being set upon. I want some answers."

Eva knelt down next to the moaning man. "And you are going to give them to me, or go straight to your Hell."

CHAPTER NINETEEN

Madden slammed the door on the apparently petrified 'demon' and shot a warning glance at Eva. "This is madness. You don't know what danger you could be placing yourself, and us, in."

"No more than I already am," Eva muttered back. "I won't hear it, Madden. Whoever is after us, I want information. We interrogate on the move."

"You used to interrogations then?"

"In a manner of speaking, yes. I have interviewed countless criminals. How is this guy any different to them?"

"Well first, he appears to be some sort of demon. Just thought I would mention that for starters. Second, did you see their clothes? It's safe to say he's not from around here."

"A foreigner?"

"Not geographically at least."

In the car, Eva found one terrified captive bound and gagged, squirming to get as far away from Janus as possible. For his part, Janus sat opposite him staring, eyes barely blinking. Madden got in behind the wheel and pulled out past the cabin and a still-present teenager who judging by the front of his trousers had witnessed a bit too much than was good for him.

May that be all you see, Eva prayed in silence.

They passed without incident through the rest of New Market, pulling onto the interstate and resuming their journey south.

Eva let the tension build for half an hour or so while observing the man. Madden was right; she could see what he meant. As with those they had seen before, this man looked to be a figure out of history. His brown uniform appeared antique. He could have been from two centuries before. Unfortunately, the damning evidence was the hood he had tucked at his belt. Eva leaned over as the terrified man stared at her and retrieved it. The hood was burlap, with eyeholes and a larger gap for the mouth cut in one side.

"I see what you mean," Eva said to Madden, who stared straight ahead, not responding.

She turned to the man. "You are of the Klan. What is your name and rank? Janus, remove his gag."

Janus leaned over, and ripped the tape he had used from the man's mouth before he had a chance to tense, settling back on the other side of the back seat.

"My name? You may call me Jack Crow." He then laughed uproariously at some self-perceived joke. "I am a redeemer. What is this? Some sort of carriage? Why are there no horses? Who are you, eh? What right have you to entice me here? Who do you work for? Grant?"

"See," Madden said without turning his head.

Jack Crow peered around him. "This is exceeding soft in here. This must be your powder room. So does General Grant allow you a man slave and a retard? Perchance your horses are decked with pretty pink ribbons too?" More raucous laughter.

"You have a lot of questions for someone in your position, Mr. Crow."

"You aren't here to scare me, lady. I have seen true fear. I have witnessed it. Whoever you are, and wherever this is, I don't care."

"That's fine, then. We will stop here, and execute you now."

Eva said this in such an offhand way Crow was completely caught off his guard. "No! There are rules now, even if I despise everything you ragamuffins stand for. You can't do that."

Eva pulled out the mysterious book and handed it to Janus. "Let's see, given what we have been through, just how much we are prepared to stick to the rules."

Janus took the book, and pushed it against Crow's face. The effect was instant. Smoke began to boil from the point of contact, and Crow screamed. The stench of burned flesh quickly filled the car.

"Enough," Eva held out her hand and Janus returned the book to her. "How did you know we were coming?"

Crow panted for a moment as he stared at her in undisguised terror. "We... we... had no idea you were coming. We were left here and instructed to bar the way of any we felt needed it." Crow jutted his jaw at Madden's back. "We felt him coming. He is like a beacon."

"How so?"

"He is weak, insignificant. Anyone stronger can sense him. We prey on the weak. You must have barely done enough to get into the Kingdom since they forced you back out so quickly, my friend." The last comment was clearly aimed at Madden, who gave no response.

Eva changed subject. "Jack are you in pain right now?"

Crow cackled once more. "Always, but a little pain is better than what is worse."

"Worse? The portals? What is through there?"

Crow screamed, a noise so high-pitched Eva had to cover her ears. "Damnation, woman! Do you not understand? Do you not see it? I was in Hell. How am I here, in this verdant land? I have no idea. But I can impart this to you. There is worse down there than me."

"Like what?"

"You shall see. You think us alone? He who came before saw to it we are everywhere. Our efforts go unnoticed."

At this, Madden barked a laugh. "Not if they dress like you. Sorry, Klan boy. Lee died, Grant won, and you are well over a century out of fashion."

The effect was instantaneous. Crow hunched up, flexed, and attempted to hurl himself at Madden face first, his teeth the only available weapon. The back of the driver's seat deflected most of the effort, but a split second later, Janus had Crow in a headlock, most of him shoved down in the foot well behind the front seats.

"Time to send you back where you belong," Eva decided. "Madden, find us a place to stop."

Then something strange happened. Crow began to stretch, his features distending. "You won't send me back there!" He roared. His mouth began to open wide, and did not stop as the jaw lowered beyond that which was possible for a human. His eyes widened as well, threatening to pop out of their sockets. Lumps began appearing on his forehead, shifting under the skin. His chest swelled, threatening to break his bonds.

Janus was threatening to lose his grip on Crow, and Eva did the only thing possible. "Madden, stop. Now."

Not seeing all that was transpiring, at first he just looked at her.

"Now!"

Madden slowed and stopped the car. The being that was Crow writhed and struggled, a fluorescent ichor dripping from his mouth and leaking from where the bonds were now too tight. Fortunately, Janus was well ahead of Eva in terms of necessity and opened the car door with one hand while manhandling the Crow-thing with the other. Once outside, Janus dragged the bloated body with both hands, leaving a trail of ooze behind.

"The second he gets in, floor it," Eva instructed.

Madden just nodded.

Janus reached in, pulled the slime-covered foot mats out and then jumped in, pulling the door behind him.

Madden planted his foot on the gas pedal, and the car roared off. In the side mirror, Eva watched in horror as whatever they had dumped continued to expand. They were perhaps a hundred feet away when there was a yellow burst, followed by a roar that shook through the car, louder than the engine at full rev.

"Crap. Crap. Crap." Madden had seen the fluorescent explosion behind them, and to Eva's trained eye was scared witless and in danger of losing it.

"Listen to me Madden, take deep breaths, nice and slow. Calm down. Keep your eyes on the road and pay attention to my voice."

"Eva, you saw what was happening to him. He is like me. Is that my future? Is that all I can become? There is something inside me, buried deep. I can feel it now. It responded to whatever was happening in the back of the car. I'm a danger to us all."

Eva responded by reaching over and laying her hand on

the back of his neck, soothing him. "There is nobody I would rather face danger with."

This mollified him somewhat. He was quiet for a while, and then began to chuckle.

"Did you see the sign that flashed by?"

"No?"

"Lexington. That's where General Lee died. If our Crow hadn't gone supernova he could have gone visit him for some inspiration."

The inside of the car began to flicker red and blue. Eva turned to check the rear window. She breathed a sigh of relief, having feared the worst. Her rational thought was not working at its best, she admitted.

"Thank God, it's just the police."

"I don't want to see another bright flashing light as long as I live," Madden growled. "Let me handle this."

They slowed and Madden parked the car on the side of the road. The police car stopped close behind, lights still flashing.

Madden wound down his window. A female police officer stood there, an Alsatian at her side. "Evening, officer. What can I do for you on such a fine night?"

"You could give me an explanation, sir, of your need for such reckless speed on the interstate in the middle of the night. Then once you have done that, you could pass me your license and registration, and finally, sir, you could step out of the vehicle. I am sure you are well aware of the speed limits in the state of Virginia."

"I could do all that, ma'am. Or instead I could perhaps direct you to the fact I am driving a vehicle bearing federal plates, and, as such, you are not authorised to stop me, rather assist me in any given way possible."

The female officer looked crestfallen. Her dog, presumably unused to seeing her in anything other than a position of command, barked and then whined. She reached down to mollify it with a vigorous ear rub.

"Right you are, sir."

"Slow night?"

She sighed. "Graveyard shift on traffic patrol. It's a killer."

"Let's hope not," Madden disagreed. "Look, while I have you at my disposal, is there a motel nearby?"

"Not for maybe another fifty miles, up near Mount Rogers."

"Mount Rogers it is then," Madden decided aloud. "Thank you officer, you have been most helpful. Have a good night." Madden rolled up the window and turned to grin at Eva.

"Speeding in a federal vehicle is allowed?" She asked.

"No idea," Madden replied, "But she didn't have a clue, and people like that will always be persuaded by a voice of authority. Besides, she will have forgotten us in moments. Best speed to the hotel? I don't know about you, but my demon and I are wrecked."

The next morning while three very tired people were still asleep, several police cars gathered not far down the interstate from where they had been stopped the night before. A tent had been erected at the side of the road, and several unnerved state troopers guarded the outside, including the young woman who had been on patrol during the night.

"Any idea why they want us here?" One asked.

"Have you seen inside? Looks like somebody was ripped apart from the inside out."

The entrance to the tent rippled, and three men emerged. The lead figure, a tall man with an imposing stare, regarded them.

"Tilly Cark. You filed a report late last night about a speeding car, yet you never followed up with any detail. Would you care to elaborate?"

Before Tilly could frame a reply, Dozer, her canine companion, began to growl at the man. A sharp glance, barely noticeable, set him to whimpering and he cowered behind her legs.

"I'm sorry sir, but who are you?"

"My name is Gideon Homes. I am working with the F.B.I. on unusual cases such as the one we have here."

Tilly began to feel an overwhelming compulsion to speak the truth, to tell all to this man. "I'm sorry sir, but I don't have any memory of such an event."

One of Homes' companions, a shorter man with grey hair, pulled out a device and depressed a button.

"Dispatch, this is eight-foxtrot-twenty on route eighty-one. I have a five-ten in progress. Black sedan in excess of eighty miles per hour. In pursuit."

"Acknowledged eight-foxtrot-twenty. Dispatch out."

"That is it as far as the recording goes, Patrolwoman Cark." The small man put the device away. "We were hoping you might be able to shed a little light on the particulars of said sedan, at least if you do not want to spend the rest of your career behind a desk."

She tensed at the thought. Trained to recognise the slightest of changes in her stance, Dozer stepped forward, growling.

To his credit, the detective stepped back.

"I am sorry, sirs, but I cannot offer anything more. You have evidence there I pursued a car, yet I have no memory of the incident."

"This is bull," burst the third man, full of muscle turning to fat. "She knows where they went. I want my wife back."

"Brian, hush now," Gideon spoke as if calming a pet. It appeared to Tilly it worked, and this Brian faded into the background. "They are leaving a trail a mile wide. What others forget help us remember. They are going exactly where I want them to go. We don't need to follow them anymore. I can go straight to Sloss and prepare.

What we have here is an emergence. It is what happens when one loses control. They can be very useful in the right place. Unfortunately, there are those that are not strong enough to resist. We shall bring back those that are stronger. I am more than a match for one puny return and two humans."

Gideon turned to the troopers. "Boys, make sure Tilly here recalls none of this. I want no trace. Remember who you serve."

Tilly watched in mute horror as the colour drained from the eyes of her three companions.

As one they intoned, "Yes, Lord Iuvart," and surrounded her.

CHAPTER TWENTY

Eva woke to the sound of the television churning out early morning commercials. She sighed.

"Another morning, another hotel." It seemed to her since Worcester, she had lost all sense of identity. Not all of that had been because of the anonymity that radiated from Madden, but it had had an effect. With the revelations in her life, she had had no choice.

Throwing on some clothes, Eva opened the curtain and delighted in what Madden had promised would be a spectacular view. The Chattanooga National Park, dominated by the majestic Lookout Mountain lay in front of her. Forests at the base led to scrub and tree-laden slopes, with the grey behemoth dominating the middle. Even from this far away, it made Eva feel insignificant.

It was not the first time in the past few days she had felt that way. Since waking up in the shadow of Mount Rogers a few days ago, their travel had been bordered by mountains the whole way. Even when Madden had insisted they detour to stop at an old friend's house in Knoxville, it turned out to be the grandest of mansions. Then the friend had insisted that despite Eva's urgency, they take a trip into the Smoky Mountains. She could not avoid feeling small and out of control.

As if to remind her of what she could not control, Jeanette Gibson appeared on the screen. Eva had not seen any news in the past few days, a fact for which she was as thankful for as being free from apparently resurrected antiquities. She decided to watch.

"Welcome to a special ABC World News report. I'm Jeanette Gibson. Today's story: The ongoing unrest in North Eastern America and its wider implications across the globe.

First, a naked man has been shot and killed in Boston, Massachusetts. Harold Fronhouse, having shed all of his clothes, surprised the owner of a local bar, beat him to death with his bare hands, and was feeding on him when he was cornered by police. He was shot trying to escape the scene of the crime. Daniel Collier, his victim, was pronounced dead at the scene by coroners. Fronhouse has been linked to a series of cannibalistic attacks in the state, ranging over the past few days to his release from an asylum by this woman: Dr Eva Ross."

A less than flattering photo of Eva, taken by Brian and seemingly donated by him, filled the screen. Fortunately, the photo was blurry and she was wearing sunglasses.

"Dr Ross is thought to be the ringleader behind many of the unusual attacks occurring, ranging from bizarre stunts such as the entire workforce of Macys in Worcester oiling themselves up and putting on an ad-hoc 'Mr Universe' show, to the more macabre, where a mob ripped apart a small child. She is currently on the run and her where-abouts are unknown. If you think you see her, she and any companions are considered highly dangerous, and should not be approached. Please contact this station at the number you see on this screen."

"Funny," Eva said to herself. "You normally contact the police."

"Isn't it just?" Madden agreed as he opened the door. "I thought the same thing earlier."

"What do you think a TV station wants with us?"

Madden watched the screen a moment longer where the Caruso and Gideon interview was being replayed. "I have no idea. I can tell you one thing. I'm not about to find out. The further we get away from that place the better. Breakfast?"

"In a moment. I just want to see the rest."

"We also have sketchy but confirmed reports of a large scale disturbance in Cambodia. Locals there have been talking about an earthquake, and the appearance of hundreds of, if the witnesses can be believed, soldiers who ravaged the area during the Sino-French war in the nineteenth century. We have been handed transcripts of what was recorded, and experts have concluded the language is a rather formal form of modern day French. Cambodian forces moved on the army, and after a brief battle, were easily victorious. Most strange, was the lack of any bodies, but nobody can confirm if this is because they have been taken for examination."

The screen flicked to jungle and clearly visible were the smoking and charred remains of trees caught in the conflict, but no bodies. Several very confused Cambodian soldiers wandered aimlessly about, and on several tree trunks ice was visible, the leaves frozen.

"No bodies, and frozen trees in tropical jungle." Eva turned to Madden. "It's spreading."

"That it may be, but I'm hungry. It can wait."

Eva leaned down to switch off the television. As she did, the voice of the reporter whispered, "Be careful Eva, they are still out there."

Eva froze a moment, and then when nothing else was forthcoming, switched off the set and went with Madden.

"What happened there?"

Eva looked back at the door to her room. "Just something on the report I was listening to. You know the strangest thing was I never had the TV on last night."

"Maybe there was an alarm on it."

Eva was not convinced, but let the conversation drift off to silence.

In the restaurant Eva sat opposite Madden at a table that delivered yet more stunning views of the nearby National Park. Feeling hungry, Eva ordered coffee, orange juice and a full cooked breakfast.

"Are you all right?" Madden asked as their waitress walked off with their order. "That's a lot, even for me."

"I'm fine, just a little tired. Where's Janus?"

"He wasn't in our room when I woke," Madden admitted. "I spoke to Mindy, the waitress, and she said he had been here earlier. I guess he is just around the place somewhere."

. . .

They ate breakfast mostly in silence. Eva ran the report through her head time and time again, struggling to make sense of what she thought she heard.

When they had finished, Madden paid the bill and tipped the waitress, who flashed him a smile that did not escape Eva's notice. It appeared the waitress had not even noticed she was there. Her choice not to comment left Madden floundering for something to say.

As it transpired, they found Janus sitting outside the hotel on a bench at the side of an empty swimming pool. Following his normal behavior, he was gazing off into the distance, where the road faded into the distance.

Eva sat beside him, holding one of his hands in her own. "Janus, was it you? Did you put my television on?"

There was no response at first. In truth, Eva hadn't expected there to be any, but Janus shifted his gaze to the road they had come in on.

"They are coming. You think you are alone on this journey?"

It was the first time Janus had addressed her directly. Eva knelt down in front of him, looking at his face.

"Janus, who is coming? The police? My boss?"

Janus looked at her. It was so unexpected Eva flinched.

"All of them. They are going to find you." With that, he looked off into the distance again.

"Lucky we have you and your shovel then," Madden quipped. It was a comment intended to lighten the mood, but the fatalistic way with which Janus had pronounced her doom made the day much colder for Eva. One way or another, this journey was soon going to end.

"I'm just wondering why Sloss of all places?" Eva considered aloud. "We have been driving for days, and we still aren't there. Surely there must have been some scary place closer to home?"

"Given what we have been through, I would say there are plenty of places, so this must be of much greater significance."

"Do you know much about it?"

Madden grinned in that frustratingly disarming way he used whenever he knew something she did not. Was this what it was like for Brian?

"Actually I do. They have a Halloween event there every year, the 'Sloss Fright Furnace'. It celebrates, in its own macabre way, the history of the furnace, and propagates the legend of the haunting. A lot of people died there when it was in production. The overseers were not gentle. It stands to reason many of those that died were no saints either. If they want to bring somebody back, why not go to a place that is going to maximise your chances of success?"

"That doesn't explain Janus and Mohammed. They have no business being there."

Madden waved the report under her nose. "Have you read this? It's crazy. Makes your pal look like a madman. I suggest you study it. Maybe you can read something from it I can't.

One thing it does confirm is we have been driving along a metaphorical river of blood pretty much since we left Worcester. The bloody history of this great nation has had us treading ground that has seen countless deaths. The indigenous people, the Klan, the civil war. Even now, we are looking out over a scene of historical carnage. The battle of Missionary Ridge was fought right out there. Basically, General Grant versus General Bragg and a whole lot of death. And the trail we follow has us pointed like an arrow towards Birmingham, Alabama. What are the chances there are other such arrows headed towards that mark?"

"It sounds like we should find an answer there then, one way or another," Eva decided. "Don't you want to know, Madden? We have dead appearing for no apparent reason. We have these bizarre portals swallowing them up. You walk around with this mysterious cloak of invisibility thrown around yourself."

"Not to you, though."

"No, not to me. And there is that very fact, too. Why me? Why am I so very special that Gideon wants me caught?"

Madden slumped next to Janus, who still looked east. "As it is, were it up to me, I would abandon this and strike out in a completely different direction. I don't like being herded. Hell, the way the situation has turned out down here, there's probably someone watching us from Lookout Mountain right now, or someone just round the corner waiting for us to leave. Every turn we make leads us into more trouble. These hellbounces are not isolated. They are linked. Why do we feel a certain way? Why did those people eat that child? Why did that guy from the hospital chew someone's face off?"

Eva chuckled. "Why did you call them 'hellbounces'?"

This caught him off guard. "Well... I... It seemed appropriate."

"In your case especially, if what we have been told about your experience in the great beyond is accurate. You quite literally bounced in and out."

Eva reached over and took Madden's hand. "All I want is an answer, then we can go wherever you like. I just need you guys to stick with me a little longer."

"And if it just leads to more questions?"

"Then I am glad I have you with me, demon or not. Did you ever consider there was a reason you came back?"

Madden did not answer, lost in thought. He shepherded Janus into the car, climbed in and put his hands on the wheel, as if reluctant to do any more. Eva knew he would.

"Let's get underway. I want to see what all the fuss is about."

CHAPTER TWENTY-ONE

THE JOURNEY, ALTHOUGH ONLY JUST OVER A HUNDRED miles, took several hours. Eva felt a growing sense of frustration as Madden simply would not drive any faster.

She knew why. Whatever he was, be it human or otherwise, he thought he was driving to his end in Birmingham. The traffic around them bustled by, and despite the companions within the car, and the strangers without, the foreboding began to press in on Eva.

In time, the heart of the city became visible. If anything, Madden tried to slow even more.

"If you keep that up, they will stop us for holding up traffic," Eva warned him. "Where will that leave us except directly in their hands?"

Madden shook his head, his gloomy thoughts disrupted. "What? Oh. I'm sorry, Eva. I'm a little distracted."

"Still thinking about what's ahead of us? It's okay to be afraid. It might actually help us."

"No, that's not it. We aren't alone here. I can feel them. They are everywhere. Eva, it feels like we are driving into a nest of demons."

"Could be a good thing," she replied.

Madden looked aghast. "Eva, how could that possibly be a good thing? There's no way out."

"But if there are so many, then they might be so busy feeling the influence of each other they won't notice you. You are weak after all, apparently. Can you feel where they are most concentrated?"

Madden gave her a look that spoke volumes.

"Directly ahead of us then, in the middle of the city."

"I would say if anything there is a ring of them. I feel once we are inside, there will be no escape."

"Just make for the middle of the city and let's see what we can see."

Half an hour later, in the early afternoon, Madden slowed the car at traffic lights. To their right sat the steel monstrosity that was Sloss Furnace. Disused chimneys stabbed upwards, and the famous white water tower bled the word 'Sloss' in rusting letters. Despite the sunshine, the furnace oozed menace.

"You sure you want to do this?" Madden said without taking his eyes off the structure.

"Not right now, no."

"Good time to tell me that now we are here."

"No, it's not that. Look."

Eva pointed past Madden, to a distant part of the furnace. In the parking lot that was partially obscured by one of the chimneys, there were at least a half a dozen state police cars.

"If there are cars, there are cops. If there are cops, they know we are coming. We have to come back later."

"In the dark? Woman, are you crazy?"

Eva put on a mock pout. "Ohh is my widdle demon scared? I promise I'll hold your hand."

"Yeah, go on and mock me. Like you aren't, too."

"Honestly? I'm not."

Madden laughed. "Bull."

"I'm not, because I have you with me. What have I to fear that I haven't already seen?"

"All right then, what do we do now? We have hours until dusk."

"First let's ditch the car. Get a new one. We have had this long enough that the chances are pretty fair at least somebody will have escaped your magic trick. After that, food, and then we wait."

Finding a car rental didn't prove much of a challenge, nor did finding a place to ditch the car. Central Birmingham did not lack for unused warehousing. The main problem was shifting their gear and more importantly Janus, who refused to move for a good hour or more. In the end, Eva had to sort through her clothes and leave at least half of it behind. She favoured the clothes she had bought while with Charlie. Madden was less fussy, and when they finally persuaded Janus out with the promise of food, they looked like a party on vacation, albeit a bit lost.

"Do we burn it?" Eva asked Madden.

"Why bother? Whatever they are after, it certainly isn't our fingerprints. The car is hidden in this garage well enough. Let's just keep moving."

The walk to the car rental was only a couple of blocks, but with Janus dragging his feet, it felt like a marathon. In time, they rounded a corner to find an open lot full of cars.

"I presume we want no fuss here?" Madden asked.

"Why, what do you have in mind? I know we are starting to run a little thin on cash, though this is probably not the place to start testing the validity of that letter."

Madden stared over the road at the car lot. "I thought I might use my gift." He paused, expecting her to say something.

"Why not? If you have come back from Hell already, you can hardly be accused of sin by doing that."

Surprised, he led them across the road and into the office.

Inside, one woman behind the desk read a magazine, paying no attention to them whatsoever.

Madden approached her. "Excuse me, could I possibly have a look at one of your Chevy's?"

The woman looked up, appraising Madden as women seemed to do. "Sure, hun. Let me get you some keys." She smiled while she tried to reach behind without taking her gaze away from him.

Madden took the keys with a nod, and walked out of the office.

The woman watched him until he disappeared from sight, and then a strange thing happened. Her face went blank, and her eyes unfocussed. It only lasted a moment, and when she came back to herself, Eva walked up to the desk.

"Help you?"

Eva put on her most vacuous smile. "Hi there. I was looking for a friend of mine. Her name's Mindy. She was supposed to be getting a car. Has she been in here?"

"Sorry, hun, there's been nobody in at all. Slow day." Clearly disinterested in any more conversation, the woman went back to her magazine.

"Thank you, anyway," Eva replied, determined to at be polite, even if she got nothing back. The woman grunted a dismissal and Eva left.

Outside, Eva found Janus leaning against the wall, shovel beside him. Madden waited in a chunky Chevrolet four by four.

"That'll do," Eva decided, and nodded at Janus to get in, who complied without fuss.

Madden gave her a questioning look.

"Food. We promised this guy food, and it's time to deliver." Eva was about to say more when a man began to shamble past the parking lot. She went cold and her heart began to pound.

"Madden, drive. Slowly, but get us out of here, now."

Madden pulled the car out of the lot, and mingled with the traffic. "What?"

"I just saw a face I recognised. Paul Shields, patient three-D. A nasty piece of work at the best of times. If he is down here then they know we are around. Did you feel anything when he walked past?"

"I can't be certain," Madden admitted. There's so much interference. It doesn't look like he saw us."

"Too late to worry now. How's about that place for some food?" Eva pointed out a restaurant bearing the name 'Fifes'."

"You sure? We are only a couple of blocks away from the old car, and only one from the rental lot."

"Yes, I'm sure. They will expect us to go charging off, so we are going to hide close, in plain sight."

Madden parked the car round the far side, and they entered the restaurant, Janus needing no encouragement and leading the way. Inside an elderly woman, welcoming them with open arms and inquiring as to their needs, greeted them.

Eva ordered coffee, and they sat down in a booth on the far side from the counter.

"That looks fabulous," commented Eva as the waitress carried a stack of pancakes and what appeared to be an enormous steak slathered with vegetables to another couple in the restaurant, which was about half-full.

"Be with you in a sec, dear," called back the waitress, who clearly did not miss a beat.

And in a moment, she was, as promised. "Hi y'all," she said in that easy-going accent so typical in the South. "I'm Peggy. What'll it be?"

"Those pancakes look just amazing."

"Aw honey, they are to die for. How many would you like?"

"Whatever is typical."

Peggy laughed. "Darlin', you ain't never been to Fifes before, have y'all? What you saw was typical, fried with cheese and bacon, covered with syrup. It's a lot for a little lady." As Peggy was saying this, she was eyeing up Madden who annoyingly remained oblivious.

Refusing to back down from the challenge Eva said, "That's fine."

"How about the rest of y'all?"

Madden ordered fried chicken to the audible approval of Peggy, but it was Janus who surprised them all, breaking from his normal reticence to order.

"Hi, Peggy. I'd love barbeque pork, squash croquettes, collard greens and cabbage, some veal parmesan and strawberry shortcake." He said all this with a charming smile that left Eva stumped, and Madden sitting there with his mouth hanging open.

"You got it," Peggy drawled as she made a note of the orders, and then sauntered off to the counter with a glance back.

Eva could not be sure if it was for Madden or Janus, but as she turned from watching the waitress, Madden was the one looking over, while Janus had reverted to his normal self, staring at nothing over her shoulder.

In a pleasantly short time, their table was stacked with plates of food, most of it for Janus. Oblivious to anybody else, he tucked into his meal as if it were his last. Eva shared a smile with Madden, the silent exchange warming her.

"So what's the next part of your insane plan?" Madden asked in a voice that barely carried out of their booth.

"I was thinking of walking there. It's not too far away."

"True. But what if there is trouble. Wouldn't it be advantageous to have some fast means of escape?"

Eva sipped at her coffee while she considered this. "Who is to say we are going to be able to get away?"

Infuriated, Madden slammed his drink down on the table, causing a few nearby customers to glance in their direction. "Your plan is to go there and what? Die? Live as a hermit with the ghosts?"

"I have no idea what my plan is. Somebody has pointed us in this direction and I'm going to damned well play out the endgame on my terms, not theirs. I am not going to set us up to flee right into their hands. The only way to do that? Be contrary. Do something they won't expect."

"Well they are certainly expecting us," Madden said as he stared over her shoulder. "Look, but turn slowly and be circumspect."

Eva did as she was told, to see on the screen of a television the car they had only just dumped, along with the words 'Murderer hunted in Birmingham, AL'. In muted tones, the reporter detailed all the events leading up to the capture of the car, and all the usual crimes that had been linked to Eva, including the death of Cathy Knott.

As they watched, the report detailed all of the supposed crimes: the cannibalism, the disappearances, the murders. The pictures painted her in the worst possible light. The hypothesis was now she was a representative of an organization creating chaos across the world, since events of unparalleled bizarreness were beginning to crop up on several continents.

It was all getting to be too much. Eva placed her fork on the plate and turned back to Madden. His face has gone pale. This was no longer a game. Somebody they had known, somebody good to them, had died.

"I need some air," she said, and exited the booth, making a beeline for the door.

Outside Eva doubled over, hands on thighs, and sobs racking her chest. She felt sick. Determined not to throw up, she forced herself to take great gulps of air.

Hands touched her shoulders, and, as always, the worries became that much less. Eva turned into Madden, sobbing gently.

"Are you worried they will catch us?" He asked, brushing her hair back from her face.

"No. I'm not. I'm worried we will fail. They are setting everyone against us and we are still here. If this were just me, I wouldn't have made it out of Worcester. Brian would have found me, and locked me in that house to raise another woman's child. As long as I have you with me, there is still hope."

Madden hugged her close. "I'm going nowhere without you."

Inside, oblivious to his surroundings, Janus continued eating. He had chosen his favourite meals, food he had always loved. Nothing else interested him but the need to consume. No moment existed beyond the next mouthful.

At length, his peripheral vision registered he was no longer alone, but he did not look up past the plates. The woman had left food and so had her companion. He decided to move onto their plates.

A flurry of activity brought more bodies around his table, but Janus focussed on the pancakes. A force was driving him to eat his fill, one he could not help but obey. He reached for another mouthful of the delicious pancakes, and a hand clamped down over his own.

Forced to look up at those by him, an act Janus had always avoided where possible, Janus beheld an elderly man with surprising strength.

"Ah said, boy, that ah love to see a lad with an appetite, but ah hope y'all can pay for this."

Janus stared at the man, failing to comprehend the meaning behind his words. He noticed his companions were no longer there, and the something inside had made him feast now directed him to follow. He stood, and when the man failed to remove his arm, Janus reached over with his free hand, and plucked it off.

The man cursed, cradling his ruined hand. Janus just stared at him, unblinking, unmoving.

Comprehension and then eventual understanding filled the face of this stranger. "It is you," he said, momentarily forgetting his hand needed attention. "My apologies. It is all on the house." The man shuffled away, and beckoned his staff to follow.

Janus sat once more and resumed his meal, preparing to clean every scrap from the plates. It was still too early.

"I tell you, they swarmed him and just as quickly left him alone. He did no more than stand up."

Madden was watching the restaurant with impatience, though to Eva it felt like a nervous energy was filling the car. They were close to finding an answer.

"You want to go in there and get him?"

Madden sighed. "No. They will have forgotten me by now, long ago in fact. I don't want to remind them since he apparently has them so well cowed."

"I don't suppose you have the power to stop the sun?"

Madden stopped fretting and reached over to touch her face. "Scared?"

"Of course," Eva admitted.

"Want to blow this off and run?"

"Never."

Madden leaned back. "Well take a load off and shut your eyes. We aren't going anywhere until Janus joins us."

Eva did just that.

· · ·

It must have been quite a while later that Eva woke. The grey skies had dimmed, and the occasional light shone in the distance.

"We have a guest," Madden announced.

Eva turned in her seat to find Janus behind them.

"Sunset. It is time."

CHAPTER TWENTY-TWO

THE APPROACHING FURNACE FILLED EVA'S VISION. Even if she turned her head, it did not help. It loomed large, dominating the skyline, a metal trap waiting to snap shut the minute they entered it.

"Still having doubts?" Madden asked as he drove.

"Are we being herded, or is the trap waiting for us on the chance we fall in it? I'm certain there's something more here, but I can't see it."

Madden tapped Mo's study paper, still on her lap. "Read all of that?"

Eva nodded. "You are right. It goes against everything I know about him. He sounds like a lunatic, not a doctor. But there is more. I don't believe Janus was a test subject. I think he was protection." Eva expected Madden to scoff at this idea, but he nodded.

"He certainly has the skill set. I swear he could kill somebody with harsh language if the mood took him. If he is protection, then protection from what?"

"Demons." It was Eva's turn to laugh. "Two weeks ago I would have had myself committed if I thought for a second I believed such thoughts to be true. But, that has to be it. You said lots of people died at Sloss."

"That's right, but they were mostly black labor, forced to keep the furnace ticking over at night. Granted you must have had a few who stepped on the wrong side of the tracks, but for the most part they were innocents, trying and, in many cases, failing to earn a living to feed their families. This was neither a good place nor a good time to live in."

"And who made it that way? There has to be somebody behind the problems."

Madden regarded the ever-approaching furnace for a moment. "Those in charge looked the other way for the most part. As long as production continued, they did not care. But, if you are looking for a primary antagonist, there is one. James Wormwood, known as 'Slag'."

"Slag?"

"Probably something to do with the crap leftover from the blast furnace. Nobody can be sure. He was responsible for the graveyard shift, an overseer and a bully. He was responsible for the death of dozens before his own life was taken. He burned to death in the molten iron of the furnace. It was never proven if he jumped or was pushed."

"Surely he must have been pushed? How else would you get close enough?"

Madden smiled. "Eva, it's surprising how close you can get to the furnace. When I was younger, I took a tour with the Governor and my parents around a working steel mill. In the furnace, it's a dry heat. You can get pretty close. If you want something that really saps the energy, try going to a hot rolling mill where they pour gallons of water onto the steel to cool it as it is rolled into coils.

Anyway, I digress. Wormwood was a right nasty piece

of work, and after he died, all sorts of strange things started to happen."

They had pulled off the highway and were now in the shadow of the furnace, its cold metal skeleton casting darkness amidst the remnants of the day. Madden pulled onto a track that took them to the west end of the monument, as far away from the cops as possible.

"Once he had gone, there were reports of strange unexplained occurrences. People went missing and found locked up with no memory of how they got there. Strange voices shouting with no source. Constant whispering driving people mad, and worst of all, a report in the seventies of one guy getting assaulted by what he called 'half man half demon'."

"Well from what we have seen, wouldn't that mean he is back already?"

"That, or he is either strong enough to pierce the barrier from the other side, or more worryingly, that Slag Wormwood can come and go at will."

Madden stopped the car under the shelter of the freeway above, having already turned it in the direction of their potential escape.

"Well, here we are, Eva. Now what's your plan?"

Eva looked in the rear view mirror at Janus. Still oblivious, he gazed unperturbed at the furnace.

"We go in there."

"That's it? Just 'We go in there'?"

"Yep."

Not giving Madden a chance to argue, Eva climbed out of the car, being careful to close the door with care. Madden and Janus did the same, and not giving them time to think, Eva led them towards the western side of the furnace.

"You have to wonder at their logic in bringing us here," Madden whispered.

"Do you?" Eva answered. "I think logic contains all the answers. First off, if Mohammed's prose is to be believed, and our own conclusions prove to be correct, we have a demon of incredible ferocity and viciousness that can enter and leave Hell at will. Second, we have you, with at least some demon in you. Been to Hell, but not long enough to notice. Weak as you like from what they tell us, and like catnip to demons..."

Eva stopped. "Oh dear God, how could I have been so dense?"

"What?"

Eva turned, putting her hands on his chest. "You. You are the key. You said it yourself. If this Wormwood could enter and leave at will, and if the goal is to bring more through, what better incentive for them to come than..."

"Than easy prey waiting on the other side," Madden finished for her. "They wanted me here from the start. They want to use me to pull something through into this reality. We need to get out..."

"Too late," Janus interrupted, pointing to the end of the walkway. "They surround us. Watch."

In the failing light, there was a shimmer in the air. Beyond, it appeared there were beings running about, black forms distorted as they flitted in and out of direct vision.

"This way." Janus tugged on Eva's hand and pulled her in the opposite direction, towards the main furnace. She followed, not having any choice in his iron grip.

"So you talk now? Or is this another lapse." Madden's tone was acid, probably because he was as afraid as she was.

"I talk, demon," Janus replied. "I talk when required. Now stay silent or meet the ice all the quicker."

Eva glanced back. The shadows were still outside the warehouse through which they hurried but even from this distance, Eva could see there were many more. Janus pulled her onwards.

They exited the warehouse, and entered a maze of pipes that surrounded the many chimneys. The presence of so much cold, dead metal chilled the air and Eva began to shiver. She no longer felt they were the only three in this space. It might have been the wind, but she was sure she could hear somebody speaking to her in a whisper just too quiet to be audible. Eva tilted her head to one side in an attempt to listen to the whispering

"Don't," Janus warned. "We are in his lair. He is the master of all here, and tonight he has the strongest of princes to aid him. If you listen, it will be the last thing you do."

"Prince? Madden is a prince?"

As Madden began to puff up with pride, Janus gazed at him. "No, this sorry creature is nothing but a lure. He who drove us here has power. True power. Iuvart, the fallen. If you were widely read you would know he is the focal point of the infernal angels, servants, and vassals to the other lords of hell. There are more than baby demons focussing their attention on you here."

They rounded a corner, and Eva was grateful to see lighting. They approached a board filled with text about the furnace. Eva stopped to glance at the information.

There was a keening in the air, and the light bulbs exploded, causing Eva to scream. Madden shielded her while Janus stood above them.

"He has been summoned. He comes. The gateway opens."

The whispering grew, and the keening became a loud hum. It sounded to Eva as though the furnace was coming to life, but when she touched the pipes, they were ice-cold, much too cold for the air around them. A mist began to form on the ground, gathering about their feet. Madden pulled out a couple of flashlights and handed one to Eva. She nodded silent thanks. Then the noise began.

It started as an insistent tapping on the pipes around them, high-pitched and barely noticeable.

"What is that?" Eva whispered.

"Recognition," Janus replied. "He knows we are here?"

Very quickly, the tapping increased in intensity, until it became a loud hammering, reverberating off the pipes. The sound terrified Eva. It was angry. Rage spilled into the air around them. Each bang made her ears ring, as if struck right by them. There was a note of finality in it. Somebody wanted them to know they were heading to their end.

Above the cacophony, Janus yelled, "They are here! Go ahead. I'll slow them down."

"What do we do?" Madden yelled back.

"Whatever you can. Think of something!" Janus turned and grabbed a loose piece of pipe, wrenching it from its mountings "Go!"

Confused at the sudden awakening of this previously docile individual, Eva paused. The lamps, having already exploded, burst alive, beams shooting out and filling the corridor with a fetid yellow light. Behind them, they could now see bodies packed from side to side, writhing and fighting to get closer. Not waiting another second, Eva turned and pulled Madden along with her.

Howls of rage erupted from behind as Eva pulled Madden on, but they remained alone.

"He's fighting them all." Madden's voice showed how in awe of Janus he clearly was.

"Yes, and if you could stop dragging your feet, maybe we could put some distance between them and us."

Madden blinked, recognizing the peril. "Yes, sorry. You are right."

He took the lead, twisting through the labyrinth of pipes until he found some steps down. "Under the furnace. Great place to hide." Not waiting for Eva, he descended.

They emerged from the steps to a tunnel that appeared to run the length of the furnace. Metal grating had been spilled on the floor to provide a walkway, and the intermittent lamps hung from the ceiling provided some means of lighting. Water dripped from cracks, pooling under the grating. Much of it was frozen.

"Funny," Madden said as he poked around at some of the ice. "It doesn't seem cold here."

"Well, which way do we go?"

Madden looked up and down the tunnel. "Car is back behind us, but so is that host of demons. We go on."

They crept forward, Eva avoiding the decay on the walls and the pools of stagnant water, some blood red with oxidised iron, as if the furnace itself were bleeding.

Stairs came into view, and Eva breathed a sigh of relief. The sense of oppression, and of not being alone, had not lessened.

"Shall we go up?" She asked Madden. There was no reply.

Eva turned. Madden was standing behind her, about

ten feet back down the tunnel. "What is it?" Eva ran back to him, but hit something invisible and bounced off, landing on her rear in the blood red water she had been so careful to avoid.

Madden's face was a horrific mask of pain and fear. "Go," he said. "Can't move. Get...get out of...here."

"No!" She screamed, and launched herself at him. As Eva reached the barrier, something deflected her, pushing her to the ground, and keeping her there with pressure on her neck.

The ground shook and the lights flickered. The pressure became a wind, roaring with hunger, squashing Eva down and pushing her into the water. Eva turned her face a fraction to stop from drowning. The air went from frigid to the blast heat of a furnace and back again in seconds. The whispers in the air became screams. Eva thought she was going to lose her mind, but continued to fight against the pressure keeping her pinned.

The rage behind the oppressive nature began to manifest as disjointed and random slashes in the air. From her position Eva witnessed a scar appear down the side of the tunnel, and screamed as another caught her leg, evidently gashing it open. She wriggled, trying to force the pressure back. She felt blood trickle down her leg, and the pressure stopped.

The oppression became rapture as something nearby changed, and a sick feeling of dread threatened to overpower her.

"It is open," a voice celebrated from inside her and all around her. "Your lifeblood, little human. It is the key."

The pressure released, but Eva stayed down. Her leg throbbed as blood seeped through the wound. "Get up, child. Come to me. You are mine."

Eva rolled over, lying on her back and gasping for air. In her peripheral vision, Madden was staggering towards her, his own legs bearing the brunt of the viciousness just unleashed.

He collapsed to his knees beside her, cradling her in his arms. "Are you all right?"

Eva smiled briefly and nodded. "Think we can get out of here now?"

In response, the lights down the tunnel began to flicker and die, darkness encroaching upon them from each end. Soon the only light left on was the one above them, and that soon began to fade. In the darkness beyond the edge of vision, there was a feral growl, as if a shadow waited for utter darkness to unleash it.

"What's wrong?" Asked the voice, this time from the distant end of the tunnel. "Do you need a little incentive?"

Lights popped on in the distance, and under them, a host of shapeless beings shambled forwards, gibbering and hooting in some unknown language. Even from this distance, their faces were a horror to behold, misshapen and oozing blood. There was a hunger about them, and upon seeing Eva and Madden, they lurched forward at a shambling run.

Madden pulled her up. "We go," was all he said.

Eva was not about to argue. Her leg still throbbed, but the bleeding had at least slowed. Madden was in a worse way, and Eva helped him climb the stairs.

The door was stiff, and proved hard to tackle. Eva yanked at the rusted handle, desperate to force it to move. Madden tried to help but his legs were weak and threatened to give way. Below, the creatures shambled on, gathering at the foot of the stairs.

Eva caught a glimpse of one as it tested the first step as

if never having seen one before, and fought the door handle, forcing it to shriek in protest. The handle snapped down, and the door flew open, pulling Eva with it. Madden followed closely behind, and they shut the door and locked it again, trapping the creatures in the tunnel.

Even as they pounded against the other side of the door, Eva leaned against it, catching her breath, and Madden shifted an empty oil drum under the handle.

"They won't get through there in a hurry," she said.

"I don't think they are meant to," Madden replied, and gently he turned Eva away from the door.

She felt the blood drain from her face as her heart nearly stopped. Ahead of her on a scaffold perhaps eight feet above the floor, stood a being only the most sick and depraved mind could imagine. It pointed, and her heart went cold.

CHAPTER TWENTY-THREE

WHAT COULD ONLY BE DESCRIBED AS THE REMNANTS OF a man glared down at them, a grimace frozen on its undead face. Wherever skin showed, it was charred and blackened, or red and festering, oozing a fluid that may or may not have been blood. The clothes were as ruined as the skin, and black flakes cracked and fell whenever it moved. Each breath came with a rattling wheeze.

These were all aspects of the creature Eva had noted in the moment before she looked it in the eyes, and that was what held her in place. The pupils glowed red, the whites were dark, almost purple.

"You..." spoke the gravelly voice. "You have been chosen above all humanity to witness my rebirth and ascension. Here, where I triumphed in my first life, so shall it be my throne in my second."

Then for no apparent reason, it turned to the left and shouted, "Get back to work before I hurt you!" Turning back, it fixed Eva with its baleful stare once more. "You have been judged, daughter of David. You have been judged and you have been found worthy."

Finding her courage, Eva shouted back, "Worthy of what?"

The demon laughed, a wheezing, guttural noise akin to perforated bellows. "Worthy to be the mother of my army. With your blood, we shall open this gateway forever. With your pet demon we shall keep a path open from the lower realm, and the army shall cross the barrier until they outnumber mankind." The demon raised its arms in triumph. "This shall be the new unholy Eden!"

Once more, it turned aside and shouted, "Push some steel before I come down there and make you wear it!"

"If this is Wormwood, I would say he's not completely in this realm," Madden whispered.

"If he was like this in life, I don't think he ever was all there," Eva replied. As the words left her mouth, Eva felt herself thrown to one side as a force pushed her.

Madden joined her shortly, dumped in a heap. "Powerful though, and great hearing," he said through teeth clenched in pain.

"It's a good diagnosis," said a voice from nearby, the same voice that had spoken from within the tunnel. "Clear, concise and simple. Lacking in any depth or actual perception. Just like your entire career, Dr Eva Ross."

A tall figure emerged from the shadows, smiling with smug self-satisfaction. He came to a stop next to Wormwood, and the demon bowed his head in a clear demonstration of deference.

"Gideon? What are you doing?"

"What does it look like I am doing? I am doing the same as you, Eva. I am consorting with demons. I am returning them to their rightful place, long denied us, that we may sit in judgement over the pitiful infestation that plagues this realm."

Eva had suspected it at first in the altar room of the hospital, but now her fears, the documentation, the abductions and chases, it all led to one conclusion.

"You aren't Gideon Homes."

The man on the scaffold laughed. "Ah Gideon Homes, what a pious man, what a scientist. You would have been a worthy successor to his position, and his work. Pity. No, I am not him, nor am I any of his predecessors. I go back further than that, a lot further. I go back to the very beginning. I hovered unseen when this world was spun out of shadow. I was there when the sun rose the first time over the pond scum that infested the earth. I stood at Pontius Pilot's right hand when he condemned your saviour to hang by the cross, and I watched the life ebb away from him. I am not anything you can connect with, you wretched excuse for a soul, with your values and your noble suffering. I serve a higher power. Tell them who I am worm."

The Gideon-that-was directed this last comment to a point behind Eva, and she turned.

Janus crept out from behind the maze of pipe work, a frostbitten pipe in one hand.

"TELL THEM!" He roared, when Janus appeared to hesitate.

A strange look of defiance came across Janus's face. "His name is Iuvart."

Eva and Madden looked at each other, and then back at the scaffold. "I'm sorry, is that supposed to mean something to me?"

Before the newly-revealed Iuvart could say anything more, Janus continued. "Iuvart was an angel. One of many who fell from Heaven. He is their prince. He can take the forms of others, and his kind are servants and vassals of the greater lords of Hell. Merely servants, I should add. For as much as Iuvart considers himself above others, ultimately he is a mercenary who does the bidding of whomever he deems in prominence. We don't know who that is."

"Let me fill in the gaps for you, little mortal," Iuvart suggested, and walked past Wormwood, who stood eyeing Eva in covetous silence.

In the moment he moved, Janus was quicker, hurling the pipe with deadly accuracy at Iuvart's head. The pipe whistled through the air, a trail of frost billowing in its wake. As the pipe reached Iuvart however, the pipe began to glow, and incinerated right in front of his face.

Janus stood in shock. "No."

Iuvart chuckled, a low, throaty noise. "Quote the scriptures, mortal."

Ashen-faced, appearing defeated Janus took a steadying breath. "Iron he treats like straw, and bronze like rotten wood. His breath sets coals ablaze, and flames dart from his mouth. If you lay a hand on him, you will remember the struggle and never do it again!" Janus staggered, and Eva caught him by the arm. "Dear God, he is aligned with Leviathan. Do you know what that means?"

"Sorry, no I don't."

"Tell her," taunted Iuvart. "Tell her all."

"Leviathan is the demon Lord of Envy. If he comes into this world, chaos will be let loose as people turn against each other. More importantly, Leviathan is the gatekeeper of Hell. If he arrives, the boundary between Hell and Earth fails." Janus faced Iuvart. "So this is what you have been doing. Seeking a way to bring back demons at will."

"And now I have it," Iuvart triumphed. "The weakest of our kind as sacrifice, and the blood of David's child. Wormwood, show them."

Unleashed by the command, the demon jumped the

barrier and had hold of Eva before anybody could react. In one brutal motion, he had ripped the back of her shirt, exposing her shoulder.

"See there the Star of David, branding her of the true line through her birth."

Eva tried to look over her left shoulder to where she knew she had an unusual mark. It had never bothered her since it was mostly out of sight. She had rarely worn strapless dresses so nobody had ever been given cause to comment, and Brian's imagination was so limited and brief that his attention rarely strayed during sex.

"It's just freckles. A skin blemish, that's all."

"How wrong you are, Eva. You are marked. You are mine."

Wormwood leaned close, its breath carrying the reek of carrion. Eva had no choice but to study him up close. Teeth were missing, and the jaw clenched and unclenched repeatedly with suppressed violence. Eva wondered how long this rabid dog would be kept on his leash.

"So this is your grand scheme? To resurrect demons? With the ease of which they are sucked back to Hell, I don't think one more demon is much to worry about."

"You don't understand, mortal. You couldn't. Let me give you a glimpse of your future. When enough are through, the balance of life shifts. For now, it pains anything less than a true demon to be in this realm. Look at Wormwood here. Look to your lover. They both suffer. When the balance shifts, the returned demon kind will shed their false skin and release their true selves. For in that state they are forever. Immortal."

"You can't do all that with one burned out husk of a steelworker."

Iuvart cackled, looking strangely out of place on the

face of the Gideon she had known. "Alone? Who said anything about that? There are seven Lords of Hell, and you have met two. Think back to how you were set upon this path, Dr Ross. Did you not reach heights of uncontrollable passion? Were you not at a grand feast in Worcester?"

"Asmodeus! Belphegor!" Janus whispered with just enough alacrity that Eva heard him. Nobody here was the person they claimed they were it seemed.

"Two of the Lords of Hell in your realm. One more and the balance is even. Then we only need let one more through and your earth is no more."

"But that means there are only six..." Janus wondered aloud.

"You have studied us overlong, little knight," Iuvart decided. "Wormwood, time to show Janus just what strength you have. I release you from this mortal skin!"

Wormwood roared with pleasure, and his face began to stretch in unimaginable directions. Eva stepped back, but his fingers elongated and grew claws to clasp at her. The skin began to split. Wormwood grit his teeth and began to take deep breaths, swelling with each inhalation.

Janus looked at Eva and shook his head. There was nothing he could do.

Then something strange happened. There was an explosion. Wormwood's shoulder disintegrated in front of her, blood and black gore splattering all over the metalwork of the furnace.

"No!" Screamed Iuvart from the scaffold.

A shotgun pushed forward past Eva. One lone cop, a young patrolwoman, pointed in defiance at Iuvart.

"Next time you try to kill me, maybe you should hang around to see the final act." She pushed her rifle at the stunned Wormwood, caught mid-emergence, and pulled the trigger.

Wormwood screamed in pain as his middle erupted and pasted everything behind in gore.

Knowing what was about to happen, Eva tugged Madden's shirt. "Time to get out of the way."

He responded, letting her guide him away from the writhing Wormwood. "I suggest you get back," she said to the cop.

Up on the scaffold, Iuvart paced impotently as his work was undone. He turned away from them. "No, I won't let you claim him," he said to empty space, and spread his arms wide. "He is mine!"

From a vantage point a short distance away, Eva watched the scene unfold. Much like earlier, a bulge appeared in the air, attempting to displace reality. In the dimly lit furnace, it made the pipes and wheels beyond bend. Ripples appeared, and for a moment, the bubble was contained by Iuvart's power. But a moment was all it took.

Jumping up from their hiding place, the cop pulled out a handgun, took aim and fired a round. The bullet hit Iuvart in the back of the head, causing him to flinch.

"It won't make any difference," said Janus. "You can't damage him that way."

"I don't need to," she replied.

In the moment the bullet had distracted Iuvart, he had seemingly lost control in the battle with the portal. It burst open, flooding the furnace with its eerie light, and sucking the air into the vacuum beyond. The portal was larger than any Eva had yet seen, and the tentacles much, much thicker. Some slithered across the floor to engulf Wormwood, who croaked in agony. Others reached to seize Iuvart.

He retaliated, his hands glowing white hot, grabbing the

tentacles and pulling on them. The snakelike appendages began to smoulder, and an inhuman shriek of agony filled the room.

A voice cut through the air, causing Eva and those around her to scream in pain as it tore through her soul and threatened to rip her sanity away.

"**Impotent Godling. Do not think you can escape us, not even here. There is no realm beyond the grasp of the ultimate death. See how futile your attempts are and witness your inevitable failure.**"

The tentacles flexed, and the burning melted away. One whipped at Iuvart, sending him crashing along the scaffold. Those that held Wormwood reached into the cavity left by the gunshot and stretched the remaining flesh beyond the limits of a recognisable shape.

Wormwood shrieked, and raised his hand, pointing at them.

"You... are one... of...us..."

Instead of the tentacles pulling Wormwood through the portal as had happened in the past, this time they ripped him asunder. The portal, normally an unhealthy shade of white, went dark and cleared, revealing row after row of scythe-shaped teeth. The tentacles withdrew, hurling the remains of the demon Wormwood into that cavernous maw. Once done, they shot back into the room, searching in the direction of their vantage point.

"Janus, they aren't stopping. What do we do?"

Janus shrugged at her. "I do not know."

"I do," offered the young woman in uniform, and fired off a round at the portal.

Eva was about to suggest that choice of action was

pointless, but the bullet hit one of the teeth, shattering the end into splinters. A roar of pain made the very room shake, and the tentacles withdrew. Something colossal beyond the portal shifted. An enormous eye replaced the teeth, fully ten feet across, pupil fixed on them. Eva felt miniscule as a stygian being straight out of nightmare, something too hideous for its enormousness to be fully grasped, beheld humans for the first time, and hungered.

The cop, hand trembling, let off another shot, and this pierced the eye, causing a scream of pain that had them all holding their ears. The body beyond moved and the portal collapsed, causing the scaffold to disintegrate as everything nearby was sucked through.

Silence descended on the furnace. Metal groaned as it settled in the aftermath of the explosion. Eva feared to move, even to breathe.

It was Janus who made the first move. "Have you seen enough? I think we can leave now. It looks like the place is about to come down around our ears."

A deep chuckle came from amidst the carnage in front of them. Metal was pushed out of the way as Iuvart, wreathed in shadow, stood. "I don't know if I should commend you for saving me, or destroy you for ruining lifetimes of preparation."

"Perhaps I consider you the lesser of two evils," Eva shot back.

"Oh no, there is no lesser evil. There is only hunger to conquer. You have brought me the key, Eva Ross. You shall not leave this place. It is too late for you."

Iuvart continued ranting, but Eva's attention was distracted by Madden, who edged up behind her.

"Wind him up."

"What? Are you insane?" She whispered back without moving her lips.

"Look around. This place is falling apart. One good knock would collapse this furnace on top of him."

Eva turned back to Iuvart, who waited for the answer to a question he had apparently asked. She put on her most innocent expression, one she knew had irritated Gideon from the first time they had worked together.

"I'm sorry; I don't consider you a threat. I was listening to somebody that matters. You know, somebody important. Somebody who can actually influence what is going on. What was it you said?"

The effect was instant. Released of the confines of Gideon Homes and his controlled emotion, Iuvart flew into a rage. His eyes and hands began to glow, outlining a creature with leathery wings wearing a face of fury. "He is mine! You will give him to me!"

"Now!" Janus yelled, and Eva found herself borne backwards by the two men, the cop following behind, shotgun in hand.

As they made their way towards the tunnel, a beam of heat passed over their heads.

"One of the lines describing Leviathan is 'His breath sets coals ablaze, and flames shoot from his mouth'. You do not want to be there for that." Janus opened the door.

They descended the steps, and started back down the direction they had come.

"No, wait!" The cop shouted. "This way!"

"The car is at the other end of the tunnel." Madden shouted back, above the noise of collapsing metal. Clearly, Janus was right.

"Not mine. It is close. Do you want to get out of here

alive?"

Heading off any argument, Eva started up the tunnel with the cop. "We can get our stuff if we survive this. Let's just get the hell out of here!"

Flashlights in hand, they ran maybe a quarter of a mile until the tunnel opened out on a parking lot. The cop urged them into her car. In moments, they had screamed round the dirt track to their rental car, and were grabbing their belongings when the furnace began to warm. Beams of light shot out of the middle as ironwork, unused for decades, glowed a sooty red. The entire plant reflected the rage Eva could feel from its core.

Red metal became orange, and then white. Eva filled the trunk of the car and climbed back in. "That's the lot. Go!"

"Where are we headed?"

Eva looked to Janus for an answer. "Got any clever plans now?"

"The airport," he replied after a moment. "Get us out of here first, airport second."

Not wasting another moment, the cop threw the car back along the dirt track with fervor, the impetus being survival. As the furnace glowed orange and then white, it began to collapse in on itself.

The sound was unmistakable. As metal disintegrated, they all heard the wailing.

"Noooo!"

As they hit the interstate, the furnace erupted, a shaft of light piercing the night sky. The heat radiated through the windows, but lessened as the car accelerated off, sirens blaring.

Eva turned to Janus, who waited patiently as if this were all natural. "Okay then. What is your story?"

CHAPTER TWENTY-FOUR

"MY NAME YOU KNOW," JANUS BEGAN. "I AM OF Polish-German descent, my family having moved here after the war. I am thirty-seven years of age.

When I was young, it was recognized I had, shall we say, certain skills others did not. I showed an extreme lack of fear, and strength disproportionate to my size. You can see I am not the biggest of men. I was taken in and given training to augment the raw talents I showed."

"So what were you doing at the museum?" Madden asked.

"Don't jump ahead," Eva said with a frown.

"I can think of a much more pertinent question," Janus replied. "Who trained me? The time has come for you to be given some answers. The organisation I represent is known by the acronym 'ARC'." Janus waited, looking between her and Madden, seemingly for them to register some knowledge of whatever ARC was.

"Never heard of it," she finally said.

Madden shrugged. "Me either. Should we have?"

"Maybe. It is not commonly known, yet unusual given

the company you keep. ARC stands for 'Anges de la Résurrection des Chevaliers'. In English, 'Angels of the Knights Resurrection'. It is an organization that has monitored and prevented exactly what you saw here tonight on countless occasions. It has links within just about every major security organisation on the planet. Interpol, CIA, Mossad, even MISIRI of Iran. ARC supersedes them all."

"To what end?"

Janus looked her square in the eye. "To prevent the apocalypse."

After a moment's stunned silence, Madden burst out laughing. "That's ridiculous," he scoffed.

"How can you say that, knowing what you are? You, who have been to hell and back, refuse to believe what is right in front of your own eyes, even after the very agent of chaos himself laid it all out for you?"

"Is that why you went there with Mohammed?" Eva tried to change the subject. They might have escaped the furnace, but she still felt in danger. Talking helped.

"I was conditioned in other ways. You must understand ARC is an organization without limit of ambition, goal, or resource. I can only tell you what I can, *when* I can, because it has been deemed right that I do so." He tilted his head to one side, exposing a small scar at the base of his neck.

"There is a chip in my head. It activates repressed memories and controls behaviour. Designed and administered by the best neurosurgeons on the planet." His eyes widened in realisation. "I never knew they could do such things, an example of information given to me when I need it."

"And the autism?" Eva asked. "I am a trained psychoanalyst. You weren't faking."

"That's the beauty of the whole process. We don't need

to fake a condition because we believe we are that way. Until the other day, I knew that change was unbearable, people I didn't know made me unbearably nervous, and only a few could be trusted."

"You recognised me from the start," Madden accused.

"That is the other skill I possess. I can read auras. I can tell when somebody is in pain, no matter how they hide it. You reek of demon, no matter how you choose to conceal yourself. Your aura is bright red. It gives off pulses of etheric energy anybody with my gift can sense. I knew you were coming, along with every other demon within a 5-mile radius. Much as you can feel their auras, so can I." Janus paused and looked out of the window. "I don't sense the trap any more. That is good."

Madden did the same. "He is right. It's different out there."

"Janus, when you left us, how many did you kill?"

"Too many," he answered her, "and not enough. Whatever that thing is that's disposing of demons decided to take matters into its own hands once I had maimed a couple of dozen. It sucked the rest of them out of existence."

"So much for the injury theory," Madden commented.

"It was never concrete," Eva disagreed. "The things reached for you on more than one occasion."

"I saw that, too," said the cop, who had until this point remained content to concentrate on the road. She had evidently decided now was the time for her to get involved in the conversation.

"Where?" Madden asked.

"When that whatever it was on the scaffold left me to die with three of my colleagues who turned out not to be quite what I assumed. I had reported an incident and then forgotten what I was talking about. They had a recording of the call."

Madden's eyes narrowed. "Who is 'they'?"

"Him, some short detective, and this big muscly guy who spent his time trying to throw his weight around. Nobody took that one seriously."

"It seems we have all underestimated that one, for him to be keeping such illustrious company." Eva agreed.

This shocked the cop. "You know him?"

"Yes, I have the displeasure of being his wife."

The cop turned in her seat. "You... you are Eva Ross. You are in terrible danger."

Eva laughed. "You think? What do we call you?"

"Tilly. State trooper Tilly Cark, though whether I am still that after this remains to be seen. Anyway, they knew you were coming to Birmingham. According to that tall guy, it was always expected you would come here. He refused to let the others accompany him into the furnace. They were to wait nearby. Once they left he had ordered the others to kill me, to hide any trails and presumably from what I have seen, pin the blame on you."

"You had a dog, what happened to it?"

Tilly looked about her in confusion. "How do you know that?"

"This is not the first time we have met," Madden informed her. "You reported us for speeding."

"Demon lore one-oh-one for the uninitiated," said Eva before anybody else could speak. "It seems demons are real, and when they come back, they for the most part exude characteristics that align them for whatever reason with one of the seven deadly sins. There are some, anomalies if you will, that do not follow this pattern. Madden is one such anomaly. If you meet him, you won't remember it. His characteristic is anonymity. As far as I am aware, there is no obvious way to tie that in to any of envy, wrath, pride, greed, gluttony, lust or sloth. Come to think of it, I wonder if that is part of the reason they are all after you."

"And yet here you all are together."

"Let's just say familiarity and a certain amount of emotional attachment lessen the effect. If you were to drop us off now, you would probably remember us for a while, but not for long."

"Unless you call fighting off a demon while a blast furnace turns white hot around you the massive emotional experience necessary," Tilly noted. "You asked about my dog. He died."

Eva put her hand on Tilly's shoulder. "I'm so sorry."

"He saved my life. He took down one of the three left to kill me, and that was when your portal opened, and tentacles took them, so close were they when kicking him to death."

There was silence for the moment, and Eva could see tears running down Tilly's cheeks in the rear view mirror.

Eventually Tilly spoke again, this time to Madden. "They have been tracking you, it seems. They noticed the unusual amnesia as far back as Worcester in Massachusetts. Even when you don't talk to people, it seems you have an effect by merely passing. As we pass these cars, they will be missing memories. Are you sure you don't steal information and keep it?"

Madden appeared confused, as if the thought had never occurred to him.

Eva rubbed her temples. "Look, it's late. This is a lot of information to process and we all need some time. Janus, I want to know two things now, if you can tell me. Firstly, you said given the company we keep we should know of ARC already. Who do we know that works for them?"

"Dr Mohammed El-Rafi. Cathy Knott, Christopher and Jana Scott. Unfortunately, Dr Gideon Homes."

The names hit Eva like hammer blows.

"Cathy," said Madden. "My parents?"

"It is what it is," Janus admitted. "You had a second question."

"Where are you taking us?"

The corner of Janus' mouth turned up in the smallest of smiles. "Me? I am taking you nowhere. State trooper Cark is driving us to Birmingham International Airport. From there, I have been instructed to deliver you to Interpol agents who will escort you to the ARC research laboratory. You have documentation that could prove crucial to the outcome of everything that has occurred here. It is documentation Gideon Homes removed from its repository. You were lucky enough to find it."

"I must say, Janus. I hate to contradict you, but I certainly didn't feel lucky when I found it."

Janus gave her a look that said he understood her meaning. He had been privy to many a conversation she had had with Madden in recent weeks since her rescue and escape from the hospital. "I suggest we hurry. Everybody will be looking for us."

As it transpired, they were not far away from the airport. Several times Eva saw fire crews, ambulances, and no end of police hurtling the other way as news about the explosion at Sloss spread. Tilly switched the police radio on, and there was no end of reports on the explosion and the so-called bomb that must have caused it. In the distance, the main terminal lit up the night, the runways bordered in multiple directions by tracks of landing lights.

"So what's the plan?" Madden asked, clearly unnerved by the prospect of being amidst so much security. "Walk in there and book tickets to..."

"Atlanta," Janus provided.

"The research facility is in Atlanta?"

"No, but the plane that's taking us all to Cairo is. This is a quick hop over, less people to stop us."

"There are a lot of people in that airport, Janus," Eva cautioned.

"We aren't going into the airport. Tilly, if you could be so kind, when we get off the interstate, take two lefts and a right. There's a road circling the airport."

Janus turned to Eva. "Our flight is from a private hangar on the far side. Lots of freight, private jets and such. They all hire the hangars. One such belongs to ARC in pretty much every major airport in the western world."

Eva was impressed. "That's a lot of money."

Showing no pride about this fact, Janus said, "Many governments may not recognise ARC as a legitimate organization. Many may even scoff at what they stand for, but all listen to those who represent us. All that happens now just reinforces the fact that we are right in our belief. If we can get somewhere a little faster to prevent the apocalypse, what is a little money to the world?"

Tilly located the roads as directed, and the light faded as they drove away from all signs of habitation and found themselves on a dirt track bordering the fencing of the airport. All fell to silence as the police car followed the track; their only guide the headlights of the car and the distant glow of the city.

As they rounded the end of the runway, the car was buffeted by the force of a plane landing. The roaring engines passed only a few feet overhead, and Eva screamed before she realised what she was doing.

"Sorry, a little tense," she said by way of an apology.

"Is there far to go?"

"No. We have to go by the end of the other runway, and the hangars are straight ahead."

Janus pointed in a general direction and Eva strained to see anything in the distance, but with the darkness, it was impossible.

In an effort to find some point of perspective, Eva looked out the back window. A brief flash of light from within revealed a car behind them.

"We aren't alone here," she warned.

Janus turned his head towards her, but Eva could see him straining for a glimpse. "Two cars, both Alabama state police. Tilly, you do not have to be part of this if you so choose. You can play the part of having captured us."

"And miss all this? Are you kidding? I want in. Just tell me what to do."

Janus indicated Eva belt herself in securely as he did so too. "When you get to the end of this track, turn left and floor it. There are a series of parking lots next to hangars. The one we want is the last next to the last hangar."

Not needing any more direction, Tilly followed the track as if they were still alone. As she reached the end of the track, she slowed, almost to a crawl.

"What are you doing?" Madden asked.

Tilly grinned. "They don't realise we have seen them. Just watch."

Slowing nearly to a complete stop, Tilly planted her foot on the gas, and pulled the brake, causing the wheels to spin and a huge cloud of dust to be thrown up. At the same time, she turned off all the lights, and after a moment, the car surged forwards, leaving chaos and confusion behind.

There was a crash behind them as the two cars collided in the dust. Moments later, lights blazing and siren wailing, the lead car surged through the dust.

"Only one," Eva called out.

"That's something," Tilly said through gritted teeth as she fought the road. "I need light."

"Do it," answered Janus. "It won't make any difference now."

The car behind had been damaged, but it still closed on them. Bullets began to fly, made inaccurate by the twisting nature of the road. One shattered the passenger window by Janus, who didn't even flinch.

"How far?" yelled Tilly.

"Maybe a mile," Janus called back above the howling wind. "When you see the hangar it will be open. Just drive right in."

More bullets peppered their car while Tilly sought to evade their pursuers. To Eva the hangars never appeared to get any closer, great black monoliths in the night as they were.

And then they were on the road that linked the hangars and warehouses. The car behind had managed to pull up close, and as Eva watched, she recognised a face.

"Brian is in there."

"You sure? Madden called.

"He's the one with the gun. Get in that hangar, or run them off the road. He means to see us dead."

"There it is," Janus pointed, and Tilly swerved for the hangar with open doors.

The sudden maneuver caught the car behind them by surprise. It had been edging past them, and it clipped their rear fender, causing both cars to spin out of control. The Alabama car flipped over a low concrete wall, its momentum causing it to land on its roof and keep spinning. In her detached state, Eva was amused.

"Hold on!" Tilly shouted and Eva braced herself. The car squealed as Tilly applied the brakes and the wheels locked. The hangar was too close and their speed too great. The car drifted sideways, and Eva could not help but watch, frozen in fear, as the hangar rushed towards them.

CHAPTER TWENTY-FIVE

Eva opened her eyes. Everything was inverted. Somehow, the car had flipped upon hitting the hangar door. From in front of her, Tilly stirred and groaned. Madden and Janus were unconscious.

Checking herself, Eva found she was mostly intact, but for a few abrasions and some cuts from flying glass. She considered what would be the best course of action. Either to escape or help those with her. They had been through so much this night the former was never really given a chance.

As Eva fought with the seatbelt, Madden's door was wrenched open, and burly arms dragged him out. The sound of fists punching inert flesh caused her to hurry, and to scream.

"No! Stop it!"

When the clasp popped, Eva fell head over heels, landing on the ceiling of the car. She fumbled with the handle, the door of which had been crumpled in the crash. Eventually forcing it open, she climbed out of the wreckage.

On the other side of the car, Brian was letting fly with all manner of invective as he punched a still-unconscious

Madden in the stomach and face. Not worrying about herself, Eva wrenched Brian off with strength she never knew she possessed and threw herself in front of Madden.

"Get out of the way, woman," Brian growled, and made to grab her.

Eva responded by pointing Tilly's handgun at him. "You move, I shoot." She pointed at a spot out on the tarmac. "Get over there and sit down, hands under your legs."

Brian smirked, and took a step towards her.

Eva cocked the gun, her arm unwavering. "Your next step towards me will be your last."

Brian stopped in his tracks. His eyes bulged with suppressed insanity. Eva had seen it in several patients over the years. She had no doubt now that Gideon, or Iuvart, had driven them over the edge. Still, he acquiesced, doing as instructed and sitting isolated on the road.

Eva now turned her attention to Madden. Despite being unconscious, he stirred in pain. There was more to it. His face was contorted, stretching in ways it should not. Eva took his hand, and it too was distended. The demon inside was taking control, seeking to escape. Maybe that was Brian's goal.

Eva hugged him close, stroking his face, seeking to calm the beast within. "Madden, if you can hear me, I think I love you. Don't give up on me. Don't throw it all away. I want to save you, but you have to fight. Do you hear me? Fight!"

She stroked his face, and gradually the demon within calmed. Madden began to smile, though the battering he had received caused him pain.

"Love... you...too," he said, and one eye cracked open before he dropped unconscious once more.

Eva lowered his head to the ground, and stood, facing

Brian. The fury that arose in her threatened to overwhelm her, and she began to raise the gun.

"Go on. Go ahead," Brian taunted her. "It is called vengeance. It is called wrath. It is as deadly a sin as they come."

Aware of what he was doing, Eva held the gun at him a moment longer, and then let it drop. "I forgive you, Brian. You know not what you do.

Since I left you, I have found happiness in the midst of all this chaos. I have seen a different world than the one you would keep me trapped in. A man who has an actual demon in him can possess my heart, while you, empty of soul and beyond saving, have nothing left to give anybody. Do you understand what it is to love? All you know is want. All you want is what you see in front of you, and like a child you reach out and grab, and cast aside as soon as the next object catches your attention. I would rather be with the spawn of Satan himself than with you."

The pain that was released with those words had a dual effect. Eva felt calm, absolutely at peace with the world. Not even the final vestiges of sanity ebbing from Brian's eyes could ruin the moment.

Something was always there about Brian Ross. There had always been a different side to him lurking beneath the surface, rearing its ugly head during their darkest times. It was revealed now in all its glory. Insanity, worn like a badge of honour. But for his repeated actions over the years Eva should have cared that the Brian Ross she had fallen for had now been utterly lost.

He began to giggle, rocking on his hands. "I've got to die. I'm gonna be reborn."

"Bad luck," Eva replied. "Not going to happen today."

Brian jumped to his feet, eyes wide, and teeth in a

grimace. A feral creature now, he sprang at her, to be met with a shotgun butt to the face. Tilly was quicker.

"Try again, meat. Let's see if you are faster than a speeding bullet."

Eva shook her head. Tilly replied with a wink.

"If we are done here, how about you cuff him to that cop oozing out of the other car and we get a move on before the other car gets here?" Janus was now awake, and a groggy Madden leaned on the car.

Tilly threw Janus a set of handcuffs. "Be my guest. Don't worry about being gentle."

Brian cackled, and then whispered conspiratorially, "Mercy is for the weak." He winked at Eva as Janus marched him to the wreckage of the other car. It did not take long to cuff him. The other cop was already dead.

"Shall we?" Janus invited them, and as one, they entered the hangar.

The doors began to slide shut, despite the damage, and they heard Brian's howls of anguish from outside.

"You just leaving him there?" Madden asked, his voice slurring with the effects of what was probably concussion.

"This is a secure unit. An army couldn't get in here." As if to emphasise this point, a second set of doors, far thicker than the first, clamped shut.

Low-level lighting came on, illuminating the hangar. Several men with machine guns, dressed black ops style, materialised out of nowhere, as did a very familiar figure.

Jeanette Gibson approached them, looking every bit in control, her television face replaced with one of expectation and genuine concern.

"Glad you could make it. We were concerned on occasion for your safety."

"Concerned?" Eva sounded less than convinced. "We

have been on a one way journey to hell and it merely concerned you?"

"You had Agent Lohnes with you. You were not really in any danger." Jeanette turned to Tilly. "Though I must admit your intervention has been timely. You have my thanks."

Madden focussed on Jeanette. "Damn if you don't look like her off the television."

Jeanette turned to Eva. "You will be expecting answers. I can give you some. Yes, I am the same person you see on the news reports. Yes it was our intention to bring you here to help you escape, and we did by aiming you in a certain direction."

"Into the lair of a demon?" Eva had trouble keeping a lid on her emotions.

Jeanette raised her hands, trying to placate them. "That was an oversight. Try to understand for all we know, there are two we don't, and ten we have witnessed. ARC is fighting a war on two fronts. The first is to keep a lid on what's really happening out there."

"And what is going on out there?" Eva's tone was tinged with scorn.

Janus stepped in. "We are seeing the first skirmishes of the apocalypse. The beginning of the end of humanity. There are demons popping into existence all over the planet. You have seen these hellbounces on the journey down here."

"Hellbounces?" enquired Jeanette.

"Dr Ross coined the phrase," Janus informed her, and received a nod of approval.

Jeanette pointed at a bank of screens, and they flicked on, each showing different scenes of carnage intermixed with her reports.

"We cover some of these to gradually introduce familiarity. ARC suppresses information on the rest. The most important thing is we have you now, and what you carry."

"You mean me?" Madden suggested. "I hope I'm not to be some specimen for study." He looked away, ashamed of what he was.

"I believe in you," Eva said by way of support.

"No, you will remain with Eva. The enemy may have miscalculated. They believe you to be a demon. I have no doubt you have it in you, but by all accounts, you weren't down there long enough to be affected in the same way. I think you are an anomaly and our enemy is clever. From what we have learned from Agent Lohnes, they had more planned for you than just becoming another minion."

"You mean Iuvart."

"Exactly. There are a number of players at this table. He is a wildcard. Unpredictable, with his own agenda. He is the reason we have to get you out of here as soon as possible."

It was at this point Eva noticed for the first time the two planes at the far end of the hangar. "Our transport?"

"Not exactly," replied Jeanette. "One thing we have learned over the years is to not leave anything to chance. Stay in the shadows and watch."

The lights in the hangar faded as the front hangar doors opened. The planes came alive, engines whining, and began to taxi out of the hangar onto the runway.

From her vantage point, Eva watched the small planes, capable of seating no more than six people each, crawling along the asphalt. The first turned and began to power up for takeoff. Against the backlighting of the main terminal, it was possible to see a figure run out past the hangar and leap onto the wing of the plane.

"What's he think he's doing?" Exclaimed Madden.

"He doesn't think," Eva replied. "He is past that stage now. It's all instinct for him. However, he got free, he is seeking me, and thinks I'm in there."

"We suspect he isn't the only one," added Jeanette.

The planes continued in their take off, despite Brian clinging to one of the wings. Both accelerated to take off speed, and left the ground. Only moments later from a different part of the airport, two rockets flared into life, one heading to each plane.

The sound of the twin explosions shattered glass in the hangar, and the wreckage of the planes covered the far end of the runway. In moments, sirens wailed as emergency rescue vehicles rushed into action.

"Now we wait," observed Janus.

"For what?" Asked Madden. "For them to start asking who owns the planes, who was in them, and who fired those rockets?"

"Should not be an issue. We have you and your legendary anonymity for protection. The planes were registered to a phantom company who have hangars elsewhere on the grounds. They were controlled by remote. If not for them being shot down, they would have crashed somewhere close by in the state, making everybody think you had been killed. A little misdirection can go a long way. Look out now – you will see already they start to gather."

Eva peeked out of the hangar. In the darkness, it was easy to observe the helicopters beginning to fill the sky. Nearby in the hangar, some of the black-ops peeled tarpaulins off a black helicopter and began to prepare it for take-off.

"We will just be another bird in the sky, with all of the others scavenging for a story."

"We will. You are all important, and what you carry especially so."

"The books?"

Janus threw the still-wrapped texts at Madden, who caught them by reflex. Instantly he hissed in pain and dropped them.

"There's a good reason for that, rubber ball," Janus said as he retrieved them. "We must go now, or see all of this destroyed. These texts might well hold the key to what has been going on."

"To Egypt? You have a strange concept of safety."

"You are here. Everybody knows it. Anywhere is safer than here. Can you not sense it?"

Madden was still for a moment. "Demons. Everywhere, but not close."

"Not close enough to stop us this time. We go to the source of these scrolls, and for God's sake try to lay low for a while."

Eva took her place beside Madden, opposite Tilly. "Not coming, Jeanette?"

The blonde presenter shook her head. "My place and my job are here. I am the face of this. You need to see me, just turn on a television. Listen carefully when you do. There may be more being said than most understand."

Slamming the door shut, Jeanette stepped away from the helicopter as the blades began to turn. She turned, and in a blink, went through a doorway.

"Egypt, eh?" Madden said with a smile. "Always wanted to see the Pharaoh's tombs."

"Best hope it doesn't become yours, too," Tilly observed. "This isn't over yet."

The twinge in Eva's stomach told her that was a gross understatement.

In the darkness bordering the crash site, two figures watched a black helicopter lift off and join the growing flock in the sky above, lost in the night. They turned as one and surveyed the wreckage.

"The experiment, was it a success?"

Asmodeus turned and regarded his partner. "We merely planted a seed tonight. Until they find what they have set out to find, we will not have all the necessary elements. We cannot reach it alone, so there is no point concerning ourselves over it."

Belphegor did not turn; instead, she regarded the flames. "So reminiscent, don't you think?"

Asmodeus chuckled. "You were always one for the fire and death. We have been at this task for a long time now. Soon the sky will rain brimstone and fire. The seas will boil and we shall be free, masters of a new realm with none to follow us."

"And what of Leviathan's agent?"

"His plans have been quashed for now, but he shows promise for one of the Third Hierarchy. I would not want to be the mortals when he catches up with them. We have time."

"No Asmodeus, we don't. We were too close before." Belphegor held up her hand. "It is taking me. The ice spreads."

CHAPTER TWENTY-SIX

EVA RAN HER FINGER ALONG THE BALCONY RAIL OF THE apartment she shared with Madden. The mortar underneath the whitewash was dimpled and the feeling not unpleasant. It was sunrise, the sky was clear and the magmatic luminosity of the sun was erupting over the horizon. The air was still warm. It never seemed to get cold in Cairo.

She smiled as the bells began to toll, calling the Muslim population of the city to morning worship. The azan echoed out from loudspeakers all over the city. Cairo was a noisy place, full of character, full of soul. Eva loved it.

In truth, it was her main connection with the population around them, since part of their agreement with Janus had been to lay low. She had not had much of an opportunity to explore Old Cairo, in which their apartment was housed. Not that it was much of an issue. She had been very tired lately.

As always, when Eva had any worries or fears, Madden appeared, slipping his arm about her shoulders. She turned to regard him. He looked very fetching in the bleached linen shirt and trousers he had chosen to wear today, hair tied back exposing the lines of his neck.

Eva snuggled into him, the scent he wore catching in the back of her throat. "Mmm. I approve."

He wrapped his arms about her, dispelling any trace of the cold. "Well when in Rome..."

"Funny you should say that. I heard from Janus the Coptic Pope died recently. They are in a transition period, choosing another though I don't think it's as grand as all the pomp in St Peter's Square."

"To them it will be."

Eva could feel the tension in his arms. "You are restless. What is it?"

"This place. Most couples would give their souls to have this to themselves, this whole building. You could house countless families from the slums here. And yet the one place I want to be is anywhere but here."

"Are we safe?"

Madden closed his eyes, reaching out in what way Eva had no idea. "There are some in the city, spread about. None near here though which is odd. This is the most ancient part of Cairo and must have seen the most death."

Eva tried the same thing. It felt as though something was out there, but she didn't know why. She opened her eyes, looking up at him. "I don't care, as long as we are safe. I enjoy that feeling."

Madden didn't look convinced. "If we are safe, then why do I still feel uneasy?"

Eva took his hand and led him away from the distant cacophony. Not stopping in the room in which they had enjoyed many intimate nights together, she walked down the stone stairs and into the inner courtyard of their white-washed refuge. It was quieter here, and as much as Eva enjoyed the dawn call to prayer, this was the only real refuge from the noise.

Cushioned benches allowed them to lean back and enjoy the mosaic of buttressed wooden shutters that patched the inner walls. Their building was typical of this area of the city: random, disorganised, but with purpose and a sense of belonging to the larger scheme of things.

They enjoyed breakfast, a mix of fruit, hard cereal that tasted indefinably exotic and good strong coffee, as they had every morning thus far. During breakfast, Janus joined them as he had sporadically since they had arrived under cover of darkness, surrounded by ARC black ops.

He poured them all coffee, including one for himself. "How are you feeling today, Dr Ross?"

"Content, at peace with the world. The clothes you had provided for us are magnificent." Eva hoped she sounded convincing.

Janus sat in silence, observing her.

Eva stared back, it was clear he didn't believe a word she had said. At length, much to the amusement of Madden, she added, "Bored, confined. Worried about Tilly. Is that better?"

Madden beamed a grin, the stubble he had taken to wearing broadening his smile.

"Much, though I was merely enquiring as to your well-being. Tilly, as I told you before has been assigned a post where her particular skills can be of use."

It was Eva's turn to grin. "Now you are the one being elusive. You never do anything without purpose."

"True. One of the drawbacks to you knowing my nature. I have arranged for access to the research lab for you both. It has taken time because of the sensitivity needed. You are aware I believe of the recent passing of the Holy Father?"

"I am. What has that to do with letting us out of here?"

"You will find out in due course. Pack your things after you are finished here. Bring the texts. We will not be coming back."

"More cars and black ops then?" Madden asked.

"No, not at all. The lab is inside the Coptic museum. You can see it from your room. We are quite safe here. I thought you might appreciate the walk."

Eva glowed at the prospect.

An hour or so later, bags packed, Eva waited with Madden inside the entrance to their refuge. Having arrived in the dead of night, she was excited to get out and see anything. The sounds of early morning bustle called to her after so much silence. The heavy bolt on the door opened with a 'clunk' and the noise flooded in.

Janus appeared in the doorway. "Are we ready?"

Eva was straight to her feet, so fast in fact she had to lean on Madden, her head dizzy. "I'm fine," she said in answer to the unspoken question from both men, and led them outside.

The vibrancy of the street outside was matched only by the diversity of the people it contained. Just from their dress, Eva spotted Muslim mingling with Christian, the cross proudly tattooed on the hands of the many Coptics. European tourists nosed through the bazaars while the locals went about the normal business of the day.

Eva realised as they walked that their refuge was a sanctuary of peace in the middle of a nest of chaos. Buildings were high and cramped, leaning out over the streets and seemingly connected to each other by masses of power cables hanging everywhere the eye could see.

They passed one particular bazaar, and Eva stopped. Closing her eyes, she breathed deeply, the heavy musk of spice filling her nostrils, and catching on the back of her tongue. "That is gorgeous. What is it?"

Janus had a sniff. "Egyptian licorice root. They make a tea from it. Would you like some?"

Moments later, with Madden weighed down by the purchase of many more spices than Eva had first noticed, they continued their exploration. Janus led them on, seemingly taking turns at random through the busy throng, allowing them next to no time to stop and look. At one point, he reached out and grabbed a small child by the arm, saying something sharp to him in what Eva presumed was Arabic.

"Janus, what are you doing?"

The child, eyes wide with fright, pleaded silently with her while trying to twist from Janus's iron grip.

Janus repeated the phrase. Defeated, the child slumped, and pulled a wallet from under his robe, holding it out to Madden.

"Hey! Where...? When...?" Madden took his wallet, checking the contents, and pocketed it deep.

With one more word, Janus sent the child scurrying off. "Linen. Not the most secure fabric in the world," he observed. "Best not to hang around here for too long. There can be many dangers in a city like this."

Slinging the bag of spices over his shoulder, Madden grunted in agreement and shoved his hands in his pockets.

"The worst fact about it is even were he to learn his lesson, it's me. He won't remember having even lifted my wallet."

With only a few more twists and turns, and a foray into one more bazaar that netted a bolt of white and gold fabric that whispered over Eva's fingers and made her tingle, Janus led them out onto a busy street, cars packed head to tail along the entirety of its length. Across the street was a stone gate, and beyond, a white church that gave the illusion of being suspended in the air.

"Isn't that beautiful," Eva breathed

"That is Saint Virgin Mary's Coptic Orthodox Church, the Hanging Church, El Muallaqa. It is the official residence of the Coptic Pope, and the home of Coptic Christendom on earth."

"A lot of names," Madden observed.

"An important place," Janus agreed. "It was built on a roman fortress, which, you will find, is very significant. This is a very Holy place, full of ancient relics, a museum unto itself. Of course, with the passing of the Holy Father, there is a lot of uncertainty and tension is somewhat high."

"Meaning there are a lot of eyes on this place right now," surmised Madden.

"Most certainly."

"And you expect us to just walk in there? Unnoticed?"

Janus put his hand on Madden's shoulder. "Demon, trust me when I say you have no chance of passing unseen by certain eyes. No choice either as it is. They want to study you. It's not often the organization gets this chance. As for the rest of them, you will probably pass unseen as you are used to doing. For that matter, we all will. Let us go in, and you can see for yourself."

"What guarantees do we have?" Eva was suddenly suspicious of this whole affair.

Janus considered the question for a moment, his eyes fixed on a point high on the church. "I cannot offer you any that come to mind. This is your one invitation to help make a difference. Maybe we shall succeed without you; maybe we shall not. But may I offer you this much: you have come this far. Why give up now?"

The request appealed to Eva's curiosity, as she suspected Janus knew it would. Despite this, she couldn't think of one reason to say no.

"Go on, then, but know this. If whatever shows up in these books turns out to be important, remember I rescued them for you. I don't want to be kept in the dark."

"That will not be a problem, Dr Ross. Shall we?"

Janus led them through the traffic and under the stone gate. In the forecourt of the church, they joined the back of a tour party being led by a guide more concerned with shouting than who she was shouting at, facing away as she was. Eva listened to the bored-sounding guide while Madden toyed with thick-leafed vegetation sprouting from a clay urn. Janus waited passively for the party to move on.

The tour guide waved them forward, warning the party not to touch the many artifacts on show in the church, and sat to light a cigarette as she took a break from her shepherding duties. The acrid tobacco stung Eva's eyes as she passed into the church, but the aroma of incense quickly replaced it.

The party broke up into smaller groups as families sought to tame wild children and elderly couples shuffled off to find a pew to sit on or pray.

Janus leaned in close. "I will arrange for our entry to the

laboratory. Bear with me." Before Eva could reply, he had disappeared.

"Where is he?" Madden asked upon finding her alone.

"Unlocking the door," Eva replied with a smile.

"Oh no, dearie, nobody should be unlocking any doors," a small voice croaked from beside her.

Eva turned to find a pair of elderly women smiling, from their accents clearly part of the tour. "Have you lost your son?" One of them asked. "Is he trying to get into places he shouldn't?"

"I'll bet he's a handsome little devil, with your dark hair and your husband's shoulders," said the other.

"Oh he's been found," said a familiar voice from behind them. "If you ladies wouldn't mind moving along, I need to have a word with these two about losing their children."

Caught in the tourist-trap mentality of being ordered and ushered everywhere, the old ladies shuffled off obediently, leaving Eva staring into the smiling face of Tilly.

"There you are! I knew I had left you two around here someplace."

Eva hugged the former state trooper close. "It's so good to see you! You look well. Nice uniform."

Looking very girlish, Tilly turned, arms spread out. She wore a mixture of khaki and black in a figure-hugging dress, with matching beret, a small but unique-appearing pin decorating the front. At her side, she wore a holstered handgun. "You like?"

Eva glanced at Madden. He definitely liked it. "You can put your tongue away now, Madden," she said, and both women laughed. "Are they treating you well?"

"Not here," Tilly replied. "Too many eyes and ears. You have heard something about what is going on hereabouts?"

"We have."

"It's getting to the point of reaching a climax. You will know the rest soon enough."

Outside, a voice lifted in song, a solemn, sad tune.

"Everybody, you won't want to miss this," called the tour guide from the entrance. "Come on now."

The congregation shuffled towards the exit, little old ladies bustling by in a hurry. Tilly placed a hand on Eva's arm, and did the same for Madden, holding them back.

"Entertainment for the masses, a lament to the Holy Father. Diversion for us. Please, follow me.

Tilly led them to a series of alcoves in the nave of the church. They approached one such, and Tilly turned, pointing to her beret. "Wherever you see that, you will find sanctuary." She looked upwards, and Eva spotted a similar shape engraved in the wall above the alcove.

The doors at the entrance to the church boomed shut, and as they did so, the wall in the alcove slid back and to one side, revealing a well-maintained corridor. Four men in similar uniforms to Tilly's stepped out, each bearing a machine gun trained at them. Eva's heart upped its tempo as she remembered the last time she had gone down such a path.

"Please," said Tilly, "won't you come join us?"

CHAPTER TWENTY-SEVEN

With Tilly in the lead, Eva followed Madden through the passageway, the alcove door sliding shut behind them. The air in this new part of the church was clean, if there was such a smell. None of the odours and dust of the outside pervaded here. The walls and ceiling were made of stainless steel, polished to a shine.

Eva reached out to trail her had along the shimmering surface, only to be stopped by one of her escorts. "Sorry, Dr Ross. This is clean room atmosphere. Try not to contaminate more than possible." The voice was Egyptian, but the accent was only very slight.

"I'm sorry," she replied, "I didn't know."

"Always sticking her fingers into pies," Madden whispered just a little too loud, bringing a muted laugh around them.

"Actually, it is ARC policy to keep everything as sterile as is possible with so many around, and for good reason." Tilly explained. "A lot of old stuff in here, so they say."

"Really? Have you seen a lot of it?"

Tilly shook her head. "I have been training in a different location. I only came down here for the first time yesterday. I'm hoping they give you the grand tour and I can tag along."

They descended several flights of stairs and entered a maze of rooms, Tilly explaining the history of the fortress and ARCs role within it. She led them into what appeared to Eva to be some type of control room, where a stocky blonde man of medium height and a strangely self-satisfied look smiled and approached them.

"Ah, there you are. I had feared the church tour was never going to end. May I introduce myself? My name is Swanson Guyomard. I am the chief administrator of this ARC facility. And you must be the famous Dr Eva Ross."

Eva shook his outstretched hand. "I don't know about the famous bit."

Without turning, Swanson pointed a device at the bank of screens behind him, and the large screen in the middle flicked on, revealing the ever-present Jeanette Gibson. Pictures of Sloss intermixed with a very confused-looking Detective Caruso. There was no sign of Brian or Gideon, but the caption read 'Fugitives presumed dead in night plane crash'.

Eva put her hand over her mouth, covering her shock.

"The best they could do, I'm sure," Guyomard said in genuine sympathy. "You had quite a ride there with Agent Lohnes."

"Had?" Madden said without humour. "I would suggest we are still right in the middle of it."

Guyomard noticed Madden for the first time. "You are the demon."

"Yeah, so they tell me."

"We have experience of your kind here, hell spawn. Tell me. If you are so tame and congenial, what is your skill?"

Madden pointed to the door. "Go out there and wait a minute."

Amused, Guyomard did just that. After a couple of minutes, to the astonishment of everybody in the room, except Eva, Madden and Tilly, he returned, and upon seeing them, he smiled and approached. "Ah, there you are."

"Again," Eva replied.

"Excuse me? Have we met before?"

"Play back the last three minutes of recorded footage from the control room," Janus, who had followed Guyomard into the room called out.

They all watched the previous introductions with amusement, except for Guyomard, who studied the picture intently.

"Astonishing!" He exclaimed when it had finished. "And it is all passive?"

"I believe so. I have never had cause to actively try and wipe somebody's memory."

"Non-confrontational," Guyomard mused. "We will have to try something. Ah! Here you are!"

Eva turned to the opening glass door, where a slim woman with short dark hair stood, a short man of clear Egyptian heritage behind her.

"Dr Ross, I have the pleasure of introducing you to Dr Gila Ciranoush, curator of the Coptic Museum, and head of ARC research into literary works."

Gila stretched forth a hand, which Eva shook. "It is such a pleasure to meet you, Dr Ross. This is Ali, one of my research assistants. The whole department is abuzz with what you might be carrying. Is it really true?"

"I'm sorry," Eva said, instantly liking the curator, "you have me at a disadvantage. I have some documents certainly, but what they are I have no idea. Here, have a look."

Eva reached into her bag, withdrawing the carefully-wrapped texts she had removed from Gideon's crypt. She still had trouble admitting he was anything more despite all the evidence to the contrary. The mood of the whole room changed as the texts were revealed, becoming one of anticipation and wonder. Suddenly the text felt much more delicate to Eva. She could feel the binding being squeezed and starting to crack under the pressure of her hand.

"Here you are," Eva said and handed the documents to Ali, who recoiled from them.

"No, I'm sorry. I cannot touch these."

Gila pulled on a pair of surgical gloves, and held her hand out. "Why don't I take them? He is ever afraid of contaminating artifacts."

Eva shared a look with Madden and he nodded imperceptibly at her. He had seen the assistant flinch upon being offered the documents too. Ali was afraid, but to Eva's trained eye, he hid it well.

"So what might these be?"

"There is a place a few hundred miles south of here called Nag Hamaddi." Gila began.

"That explains a lot," Madden said.

"You are aware of it?"

"Madden was captured back in the states. Rigged up to a cross and tortured. It looked like some sort of ritual. I think they were going to bleed him to death on a granite altar. The torturer kept screaming about Nag Hamaddi."

"Do you remember what he said?" Gila asked Madden, who shook his head.

"I do," Eva volunteered. "It sounded like 'Dyaa hoo-ah in tocholin Nag Hamaddi'."

"Where are the Nag Hamaddi scrolls..." Gila said in wonder. "Others knew you had them. Others guessed their nature."

"What are they?"

"Well in 1945, two brothers discovered a cache of leather-bound papyrus codices written in the Coptic language. Through various means, most have ended up here at the museum, but there was rumour some were lost, or destroyed because their content was sacrilegious. In the thirteen other codices we have studied, there is reference made to an apocalypse. This is biblical in nature since the codices also contain references to Gospels and Apostles. Ultimately, the truth is revealed that there was a fourteenth that held the blasphemy in complete form. It was this codex that was reported destroyed, though on occasion information would surface that appeared to have originated from these codices, yet we could never trace the source."

"And this might be the fourteenth Codex." Eva felt a wave of guilt wash over her as she recalled how she had leafed through the book, uncaring.

"At the end of the thirteenth Codex, it refers to 'The Origin of the World'. It is my belief that if this is the lost Codex, it might contain many of the answers we seek."

"Can you translate it?"

Gila smiled. "If anybody can. We have the best Coptic translations here in the world. I need to get to work on this. It could be critical to everything we do. If I may take my leave of you, I'll get started right away."

Not waiting for any assent, Gila grabbed Ali and the two of them left the room.

Swanson chuckled. "You may not think much of that little exchange, but you have just given Dr Ciranoush the most treasured document she has ever known. I thought she was ready to burst."

"Is she as good as she says she is?" Madden asked.

"Oh yes. I can guarantee you two things. First, she will have a complete translation for you. Second, she will not sleep until it is done."

"Harsh," Madden observed.

"Oh quite the contrary, my little phoenix. Much as you have risen from the ashes, so will the words of the ancients be lifted from those pages. The most important aspect of ARC researchers is enthusiasm, and she has more than most. Over the years, we have made many miraculous discoveries and many terrifying ones. If you will come with me, I will show you what I mean.

Swanson led them out of the control room and through a corridor filled with glass windows. The rooms beyond stretched into the distance and were filled with banks of cabinets and what looked to be recording equipment, network servers, and all manner of gadgetry.

Madden let out a low whistle. "Quite an operation."

"What are you recording?" asked Eva.

"Everything," said Swanson matter-of-factly, as if the question were asked every day. "Every television channel in every country. Radio too, and every security camera we can patch into, which is most of them. If the world ends tomorrow this lot will be safe, transmitted in an instant to a secure server. If anybody survives, eventually they will find this and start again with the knowledge of what ended it before."

A wave of foreboding washed over Eva. "You think it's going to, don't you?"

"One never knows, Dr Ross. This is but the latest chapter in an event that has been happening for generations. It may continue long after we are gone. But we are not just recording history. There is method to our madness. Let me show you a recording from a year or so back."

Swanson led them to an adjoining conference room, where he flicked on a large screen.

"There are refreshments here. Please help yourselves."

On the screen, a scene materialised. Thousands of people milled around a central area of tents. The crowd stretched on for perhaps a mile, funnelling in from several street-lit avenues that reached into the distance.

"This is Tahrir Square, in central Cairo. You may remember it from such recent excitement as 'The Arab Spring'. This was one of the key melting pots, but it was not what it seemed, though it started off with noble intentions."

On the screen, the crowd milled about, restless.

"There's nothing obvious there," Eva observed.

"True, but watch this." Swanson pressed the ever-present control, and the screen changed colour, looking more like a thermal camera. "Now you are watching auras. As you are aware, there are those among us who can sense the energy around a being. It is an offshoot of holistic medicine; we were able to exploit with research and enough funding. We like to call this the science of the Apocalypse. Look closely."

Eva stepped in front of the screen, Madden and Tilly to either side. Most of the crowd had a yellow gleam to them, but that changed, and Eva's heart nearly stopped. All noise disappeared as Eva focussed on the screen, as a being of violent, angry red entering the square from one of the avenues. The aura was so vivid it outshone all those around it, leaving them tainted.

"Is this what you look like?" Eva whispered to Madden.

"An appropriate color, no?" Swanson said from the other side.

More of the red figures entered the square, each from different avenues. As they passed, a visible restlessness followed in their wake. The level of noise began to rise. The red figures ambled in random directions or so it seemed. They came to rest at equal points in a circle around the center of the square. Then the strangest thing happened. There was a pulse of red and Eva jumped back, somehow feeling it. The aura of the crowd had turned from yellow with a few eddies of red into a deep orange in a moment. Violence began to erupt simultaneously across the square. In moments, the all-too-familiar running battles that had been shown on television filled the screen.

"There have been many sinners in the history of this country," Swanson observed. "There you see but a few. Imagine how many more are out there, on the other side, just waiting for their opportunity to come back here and help tip the balance."

Eva glanced at Janus, who nodded. They both recalled what Iuvart had said at Sloss, where he used those very words. She turned to speak to Madden, and no sound came out. Pain erupted in her side, as if she was being torn open.

Eva dropped to her knees, clutching her side, trying to hold it all in.

"Eva? Eva!" Madden dropped to her side. "What is it?"

Pain throbbed in her middle, and tears came to her eyes, but Eva could not speak. A dry, dusty smell wafted around the room. Strange she could smell that after so long. In the moment it took Eva to topple over on her side, she saw the screen change from Tahrir Square to their own room. Madden was by her side glowing faintly red. In the room, there was a second figure, a much stronger hue, exuding menace.

CHAPTER TWENTY-EIGHT

DAYLIGHT INTRUDED UPON EVA'S SLEEP, CAUSING HER to stir. She could feel the warmth on her eyelids, enticing her to wake. Wherever she lay, the room smelled like the rest of the ARC facility. She had no idea why she was lying down.

She groaned and tried to stretch, when a sharp pain in her hand caused her to pull back.

"Steady there, you don't want it coming out again."

Eva opened her eyes a crack, focusing on her hand. Underneath surgical tape, a tube emerged, connecting her to an intravenous drip at the side of her bed.

"Coming out?" she croaked. "What is it doing in there in the first place? Where am I?"

"You had a fall," the male voice explained. "Given the nature of our location and the recent company you have been keeping, it was deemed best if several tests were run."

Eva moved her free hand to her stomach. "The pain," she groaned. "I have never felt anything quite like it. I thought I was being ripped apart."

"You had a bleed," replied the voice. "It is not uncommon in the early stages of pregnancy, and can often be purely incidental. Yours was fairly major. Still, everything is fine inside. You are both perfectly healthy."

The words took a moment to hit home. Eva was so focused on the word 'bleed' she almost missed what followed.

"I'm what?"

"Five or six weeks pregnant, judging by the scan. Congratulations, Eva. You are going to be a mother."

Now she thought about it, the voice did seem somewhat familiar. Eva opened her eyes fully and regretted as the lights overhead nearly blinded her.

"Here, let me," said the voice as she tried to shield her eyes with her taped hand.

The lights dimmed, and Eva was able to see. A smiling face came into focus. "Mohammed El-Rafi. What in the world are you doing here?"

Mo perched on the end of the bed and held her free hand. "Every ARC operative has full access to everything going on within the organization. Do you think I would let anybody else on this planet care for Eva Ross? Especially after she concluded the work I began in Birmingham?"

"I read your submission. I thought you were insane."

"And what do you think now?"

"Mo, I think we are in a lot of trouble. My entire career, I worked for Gideon. I respected him. I endeavoured to be more like him, following his guidance. And now, I find all this time I was taught by what amounts to a demon prince. What does that say about me, about my methods? Is my perception twisted?"

"No, I do not think so, Eva. In many ways you have

changed since grad school, but from an outsider's point of view, you still see the world through your own eyes, not through the cloud Iuvart wished to place there."

"And yet it seems I am a target, because of a birthmark?"

"Which is why we have to keep you safe. Tell me. Your companion, is he the father?"

Not ready to admit to this just yet, Eva said, "Mo, I am still married. He is not my husband."

Mo said nothing more, but gave her a look as clear as daylight that said he did not believe her. Eva surmised they had had a long time on the road with Janus, and even if he believed himself to be autistic, he could have been recording information the entire time. It was too late to worry now.

"Where is Madden?"

"The invisible man? I don't know, to be honest," Mo said, as he checked the drip. "He came here with you, but hasn't been here since. Quite frankly, were it not for all the cameras, I wouldn't remember him at all. I have no memory of his visit in Allentown. Keep your hand still. Let's get you detached from all this machinery."

Eva allowed Mo to remove the needle from her hand. "Not your usual brand of medicine."

"Not the one I study, for sure. However, we have many skills. ARC isn't for the limited. The Battle requires many talents."

"The Battle? A rather grand term."

Mo smiled. "I have always found it to be appropriate. It's what we do. There nothing on this Earth more important than The Battle. Whatever is going on 'down below', is affecting us all. If I said to you that global warming was theorised to be directly related to demon activity in this realm, you might be inclined to scoff at the idea. Yet, there are many in the organization that believe it is so."

Mo finished applying a bandage to her hand. "There. All done."

"Can I get up?"

"Of course, if you feel up to it. Your clothes and all you brought with you are stored in the closet. All I would ask is don't over-exert yourself, Eva. All life is precious, and you are at a very delicate stage. Babies have been lost for doing a lot less. I'll give you some privacy. Come join me outside when you are done."

Mo left the room, and Eva sat up, swinging her legs over the side of the bed. Touching the floor, Eva pulled her feet back as the icy cold caught her by surprise.

Trying again, Eva was this time prepared for the shock. The floor had the same pitted texture as her balcony, and in a strange way she enjoyed the feeling. It gave her a sense of continuity.

Standing up, Eva felt her legs wobble and had to sit once again. Reflexively, Eva put her hand to her middle, as if the cold and the fatigue were a direct challenge to her unborn child.

With nobody nearby to help her, Eva resolved to dress in between rest breaks, but by the time she had stood again and steadied herself, she was feeling a lot stronger, her thighs burning a lot less from the strain.

"Little steps, Eva," she muttered as she made her way across the room. Choosing a linen skirt, and donning a blouse that wrapped about her like gossamer, sliding over her skin, Eva defied all sense of fashion by pulling on a pair of running shoes she found comfortable.

Feeling more confident about facing at least a little part of the world, Eva opened the door.

. . .

Outside, the false daylight was supplemented by a series of small windows, opening out onto remains of the Roman fortress and allowing the sunlight reflected from the white-washed walls to give the room an eerie glow. Eva found Mo sitting by a table loaded with food.

"Thought you might be hungry."

In response, Eva's stomach growled. "Excuse me."

Mo laughed. "No need. What's a growl between old friends?"

Eva sat down, and looked over the bounty. "So where to start? Lots of vegetables here."

"If I were you, I would get my energy back before tucking into them. Here, try this."

Mo handed her a plate upon which sat a square of what appeared to be moistened cake. "And this is?"

"We call it 'Basbousa'. It is a spice cake made from semolina soaked in syrup. This will get you back on your feet."

Curious, Eva took a fork and sliced a corner off the cake. The syrup and spices were just rapture, making her whole body quiver in delight. "That is wonderful."

Eva attacked the cake and had devoured it in no time. She reached for another slice.

"Steady," Mo warned her, "don't want you making your-self sick.

Eva acquiesced, and instead, filled a plate with the vegetables and lentils she had become accustomed to while in the house. Lingering over the food now she was finally eating, Eva looked around the room. Down the corridor, there were entrances to three other rooms such as hers.

"Still in the complex. I haven't come far."

"What need has ARC for a specific medical base? We need to be ready for all eventualities."

"Who is that?" Eva pointed at a portrait of a man dressed in suit and waistcoat, astride a horse, long black cloak draped behind him. "He looks very grand, and sort of selfless."

" Jerome Guyomard, the patriarch of Anges de la Résurection des Chevaliers. An explorer and philanthropist, he was the first of us to witness what you so colourfully termed a 'Hellbounce'. Of course, it must be saidhe had no idea what he had encountered. He was an explorer, and he was in, what was then, the deepest darkest Africa, looking for new species. It was all the rage in the nineteenth century. Suffice it to say he encountered a species he did not expect, in a settlement near what is now Kinshasa."

"What happened?"

Mindful of the fact Eva was still eating, Mo opened a laptop and placed it next to her. "Have a look for yourself. He was French, but of course with modern technology, it was accurately translated long ago."

Tucking into her third slice of Basbousa, Eva began to read.

The natives, simple as they were, nonetheless had complexities in their history. We had employed several such as porters as we sought a route through the denser parts of the jungle. Upon crossing an invisible line of demarcation, the porters, as one, dropped their assigned crates and fell to their knees, begging us to take a different route. We stood resolute to continue on our chosen path however, and following extensive discourse with the porters, offered them such trinkets that made them override their instinct to depart and continue with us on our journey.

Now we had not been on the trail for more than a day

when the lead tracker was assaulted by one of their fellows, who appeared from the foliage, covered in mud and screaming with a crazed demeanour. The remainder of the tribe scattered, vanishing into the foliage, but the exploration party remained steadfast. Even as the newcomer, clearly lacking in sanity, ripped his associate asunder, Monsieur Philipe LeClerq equipped his rifle, and fired a round, throwing the assailant back fully ten feet.

Eva began to grow cold with anticipation. The sunlight from outside felt as though it had dimmed. She read on.

The Wildman, now defeated, lay prone in the undergrowth. As we summoned the courage to investigate, a yawning maw opened up in the air right before us, sending forth a light such as burns from a ship's lantern, smoky and fey. The body of the Wildman was lifted by unearthly forces and sucked into the mouth, which then closed, never to open again.

When the porters regained their wits, they explained their avoidance of the Wildman. It was said he resembled a village elder, who had died five years before.

Eva looked up. Mo was watching her, concerned.

"I'm fine. It's just chilling reading such an old account. Did he find any more?"

"Not that we are aware," said Swanson as he entered the room with a couple of strangers in tow. "My ancestor was never so lucky. Despite being rich, and having extensive influence, he was a very intolerant man, never having time for those who couldn't understand his concepts or motives. He died following a confrontation with one of his colleagues, who took exception to his quite frankly grating personality and continued barbs."

Swanson paused to glance at the text of the screen. "People are never perfect, and often they do more harm than good, but despite his imperfections he got us off to a good start. I like to think he would be proud. Eva, I would like you to meet doctors David Fleming and Samantha Stack. They are ARC researchers working in different areas of interest, but who have been called in following your discovery to follow up on the initial findings."

Both doctors nodded a greeting. Eva smiled back. She could sense the excitement in Swanson's voice. "You know something then?"

"Yes, we know something, at long last. But I think it should come from Dr Ciranoush. It is her project. If you would like to join us, we are going to head over to the museum. We will wait outside for you to finish up here."

"Just one thing before you go. Where is Madden Scott?"

Swanson shrugged. "No idea, I'm afraid. He left shortly after you took ill. Said he had to see someone in the city and he would be back."

"And you have no idea as to his whereabouts?"

"Sorry, we lost track of him. Must be that damned ability of his to disappear. We will be outside. Dr Rafi, would you join me for a moment please? Take your time, Eva."

Finding herself alone, Eva chose to continue her meal. The laptop had locked itself, so she found no further distraction there. At length, and given no other reason to do otherwise, Eva returned to her room, packed her belongings and made to leave the infirmary.

As Eva walked down the corridor past the other rooms, a whispering made her pause.

The voice was nowhere, and yet came from all around her. *"Eva Ross, I know you. I know what you carry. You can be the salvation of us all, or the damnation."*

"Who are you?"

The sibilant whispering clawed at her mind, threatening to rend her sanity. *"You must be freed of all choice. Only then can all be saved."*

Pressure began to build in Eva's stomach. Something that had evidently begun its job several days before sought to finish the task. Eva sank to the ground, her hands protecting her stomach.

"You won't take my baby!" she cried in defiance, at whatever sought to assail her.

The pressure grew, and Eva screamed.

Suddenly, and she had no idea of comprehending why, but Eva no longer felt alone. There was nobody else in the corridor, but Eva had company.

"You will not hurt her any more. This mortal is under my protection."

"You cannot!" The first voice raged, and pressure not unlike the feeling in the tunnel under Sloss assailed Eva, forcing her down under a barrage of imagined wind.

"There are stronger forces. You cannot defeat love."

From within her, there came a warmth. Eva closed her eyes and imagined a glow. The light enveloped her and deflected the wind, allowing Eva to stand. Eva felt a bond, and unlimited love. More, she felt trust.

"Who are you?"

"We shall meet soon. Stay steadfast. There are many trials ahead, and many that would use you. Gird yourself against them, and know I love you."

The glow intensified, and the hostile spirit fled wailing.

Then all hell broke loose. Alarms sounded, and Eva, leaning against the wall as she tried to make sense of what had just happened, felt people rushing past. The door opposite was thrown open to reveal a body lying still in the bed, the sensors indicating he was flat lining. It was Gila's assistant.

CHAPTER TWENTY-NINE

THE BODY LAY PRONE, UNRESPONSIVE. THROUGH THE doorway, Eva watched as faces turned towards her.

Swanson and Mo came back into the corridor.

"What happened, Eva?" asked Mo.

Stunned to silence, Eva tried to ask herself that same question. As hard as she searched for an answer, it eluded her. The only thing she knew was she was no longer afraid. Fear had evaporated. All she could say was the truth, as they would expect to hear it.

"Somebody... something spoke to me. I had a pain and collapsed. The voice went silent, and I felt better. Then your staff all burst past me. Isn't that Gila Ciranoush's assistant?"

Swanson appeared grim. "Yes, you are correct. Ali fell ill shortly after you, and we had him under observation here. Are you okay? Would you like to rest more?"

"I'm fine. This isn't the first odd experience I have had, and hanging around with you lot, I am damned sure it won't be the last. You were taking me to the Museum. Shall we go?"

Not waiting for an answer, Eva marched past them.

Finding her way out of the facility and into the church was not hard, the only issue being the over-abundance of gun-wielding ARC soldiers who constantly challenged her before Swanson appeared. As Eva passed through the hidden door, she was relieved to see the church empty.

"Where to then?"

"Down behind the altar." Swanson pointed off to their right. "Doctor Rafi, would you please supervise the post mortem of Ali."

Mo nodded, and with a wink for Eva turned and left.

Swanson took the lead. "We are lucky to have him with us. Too many have died recently during your little jaunt in the States. A lot of important benefactors."

Half listening to Swanson, Eva became absorbed in the magnificence of the architecture around her. The walls of the museum were buttressed at intervals, and the panels between decorated with frescos, in front of which stood glass cabinets filled with treasures.

"Impressive, isn't it?" Swanson said, bringing Eva back to herself.

"It's stunning. Not very busy though."

"The museum is officially in a period of renovation. As you well know, there are currently more important issues than public access."

"It's so peaceful," Eva said, revelling in the serenity of the building. The silence comforted her. "We will be thankful for such moments in times to come."

"My sentiments exactly. Now, let's find Dr Ciranoush."

Swanson led Eva through more of the Museum, moving at a pace that allowed her to take in the sights, but not study the artifacts. At length, he came to a thick acrylic screen behind which Gila Ciranoush was studying documents. Without looking up, she pressed a button and waved them through. Swanson took a door to the right, seemingly moving off in a different direction. Eva followed and found herself in a corridor. One more door later and she was on the other side of the screen.

"Security," Gila said by way of explanation. "The manuscripts here, aside from being priceless, are ancient beyond measure and very sensitive to changes in temperature and humidity. The fact you disturbed this scroll repeatedly and brought it through so many adverse conditions is a minor miracle in itself."

Feeling guilty about the number of times she had looked at it, Eva sought to change the subject. "Have you translated the contents?"

Wiping a hand across her fatigued brow, Gila nodded. There was an air of excitement about her, a glimpse of a smile, and jerky movements of somebody so nervous they could barely contain themselves.

"The dialect is Bohairic, an ancient Coptic version of Egyptian. It is most similar in style to the thirteenth codex, which hints at a similar time of creation, if not the same author. It has nothing to do with the Origin text found in thirteen. It talks about the return of demon kind to the earth. It speaks of another scroll, a sealed scroll. They mean to enter this realm by force of will."

"He knew. Damn it, he knew!" Eva thumped the desk on which the scroll rested, causing Gila to protect it with her arms by reflex.

"Sorry," she said, embarrassed. "I can't begin to think how sacred this is to you all, but it is just another piece of the mystery. When I found the scroll, there were corpses.

They were the remains of all the previous hospital administrators. Iuvart was taking them and assuming their place. In return, he had them locked up in a room until death, working on trying to decrypt a document, presumably the scroll. One had left a note attesting to such.

I think back to all I have seen. The sacrifices, how Wormwood appeared in Sloss. Iuvart was trying to bring the man back pure. We have seen demons in pain here, and any serious injury sucks them back to that wherever-it-is. We have seen evidence they can force the human shell asunder, although what happens after I could only guess at."

"They don't last long," Swanson supplied, and flicked a computer on. After a moment, he had found what he sought, and Jeanette appeared, providing commentary on what appeared a massacre, malformed humans with grossly distended limbs, and all lying dead. "It seems once they are released from human form they have immense power, but at a cost. They die within minutes."

Eva went cold upon hearing this, acutely aware of how close Madden had come to losing control.

"They tried to do the same thing to Madden. All I have seen has pointed at attempts to use hellbounces to stop us, and yet Iuvart himself claimed Madden and I were crucial. He called me a child of David. Does that make me Jewish?"

"Not necessarily," Swanson replied. "It could be your family originated in this direction. You can choose your religion. You can't choose where you are born."

"I had a feeling before that Madden and I were coming into this at the end of the story. Nothing has changed to convince me otherwise."

"I think you are not as far along as you suppose." Gila trailed her finger down the papyrus manuscript. "You wanted to know the contents of this scroll, well here it is. It is mostly an existing Gospel, that of Saint Thomas. I was able to skip through large parts of it, knowing the passages. What is interesting are the passages interspersed amongst the gospel. It talks about buried texts, about information so revealing and so terrifying that once the author had written it down, he realized it could not be shared. He buried it. This was one of the scrolls they claimed was burned by the mother of those that made the discovery. Now you have to ask yourself what information is so dire the author did not destroy it, and yet not only left it in this world but left indications as to its whereabouts. This is the key to a bigger secret."

"The author was a demon."

The two ARC operatives looked at Eva in silence.

"You said it yourself, Gila. They did not destroy it after having written this momentous information in their trance, or religious ecstasy, or however you describe it. Therefore, they must have had a purpose for the text. If that was what Iuvart was seeking to unlock, it stands to reason it was written by a demon for a demon. They wanted it found."

Swanson's phone rang, and he stepped off to one side to have a conversation.

"Eva, you do realise what you are saying is as about as blasphemous as it gets?" Her face was grave. Gila had an earnest belief in whatever faith she followed.

"Blasphemous to who though? If one follows Christianity, Judaism, Buddhism, are there not parts of the text for one that contradict others? Who is to say demons don't have a religion? This might be holy to them."

Gila looked like she wanted to say more; a glance at Swanson betrayed her. These people all knew more than they were letting on, Eva decided.

As it was, Swanson chose this moment to put his phone away, and switch on a bank of screens located to one side of the room. He said nothing as the screens flared into life, each looking out from the museum and church at a different angle.

"What is it?" Eva asked.

"Not sure," was Swanson's answer. "We may have a problem."

The cameras came into focus to reveal on every screen a mass of humanity, bodies packed together in all streets and alleyways. Even though the view was just a glass screen, Eva could feel the violence in the mob outside.

"Demons?"

Swanson pressed a switch, and the filter was applied. On every screen, there was at least one demon presence, swirls of orange permeating the aura of all around them. "Some, but that's mostly people, albeit under an influence."

The mob became restless, pushing forward, and then surging with no care for any that were crushed. The reason for the surge became apparent when alarms started to screech all around the museum.

"Security breach!" Swanson yelled above the noise. "Somebody has let them in!"

On the screens, the mob became a torrent of bodies, raging forward; unmindful of any that fell and were trampled underfoot. As yet, nobody approached them in this distant part of the museum.

"How long?" Eva shouted.

"At that pace, maybe five minutes." Swanson depressed a button and the alarms stopped. "No point having that deafening us as well. We will know how long we have when the barriers come down. They are set to trip the moment a demon or anybody under their influence passes the entrance."

As was typical, the moment Swanson said this, barriers began to seal off every alcove.

"Don't fret. We should be well protected in here."

A flashing light above one of the screens caused them to look away from the gloom of the museum. Swanson flicked a switch and spoke into a microphone. "Report."

"They have found the entrance sir, but can't figure out how to get in. The sheer weight of numbers is going to make it difficult to co-ordinate a counterattack." It was Tilly on the screen.

"Seal the door, and get everyone out," Swanson ordered. "We will just have to hope they are too preoccupied with us to worry about trashing the Hanging Church. I will open every access point to get them in here. Everything is well protected. We will rendezvous with you at the monastery."

"Sir," came the reply. Tilly spared one moment to wink at Eva, and the screen went blank.

Swanson paused for a moment, muttering under his breath. He then flicked another switch, causing a screen to rise from the control panel. The face of an elderly man appeared.

"Report," he said in much the same tone as Swanson just had.

"They have taken Cairo. We have minutes left. Regrouping to the secondary location."

The old man swore. "There is no hope for salvation?"

"No. A mob under influence is passing through the church and into the museum."

"And do we have confirmation?"

Swanson sighed. "Yes father, we do. We have at least two loose, and a third player trying to introduce more. We have lost agents in the USA but picked up valuable intel. We have the key." Swanson nodded in Eva's direction.

"Keep her safe, son. She may be the salvation of us all."

"And the experiment?"

"One has failed. The other is ongoing."

"Keep me apprised. Good luck." The screen went blank and lowered back into the console.

"So what do we do now?" Eva asked of them both. "Do we sit here? Wait in this plastic box for someone to find us?"

"That is the plan, yes," Swanson affirmed to Eva's dismay. "We need to trap the mob in the Museum. We owe the Coptic Church that much. They have been very great benefactors of our organisation for a long time, and as long as demons are hunting us, they aren't causing any more than superficial damage to the Hanging Church. Could you imagine letting someone trash the Vatican, or Mecca if you had an alternative? Besides, we have a way out. We only need wait long enough for the bulk of them to reach us."

"And if they catch you before you get out?"

Swanson placed one hand on Gila's shoulder. It was clear to Eva this had been considered. "Then we will have played our part. Others will take up the struggle."

A movement in the shadows on the other side of the screen distracted Eva from what appeared a very private moment between Swanson and Gila.

"Somebody's out there," she said, feeling very claustrophobic in this giant plastic box, like a trapped animal waiting to be put out of its misery.

Swanson stood beside her. "It was always going to happen. Gila, secure Codex Fourteen. Let's be as ready as we can be."

Again, at the edge of her vision, a figure moved, initially hesitant, and then when it was clear there was no resistance, with increasing audacity. A drip became a trickle as more found their way into the depths of the museum. The trickle continued until bodies were pouring down the corridor.

"Don't move," Gila cautioned Eva. "They might not have seen us yet."

But, it was already too late. The foremost figure had spotted them behind the screen, and hurtled towards them, pulling others along with a scream that could even be heard behind the thick security screen. Not stopping, he ran until he collided with it, the impact crushing his nose and sending a spray of blood across the glass.

Others followed, and either collided with the glass or began to hammer at it, using anything they could lift, or just their bare hands. The press of humanity was overwhelming, and pretty soon, the entire screen was filled with faces, snarling, angry, or utterly vacant. Eva did not know what was worse, but stood her ground. The scent of dry dust was thick in the air. Demon kind was once again seeking her.

Eva turned to say as much to Swanson, but a quick glance told her they were preoccupied, staring in terror at the glass.

"How can it be?" Swanson whispered. "You died. You already came back. You cannot come back again."

Eva followed his gaze, to find the man who had initially assaulted the screen standing there, grinning at them, teeth missing, his face smeared with blood and his nose a mere memory of the shape it had been.

"Swanson, tell me that is not who I think it is."

The ARC director lowered his head, shaking it, not saying a thing.

"God preserve us!" Exclaimed Gila. "Ali?"

The figure on the other side of the glass turned and leered at Gila, eyeing her up and down in a way that left no doubt as to his intentions, and then began to hammer on the glass. Those about him took up the rhythm.

"I saw him dead," Eva said aloud. "He was on life support in the room next to mine, and yet when we got here, he was in the room with us all. The sensor picked him up as demon from the aura. There were two in the room with us."

Eva grabbed Swanson by the lapels on his jacket and shook him. "There were two in the room with us, Swanson! Jesus Christ, what have you done?"

On the other side of the screen, the wall of flesh pressed so hard, and with such force the screen began to creak. Even demon kind were being crushed, and those that did were caught up in a maelstrom of white as portals opened in the midst of the mob and pulled them in. Tentacles whipped against the glass, one causing a fracture. It was so commonplace for Eva now she no longer considered what was on the other side, but the fracture in the glass was noted and the pressure increased. It began to tell, the fracture spreading.

"Let's get her out of here," Swanson instructed, avoiding Eva's gaze but having gathered his wits enough. "We have to get to the Monastery. Dr Ciranoush, do you have all you need?"

"I do."

Swanson pushed a button and part of the rear wall detached, leaving an opening. Gila went first, Eva followed, Swanson close behind.

Eva glanced back past Swanson. Even as they fled down the tunnel, she could still see the raging mob attacking the glass. Ali stood in the midst of it all, staring down the tunnel after them, oblivious to all else. He was watching her.

CHAPTER THIRTY

THEY FLED AS FAST AS THE SPACE ALLOWED, EVA having to duck in several places. They could have been two or maybe three hundred yards away when the screen finally gave, the glass smashing to the floor with a noise that echoed down the tunnel and made Eva's already thumping heart beat that much faster. Howling voices echoed from behind, and the distant sound of footfalls signalled the pursuit.

Then they were out in a bigger room, emerging from what looked like a safe.

Swanson swung the door shut and rotated a huge wheel to lock it. "They aren't getting through now. Out there. Get in the car."

Swanson signalled, and Eva did as instructed, emerging onto a side street bathed in late afternoon sun. Outside a range rover in desert camouflage colours waited, door already open, and ARC security stood beside it.

Not waiting, Eva jumped in the front passenger seat, and Gila climbed in the back. Swanson took the driver's seat.

"You know what to do," he said through the open window to the operative.

"Yes sir, it is already being done."

"Good." Swanson spoke no more, accelerating away into the afternoon traffic.

As they climbed a ramp on to what must have been the Egyptian equivalent of an interstate, Swanson pressed a button on the panel in front of him.

"Agents EC one and ES six en route to secondary unit. Package is secured."

"Acknowledged," a voice answered from speakers around the car. "Proceed with all haste. The situation is critical. The experiment was a failure."

Swanson paled at this cryptic message. "I disagree. The experiment was a success. It proved the enemy can infiltrate our most secure compounds. But, at the same time, you are correct. It was a colossal failure."

"You knew he was a demon and yet he still managed to winkle you out of ARC Cairo. You have the package now. Make use of it and fly directly to Geneva." The line clicked and Swanson pressed the button once more, ending the communication.

"I think you owe me some answers," Eva said, feeling betrayed but not fully understanding why.

Swanson kept his eyes on the road. "We are as likely to be killed on the road by some lunatic driver as we are by a demon mob. Now really is not the time."

"Oh, I beg to differ. You can't escape me or weasel out here."

Swanson sighed. "I guess you are right. What did you want to know?"

Eva looked over her shoulder at Gila, making it very clear she was included in this. Sweating, despite the comfort of air conditioning, she merely nodded her head in acquiescence.

"Ali. You created a hellbounce."

"We did. It was our first major success."

Eva felt sick. "These things are popping up all over the world and you wanted to create one?"

"He volunteered. Ali knew the risks involved. He was a convicted murderer given a second chance at life, if he returned."

"What kind of sick and twisted people are you? Hell is coming to earth and you are chancing on turning a murderer into a demon."

"I don't expect you to understand. ARC defends humanity in any way possible. Sometimes that means we don't use what could be the most ethical of methods. What matters is we get results. Ali was facing the firing squad. We negotiated a different end for him so we could control the time and place of his death. He died in that room. The body was brought back to life and left in a coma. For twenty years, he lay there. Then in the room where the body had died, the man existed once more."

"Did he know you kept his body alive?"

"No."

"Did he know his body was capable of speaking to people?"

Swanson turned to her. "Explain. Is that what happened in that room?"

Eva watched the evening sun as she considered what had happened, its ruby gaze dazzling her momentarily. "I felt someone speaking to me, trying to overwhelm me. When it all ended, that's when the chaos happened." She didn't feel comfortable telling them about the other voice. Eva put her hand to her stomach in reassurance. She was pregnant and Madden was nowhere to be seen. It was down to her and her alone to protect the life growing within.

"He wasn't the same when we saw him in the museum," said Gila. "Up until then he was calm, and constantly monitored."

"You don't think the death of his mortal body, after he had already returned had an effect?"

"Maybe," Gila conceded. "He was always strange around the texts we researched. He kept on about being unworthy of touching them."

"I don't doubt it. Anything holy would cause a hellbounce pain. I thought you scientists would have known by now. You wonder why he wouldn't touch any of the scrolls? When Madden touched it, the scroll burned his skin. I saw Ali flinch when I tried to hand the codex to him. You probably just observed his normal reaction."

Eva looked out over the Nile, yawning wide and lazy to their right, its dark waters dotted with a flotilla of small sails that danced in the late afternoon breeze. If only those aboard knew what she knew. They might not seem so carefree.

"We just never knew," Gila admitted.

"There is a lot you don't know for a so-called last line of defence."

"Science is sometimes best guess," Swanson growled. "Those words count for a lot with the unknown and have led to many a breakthrough."

"Well here is my best guess for you. Let's test your theory and see how close to the mark I am when it all pans out. Madden didn't leave, you had him moved while I was unconscious. That mysterious message you received attested to that fact. It also ties in with what Iuvart said to us in Sloss. It seems we are both needed. You would be wise to keep us together."

"Or to keep you apart. Have you not considered the possibility that if you are nowhere near each other, then what could come to pass may never happen?"

Eva shook her head in disbelief. "Are you really that naive? Do you think if they are this close to getting what they want, that the small matter of distance will prevent them from succeeding? I doubt there is anywhere on earth you can hide us."

"Maybe you are right," Swanson admitted grudgingly, "but for now how about we keep you alive long enough to figure this out? We have guests."

Eva turned in her seat to see Gila already looking out the rear window.

"Where?"

"Three sedans, all beat-up looking. They are a couple of cars back, all sticking pretty close together. They have been that way for the last couple of miles. When we move, they move."

"They must have been waiting for us to escape the museum," said Eva, tired already of the endless succession of car chases.

"Most likely," agreed Swanson. "Most of that lot have not a brain between them, but there are definitely some advanced thinkers on the other side. That means not only did they expect us to escape from the museum, it would suggest they intended for us to head towards Nag Hamaddi."

"With the Codex in our possession to boot. Well what can we do?" asked Gila.

"Not a lot. We don't have any weapons, and if we did,

we sure as hell couldn't use them. ARC might count all major governments and agencies amongst its subordinates, but your local Cairo police are less likely to be friendly. We have a long way to go yet. Let's see if we can put a little distance between them and us."

Swanson began to accelerate as much as the traffic allowed. It was late afternoon and the roads were busy but negotiable. Several times, he managed to put some distance between their car and the pursuers, but each time this happened, within minutes the tailing cars had closed the gap.

Swanson flicked the speaker on once more. "This is agent EC one en route to secondary unit. We are being pursued. Three unmarked vehicles."

"What is your location EC one?"

Swanson glanced around. "Street Corniche El Nile, south of primary unit. Other side of the river from Al Hawamidiyah."

There was a short pause. "Agent EC one, you are instructed to proceed outside of the city using any and all means short of lethal violence."

"Yeah I know, can't involve the locals. Thanks."

Swanson switched off the communicator. "Well, it was worth a try. Hold tight."

There was no subtlety to his actions this time. Swanson floored the gas and what Eva had thought to be lumbering beast of a vehicle roared in response. They surged ahead, and traffic melted away as each driver recognized the peril. Behind them, the three sedans were slow to respond, not being a match. The surprise was evident in their response. As Eva watched in the side mirror, it exploded as a bullet hit it.

Other shots ricocheted off the panels.

"Windows and panels are all bulletproof," Swanson advised. If that's all they have, we are quite safe."

The three cars, despite the speed and traffic, now began to close in on them. No more shots were fired, either because those behind realized the futility, or because they had run out of bullets. Eva suspected the latter.

Two of the cars pulled along either side of them, while the car with the gunman remained close behind. The cars to either side began to close the gap.

"They want the Codex," Eva realised aloud.

Gila put her arms around the case containing the Codex, protecting it.

Swanson added, "And they want to slow us down in order to get it without damaging it. Hold tight."

Eva barely had time to grab the seatbelt before Swanson swerved the car first left, and then right, causing the cars on either side to veer off. It took only a moment for them to recover, and Eva screamed as they closed once more.

In the car to their right, the driver was shuddering at the wheel, his eyes wide, and his teeth in a grimace. He shouted something out the window of his car at her, but she could not tell what it was, nor if it was even English. His face began to stretch, distending as Eva had seen others do, but unlike them, this time it did not stop. His face was elongated, a macabre parody of a human, and his shoulders began to bulk out.

Gila screamed, and Eva knew without looking that they all were changing. Whatever had precipitated this was not clear, but Eva could not tear her gaze away from the driver nearby. His eyes became bloodshot, and the stretched skin of his face ripped as a demon, too large to be contained, forced its way out.

Blood and gore washed the interior of the car and Eva

watched, transfixed. From the noise behind her, Gila was hysterical at the sight. Eva had never seen the change up close. The bulk of the demon that now struggled to control the car was matched by those behind it in the same car, and as Eva glanced around, was at least equalled by those in the other cars.

The grimace of the demon closest widened, and it sought to open the door. The creature was too bulky, and Eva surmised the car still moved only because the foot was wedged in place on the gas pedal. Still, it thrust an arm through the open window and clawed at the side of their car.

"Swanson, get us out of here!" Eva yelled, a comment echoed by Gila amidst her screaming.

All around them, the road was becoming chaos as more people saw what was occurring. Cars veered off in every direction, some skidding to a halt, others speeding off in front.

Sirens wailed behind the trailing car and in response the demons screamed, an ear-piercing sound that began to shatter the glass of their vehicles and of those around them. Eva put her hands over her own ears, and then thinking better of it, covered Swanson's instead.

They were out of Cairo by now, and Swanson pushed their car still faster. Their three pursuers became erratic, and the police made it through behind them. The passenger signalled for them to slow, waving with a gun, and then threw his hands up as one of the demons finally made it out of their car. Jumping across, aiming for Gila, the demon miscalculated, landing atop the police vehicle, crushing the hood and causing it to flip over. The police car somersaulted atop the demon car to the left, the rear car crashing into the last.

As carnage erupted behind them, the ARC car shot forward onto clear road, all other traffic having been caught in the crash. Swanson was keen to put some distance between them and the accident, keeping his foot down.

"Ease back." Eva put her hand on his arm to soothe frayed nerves, and Swanson jumped.

"What?"

"I said ease back. We are beyond their reach and they most definitely are beyond ours. No point getting us killed too."

Swanson did as asked, and pulled the car over to the side of the road. As soon as they had stopped, Eva got out and walked to the back of the car, looking back up the road.

The sun was now a deep red as it sought the horizon, its russet glow rippling across the Nile. They were perhaps a half mile from the wreckage, and even in the failing light, a miasma could clearly be seen gathering about each car.

The breeze blew the scent of the endless Sahara across her, and Eva could not help but notice the tinge of carrion from the distant fog.

"Is this what happens?" Gila spoke in hushed tones.

"Not usually. This is something else."

They watched in silence as a portal opened up above the fog, blue light circling a white center. This time it was horizontal, floating above the wreckage like the underbelly of a perceived flying saucer. The whole fog bank lit up a pale blue, and even from this distance, it was clear there was fighting going on within. The tentacles reached through, stabbing into the cars and pulling them aloft and into the portal. But, unlike before, it didn't end there. The tentacles paused for a moment, and then grabbed at several other cars, still full of terrified people. These too disappeared and the portal winked out, leaving the screams of those spared the gruesome fate.

"That's never happened before," Eva observed.

"What?" Said Swanson, still shaken if his voice was an indication. "What never happened?"

It all made Eva furious. She poked his chest, the linen pushing into plump flesh underneath. "You make demons, with no thought of the consequences. What sort of an organization are you?" Eva flung her hand out towards the distant carnage. "That. That has never happened before. When a hellbounce is injured, as you saw in the museum, it is sucked back to Hell. All hellbounces seem to suffer on Earth. But when the demon inside escapes, they are doomed to die. Iuvart wants to open a portal to Hell to bring demons back without the limitations of a human shell. Whatever those portals are, they remove the demons, but this time they also took people, and cars. Something new has piqued the curiosity of whatever is moving those tentacles. If you know anything of use, you had better tell me, and maybe I can make more out of it than you appear to have."

Swanson swallowed, and looked at Gila briefly. "Eva, we haven't told you the full truth. I promise you we will, but we need to get to Nag Hammadi. Fast."

"Why? Are the answers there?"

"Perhaps. But that's not the only reason. Eva, they are going to execute Madden."

CHAPTER THIRTY-ONE

THEY WERE ON THE ROAD FOR TWO DAYS FOLLOWING the incident. At first, Swanson had been keen to put as much distance between them and the site of the portals as quickly as possible, but in the utter darkness of rural Egypt, driving at high speeds became much too hazardous.

The first night they stopped at a hotel in the town of Beni Suef, across the river from their initial route. They stayed to the west of the Nile the following day, tracking it as far as a town called Sawhaj, where again they spent the night.

"How far are we away?" Eva had no other thought than to reach Madden from the moment Swanson had pronounced his sentence.

"Perhaps ten or twenty miles," Swanson responded, still distracted by what he had seen; he hadn't spoken at all in the car, and barely said a few words in the evenings since Gila spoke all of the local dialects and assumed the role of translator. He had a haunted look in his eyes.

"Then why can't we go now?"

Swanson refused to look up. "Because it's on an island,

and the ferry will not cross at night. They will not do anything without my authorization, and the plan is for me to be present. Within a certain time frame." Swanson said no more, choosing to leave the two women alone and retire to his room.

Eva toyed with the smooth porcelain cup she had been given, and then took another sip of the dark tea it contained. Enriched with cane juice, so Gila had informed her, the dark tea was sweet, rich, and complemented the aroma of spice that wafted around the bar and caught in the back of her throat. It almost made her forget there were bigger issues to worry about. Almost, but not quite.

"What does he mean about a time frame?" Eva asked, leaning forward.

Gila looked about the bar. Nobody was close, so Gila leaned across the table, closing the distance. "He means that after a termination order is issued by an officer, if it is not enforced personally then subordinates have leave to act on their behalf. I'm sorry, Eva. We might already be too late. It depends entirely on who is in charge on the island."

Nothing more was said on the subject. Eva nursed her tea, and Gila had departed for her bed many hours before Eva sought her own.

Despite the comfort of fresh cotton sheets, smooth and cool against the heat, Eva barely slept that night. Her worry for Madden was so great, even the child growing in her womb seemed to sense it, causing waves of nausea to accompany her disquiet.

They met in the bar the next morning and ate in silence, the normally delicious fresh fruit tasting bland and unmemorable. Without any knowledge of Madden, Eva was caught in limbo.

The sun was barely above the horizon when they set off. Every second of the journey, every mile that passed, Eva willed them closer.

After what could have been an hour, an island began to appear in the middle of the Nile. Upon seeing this, Swanson took a left turn and they crossed a bridge over the river. Heading east, the road bordered on desert, eschewing the lush vegetation of the far bank. With mulish reluctance, the island continued to grow.

"Welcome to Tabenna, home of the Monastery of Saint Pachomius," intoned Swanson.

"I've never heard of him," Eva admitted.

"It's not a surprise," said Gila. "Few outside of either this immediate area or the ARC organisation have. Pachomius was a monk who lived in this region around three hundred years after Christ existed. He spent his life a nomad until he found this island. The recorded history tells he was praying here and a divine voice spoke to him and asked him to remain here and build a community. He was directly responsible for forming the first communal monastery, right there on that island."

The morning sunlight glinted off white buildings, setting them aglow.

"It doesn't look like its seventeen centuries old," she observed.

"Well no, over time the order spread to other communes, and this particular monastery was abandoned. ARC resurrected it about fifty years ago to become a self-sufficient commune, a last refuge, if you will against all that is to come. It is a farming community, wholly self-sufficient.

In truth, it is the primary ARC outpost in this country, though many would argue contrary to that."

A snort from Swanson indicated he agreed with Gila's last comment.

Gila continued. "The only way on or off is by ferry, and that is once a day, if at all. We walk from here."

Swanson pulled the car to a stop, parking it in one of a series of bays marked out with chalk. There was one other vehicle next to them, a goods van with blackened windows. Maddens prison.

Eva stepped out, relishing the scent of the river as it flowed by. There was no dust in the air this close, and no reek of death. The island reached out to her with a sense of serenity. Even from this distance, it truly did feel like a bastion against the troubles to come.

A jetty poked out through the reeds, at the end of which waited a small boat with an outboard engine. In complete contrast to the surroundings, a black-ops ARC soldier awaited them, giving lie to the humble truth around them.

The soldier inclined his head to them. "Directors, doctor. If you will be careful boarding the boat, I will see you safely across. They are expecting you."

"Have you killed Madden?" Eva burst out.

At a nod from Swanson, the soldier replied. "Ma'am I'm on perimeter duty. Last I heard they awaited the director before completing the experiment. If you would climb aboard, please?" The way he answered her spoke volumes about his distaste for the subject.

The trip over the river was brief, the distance between shore and island no more than three hundred feet or so. As they disembarked, Eva was hit with a barrage of scents.

"What is that?"

"Herb garden," Swanson answered. "This island is only a couple of miles at the absolute most from end to end. We use every available space for something here. Herbs were growing here when the island was resettled, and here they remain."

The heady mix of scents continued to assail Eva as they climbed steps carved into the rock. "What herbs do you use?"

Swanson beckoned to a man tending the garden, who strolled over, smiling. Upon hearing the repeated question, his smile bloomed into a grin.

"We have fennel, hyssop, cumin, and aloe in the garden here," he said in a friendly Egyptian accent.

Eva trailed her hand along a beautiful grey green plant that grew alongside the path, its bitter scent contradicted by the beautiful yellow flowers. "And what is this? A weed?"

"Everything has its place on the island," the gardener replied. "That plant is green ginger. I believe elsewhere it is known by its biblical name: Wormwood."

A face flashed into Eva's mind. Empty, soulless eyes. Red, angry scar tissue. A maniac's grin, devoid of humanity. The memory of Sloss would never be forgotten. Eva let the plant fall from between her fingers, stained the second she had heard the name.

"We aren't safe here," she said to her companions. "I suggest we get what should still be here and depart."

Eva let Swanson take the lead, and as they walked to the center of the island and the pseudo-monastery contained thereon, she only had one thought. *Janus. How could you let this happen to us?*

In time, they reached the focus of the island, a walled compound full of buildings organized into clusters around a central hall that was clearly intended for use in worship. As they passed through the gate, three people met them there.

"Director Guyomard, welcome," said the lead figure, a tall greying man with fierce eyes. "I trust you are here to complete the experiment. I can confirm the subject is in the appropriate state for a portal to open. I saw to it myself."

Without thinking, Eva stepped forward and slapped the man across the face, sending him reeling.

"Eva, no!" Swanson yelled, grabbing her and preventing her from going after the man, who recovered, balling his fists for a fight.

He began to laugh, and it was not a pleasant sound.

"Well, you can tell when someone has a bit of demon in them, or has had." He looked her up and down, leering. "Tell me, was whoring for a demon any more satisfying? Does carrying his progeny fill you with dread?"

"Administrator Sarch, enough." Swanson said in a tone that brooked no argument. "We are here to end the experiment."

"Excuse me? That was not the order handed down from Geneva."

Swanson put his arm about the older man's shoulder. "See that's the thing. Somebody sitting in a cave in Geneva is not somebody here on the Tabenna, and I am in charge here. Do you dispute my authority?"

"No, but..."

"Good. That's settled then." Swanson motioned to Eva and Gila, and they continued past the soldiers and the baffled man. "Ivor Sarch, what a card. However did I promote that one?"

The administrator ran down the path, pursuing them. "Wait. You can't. I have seen the broadcasts, and not just those sent to the public. We have demons popping up all over the world. In every area of recorded major conflict in the past thousand or more years, we are seeing new incidents. The Middle East, North and South America, Eastern Asia. Before, it was examples of strange occurrence that were thought to be isolated and comical. Now we even have your demon-infested traffic jam from two days ago."

Eva stopped and turned, her heel spinning in the dust. Already the morning sun had caused trickles of sweat to descend her back, but the moment he mentioned the chase, her blood ran cold. "What did they say?"

"That a car escaped. That Cairo police were killed. Most importantly, those two dozen innocents were, according to over a hundred eye witnesses, pulled through a portal by tentacles. This was not an ARC sanctioned broadcast. This was not Jeanette Gibson. This was local news. This is the first of many, Swanson. You know what a wildfire this sort of thing becomes. We need every advantage we can get."

"Killing Madden will get you nothing other than another portal to study."

"You haven't told her the plan, have you?"

Eva turned to Swanson. "What plan?"

Unable to meet her gaze, Swanson mopped his brow with a handkerchief. "The plan was to open a portal and send instruments through to the other side. The goal to see what is there and try and gain an advantage."

"Swanson, no! I won't let you."

Sarch appeared very satisfied with her reaction. A small victory in return for her violence.

"Sometimes the best course of action is to take no action," Swanson said, agreeing with her. "It won't do us any good."

"The hell it won't," argued Sarch. "You have seen the local unrest."

"We have seen more than that," Eva countered. "You think in such provincial terms. We came to Egypt to hide from Iuvart. Studied your textbooks? Demon of the third Hierarchy? He wants to open the gate to Hell and needs Madden and myself to do it. With that story all over the news he will be making a beeline for Cairo and then us."

"Yet you would choose running around with a demon over sanctuary here?"

Eva stepped forward, squaring up to the taller man. "I would rather take my chances with someone I know and trust than members of a faceless organization that has no feeling toward the sanctity of life by putting innocent people at risk. Now, where is he?"

Sarch stood defiant, staring her down. "He is contained in a secure unit. Underground."

"Well, take us to him," Ordered Swanson, who turned and resumed his walk to the building at the center of the complex.

With Sarch and his entourage following them, Swanson led Eva and Gila through the chapel and downstairs into a complex that was very reminiscent of the labs in Cairo.

"This was the original," Swanson said as he noticed Eva staring.

"Where is he?"

Swanson waved Sarch forward, and reluctantly, he pressed on a panel in the wall. A light moved down his hand and hidden sensors behind registered his handprint. A section of the wall popped forwards and slid to one side, revealing a room too small for a prison cell. Inside, Madden was propped between the narrow walls, arms chained behind his back.

"Free him," demanded Eva.

Sarch had barely released the lock when Eva shoved him out the way to help free Madden. Unchained, he rolled in the available space and groaned. His face was encrusted with dried blood, and as Eva tried to sit him up, he winced, protecting his ribs.

Madden opened one bruised eye, and a fleeting smile crossed his face. "It's you."

"What have they done to you?"

Madden groaned, resting for a moment. "They tried to beat the demon out of me, but it won't work. They have all auras dampened on this island somehow. They see me, always. The portal. I can feel it wants to open. It is there, waiting for me. They said if I went with them, you would be left alone, and they wouldn't take the demon from within you. Our child."

Eva's hands drew protectively to her belly. "You know then?"

Madden nodded. "I know. I waited by your bed for several days after you collapsed. They said they were keeping you under while they examined you. They said it was going to be days. I have been here... I lost track of time. This whole area. The island has auras dampened. Like Cairo."

Eva felt rage. Fury and a sense of betrayal rose within her. She turned to Swanson. "How long?"

He raised his hands in a futile gesture of placation. "We were only trying to help."

"How long!"

"Three weeks. You were sedated for three weeks. It was in your best interests."

Eva's eyes unfocussed. The room became a blur. She

was completely taken aback. Swanson tried to make more excuses but she didn't hear him.

"So I am nearly two months pregnant, and for half of that you have had me drugged, while Madden was being beaten to a pulp." Eva focussed on Gila.

"I swear to you, Eva. I did not know. They gave me the book and I deciphered it. I did not see you again until you awoke. For all I knew, you weren't even in the facility. They do not tell me anything they don't wish me to know. ARC isn't the all seeing all knowing organisation they think they are. There are always divisions."

Eva pointed to one of the soldiers. "You. Grab Madden and get him seen to. Get him fed and bandaged."

She turned to the rest of them. "With what is coming, you had better hope there isn't a portal waiting for him when we get off this island, or I swear to God I will see you all in there with him." Eva moved out of the way so they could attend to Madden. She collared Swanson.

"Did you plan the riot to get me here?"

"No. That was a mole hunt, pure and simple. Proof of his effectiveness lies in the destruction of the base. The artifacts in the Coptic Museum are beyond worth but the text in the Codex is far beyond that. Demons are popping into existence all over the world and we have a chance to reverse this utterly. You have come too far and seen too much not to believe."

"Right now, I don't believe a single word you say."

Eva turned to Gila. "Why don't you fill me in? What else did you presumably not tell me about the Codex?"

"It is what we needed to get you here for. The island is a haven from unfriendly ears." Gila drew Eva away from the cell, and to a table where she opened the Codex, and pointed at indecipherable characters.

"This mentions a gatekeeper, he being responsible for breaching the barrier. He is old, and has lived many lifetimes. He has been many people."

"Iuvart."

At this name, those still in the room visibly paled, one of the guards making the sign of the cross.

Swanson shook his head. "The Infernal Angels have plagued us for years."

"You didn't know about this?"

"No. I asked Gila to keep it to herself until we arrived."

"What else does it say?"

Gila moved to a passage later in the text. "This mentions a guide from beyond the breach who lives beyond sight. He is here to take us all to Hell. He is slain, but standing."

"Madden," Eva breathed.

"It tells of Hell's chieftains and the tragedy yet to come. It says those already here can come and go at will. It mentions one who understands the nature of man, who will discover the secrets of the scroll and close the breach. Finally, it mentions the true angels, the defenders of the mortal realm. It doesn't say how many, just ends with a note that this was given to the author in a dream by an angel. An ancient angel who walks the earth yet."

Gila closed the Codex. "There is more. But even here, you cannot be told. This scroll mentions another. This is not the solution, but confirms what I suspected. I have to show you something before I can tell you more."

"I don't see any reason to trust the lot of you.

Gila took her hand. "Please, Eva. If this is not enough to convince you we want to help, I don't know what else to do. I saved your life."

"Save his. If you believe in me at all, if there is to be a

way out of this, a solution to stop demons overwhelming us, I want you to save him. I want you to use your science."

"And we will, but first we have to get off the island."

"And go where?"

Gila looked at Swanson, and he nodded. "The Sanctuary."

CHAPTER THIRTY-TWO

THEY REMAINED ON THE ISLAND FOR ANOTHER DAY, Eva fretting every moment over Madden who, freed from his cell and given plenty of exercise and nourishment, recovered with remarkable swiftness.

As they lay together at night, Eva could barely sleep. She watched Madden, taking in every line of his face, the way his breathing was difficult because of the ribs, the pain of his mere existence that shone through when he wasn't guarding against it. Only in sleep was the true face revealed. The scent of stale sweat still lingered where he had dumped his clothes. Eva couldn't fault him for that. He was exhausted.

The next morning, Madden appeared almost back to his normal self, but for small bandages round his wrists and a slight wince when he turned. He said nothing to anybody during breakfast, or the trip back across the river. A small smile for Eva was all the emotion he showed.

Eva knew why. Madden feared the moment they came out from the umbrella of the island's protection. Agitated, he kept casting overt glances behind.

"Every time you do that you make the boat wobble. If you want to swim to shore, why don't you get out and do so? I would love however to reach the shore dry."

"It's there," he said. The worry in his voice indicated he at least believed it.

"There's nothing behind us."

"Why can I feel it pulling at me then?"

Eva ran her fingers down his face, catching them on the bristles he had missed shaving. "Because you fear it. You are stronger than that. Don't give in."

Nothing happened as they reached the far shore, though Madden was not convinced and still looked back at the island. Gila looked as perplexed as Madden and Swanson contented himself by avoiding them all. The strange thing was the slightest scent of carrion mixed with dust. It tickled at Eva's nose, disquieting her. It was the smell of demons, the reek of death. And there were neither demons nor a portal.

Eva ushered Madden into the car, seating herself beside him in the back.

"Plush," he observed. "Better than a box, eh Director?"

"I can only apologize again," replied Swanson. "It was a gross error in judgement." He started the car and they drove off, heading towards the dazzling sun in the East.

"Do we have far to go?" Eva asked.

"Ten miles or so," Gila replied, and handed her a book, already open. "Here's some reading material. Read the book awhile."

Without looking at it, Eva hefted the book. "In the time it takes to cover ten miles?"

"You will see what I mean."

Eva glanced at Madden, who had already begun to edge

away, and then down at the book. "The Book of Revelations? You would have me read the Bible?"

"Just one book. It's an abridged version and shouldn't take you long. It's important."

With no more comment, Eva settled back and began to read.

Ten miles or so later, Swanson pulled off the road to head North on a dirt track. Eva was still reading, and whereas the smooth road was fine for this, the random jumps of the dirt track soon had her stomach churning. Eva clamped her mouth shut and closed her eyes, trying to calm herself. It wasn't working.

"Stop the car!" Madden shouted.

Swanson slammed the brakes on, causing everyone to lurch forward.

That was enough for Eva, who shoved the door open and jumped out, making it not more than five paces before she threw up.

Swanson came round to see to her, silently offering moistened cloths for Eva to sort herself out.

"You okay?"

Eva coughed, and retched again. When she came up for air, she said, "Yes. I don't know how much experience you have of this, but people in my condition sometimes do this, especially when being thrown around inside a car whilst trying to read. How far do we have to go?"

"Another mile or so, but I can take it easy. This valley is called a wadi, an ancient riverbed. The sediment can be soft so it helps to be careful."

Eva nodded her thanks, scuffed loose dirt over the mess she had made, and climbed back in.

They trundled over the packed dirt and the track lost its identity, becoming a wadi at least six hundred feet across, surrounded by ridges of weathered stone. The reading didn't get any easier, but with an empty stomach, Eva was at least able to complete the Book.

"So I'm done," she announced. "Do you want to tell me why I just lost my breakfast over the mythical end of the world?"

"Because it is no myth," Gila replied as she watched the horizon. "The Book of Revelations details the way to stop hell coming to earth."

"Sorry Gila, I just read the Book. It says no such thing."

"Not in so many words, but I did tell you it was the abridged version. All versions are abridged, so as to not reveal the true meaning of the document. We have the original. Here is the first part. Before you come any further you must read this."

Gila handed her an electronic tablet one side of which had a photo of a document, the other side a translation. A spider web of lines crossed the two documents, indicating points of correlation. Eva began to read, and within moments, she was picking out differences between the first version and this. As she got deeper and deeper into the document, her breathing slowed. By the end, she was awed by what she had read.

"That is the truth?"

"Every word. I translated it myself. The book of revelations is in fact an accurate account of the last time this happened. There is only one way to stop demon kind flooding to the earth and displacing humanity."

Eva scanned back through the document. "From what this says, the gatekeeper was defeated during the period when the sun became black as sackcloth of man." Eva looked up. "An eclipse. Are there any due?"

"One, across the subcontinent. In a fortnight."

Eva watched the approaching ridge. All of a sudden, the chaos she was centered in became much more profound. "So either way, this all ends in two weeks."

"Let's hope for the right outcome, keep a little optimism," urged Swanson. "Remember, this was done once before. We have the document. The scroll. It was resealed. This isn't just faith any more. It is fact. The Nag Hamaddi codex you brought to us shows what could be a new Gospel. It is a set of instructions. But if you think about it, isn't that what the Bible is anyway? It is ultimately a set of instructions on how the authors believe one should live their lives. All Holy books are exactly that. This is just a little more specific."

Eva scanned back through the documents. "Where are you going to get a lamb from?"

Swanson stopped the car and turned to her, a look of utmost seriousness on his face. "We don't need one. You, Eva, are our lamb."

"What? Are you crazy?"

"No. I am as serious as I could possibly be. The mark on your neck confirms it, as is written in our texts. The Lamb, of the tribe of Judah and the root of David, will be revealed by his Star. There can be no mistake." Swanson pulled up his shirt sleeve, revealing a small cross on his wrist. Gila did the same.

"You are Coptics..." Madden wondered aloud.

"We are," Gila confirmed. "Our people have been persecuted for generations. We know when to exist in the background if necessary."

"Well that's good," Eva replied. "If what happened in

Cairo is anything to go by, we are going to have an army of demons from Cairo converging on us at any moment, and that's not even thinking about what Iuvart could be bringing. We could do with some hiding in the background. But how are we supposed to do that if your vaunted ARC cannot protect a single facility?"

"You have to consider the bigger picture. We were prepared to draw them in, let them reveal their hand, just to answer a question. That's why we were there, because it's the Coptic center of the world. It's where the answers were found, proving us right. It's where the new Pope will be chosen, coming from the ashes of a demon invasion. That's why we are here. To protect the scroll and if needs be, to open it. Time to get out."

Swanson had stopped the car at the foot of a small ridge. The sun was high enough for the ridge to offer no protection against its pounding heat, and Eva wrapped a headscarf about her as she got out.

"Up there, couple of hundred yards climb if you feel up to it." Said Gila.

"You couldn't keep us away," Madden declared, and took Eva's hand to lead her up.

She noticed the curious look that passed between the two ARC directors following at his comment but chose to remain silent. After about ten minutes of ascent, during which Madden did his solicitous best to ensure that despite her protestations, she take as easy a route as possible, the small trail disappeared behind an outcrop.

Swanson took the lead. "Careful now, the entrance is a bit tight. May I welcome you to the tomb of Saint Pachomius?"

Eva ducked as she followed, but the narrow passage soon opened out into a large cavern. The ceiling disappeared off into the darkness. Eva used her hand to guide herself round the edge of the cavern, rock polished smooth passing under her fingertips. The air tasted stale, despite the opening. It was as if the opening was temporary, or recent.

Echoes of steps preceded a metallic 'thunk'. A beam of light appeared, throwing the cavern into stark contrast to the darkness as Madden switched the flashlight on and nodded thanks to Swanson.

"Not a lot left of him," Madden said as he looked around.

"It wouldn't be that easy," Swanson replied. "Try having a look around the place."

Madden noticed her along the edge of the cavern, and brought the light to her. "How about we explore the cracks together?"

Eva smiled in response, his easy charm warming her. They followed the wall around, noticing nothing out of the ordinary. Eva had taken a couple of steps ahead, and was poking at a gap when Madden dropped the flashlight.

"Are you all right?"

"I don't really know. There's something in front that's repelling me. It's painful, but not unbearable."

"And there you have it," Swanson said from behind them. "Imagine if we let any creature other than you, so tightly on a leash, near here. You are as faintly demon as we have ever seen, and yet it is difficult for you to bear, no? For those stronger than you, it is agony. It's what will keep us safe at the end."

Gila pressed a seemingly innocuous section of stone, which popped open to reveal a small panel.

"Gila Ciranoush. Agent ES six," she whispered into the panel. Red light scanned her eye for a moment.

"Retinal scan, breath sample, voice modulation confirmed," a cold computer voice intoned. A series of clicks indicated a complex system of locks was moving, and a few moments later, twin doors opened on silent hinges.

The opening doors caused an immediate response to Madden, who screwed his face up, cringing in pain. He took a step back.

"What have you done?"

"Sanctified the corridor. It is anathema to hell spawn. You could see it as a mystic barrier for what it is worth. Consider how you react to holy texts. They burn you. Imagine passing through a hallway built entirely from bibles."

"I need to go through," he insisted. "Whatever is inside of me will just have to suffer." Madden took Eva's hand. "Help me."

She nodded, and kept pace as he ran to the doors. The hallway was no longer than four or five yards long, but as they passed through the roughly hewn rock, a high-pitched squealing began to pierce the silence. Eva turned to Madden, pulling him on, and realised the noise was coming from him, but from within him, not from his mouth.

They reached the end of the hallway, and Madden collapsed on the ground, panting, in front of another door.

Gila leaned forward to repeat the retinal scan, while Swanson knelt beside Madden.

"Imagine, if it did that to you, what it would do to your brethren," he said softly.

More locks clicked their way open, and this time the doors slid apart. About to enter, Eva stopped in her tracks.

· · ·

"I have been here before."

"Impossible!" Swanson was ready to argue the point further, but Eva held up her hands.

"Wait. I know this place. I have been here before, but not as you know it."

Eva wandered around the room. It was lit by the same eerie fluorescent glow. It gave her the same feeling of unease.

"This is what I found behind Gideon's," Eva corrected herself, "I mean Iuvart's office in Worcester. It was identical, with the altar, and the six platforms arranged just so. What I don't understand is why."

Gila moved to a series of ancient shelves along one wall, indicating them to Eva. "This is a repository, built against the end of days. Our Father of Fathers, Pope Theophilus sanctified it personally in 391 AD. Word has it in that year, he discovered a hidden pagan temple, removing artifacts, and causing a conflict between the Christians and pagans. The Roman Emperor Theodosius decreed the temple outside should be destroyed. This is all that is left. It housed a significant portion of the great Library of Alexandria, and has ever been a repository for our most sacred texts. Modern security mixed with ancient wards. This is the last place that will survive should Hell come to earth."

"And nobody has ever gotten in here?"

"Not in here, no. This altar has always remained free of invasion." Swanson pointed behind them. "Out there, only once. According to our records, what was termed the 'Nag Hamaddi find' was actually a lapse in security. Two men broke in and took whatever they could lay their hands on. It just so happened to be the entire collection of codices. Most we now have back. Two were never recovered."

In the midst of so much ancient history, Eva found herself caught up in the story. "What happened to them?"

Gila patted the bag at her side, withdrawing the ancient text and placing it with reverence beside similar scrolls. One gap remained.

"The first you have brought so fortuitously to us. The second... Well the second we now know the location of."

"The location described in Codex Fourteen," Madden wondered aloud.

"Exactly," Agreed Gila. "The contents of Fourteen you will agree are dire enough in themselves. It is said the contents of the last Nag Hamaddi scroll are enough to render sane men mad."

"As futile as you think we are, ARC is a diverse group of people, and our resources are vast. We have been at this for a very long time. How else does one fight the forces of hell on such a broad front?"

Eva wanted to believe Swanson, but too much had happened for her to be convinced easily. She touched Madden's hand for reassurance. He squeezed in return, weak from the ordeal of the hallway.

"This room. I don't understand it. Why would Iuvart build it. How could he build it?"

"Why?" Gila tapped on the tablet she had brought with her. "Maybe to try and predict where in here we would store what he needs. He can't pass through the hallway. No demon of any relative strength can." She turned to Madden. "Sorry, you are a weakling, it seems."

"Under the circumstances I'm happy to be so."

Gila turned back. "As for how, read this. Second page, about halfway down."

Eva took the tablet, and for the benefit of Madden, read aloud.

"Accompanying the men was Iostus, a local magi. He behaved contrary to his nature as if... As if he were another man wearing the skin of his brother."

"My god, he has been here," Eva interrupted her recitation to exclaim!

"Not in here, but he has been outside."

Eva's heart began to thump harder. "He knows we're here. We have to get out!"

"Maybe," said Swanson, "but he is patient. He has been at this for millennia. He has been here since before the scrolls were written. There are bigger goals. You have seen them yourself. Lust, Greed. Two of the seven deadly sins. There are demons associated with each. We think Hell is organised into castes, or clans of a type. Leviathan displaced Beelzebub for envy, Abadon rules sloth, Belphegor with gluttony, Lucifer with pride, Asmodeus with Lust, Mammon with avarice. Satan with Wrath."

"Those names, aren't they often names associated with the same creature? The devil?"

Gila took the tablet from Eva, changing the screen to a red being with horns. "'The devil' is a colloquial term for those that don't know better. To the uninformed, Madden is 'the devil'."

"The last time this happened," continued Swanson, "Beelzebub tried to lead Hell's minions to earth. The Book of Revelations, in its own way, tells of his failure and subsequent defeat by Leviathan, who we know to be the current gatekeeper to Hell. Iuvart, for whatever reason, is Leviathan's minion. What we do know is at least two of the leaders were stuck on earth after the last portal closed."

"Belphegor and Asmodeus," Eva said.

"Indeed. You have met them already judging by the

reports. Them, or their minions. They are certainly aware of you."

Eva considered this. "It may be so, if they were directly involved. There was a blonde woman who carried the girl that was devoured. There was a man paying a lot of interest to Madden and myself in that bar." Eva said the last with a soft voice. It was the beginning of her adventure with Madden, and for all of the terrors and hardships, they had enjoyed many good times, too.

Swanson shrugged. "It could be them. It doesn't really matter. They are doing one thing: preparing for the portal to open into Hell."

"They aren't searching for the key like Iuvart?"

"We don't believe so. Iuvart has a task. To open the portal. Belphegor and Asmodeus, we believe are more concerned with gathering your hellbounces and keeping the portal open once it has been activated. In order to banish the portal, it needs to be opened, at least partially. We have the means, the only means, to do this."

Swanson led them to the main altar on top of which rested a small chest. With careful hands, he unclasped it and lifted the lid.

Eva leaned forward. Inside, resting on a gold cloth was a scroll, perhaps ten inches across, worn and browned with age. It had seven wax seals inscribed with unintelligible characters along its length.

Unable to more than glance at it, Madden shied away.

"Behold," said Swanson in a whisper. "Behold the Scroll of Judgement."

CHAPTER THIRTY-THREE

Despite the scroll being there in front of her, Eva doubted her own eyes.

"Surely you don't believe this is the actual scroll."

"Oh, I believe it," Swanson said, conviction dripping from his words. "May I remind you what Anges de la Résurection des Chevaliers actually is? It is a meeting of science and faith. As such, there are certain objects we believe to be key to what is going on here, and this is such an object.

I believe it. Why? Because this is the scroll, the actual scroll taken from the Aegean island of Patmos where it lay open, all seals broken, several thousand years ago. There was nothing left, just devastation. The language therein is of unknown origin, but we believe it to be the Divine language, unworthy of our mortal eyes. It was re-sealed by one most Holy, and the woes affecting the earth disappeared. Were one to break this open again..." He shook his head. "Well, on the modern world it would wreak devastation. Infrastructure, history, society. You name it, the losses would be catastrophic, and that is before the demons come to town."

Madden began to laugh. "Before? We're already past that stage. This world is already being devastated, with mankind in its so-called ascendency. Demons have existed long before they started sucking sinners into their domain. This just brings it all to a head."

"Nevertheless, this is what we have and this has ever been our plan. The Bible wasn't just a series of visions. There was fact behind it all. Something went wrong and the portal closed. This scroll absorbed the energy of countless demon forms. As contradictory as it sounds, this scroll is without a doubt our most holy artifact. The energy locked within has no limit."

Eva knelt to examine the scroll. She felt a longing, as if she had to reach out and take it. Before she knew what she was doing, her hand had reached forward, beginning the movement that would culminate in her claiming the scroll.

"See," Gila whispered, "We chose correctly. It wants you to take it. That in itself shows the truth of it."

Eva struggled to control herself. Her fingertips brushed one of the seals, the ancient wax cold and hard, yet warming to the touch. "Does it work?"

"Break a seal and find out," Swanson said. "But be warned. There will be consequences. There were before." Swanson took the tablet from Gila, and began to read.

"I watched as the Lamb opened the first of the seven seals. Then I heard one of the four living creatures say in a voice like thunder, "Come!" I looked, and there before me was a white horse! Its rider held a bow, and he was given a crown, and he rode out as a conqueror bent on conquest."

Hearing these words froze Eva in place. She clenched her fist and withdrew her hand.

"No."

Swanson put his hand on her shoulder. "That is called belief. It is the first step towards faith. Perhaps the descriptions in the Bible are flowery for a reason. Perhaps the author misinterpreted even older text. Perhaps he found something too terrible to put in words and spared humanity unnecessary fear."

Pulling on soft gloves, Swanson removed the scroll from the chest by pulling the gold cloth up from each side, and placed it in a small case, seemingly created just for carrying it.

"Does it not call to you, too?"

"In a way, but I am not destined to open it. We have what we came for. The new Codex will be safe here."

"Safe here, with a man carrying a demon around inside of him in this place," Madden muttered.

Getting back through the hallway was even more tortuous for Madden than the first trip by his reaction. The demon within him mewed weakly the second time round. Madden collapsed to the floor gasping at the end.

Eva knelt to help him and Madden pushed her away, causing her to land on her side.

"I have to do this myself," he said, his voice brusque. "I'm not a human, I get it. But it doesn't mean I need my hand held every moment."

"It might do you good to remember you are not the only one in this room carrying something else within you," admonished Gila, helping Eva up.

"Oh yes, we are all perfect in this room," he replied through clenched teeth. "Heroes all, fighting the dark forces."

"I don't see what you have got to be so bitter about all of a sudden," Gila spat back. "You have gotten a second chance at life and from what we have heard; you have lived it to the fullest. Most aren't so lucky. A little pain is good for the soul."

"Your schadenfreude is less then becoming," Swanson said as he finished locking the hallway and joined the rest of them. "Particularly in one so learned."

"And yet you are the one who gets to carry the case, because your name is Guyomard. There are handfuls of lesser people more worthy to bear the scroll than you. Operatives who have made a positive contribution, and not been responsible for the loss of an entire ARC facility to satisfy their own curiosity."

Swanson was about to retort when Eva interrupted them all.

"Wait. Stop. Before you say another word. Everybody take a step back and take a deep breath. Do it, now."

They all broke off, and through the sheer tone of command in Eva's voice, did as bidden.

"Now close your eyes. Gila, who is Iuvart the minion of?"

"Leviathan," Gila answered.

"Swanson, which of the deadly sins is Leviathan associated with?"

"Envy," Swanson said, the sullen tone of his voice indicating the recent comments had been very close to the bone.

"And has anybody considered why the sun is no longer shining in through the doorway, given it is mid-morning?"

Madden stood, facing the doorway. "Because we are no longer alone."

The spell was broken, for the moment. Eva now smelled the familiar reek of carrion as it wafted in on an invisible fug. The chill of twilight filled the cave, only the faintest glow coming in from the entrance.

"There are many," Madden said in awe.

"How many?" Whispered Swanson.

"Too many. He is here, too. I can feel him nearby."

"How?" Gila asked as she backed away from the entrance.

Madden pointed at himself. "Demon. I feel them; they feel me. That's how they know where I am. The closer they are the easier it gets. It must have been that hallway. I should have sensed them before now. We need to go out there."

"Don't be foolish," Swanson said. "We can stay in here. We are safe."

"No, we are not. Something else has control of me."

Madden threw a punch, connecting square with Swanson's jaw. Before Swanson had even hit the ground, Madden had his case out of his hand, screaming as he gripped the handle. The look on his face said it all. He was terrified. Still screaming, Madden walked out of the cave into the gloom.

Swanson stirred and Gila helped him up.

"Don't let him get to them! Go!" Gila screamed at her, and not thinking, Eva ran out after Madden.

At the entrance to the cave Eva stopped, covering her mouth with her hand in horror. It was too much to take in. The sky was indeed dark, a grey twilight with streaks of green flashing through the heavens. The floor of the wadi was filled with faceless forms, dark and unmoving, shadowed parodies of human beings. They stretched up the sides, and into the distance as far as the eye could see. Too many indeed.

Madden stood perhaps a dozen steps in front of her, gripping the case. He whimpered in pain.

Footsteps behind indicated Gila had roused Swanson sufficiently.

"What in God's name..." He muttered.

There was a ripple in the distance, getting closer as it passed through the faceless masses. It disappeared from view occasionally as it flitted from shadow to shadow, approaching them with an increasing sense of menace.

As it closed upon them, Eva saw behind the distortion a blurred human form, strolling as if out for a walk. Only once it had passed all of the lifeless figures did the distortion disappear. At the foot of the slope, Iuvart watched them, dressed exactly as the Gideon Homes Eva remembered had done. He started up the slope towards them.

Eva put her hand on Madden's arm. "The scroll. He cannot touch it. He couldn't get in the temple. He meant for us to come here. He meant for us to bring it out."

"It doesn't matter," he replied through teeth clenched in pain. "I can't move. Take it if you can and run."

"No, I don't think we shall be having any of that," said Iuvart from just down the slope before Eva could move. "Come, demon. Come to me. You have done well, and I will be taking that now."

Despite her grip on him, Madden began to walk down the slope towards Iuvart. Eva let go, rather than risk falling in his wake.

"Good girl," approved Iuvart. "Save the last little remnant of hell spawn you can, while you can." He took a deep breath as Madden came to rest beside him, looking back up at her. "Beautiful day, isn't it?"

"It's not over yet," Swanson came to stand beside Eva, staring down at the demon.

"Is it not? And what are you going to do to change things? Look about us, you insignificant ARC worm. Where is your Holy order? Where are your champions? Are they enough to stop the twelve tribes of the damned?"

"Those are the twelve tribes of Israel!"

"Those *were* the twelve tribes of Israel," Iuvart taunted back. "You should find the complete history of what happened that day. I was there! Your twelve tribes of Hebrews were sucked into my domain along with most everything else. Now they are my playthings. You think you can best them?"

As one, the entire mass of shadowed humanity took a step forward, and the ground underneath Eva's feet shook.

"Not before. Certainly not now. With this, I am going to open the portal and welcome my brethren onto this plane. When enough of us are here the balance will shift and we will have no more need of these puny casings."

Iuvart reached out to the nearest shadow, and stroked it as if it were a pet. "You should see the tribes in their full glory. Beautiful, reborn, hungry. My master has chosen them for his own, and they wait on the other side, the vanguard ready to reclaim what was denied them so long ago. Demon kind will flourish with what has been denied to them for so long."

Eva realised Madden would live to see the end if that did happen. Iuvart must have known she was the one destined to open the scroll, and yet he did not choose her. She began to feel anger and even envy Madden would survive and she would not. He had been coerced, but that was irrelevant. He had left her pregnant and abandoned her. That he was able to do such a thing caused a rage to build within her.

"Eva, don't," Madden called. "It's him. Think about all we have been through. Think about what I can do. He is the same."

Iuvart turned, backhanding Madden, who flew back about five or six feet and landed in a heap down the slope. His words had the desired effect; all feelings of envy Eva had experienced were a distant memory. Madden was once again her main concern. A quick glance at Swanson and Gila showed faces filled with remorse. They had been under the same spell.

"Get up. Take the case," Iuvart commanded Madden, who responded with the sluggishness of one still dazed. As he gripped the handle, Madden began to scream.

"It is agony compounded," Iuvart observed, and then smiled at Eva. Wearing the mask of Gideon Homes, who never smiled, the look unsettled Eva yet more.

"He is the one I came for," Iuvart declared to them. "He is one of us, yet he is joined enough with life that this won't destroy him. The seed of life that grows within you ensures as much." As Madden whimpered, Iuvart stroked his head, as one might do a pet. "It will torture him to the point of death though, but he will live to see the end of your world. I take my leave of you now. There is nothing left on this earth for you to hope for. Take solace in the little part of him you have within you, Eva. That is all you will ever have of him, in the days that remain to you. My master is coming. Tremble and despair."

As had happened back in Sloss, Iuvart's eyes began to glow, and the intensity of the light forced Eva to avert her eyes. Screwing them shut, she wanted nothing more than to crawl under the earth and hide.

The feeling passed, and when Eva opened her eyes once more, the wadi was empty, the sun blazing down upon it. At the edges of her vision, black wisps of cloud evaporated, and the dusty stench of death wafted for a moment. Eva's eyes fixed on a spot a few metres away, trying to retain every detail of her lover. Madden was gone.

CHAPTER THIRTY-FOUR

ALONE. THERE WAS NO BETTER WAY TO PUT IT. ONE moment Madden had been alongside Eva, the next he had been ripped away from her, tortured by the burden he had been commanded against his will to bear. Eva climbed down the stone ridge, unseeing, unfeeling, and wandered about the floor of the wadi. She had never felt so alone.

She felt a hand on her shoulder. Gila was there, concern written across her face. Eva wanted to trust the woman. She had certainly done her utmost to show they were on the same team. But despite the goodwill, Gila was an ARC operative, and so far, the organization hadn't done her a lot of favors.

"We have come so far, and for what? Was it all worth it?"

"Eva, I can't begin to understand how you must be feeling right now."

"Punch through your ribs and rip out your heart. Dash it on the rocks and slice it into a thousand pieces, and you might be half way there."

"There is still hope. There is always hope. You just need to know where to look for it."

"You will excuse me if I don't share your optimism."

"We haven't yet unravelled all of the mystery. We have a fortnight until the eclipse, and most importantly, we know where it is going to pass. Ancient records show where the darkness passed when the last scroll was opened, tracking it from Patmos to a mountain range in Afghanistan. We believe the eclipse will follow the same path. As long as the scroll is opened during that particular eclipse, the portal will open."

"Great. So in the middle of one of the most dangerous places on earth, Hell is about to open up."

"One might argue it's already there," Swanson said as he joined them on the floor of the wadi. "Eva, this isn't going to be easy for you, but we need to know what's in the final codex."

"Are you abandoning Madden?"

It was clear Swanson was choosing his words very carefully so as not to aggravate her. "No, we are not. Please believe me that Madden Scott, right now, is the primary concern of the entire ARC organisation. But we are here in this place, and we have to have answers."

"I understand. Even at Hell's precipice your thirst for knowledge knows no limits."

"No. It's not like that at all. Consider this a way to help Madden by looking in a different place. We are taking the same path he is, just by a different waypoint. Look. It's hot out here; we are all shaken to say the least. For whatever reason, Iuvart left the car untouched. Let's get inside and then we can have a more rational conversation."

. . .

Eva allowed Gila to help her into the back of the car, where she did admit she felt better out of the merciless glare of the sun. Gila produced bottles of sugar cane juice from a unit in the back of the car, and they sat in silence, savouring the cool, sweet liquid.

"Do we have a location?" Swanson asked Gila, who nodded.

"Qena. The text is hidden in Qena. The codex talks about catacombs to the east, and a place of great death. There is an immense cemetery in Qena."

Eva zoned out as Gila continued her reasoning about the location of this final codex. She didn't really care, and despite being out of the sun, it hadn't changed anything for her. Madden was still missing.

From within her, the spark of life glowed warm with reassurance. It seemed to say: 'Where there is life, there is hope.' Before she realised what was happening, Eva realised she had said those exact words aloud.

"I agree wholeheartedly," Swanson said, not missing a beat.

"How are empty platitudes going to save Madden? Save us?"

"They are a start. I have no idea what the next fortnight holds for us, Eva, but I can tell you this. First, we still have the codex. Second, we know where to look for the final codex. Third, we are not dead yet. And finally, this may be the only way we can save your... 'man'. Iuvart has Madden and he has the scroll, but we have time, and we have knowledge. Our organization has studied the text in Revelations for generations, and the conclusions reach include the opinion that no demon can open that scroll, no matter how hard they try. It is the embodiment of everything sacred.

They might as well be trying to open the Arc of the Covenant."

"Do you have that too? We could use a little lightning."

"No, I'm afraid that was lost in the desert, in antiquity. They need Madden to carry the scroll because they can dominate him and he is one of them, however weak. If he tries to open it, as with any other demon, he will be eradicated. Ask yourself this: given you know so much about Iuvart in his current incarnation, why are we still alive? Why were you allowed to leave Birmingham alive? Iuvart could have left us to his thousands just then, three insignificant humans. Or... maybe not so insignificant."

"Everything has its purpose." Eva answered.

"We still have something he wants," Swanson agreed, breaking into a grin. "I daresay you will see Madden again." Swanson started the engine and began slowly to traverse the wadi back towards the road.

Gila looked up from the Codex translation. "Eva, tell me of your family, your past."

Bemused by the sudden change of subject, Eva couldn't help herself and laughed. "My family?"

"Certainly. You never know how important it could be." Gila had a completely straight face, an earnest expression. She meant every word.

"Well, I was born in Sioux City, Iowa. My father was a manager at an electrical manufacturing plant, and my mother has worked with the needy all of her life for various charities. We are fifth generation American. My current surname, Ross, is said to come from Scotland. I moved to Worcester when I was eight to live with my aunt and uncle, my mother's brother. The reason I was always told was the schooling was better along the East coast and would afford me more opportunities than Midwest farm country. I guess they were right. It certainly led me down a path I would never have expected."

"One thing you did not mention, Eva of Sioux City. Your birth name."

It had been so long Eva had almost forgotten it. For many years, she had been Eva Ross, and for countless more, she had dreamed of being that. She unwound the window, letting the breeze dry her face. Dust in the air threatened to scour her face but to Eva it felt as though she was being washed clean of both name and history.

"Maygan. My maiden name, the name by all rights I should be using now is Eva Maygan."

A small smile crept across Gila's face. "Have you ever studied genealogy, Eva?"

"A little"

"Were there many women born in your direct line of ancestors?"

"Not that I recall."

"I'll bet there weren't, or at least not many survived. So Eva Maygan, would it surprise you that your name bears a startling resemblance to the Star of David which you bear on your shoulder, known in Hebrew as the Shield of David, or Magen David?"

Eva felt foreboding. Yet again, she was caught in this inescapable web.

"It is said only the true son of David can open the seals on this scroll. Why only a son? Why not a daughter?" Gila countered.

"Now that is a real leap of faith."

Gila waved her tablet around. "I'm only reading out what the text is telling me. It reminds the reader of who is worthy, and who should believe. What is this whole endeavor if not a huge leap of faith? I put it to you both that

Eva Ross is not just a psychotherapist from Massachusetts. Unfortunately, Iuvart knows this, too. If you are who the codex says you are, then you will have to prove yourself. That means finding Iuvart, defeating him, and rescuing the scroll. It means staying alive long enough to do that in the first place. It means being strong, and not giving up."

Gila made a persuasive argument. Eva admitted she felt better than she had when getting into the car. Now they were back on the road, hurtling towards the next danger.

"Say I buy into all this. What do we know?"

"We know the sixth seal is the key. That's the point at which the portal opened last time. If you refer to the Book of Revelations, the opening of the sixth seal is when the action really gets going. In this situation, Iuvart acts for his master. You can guarantee when the seals are picked apart, there will be something waiting on the other side to come through. That will have been no idle boast. One question to consider is did the portal cause the eclipse or did it require the eclipse?"

Swanson lobbed his phone back from the front seat. "Take a look. That is a map of all recent past and predicted near-future eclipses, superimposed on a map of the earth."

Eva studied the map. "There's nothing at all over the area you mentioned."

"Swap the screens. There's another window behind what you see."

Eva did as required, and a few distinct black lines were added to the curved paths of the eclipses across the earth.

"I see."

"That is the map taken from the ARC archives. It's different to the official released version. There are those that don't want people looking too closely at the maps."

"They want to keep this a secret?"

"They want to keep the public safe. If events happen, as we expect them to, wouldn't you rather the only people in those mountains are meant to be there by design, and aren't a ragtag band of sightseers watching for the sun to go dark? If we save the world, the best thing that can happen is that nobody knows about it."

Another twenty-five miles to Qena, and Eva had to endure every moment with the thought that despite all that had been said, Madden was getting further and further away. The road followed the beautiful blue ribbon of the Nile as it wound its way down the center of its lush, green valley and she barely paid it any attention. In every reflection, she saw his face. In every child they passed, as Swanson tore through numerous villages, Eva saw her own being brought up without a father. In the distance, every dust-swamped ridge reminded her of the last place she had seen him.

In time, Eva ceased lamenting and became aware of what was happening in the car. Gila was lost in translating some document, and Swanson was on the phone.

"Yes sir, I understand. We have a few chores, but we should be there in plenty of time for the main event. You just ensure everything is ready. We will see you in Luxor just as soon as we are done."

He put the phone down beside him, and glanced in the rear view mirror at Eva.

"Back with us, then?"

"For my sins."

"Ha! 'He died for our sins'", Swanson quoted. "All this has to make you ask 'Did he really?'"

"Well if Jesus died for our sins, there was a massive backlog."

"What did Control say?" Gila asked, not looking up from her work.

"They confirmed the eclipse. Two weeks today, about mid morning. They also confirmed the location, or at least their educated guess at one. If ever there was a portal, northern Afghanistan would be the worst possible place."

"The Hindu Kush Nexus?"

"The very same."

The tone had taken a turn to the very serious now. For a moment, nobody said anything as both Gila and Swanson were left to contemplate their own thoughts.

"What?" Eva asked. "What does that mean?"

"There are certain places in the world that have always been natural points of contention," Swanson explained. "That particular area, in the mountains of Badakhshan Province in Afghanistan, has been an area in transition for millennia. It is a natural waypoint and the junction of the most extreme limits of empires. Armies have clashed there and been repelled more times than it is possible to count. The borders have shifted slightly over the years, but because of the geography of the area not a hell of a lot. Places like that we term 'nexi'. Any place where there is a great deal of death and history that crosses a line of biblical eclipse, we take very seriously. If Iuvart were going to attempt to open a portal, it would have to be at such a place. The ethereal energy would be near limitless. The Hindu Kush is a hotbed for evil, and with the untold number of deaths..." Swanson shook his head. "If a portal opened there, imagine the unholy souls that would erupt into being just through the nature of the energy being generated by such a portal. If Iuvart succeeds, they go a great way towards tipping the balance. That has always been considered one of the most dangerous locations on the planet. It is why so many have sought to own it."

"In order to protect it?"

"Yes Eva. Even back then, they knew. Imagine an iceberg. The small surface area is the knowledge in general circulation. What lies under the water is what people don't see. There are forces located there even now, up on the glacier."

"Sounds like you have known this is going to happen."

Gila flicked her computer off and placed it beside her. "Eva, call us fatalistic, but that's exactly what ARC is. This event WILL happen. It is just a matter of when and where, and being ready for it. Can we do anything about it? That we do not know. It is the reason we are searching for the last codex. If it reveals its secrets to us then maybe the when and where are confirmed and we learn a little about the why."

"And you have us looking in a graveyard. That could take some time."

"Not just any graveyard," Swanson said, and pointed out of the car where a series of monoliths erupted with waxen majesty into the afternoon sky. "That one."

CHAPTER THIRTY-FIVE

"THAT'S NOT A GRAVEYARD. IT'S A PALACE." Eva pressed the button to open the window, feeling the heat of afternoon on the breeze, followed shortly by the strong scent of the thousands of flowers growing along the sides of the road. Palm trees surrounded a mosque that could be described as nothing less than resplendent to Eva. She winced in the sunlight, unused to it with the tinted windows of the car. The mosque shimmered under the azure heavens above.

Gila leaned past Eva to breathe in the scented air, emitting a sigh of pleasure before returning to her seat.

"I love it here. So beautiful. The mosque was built in honor of the Maghrebi Abd el-Rahim. He settled here upon return from a pilgrimage to Mecca. He founded a great center of learning and prayer here, and, when he departed this earth, the great mosque was built above his tomb, in itself becoming a great place of pilgrimage for many Muslims. The graveyard contained beneath predates his death by hundreds of years and that was over a thousand years ago. The codex is older still. A description here details one specific grave with ancient glyphs as markings. That is what we are after."

"You are aware such an ancient grave is probably weather-beaten, any carvings worn smooth?"

"Perhaps, but the graves run deep under the mosque in catacombs. They haven't seen daylight in the best part of a millennium. We certainly have a chance."

"And I suppose you have a way in?"

Swanson popped the cap from a bottle of coke, draining the bottle with one thirsty gulp, even as condensation ran down the bottle onto his shirt. He held up the bottle, showing her the logo.

"We are not without resource."

"And your resource led the demons straight to you before."

"True, but here we don't need to contact anyone. We have the curator of scrolls and texts from the Coptic Museum."

Gila blushed in response. "It is fact; they do know me in these parts, and that should be enough to get us in there. We will get to your demon yet, Eva."

Swanson drove them around the boundary of the mosque until they found a busy parking lot. Parking the car into a free space, Swanson turned in his seat.

"Your turn. Show us the way."

"Wait here a moment," Gila said by way of answer and left them in the car.

After a short and apparently amiable conversation with a guard, Gila returned.

"It's fine. The mosque is busy with pilgrims and prayers, but they have agreed to show us the way down to the graveyard, providing we don't make too much of a mess."

"Do they know what we are intending to do?" Eva asked.

"You could say I glossed over the details of that part," Gila replied with a wink. "Come on."

If the mosque outside was grandiose in statement, the interior was palatial to a fault. Rows of stone columns buttressed the domed roof from end to end of the hall. In between the columns hung crystal chandeliers. The floor covered in a series of thick patterned carpets appeared to be competing with the painted frescos on the ceiling in a battle to draw the eye. Eva did not know where to look next.

"Stunning, isn't it?" Gila whispered.

"I have never before seen the like."

"The artwork on the ceiling took the better part of a century to complete. There is gold leaf set into the arches under the ceiling. They wanted to pay the Maghrebi every possible respect. If you are going to worship God somewhere, you could choose a far worse place to make pilgrimage to."

Gila opened a door that stuck out as somewhat unassuming and functional amidst all the opulence.

"This way. This is as much as we shall get to see."

Eva followed Gila down a very narrow and steep set of stairs, lit by a series of candles that had smeared the whitewashed walls with black smoke stains over the years. The temperature seemed to Eva to change with every step down, the heat of the afternoon rapidly displaced by cool, moist air. By the time they had reached the bottom, she had goose bumps on her arms.

Gila offered her a cardigan, which Eva gratefully put on. "Thanks."

"I've been down here before. I came prepared."

Eva stepped out of the light from the stairs into the semi dark, touching one of the many headstones. It was chilled to the touch, and completely smooth. "This is in good condition. Recent?"

"Nothing down here is younger than the Maghrebi's tomb. This place has been very well cared for, even back in antiquity. I doubt anybody has been down here in the last decade. They don't let many in."

Eva sighed. "That rules out lighting then. I'm getting weary of all these dark places."

Gila laughed. "Welcome to my world, but it's not all that bad." She reached out and detached an object about the length of a forearm from the wall, flicking a lighter at the same time. In moments, Gila had several brands burning. "Torches. They are soaked in some sort of oil and will burn for hours. We can light as many as we need along the way, just as long as we extinguish them on our way back."

"Won't that affect the air down here?"

"Trust me, Eva. I do not believe you have quite comprehended the size of these catacombs."

"Why don't you show me?"

Gila replaced the torch and lit a second. "Wait here."

She disappeared into the dark, her progress marked by the sooty glow of torches as she made her way through the catacombs.

"I'd give anything for a good Maglite, torches or not," Eva said while watching Gila's progress. She felt the touch of something hard and cold on her arm and turned to find Swanson offering exactly that.

"I don't necessarily buy into Dr Ciranoush's level of technology at all times. I like to come prepared."

"And yet the batteries on your glowing nightstick will

run dry far earlier than any of these torches," Gila said in response as she appeared from a completely different direction. "I've lit about a third of the way there. We will need to do the rest as we go along. Let's go. Stick to the path."

Eva did as asked. The laid brick path was amidst the graves, and appeared more recent than the brickwork that made the vaulted ceiling. With the torches alight, it made for easy going, but soon enough they reached the limit of the light.

"Doesn't this freak you out at all, being down here amongst all this death?"

"No, not at all. You have to see it from my perspective though. I work in biblical history. I spend nearly all of my time examining the ancient dead, or items that were written by or belonged to them. Being down here is just like you visiting a patient. Could you help me with the torches please? I think we will need a bit more light when we get where we are going."

Gila handed her a spare torch, lit it from her own, and moved off to the next set of stone buttresses to find more torches.

Eva touched her torch to one attached to the wall and it flared into life. She did this again, as she kept pace with Gila, and with double the amount of light, she began to see the true extent of the catacombs. Graves stretched off in every direction, but all were immaculate, serene and undisturbed. In time, even the path ended.

As Eva stood at the end of the brickwork, Swanson commented, "They don't have cause to come this far."

"Why not?"

"You see the sarcophagus to your right?" Gila called from the other wall. "That's Abd el-Rahim. If ever they come down here, they want to come no further. Only recently has anyone ever gone further. A few years ago, three Muslim brothers killed many Copts outside of a nearby church. Rumour has it they were brought down here and executed, though nobody has substantiated that rumour."

"You know you guys aren't exactly selling this experience to me. How do you know they went any farther?"

Gila pointed to the floor where tracks led off into the darkness. "Because we are following their footsteps."

"Madden, the things I do for you," Eva muttered, and lit the next torch.

As they continued, the walls started to narrow, and shouting distance became talking distance. This eased Eva's fears somewhat, though the tons of rock and dirt above her head meant the darkness was the least of her problems. The graves became far less organised and much more unkempt, the headstones showing much more of the weathering Eva had expected. The tracks continued. The musty taste in the air made Eva feel as though she was deep underground. She stopped and looked at the ceiling.

"Actually we aren't that far under." Swanson said. "The supports are much more concentrated under the mosque, but here we are past a road and under gardens on the other side if my judgement is correct. There could be only a few feet of rock above us here."

"Great..."

"Over here, you two. I've found something." There was enough excitement in Gila's voice to make Eva forget her predicament.

Stepping with respect around the remains of decayed graves, Eva approached Gila, Swanson behind her.

"The codex indicates its sister volume will be revealed with a sign."

Eva examined the wall in front of them. "I'm sorry Gila, but I don't see it."

Gila waved her burning torch at Eva. "Let's light the place up. It might seem a little clearer that way."

Eva followed Gila's lead, setting every available torch alight. There were many, and soon the most ancient of grounds in the labyrinth glowed a steady yellow.

"Now, take another look," Gila instructed.

Eva examined the wall, this time from a distance. "I see markings, but I couldn't tell you what they are."

"Good spot Gila," Swanson approved. "It's so simple and yet so profound. It makes you wonder if they always knew. Eva, let me."

Swanson pulled a stick charred black from an extinguished torch and approached the wall. He etched markings in black, moving from left to right, up to a point and then down to the bottom of the wall.

"See it now?"

With the black lines highlighting the carved wall, it was hard to miss. "The ARC symbol. Like the one in the church, but different somehow. More simplistic."

"Older," said Swanson. "You heard the story about our founder, my ancestor. This is a thousand years older, maybe more."

"How did he find the logo if this place was hidden?"

"Maybe he found the wall. Maybe this logo is in other places. Who knows? What matters is it's a sign we are close."

Eva stepped forward to examine the wall. "What are we looking for?"

Swanson tapped at the stone with the heel of his torch. "A way in."

Eva repeated the action, the metal producing a dull 'thunk' from the impenetrable stone. For the next five minutes, she repeated this action, while Gila and Swanson did the same on other parts of the wall. Nothing changed until Eva tapped a spot between two of Swanson's markings, where the 'C' of the ARC logo would have been. The stone vibrated with the impact of the torch.

"Got it," she said aloud.

Swanson reached her first and repeated the action. "Definitely hollow. Stand back."

From his pack, he produced a chisel and mallet, and began to attack the stone.

As he worked, Eva felt something brush her face. She looked up to see dust falling from the ceiling in response to the repeated vibration.

"Hurry up, Swanson. The roof looks like it's ready to collapse."

Swanson dropped the chisel and gave the fractured stone one almighty blow with the mallet. There was a sharp rapport as the stone split in two and fell out from the wall. He peered in.

"There's something in there."

"Let me," Gila offered, and donning a pair of white gloves, reached past Swanson into the hole. She withdrew a book not unlike the codex Eva had found, and holding it reverently, blew dust from the surface.

"Codex fourteen," she breathed, and placed it in a cotton bag and that into her pack.

"Done then? Let's get out of here." Swanson made to turn away, but Gila stopped him.

"Hang on. There's something else in there." She

reached in, almost up to her shoulder, and pulled out what appeared to Eva to be a large glass dagger.

Eva drew breath to make comment when a hand clasped over her mouth. Two more grabbed her arms and pulled her tight to the pillar behind. She tried to shout a warning as a figure in shadow passed her, but all that came out was a muffled grunt.

It was enough to make Swanson turn, and without hesitation, he leapt towards the unknown assailant, grabbing them it the throat, his hand with the mallet arcing round to strike.

The attacker threw out a hand to catch his arm, and the struggle was on. Clearly, a man by his size, the attacker yelled something in what Eva presumed was Arabic, and followed it with a roar. Swanson was distracted for a moment and looked towards Eva. She could not move but did not need to. The stench of carrion was so overpowering Eva would have fainted had she not been held tight. There was movement, and Eva found herself bound to the pillar by rope. The hands released her, and two more men stepped around the post. One leered at her before turning towards Gila, who had backed against the wall, dagger still in hand.

"The knife," one of the men said in heavily accented English. "Give it to me and you may go."

"I think I'll take my chances with the knife," Gila replied.

"I hoped you would say that." The speaker threw back his robe and screamed, as did the other two.

In the past, distance had withheld the true horror from Eva, but now all three men began to swell, their mouths stretching, their heads swelling in impossible directions. One looked at her and his eyes began to slant outwards. His skin, paper thin, started to rip as it could no longer contain what was beneath it. The bulkier demon form began to emerge from its mortal cocoon, born in a fit of screaming, and the blood and tattered flesh of a ruined carcass.

Swanson still had hold of his opponent even as he changed, and was having trouble retaining his hold with the blood pouring over his hands. In a move of herculean strength, he sidestepped and brought the emerging demon around to smash against the wall, driving the mallet into its face.

As if waiting just out of sight, a portal opened, and tentacles reached for the injured demon. This brought a deafening roar of rage from the free demon, who bunched its shoulders, ripping free of the final shreds of its mortal shell. It towered above them all, seven feet in height, and a deep red color, as if there was no skin to cover the muscle beneath. Crowded by the low cciling, it hunched over, and powered towards Gila. It reached for her, but miscalculated as Gila took a step towards it, driving the dagger into its middle. The demon screamed, and there was a detonation from within. The demon exploded; the force sending parts all over the catacombs, covering Eva with gore and throwing Gila and Swanson to the ground. The final demon, comprehending which danger was more real, roared in impotent rage, and dived into the portal.

The portal winked out, all enemies taken or destroyed. Dust continued to fall from the roof in several places, starting to pour in streams right over Gila. There was an ominous creaking above them.

"Swanson! Gila! Get up!" Eva continued to shriek at them until finally Swanson began to move.

"What just happened?" He croaked, his face covered with blood, both his and the demon's.

"Get Gila! Get her bag and the knife! The roof is going to collapse!"

Moving on instinct, guided by her words, Swanson shuffled to Gila, dragging her to the column to which Eva was tied. The stream of dust increased, pouring into piles on the ground as dust began to be replaced by dirt.

Swanson leaned against the pillar, attempting to recover.

A glint of light on a fractured surface caught Eva's attention. "Oh dear God, the knife. Swanson, get it. Without it, we are all lost."

Fist-sized rocks began to fall from the weakened roof as Swanson made his way back to the wall, and he cried out as several hit him.

"Hurry!" Eva screamed, but it was too late. With a crack, the roof imploded, sending tons of rock and earth to bury the catacombs of Abd el-Rahim forever.

CHAPTER THIRTY-SIX

THE LATE-AFTERNOON SUN SHONE ACROSS THE SURFACE of the flower-bedecked park that was one of many that helped ensure Qena's status as one of the most beautiful cities in the world. The park was busy, locals, enjoying the scenery mingling with tourists and pilgrims alike. However, this was not the reason for the presence of so many people.

A huge hole had opened up at one end of the park, and around it hundreds of people mingled. The opinion amongst all was the hole was part of an underground grave, or caves connected to the catacombs above which the mosque resided. The inhabitants of Qena were well versed in the lore of their city and proud of its ancient history.

There were more than a few screams then, and quite a few comments alluding to the undead when a hand reached over the edge of the hole, clawing for purchase at the turf beyond. Emerging from the chaos beneath, Eva blinked at the bright daylight, revelling in the heat after the frigid chill of the crypt. Hands steadied her as she climbed to her feet, and Eva smiled grateful thanks, unable to understand what was being said, but overjoyed to be alive.

Another set of hands, and Gila emerged, still dazed from the detonation beneath. She caused more of an outcry for the dagger she held reversed in one hand, the weapon being too big for her bag. She said a few words in Arabic, and several men rushed to the edge of the hole to offer their hands to Swanson, pulling him out.

He spared a moment to stare back down into the darkness, and then added a few words of his own, handing a card to one of the men who hurried off in the direction of the mosque.

"Come on, we need to get out of here." Swanson indicated to Eva they had to help Gila, and she did so willingly.

"What did you give to that man?"

"A card. He is an imam, a prayer leader. I told him of the danger, and informed him he can use that card to draw whatever funding they deem necessary to protect the catacombs and restore the area."

"Mighty generous."

Swanson continued to guide a near-senseless Gila towards the car. "We are all fighting the same battle now. We are all on the same side."

Saying no more, they got Gila settled in the car, and were on their way.

As the only person in full control of their faculties, it fell to Eva to drive. Reluctant to helm such a large vehicle, Eva was pleasantly surprised to find the controls near at hand and easy to use.

"This thing could almost drive itself."

"Pretty soon they will," Swanson agreed. But you have fifty miles of straight road to get used to it. We will take a plane after that, and arrangements have been made for when we reach our destination."

"Which is?"

"Peshawar, Pakistan. But we won't go anywhere until Gila is back with us, and has translated the codex. Besides, I could do with a rest myself."

Eva let Swanson see to Gila, mopping her brow with a towel iced from the small frozen compartment in the back. She was still amazed to recall him rising from the rubble of the ruined catacombs with barely a scratch. Some people just had an incredible amount of luck.

As the miles passed by, Eva settled into the role of navigator. There was nothing to it. The road followed the river remaining in the lush green belt that enclosed it. The experience was a pleasant one. In time, Swanson finished, and eschewing the final codex, sat fingering the dagger.

"Stunning, isn't it?" Eva said.

"Aesthetics wasn't your reason for keeping it. What happened in there?"

"Gila stabbed that demon. When she did so, it exploded. No portal, no tentacles. Just obliteration. What if that is meant to kill demons? Supposing it is, what if that was used in closing the portal the last time Armageddon happened?"

"A not unreasonable hypothesis," Swanson said, hefting the dagger and stabbing thin air. "It was after all found with the final codex. Perhaps the two are linked."

"Can you tell anything from looking at it?"

"Horn handle, nothing special about that. The blade though. It looks like glass. It's razor sharp. If I had to guess I would say it's obsidian, but I thought obsidian was always dark."

"It varies. It can be golden, or rainbow-coloured. Depends what's in it."

Swanson stared at her for a moment. "People never cease to amaze me. A rock hound, too."

Eva let a small smile slip, and concentrated on the road.

In time, the dense green foliage around the road became interspersed with small settlements, indicating the imminent emergence of Luxor. A steady stream of aircraft to her left showed the location of the airport, but Swanson pointed her in the opposite direction, right into the heart of the city. Eventually they pulled up in the car park of a small but pretty hotel with the name 'Kareem Hostel' in arabesque style letters on the wall. Gila was still out of it, but showing signs of coming around.

"Wait here. Keep this hidden." Swanson handed Eva the dagger, which she wrapped in her scarf. From her vantage point, she watched Swanson enter the hotel, and embrace a man she presumed to be Kareem, greeting him with warm words.

"Another ARC follower," she presumed.

The man accompanied Swanson back out to the car where they stopped beside Eva's open window.

"Kareem, this is Doctor Eva Ross,"

Kareem, with the typical head of black hair, slight build and thin beard smiled. "Blessings of Allah be with you, Doctor Eva Ross."

"Hi," was all Eva could think to reply with, but Kareem beamed when she flashed him a smile. His attention was diverted from Eva when he saw Gila in the back of the car.

"Ya Allah, what has happened to her?"

"Accident in Qena," Swanson supplied. "We need to get her into a bed."

"Come. Come!" Kareem beckoned to Eva. "We will worry about your car. And your friend first. Come."

With Swanson's help, Kareem lifted Gila and they carried her up into the hotel, placing her in a room two floors up.

"I will stay with her," Eva volunteered when the men hesitated to leave.

"Make sure you do," Swanson warned. "I'll take the room next door, but make sure you stay in here. Luxor can be a dangerous place and I can't watch your back. I need to organize an Apocalypse. If you need anything, speak to Kareem."

Both men nodded a goodbye and Swanson shut the door.

For the next few hours, Eva waited while Gila tossed and moaned in her sleep. Having been assured by Swanson there was no problem medically, and she would recover in time, all Eva could do was wait. However there was only so much mopping of the brow she could do, and eventually Eva got up to explore the limits of her new confines.

There wasn't much to the suite. Two beds, a small bathroom and a table made up their quarters. Eva was pleasantly surprised when she opened the curtains to reveal a small balcony complete with hardwood table and chairs. Slipping out as quietly as rusty hinges would allow, Eva escaped to this new freedom.

The sunset across Luxor was nothing less than stunning. Eva watched in wonder as shadows stretched long between the buildings below, interspersed with a deep red from the low sun. This caught across the west-facing walls of the nearby temples, rendering them aflame. It seemed to

Eva it was how the view would appear if they lost. A desperate kind of beauty, as if Hades had already come to town.

The stunning sight was offset somewhat by the fact they were adjacent to the main train station in Luxor. The sound of trains and crowds jostling for prominence was unending, and rose to their balcony in waves.

A creak from the door betrayed the fact Eva was no longer alone. Gila crept to her side and leaned on the balcony.

"Stunning, isn't it? I've never quite found the words to describe the Necropolis at sunset. Shame about the noise."

Eva turned to speak but Gila beat her to it. "Yes, I'm fine. Bit bruised perhaps, but God willing I'm ready to fight another day. I would appreciate knowing what happened though."

Eva laughed. "You stabbed a demon with the obsidian blade. It wasn't swallowed by the portal. It exploded and knocked you flying. Then the roof collapsed."

Instead of shock at the description of events, Gila surprised her by saying, "Interesting."

"I thought the same. There was a risk we were going to lose the dagger, but Swanson saved you and it."

"And the Codex?"

Eva pointed behind them. "Back there in your stuff, with the dagger."

Gila rubbed her head, still woozy from her appearance. "So much to be done. Well, I'd better get to it."

"Anything I can do to help?"

Gila smiled. "Only if you can learn all matter of ancient languages in the next five minutes. With this noise, I'll have to work inside. I expect Swanson wants this translated an hour ago, and it might provide the key to the dagger, and whatever is going to happen in the next two weeks."

Gila pointed down past the station. "The street full of bazaars is called Sharia al-Mahatta. Just past the station is an excellent little stall selling cold, fresh sugarcane drink. I recommend it to you. It should provide distraction for a few hours, and isn't too far away."

Gila pressed some Egyptian currency into her hands, the crisp notes folding around coinage. "Go shopping. God knows you need a change of clothes. I will see you soon. Do not worry about whatever promise you made to remain here with me. I am fine, and you can't get into too much trouble so close to the hostel."

With that dismissal, Gila left the balcony, and by the time Eva had checked her bearings and re-entered the room, Gila already had papers scattered over her bed, with her tablet on one knee, and the final code on the other. Eva paused to listen to Gila mutter words in a language she couldn't possibly comprehend, and it very quickly became clear there was nothing she could do. Trying to make as little noise as possible, she left the room, pulling the door shut behind her.

Eva made her way down through the hotel, letting her fingers linger at times over the white porcelain tiles, the only cool thing in all of Luxor so it seemed. As she passed the reception, nobody challenged her. Noise came from the restaurant nearby, so she stayed as far away as possible until she slipped out into the evening.

Outside, the street was almost in full shadow as the sunset fell to dusk. Light bulbs began to blink on as Eva moved away from the hotel. The bazaar ahead called to her, the lingering heat of the day still evident. With the onset of nightfall, other people came out, having hidden from the day's sun. Much like Cairo, Eva noted the presence of many different nationalities. As a tourist hotspot, it was expected.

For the moment, Eva found herself wandering alone, the street as quiet as the chaos ahead was balmy. The bottom level of many shops lit up the street like an arcade, the vendors lounging on steps smoking, watching her in turn, as she observed them. Eve feigned an air of aloofness, hoping to distract them from luring her into their shops.

The same could not be said of the bazaar that filled the square ahead. Stalls had erupted anywhere there was space, leaving the pathways between very reminiscent of an ant's nest. They were overflowing with cheap golden trinkets and colourful shawls. As Eva walked through the bazaar, she lost track of the number of times Arabic-accented 'Pretty Lady' was thrown at her by merchants desperate to entice her in. Incense burned everywhere, the sweet waft of sandalwood adding to the aroma of the clothes all around her, evidence that some had remained unsold for a very long time. This mixed with the pungent aroma of spiced food being cooked in several large clay pots interspersed between the stalls. The result left Eva's stomach growling, reminding her she had not eaten since breakfast.

As Eva walked past one particular stall, several men began shouting in her direction. Eva ignored this and began to walk off faster as the level of noise increased. She turned, and one had approached her, waving one arm in her direction.

"I'm sorry. I don't know what you are saying," she replied.

"He says you offend them by not respecting their traditions," a voice offered from behind her.

Eva turned to see a small Egyptian man in jeans and jacket, bearing a rather scraggly moustache looking up at her.

"I'm sorry; I don't know what they are."

He grinned. "Let us make amends for this innocent slight, and then the evening will pass much more easily for you." Turning to the merchants, he began to speak quickly, and with a certain amount of authority at them. They responded, the large man in front still waving his hand up and down at her.

"Do you prefer red?"

Eva nodded.

"Good. Wrap this about your head and shoulders." The man picked a rather luxurious shawl from the pile in front of the merchants and handed it to her.

Eva wrapped the material about her head and shoulders, luxuriating in the smooth material, not any warmer despite the heat. The small man was clearly haggling with the merchant and at length he turned to her. "He wants twenty Pounds for that."

Eva fingered through the money Gila had pressed upon her, finding a green note marked with the appropriate amount, and handed it over.

Instantly the merchant and his friends changed from ire to fawning smiles. He said something more to her and winked.

"He says it becomes you, and wishes you Allah's good grace and protection this night."

"I'm sure he does, now he has my money," Eva replied and flashed the merchant a grateful smile.

"Come; let me escort you through these thieves and vagabonds."

Beguiled by his easy charm, Eva found herself following

him from stall to stall. "Who are you? I don't even know your name."

"I am called Nassor, pretty lady. I work at the hotel in which you stay. I was asked by your scientist friend to keep watch over you since you would inevitably ignore him and leave the hotel. It appears he knows you quite well."

They stopped so Eva could buy some sandals, and when she was done, Nassor took her to a stall selling the fabled sugar cane drink. She, of course, paid.

"Are you liking our most beautiful city?" Nassor asked while she sipped the ice-cool syrupy liquid.

"I haven't had much of a chance to see it. Shame, really as I have heard many good things over the years."

"How is it a shame? You are here now. You may see it all by day and at night the temples are alight. Luxor never sleeps."

"It is a shame because I may not be here for long. I barely remain in the same place for five minutes now it seems."

Nassor's eyes narrowed. "Where might you go?" He asked innocently.

"I have no idea," Eva replied, a feeling in her gut making her suddenly suspicious. "I go where they tell me. Do you mind if we go back to the hotel now?"

"For certain. I am sure you will be missed before too long. Please, follow me."

Nassor left his drink untouched, and began to wind his way through the bazaar, passing through streets Eva had not seen before. The crowds were still busy, and Eva was so distracted by following her guide she didn't notice the hotel until they approached it from the same road she had driven down. At the entrance, he turned and bowed, palms pressed together.

"I will leave you here, Doctor Ross. I have business to attend to. I bid you a good night."

"Thank you for showing me round," Eva called as Nassor hurried off in the direction of the kitchens. He did not turn back.

Nonplussed, Eva made for her room to see how Gila was coming along with the translation. When she crept in the room, acutely aware of how people could get disturbed easily when studying, she found the room was empty. There was no evidence of Gila or her work anywhere in the room, though the beds showed some sign of use. Eva folded her shawl, and placed it in her bag under the new sandals, and sat on the bed.

"He called me Dr Ross," she said aloud to the empty room. "He knew my name and yet I never gave it. He didn't know Swanson's."

Something was wrong. Gila should have been here. Eva locked her bags in case a hasty exit was again needed, and hurried to the door, intent upon finding the only people she knew in this country.

In the corridor outside, Eva paused. Swanson should have been in the next room. She turned to check his door and it was ajar. Opening it, she found there was nobody inside.

"Swanson?" She whispered, and there was a shuffling in response. Eva fumbled for the light switch, and before she could find it, was grabbed from behind. She tried to scream, but a cloth smothered her face. The cloying smell of chloroform overpowered her, and she dropped to the floor.

CHAPTER THIRTY-SEVEN

Eva's head swam. Amongst the muddle, she wondered as to the safety of her child. It was well documented Chloroform could to lead to deformities at birth if administered above a certain concentration. Eva had no idea how much they had used. The reassuring glow of warmth from within let her know everything was all right. If a demonic presence couldn't beat her, she doubted chemicals could.

The sack was still placed over her head, the coarse fiber scratching at her cheeks, and through it, Eva could only see a series of bright lights. It was hard to keep her eyes open at all, as the burlap stank of ammonia, and stung her eyes.

Eva attempted to move her arms. The ropes that bound her hands burned into her wrists, tied so uncomfortably tight that her hands had gone numb. She concentrated on calming herself, taking slow, even breaths. This helped calm her and soon she was in full control of her faculties. Closing her eyes, she reached out with her other senses, trying to gauge the size of the room. In the silence, she sensed movement.

"Okay, since you have had plenty of time to observe me, care to tell me what I am doing here?"

"We shall be asking the questions this morning, Doctor Ross," Said a voice that was very familiar. Fake smiles and earnest intentions hid ulterior motives behind a thin and wispy moustache. How could she have been so beguiled?

"Nassor. Well, that answers that."

"Agent Nassor Fayad of Interpol, woman," said a voice with such a heavy accent it was difficult to understand, growling close to her ear. "You would do well to remember."

"Who are you, and what are you doing here?" Nassor asked, irritation at the interjection from his colleague, certainly a local policeman, clear in his voice.

Eva saw no point in lying. She was already in it up to her neck. "My name is Eva Ross and I am travelling through Egypt with friends."

"You are Doctor Eva Ross, wife to Brian Ross, of Worcester, Massachusetts in the United States of America are you not?"

"No argument there. Why am I here, being detained like some sort of terrorist?"

"You are here at my request, and because you are responsible for the heinous death of a small girl in your home city, imprisonment of several individuals in your own home, and a string of mysterious deaths stretching from Worcester in a direct line to Birmingham, Alabama. The authorities are most keen to talk to you and your male friend, but I have you first. Where is he?"

"Swanson? I have no idea. I was trying to find him when you jumped me. I can't wait to see what happens when he finds you."

"Not him. The other male friend. The one who travelled from America with you. Where is he hiding?"

"I don't know."

Eva's head rocked sideways as a heavy hand slapped her across one cheek, the fibers grinding into her skin with the force. She tried to shake them free, but the sack stuck to her flesh. A hand grabbed her thigh, and travelled up; running close enough to her groin to assure her she was in great danger.

"I assure you," Nassor said with the patience of one used to such interviews, "you will remember. Otherwise we might be compelled to encourage you to talk by other methods."

The hand lingered, desperate to explore her further.

"I told you. I don't know where he is. He was kidnapped north of here when we were travelling from Cairo."

"Where exactly?"

"On the road to Qena. I don't know the names of all the places here. It wasn't five minutes ago I was in America."

"And what were you doing on the road to Qena? Why are you here at all? You will answer me!"

Eva felt another blow coming, and tensed herself, but the blow never came. Something had changed.

"She was, and is, travelling with me."

Eva held her breath as the tension in the room ramped up a notch. Her liberation was at hand.

"Monsieur Guyomard," Nassor fawned obsequiously, "I was not aware of your involvement. She... This is only a woman. Interpol has jurisdiction here."

Eva remained still while the ropes were cut from her wrists. As blood surged back into her hands, Eva cried out in pain, but set to moving them as much as she could. The sack was removed from her head, dazzling her for a moment. When the light dimmed, Eva found herself face to face with a very tired but alert Gila Ciranoush, who checked her over. In the background, Nassor was facing off Swanson, two Egyptian police behind him attempting to look imposing. Swanson was having none of it.

"You will live, but we need to get something on that cheek before it festers," Gila said.

"I did warn you to stay inside," Swanson admonished. "You never know what cockroaches crawl out from under the rocks in places such as this."

No longer in control, Nassor bristled at the insult. "As I said, Interpol has..."

"Interpol has nothing, agent Fayad. ARC has jurisdiction over Interpol, as well as full cooperation from a dozen or more international agencies, many of the governments of the world and you damned well know it. You would drug, bind, and beat up a pregnant woman for nothing more than information?"

As Swanson said this, Nassor's eyes narrowed, and once again, Eva felt uncomfortable under his scrutiny. Why did he care if she was pregnant?

"Get out." Swanson pointed at the police, and then the door. Only following a nod from Nassor, did they move, one of them leering at Eva as he left. No doubt the man with his hand up her leg.

Nassor remained, unmoving. "You will live to regret this."

Swanson leaned in on the smaller man. "I can assure you if we all live, little policeman, this incident will come far down the list of things I come to regret. Now get out, and pray we never meet again." Swanson held Nassor's gaze by sheer force of will, a previously unseen level of command coming to the fore. This was not the man Eva had come to know. This was something else.

Backing down from the challenge, Nassor spared a glance for Eva, an insult on the edge of his tongue, but left the room without further comment.

In the meantime, Gila had begun to apply a soothing balm to Eva's face. Swanson watched the hallway for a moment, and then turned to Eva.

"Can you walk?"

"I can sure as hell try." Eva attempted to stand, but ended up back on the seat. The second attempt was much better, and with help, she stumbled out of the interrogation room.

"Where are we?"

"Not here," Swanson answered. "Too many ears."

He led them out into a narrow alleyway where their car was waiting. Once Eva was seated, Swanson took the wheel and began to drive.

"That is a holding area for prisoners of the Mukhabarat, the Egyptian secret service. They have had you since last night. Suffice it to say ARC knows everything they do, and once we knew you were missing, and who had been seen about the hotel, it was only a matter of time. Lucky, too. They are not gentle in their methods."

Eva touched her cheek. It was swollen, but not painful. "I was finding out the hard way. They wanted to know about Madden."

"I do not doubt that. Half of the world would give everything they own to know where he is. Nobody knows. But we know where he will be in thirteen day's time, and that information is privy to only a few."

Eva could sense the tension. "You have changed. What has happened?"

"An epiphany, a revelation, call it what you will."

Eva turned to Gila. "You have translated the codex? Already."

Gila's face was somber. "I have translated some. Enough that I fear what else I may find out. But first, look."

She flicked on a small screen on the back of Swanson's seat to reveal a harbor, covered with bodies. Many were human, the pools of blood attested to that. The camera panned round to show many non-humans, hellbounces who had released their demons. Some still moved, attempting to crawl to the person filming. After a while, Jeanette Gibson returned to the screen, the one constant in all of this.

"These demons have had their chance at hellbounce. They have slaughtered humans, and died in the attempt. This is happening all over the planet. That was Bristol, England where once pirates smuggled slaves. It is one of hundreds of reports. The world is panicking. This is happening soon and we may not even be able to prevent it. We stand on the edge of an abyss so much greater than we could have believed possible. Let me refer to my notes and I shall reveal what I have learned."

Eva stared at the screen, waves of pure dread threatening to overcome her.

Gila pointed at the screen. "This is what the final Codex is about. This is what it reveals."

Eva shuddered. "That's about par for the course."

"Oh no, this is not the half of it. If the Codex is to be believed, Satan is not the dark prince the world believes him to be. According to the passages contained herein, Satan was a willing sacrifice from Heaven. He chose to go to Hell to prevent something worse from breaking through into Hell and from there to the mortal realm. It seems Heaven feared this greatly."

"But why? If there is a heaven, much as there appears to

be a Hell, what do they have to fear? I mean it's Heaven! The eternal realm of the good!"

"I do not know. Perhaps this worse thing would end humanity, the source of population for both realms. Perhaps it was coming straight for them. Either way, Satan was juxtaposed against it, as fire is juxtaposed against ice, thus creating a balance. In time, others sought out the sanctity of Satan's realm, be it for dissatisfaction with the upper realm or a casting out. They believed the lower realm to be something other than it was. Chief amongst them were those most railed against Heaven. Asmodeus, Beelzebub, Abadon, Lucifer, Mammon and Belphegor. They joined Satan as chiefs in what came to be known as the seven deadly sins. They attracted those of like mind to themselves, and Hell as we know it came to be formed."

Eve struggled to digest this information, but something didn't ring true. As she watched a pitched battle between demon kind and armed forces, it came to her. "The names are wrong. It should be Leviathan, not Beelzebub."

"There is reason. The last time they attempted to rupture the veil to the mortal realm, Leviathan, then the Lieutenant of Beelzebub, fought and vanquished his master at his moment of triumph. It is well documented as you have seen. Somebody on this side opened the portal, yet here we are. As it is recorded, the demons reverted to type following the failed attempt on the mortal realm. Between them, Mammon and Leviathan conspired to topple Satan from his position of pre-eminence, using Abadon as a dupe and puppet. It involved an agent on this side attempting to open another portal somehow, but beyond that, I have not been able to glean more detail. What the Codex does reveal is that during this time, and influenced by others, Abadon destroyed Satan, tearing him to pieces. Satan fell, and

Abadon assumed his place as the preeminent force in the domain. But Abadon was not Satan. He was not a willing sacrifice, but a being merely seeking power, and as such, could not fully comprehend the role that position required. The balance shifted. The barrier Satan had kept in place, the frozen core of Hell, now showed cracks, and the force beyond started to seep through. It is a force of ice to the fire of Satan, and Hell is freezing over as the minions of this other entity find their way through the cracks of the seal. Abadon is powerless to stop the being beyond, he can only rally against it. The population of Hell is terrified, and desperate, and seeking a way out."

Gila put the Codex down, and wrapped it carefully. "This happened nearly four thousand years ago, during the time of the Assyrian Empire. Hell has had millennia to find a way through. The last time they tried a portal into this world, the record of it came to be known as revelations. The Codex says this came from speaking to a demon agent that came to earth, a survivor of the first conflict. It referred to the entity just as 'The Soulless', a being of ice, whose minions bore weapons that could cause violent death to its kind. The text here translates the weapon as 'Frozen Soul'."

Eva picked up the dagger, examining the blade. "A frozen soul. This is the weapon of our enemy's enemy."

"Yes but in this case the enemy of our enemy is still our enemy. They are destroying demons, or as we have seen, sucking them beyond hell. The ranks are swelling and the balance is shifting in a different direction."

"Balance," Swanson said from the front. "That is the key word. Iuvart said the earth becomes hell when the demon population reaches a certain point."

On the screen, the reporter was being mobbed by people clearly under demonic influence. Blood and gore spattered on the lens shortly after and the signal went dead. Eva and Gila looked at each other in silence as the buildings flew by outside. The distant airport was now much closer.

"Who is to say we are not almost at that point? Who is to say Hell is experiencing the same situation? Their attack might be survival. We cannot guess at what has happened during the millennia since this was written. I can promise you this though: we need to move Heaven and Earth to keep that portal from opening."

Eva hefted the blade, holding it up vertically so the light outside reflected from the conchoidal fractures on the edge. "Iron he treats like straw, and bronze like rotten wood. If you lay a hand on him, you will remember the struggle and never do it again! I remember the struggle all too well. We need to catch a plane."

CHAPTER THIRTY-EIGHT

Now Eva had a focus and the beginnings of a plan, she waited in the back seat of the car, restless with impatience. The scrubland around the edge of Luxor flew by as Swanson pushed the car to greater speeds. Then a thought occurred to her.

"What time is it?"

"About half past eleven. They kept you pretty well hidden," was his reply.

"And pretty well drugged. What time is the flight? I presume you have some fancy chartered jet again?"

"No such luck, I'm afraid. Qatar airways from here to Doha, then another to Peshawar. Thought since our speed didn't accomplish anything in getting you here, we might try a different approach. Besides, we have time. The flight isn't until just after seven but we have twelve days to get there. Right?"

"According to the best intelligence, that is correct," Agreed Eva.

"Then why are we driving so fast?"

"We've picked up a tail. I'm testing their resolve."

"Who is it?"

"Probably Interpol agents under Fayad. They are pretty tenacious, and out here tend to operate by their own rules. They seem to feel the agenda here needs their own personal interpretation. Either way, they won't do anything precipitous, not now I have put their boss in his place. He's probably just confirming we are actually leaving the country."

Eva watched the jeep behind them keeping pace from a distance for a moment. "I know you have said about ARC superseding all of these organizations, but until this morning I don't think I have ever really appreciated it."

"It's all political. ARC has its co-operation and resources. They understand there is more at stake than anything they are prepared to handle. We have agents who are with Interpol, and they make use of our advice. It doesn't mean everybody agrees with us of course, such as agent Fayad. Sometimes they need a little convincing to make the leap of faith."

The car behind never got any closer, and by the time they reached Luxor International airport, it had given up the chase and turned back to the city.

Swanson parked the car at the entrance to the departure terminal, waving at someone to come take the car.

"Grab your stuff, and I'll meet you inside. Keep the knife in this at all times. Keep it safe." He handed over a small case lined with foam, with a gap cut for the knife. Eva placed the weapon within and locked the case, holding it close. With Gila, she went into the terminal, passing crowd of people as they were directed to the VIP lounge.

"May as well make ourselves comfortable," Gila said as they occupied a rather plush sofa, and waved over a waiter.

Leaning back into the cushions, Eva felt more relaxed in an instant. "I could fall asleep right now."

"I'll bet. You do not want to be doing that here though Eva. In fact it would probably be better if you didn't sleep again until this is over."

Eva was taken aback for a moment until she realised Gila was joking. They both laughed.

"We are safe here. I will keep an eye out if you want to take five."

With a smile of grateful thanks, Eva closed her eyes and drifted off in seconds. Her sleep was exhausted, dreamless, and only once was she disturbed. Though she did not open her eyes, Eva heard the conversation through the fog of semi-consciousness.

"I have the tickets," Swanson said, "But we have another problem. Control has asked us to report in and they are not taking no for an answer."

"What about her?" Gila asked.

"She is fine here for now. There is no imminent danger."

"Don't be a fool. There is danger everywhere. Has the journey here not proven that?"

"Be that as it may, we might be a few hours. Give her the tickets and we have an incentive to get back. Write her a note if you must, but do it fast."

The next Eva remembered was waking up as the airport announcer called the imminent departure of the flight to Doha. Eva jumped up, panicking. Swanson and Gila were nowhere to be seen, and the only thing with her was her luggage. Tucked inside her bag Eva found the three tickets, and not waiting to see if they would arrive, rushed to the gate.

At the baggage control, there was a moment of fear as Eva watched the case go through the x-ray machine, but to her utter bafflement, when the case showed on the screen, a completely different set of contents appeared. Not pausing to consider the ramifications of this, Eva sought the correct exit.

The engines of the plane were warming up, she could tell that much from the noise coming up the walkway. Eva thrust her tickets in the direction of the flight attendant who was about to begin closing the gate.

He peered at the tickets. "You are too late for these. Others have been given your seats when there was a no show."

"But..."

"There is one seat left in economy. Take it or leave it."

Eva looked over her shoulder. There was no Swanson or Gila to bail her out this time. If she was going to get to Madden then she had to take this flight. With a resigned sigh for the attendant, she allowed herself to be shepherded onto the plane. Her seat was in the middle of a row facing an oversized television screen on the wall in front and could not have been more uncomfortable. Stowing her gear she sat down and belted herself in. With the changes in her body now becoming noticeable to a woman who was normally slim and athletic, the belt was tighter than she would have liked. Still, she was on the flight. The relief brought by that one thought was more than enough to offset the worry about where her companions had gotten.

Still exhausted, and not really woken up despite the rush, Eva began to drift again before the plane even moved.

. . .

When the plane arrived in Qatar, despite being in economy, Eva's ticket allowed her to be transferred to a luxury hotel near to the airport. It was late and she allowed herself to be ensconced in a room full of delights and delicacies, none of which she paid any attention to.

The next morning a call awoke her, and breakfast was served in her room. Eva had a minimal amount of time to check the knife, and her baggage, and to read the letter.

Eva, keep going. Stop for nobody. You know the stakes. Trust in us. We will find you.

Gila

Eva had no choice. She had been set on this path so long ago, she could barely reason why she was doing all this. She stared at the letter as if there was some hidden meaning behind the words. The paper was old, the sheet thin and scraped, fibers coming off as she rubbed her fingers over it. It had meaning. Gila would say it represented history, and if they did not prevail, there would be nothing in the future for anybody to call old.

"I understand," she said aloud to the empty room, folded the paper and set it in the bag. Her belongings packed she made her way to the waiting shuttle bus.

In the airport, Eva was directed to an area called 'The Gold Lounge' where people with far more money than sense were purchasing all manner of luxury cars shown on pedestals. Not a glance was spared for an American with a couple of handbags.

She sat out of the way, trying to remain obscure until her flight was ready. It was nine in the morning and the flight wasn't until half ten. Eva made herself a coffee from the complementary drinks, and then remembered her condition, setting the hot drink aside and reaching for a bottle of water. She was determined not to be late for this flight, and had had a good night's sleep.

When the call eventually came, Eva was the first to rise, comprehending this lot had the money to be able to get on the plane last and still keep their seats. Unlike the night before, Eva was greeted warmly by the attendant and shown to her seat in first class, of which there were three to choose from. A half hour passed before anybody else deigned to join her. When they did, they were all businessmen and far too occupied with their own lives to spare her a glance, much as they had in the lounge.

Eva ignored this, and relaxed in the comfort of the knowledge Swanson and Gila were somewhere behind her, Madden was in front of her, and at some point they would meet again. She didn't even feel the plane take off.

About an hour into the flight, Eva noticed a whispering. A sibilant conversation was being had around her, as if somebody didn't want her to hear. Surreptitiously, she looked around the cabin. The businessmen all had their noses in laptops, or were having animated conversations on their phones. None paid her any attention, yet the whispering continued.

Eva checked her bag. It had been a long while since she had used her phone; the battery had run dry back in the States. She pulled it out, and the screen read 'Brian'. Her heart began to pump. Her husband was half a world away, driven insane, left spread over a runway following an explosion. She had not spared a thought for him since Birmingham; too much had happened too quickly. Yet somebody had his phone, and had called her on her own dead cell phone.

Eva lifted the phone to her ear, and the whispering

grew louder, wisps of sound interspersed with echoes of words. She strained to listen harder, covering her other ear with her free hand.

"*Your child is dying, as your life in this world grows short.*"

Eva jumped as the words burst out of the phone, nearly deafening her.

"*You can feel it. The pain as your womb thickens, as the life within is smothered by your own defences. Your very body rejects the abomination within.*"

Eva waited for the retaliation from within, as had happened in Cairo. There was nothing. She sought inside for the comfort of her unborn companion, but all she found was emptiness. A cold nothing. The life was extinguished.

"Who are you?" She demanded of the voice in the phone, still whispering unheard as one amongst many in the background noise. "What are you doing to my child? WHO ARE YOU?"

"*I am your future. I am inevitable.*"

Eva felt a pain ripping through her middle, as the innocent within was ripped from its future. Amidst the pain, Eva felt wet spreading beneath her, and in moments her linen skirt was stained red.

As she writhed in torment, the other passengers stood to form a circle around her seat. Their faces were blank, in shadow. Through the haze of pain, she recognised none of them. They leaned in and Eva screamed.

"Miss? Miss?"

Eva turned to find one of the flight attendants at her side. Utterly confused, she just gaped and nodded.

"Would you like something to drink?"

"I... would I like a drink?" Eva checked her skirt. It was dry, no hint of blood. There was no pain in her middle, yet there was still a feeling of absence.

Putting it down to the nightmare she must have suffered, Eva rearranged herself. "Yes that would be lovely. Just a glass of water with plenty of ice."

The flight attendant smiled, a condescending face that showed she was used to dealing with eccentrics in first class and turned away to fetch the drink. Eva looked around, pinching herself to make sure she was awake. Nothing had changed. The compartment was still silent, the businessmen mostly dozing.

In a moment, the attendant returned and handed her a glass full of ice.

"Thank you," Eva said, trying to assume as normal a face as possible to show she wasn't deranged.

"Don't spill your drink," the attendant warned. "It carries all our hopes."

Unsure as to the meaning, Eva glanced back down at her glass, and it was filled with blood. In the middle fetus pulsed on a placenta attached to the glass. As Eva watched dumbstruck, the fetus opened tiny eyes and pulled itself to the edge of the glass, eyeing her with miniscule eyes. Its face swelled and fell apart, leaving a much larger head, full of pointed teeth and well-defined muscles glaring at her.

"I am your future, Mother," it hissed, and climbing to the edge of the glass it leaped at her face.

Eva threw her hands up and screamed. The businessmen to either side of her looked up from their laptops and huffed at the breach of etiquette.

"Miss? Miss?" It was the very same attendant. "Are you well? Can I get you some water?"

"Where are we?" Eva demanded. "When do we land?"

Confused by this aggressive approach, the attendant stepped back. "We are about twenty minutes from landing, about to make our descent. Are you well?"

Eva felt around her stomach. There was no pain. The swelling was still there. She was no longer alone. She realised now more than ever she had to get this done.

"I am fine, thank you. Bad dreams. I will pass on that drink. I'm not thirsty."

The attendant nodded with a smile that spoke more of relief than anything else, and backed away.

Eva gripped the arms of her seat, watching the graphic on the screen in front of her as the plane inched its away across the map of Pakistan.

Behind her, his eyes still locked to his laptop, one of the businessmen smiled.

Eva found herself alone, wandering through alien crowds in Bacha Khan Airport in the Pakistan city of Peshawar. There were armed forces everywhere; old men in faded fatigues wielding machine guns were almost as popular as the traditional baggy clothes worn by men all around her.

It was one such man that stopped Eva as she stood outside the arrival terminal, wondering what to do next. While the garb he wore was the same, there was definitely a finer cut to it, and the small ARC insignia on the left of his chest left Eva in no doubt.

"Doctor Ross?" He said in lightly-accented English.

"Yes, I am Eva Ross."

He bowed his head. "You may call me Sajhid. Can you please confirm the name of my organisation and what it stands for?"

"ARC. Anges de la Résurection des Chevaliers. The

angels of the knight's resurrection, though what angels and knights you expect to resurrect is beyond me. All I have seen so far is demons."

"And they won't be the last. This entire region is in chaos. Whatever is going on across the world, it is here in force. I am your guide in Pakistan and to our destination. Regrettably, it seems your Interpol incident sparked off larger issues, and your companions have been delayed a day. It appears their plane may not reach us. There are reports of a crash somewhere between here and Doha."

"And you don't know the specifics? That doesn't sound like ARC."

Sajhid indicated the chaos around them. "You can see with your own eyes, people are scared. They are running. Information can be hard to come by. If you had a plan, I suggest you stick to it."

"Yes, we need to keep going. It is the only chance we have. Please, if you will come with me, I have a car waiting. We can be underway immediately."

With one regretful glance at the plane landing behind her, willing it to bring fortune; Eva followed the agent to his car.

The car was a rugged Jeep, set for all terrain judging by all of the extras it carried. Wheels, canisters, tools of every sort were bolted all over. This was not going to be the air-conditioned pleasure-ride Egypt had been.

"Tough roads ahead," Sajhid said when he saw her looking over the car. "And tough neighbourhood. People are spooked."

"Let's get out of here. We don't have much time as it is."

Settling into the car, Eva found the back to be dark and

comfortable. When Sajhid turned the key, the engine roared, and within moments of them pulling into traffic; it was clear the ride was going to be a bumpy one.

"Do you have the knife?" Sajhid asked her.

Eva opened the case and pulled the obsidian blade from its foam housing. "I do. It works, if it helps you to know that."

She swore a look of fear passed over his face, replaced quickly by avarice, and then nothing. Her years in training had taught her to observe rapid changes of emotion. Why did somebody dedicated to ARC's cause fear the instrument of their salvation?

"Do not worry, we have everything we need. We are meeting a contact in Jalalabad, three days from now. He will see you to the end."

Sajhid attempted to make good time through the city, but the crowds were so ferocious it was tough going. At one point, they were held at traffic lights for a good five minutes.

"Isn't there a better way around?" Eva asked.

"So sorry, Dr Ross, but the city is full. People are terrified of what is outside. Any road out is full of people trying to get in."

The press of humanity threatened to swamp the cars on the road as more and more people tried to pile past them. The mood was fear. From her refuge in the car, Eva could feel it. These people were terrified. She hugged the case containing the dagger, the only thing in the car that ultimately mattered.

Outside, cars began to beep horns, trying to clear the road. The fear was getting to them, too. Then someone fired a gun. In an instant, the mood changed from fear to anger. Eva could feel it trying to permeate the car and get to her. She closed her eyes and took several deep breaths. The people outside began to hammer on the windows, rocking the car. Then the windows smashed. Hands reached in, grabbing for her and anything they could free from the inside. Eva batted hands away as they got too close.

When someone took hold of the case with the knife, Eva screamed "Sajhid, floor it. I don't care where you go but go!"

Sajhid glanced at her, seeing the ongoing assault, and planted his foot on the gas. The angry mob parted as fear for their lives overcame the irrational rage. One man held onto the broken window, the glass cutting his hands to shreds, covering everything in blood. His face was drained of any vestige of sanity, and against all rational judgement, still he reached for the dagger.

Eva unbuckled and moved to the other side of the car, only for another hand to grab at her. Another Pakistani man grabbed for her, teeth locked in a grimace. As he stared into Eva's eyes, his face began to distort.

"Sajhid, stop the car!"

Her driver slammed his foot on the brake, and this dislodged the two attackers. In an instant, they were off again, and the hellbounces pursued them on foot, beginning to gain.

Eva watched them, impotent in her lack of ability to do anything meaningful.

"Faster, Sajhid," she urged. The two men expanded, exploded, and started to tear up the frightened mass of humanity around them until they recalled what they were after. Howling, at a pitch so high that the people around them dropped to the ground in agony, and even from distance, Eva was forced to cover her ears, they began the pursuit.

CHAPTER THIRTY-NINE

THE DEMONS CAME ON, GETTING CLOSER WITH EACH stride. Sajhid must have been doing over sixty in the Jeep, which shrieked in protest at every pothole they hit.

Then, as with so many times before, the demons began to lose pace. Eva sighed, settling back into her seat. If she didn't make it to Madden, they wouldn't be running out of energy for much longer.

As if sensing the danger had passed, Sajhid eased back on the gas. "Does that happen a lot where you are from?"

"Only recently. They can't cope with existence on earth, not yet."

"And when the end comes?"

Eva began to pick glass off the seat, gathering it in the garment she had bought in Luxor. "Should that happen, you won't need to worry about driving fast ever again. There's something worse than Demons."

Clearing the glass proved problematic. It was everywhere. With the windows smashed, the breeze messed with Eva's hair, blowing in her eyes. The back of the Jeep was cramped for space with all of the provisions, and in the end she gave up trying to gather all of the shards, content to just tidy her own personal space.

By the time she had settled down, afternoon was descending into evening, and the temperature although still pleasant, began to drop. Eva emptied the shawl of glass and wrapped it about her.

"Cold?" Sajhid asked.

"Not unbearably so. It's just the wind. And no, before you ask, I don't want you to slow down."

"Not like back home, is it?"

Eva gazed out at the mountains growing ever nearer. The dry brown landscape was as barren as Egypt, and as alien to a city girl like her as was possible.

"Back home now it would be chilly, the night dark already, and probably raining. I have that much to thank this adventure for."

"We shall be stopping soon. We are approaching the border into Afghanistan and the Khyber Pass. I shall see us through, but it will take some time. It can get very busy."

"That's all right. I have been on planes for the past two days. I could do with stretching my legs."

A flutter in her stomach caused Eva to jump. She put her hand over the slight swell and felt it again. "Oh my."

"Is everything all right, Dr Ross?"

"Oh yes, much better than that. My baby. I felt it move. That's the first time."

"Congratulations."

As Sajhid had promised, pretty soon they were in a queue of traffic as guards checked papers for all those crossing the border into Afghanistan. Leaving him to it, Eva got out of the car. It was the first time she had been able to assess the damage to the car. There were dents and gashes all down the side where the panicked population had assaulted them, many far too severe for mere human hands to make.

Eva stepped away, gathering in the view. The road twisted off into the nearby mountains, the grey ribbon being hidden by rusting signs pointing to Kabul and Kandahar. The air reeked of diesel fumes as lorry after lorry inched forwards. Travellers and traders wandered amidst the impromptu bazaar that sprawled to one side of the road, the merchants hoping to tempt the drivers with their wares. After her experience in Luxor, she kept her distance.

Away from the road, Eva watched the behemoth of metal inching towards the border. From a distance, she became very detached. The oncoming evening lent beauty to even a queue of vehicles with this backdrop behind them. Finding a rock to perch on, she sat down. The stone retained the heat of a day's worth of sun, so enjoying the dusk became infinitely more pleasant.

A girl wrapped in a red shawl came to perch beside her. Eva smiled in welcome, sure she wouldn't have the language skills to deal with her, and shifted over.

The girl smiled in thanks, and sat down, snuggling against Eva as if the rock was not enough. It was not unpleasant. Eva wondered if this is what it would be like if she had her own daughter.

As if in response, the baby kicked once again. As before, Eva gasped and put her hand to her belly. The girl looked up at her, eyes enquiring. Eva held out her hand, indicating the girl should do the same. When she did so, Eva moved her hand, putting it under her own on her belly. The baby kicked once more, and the girl gasped in delight.

Eva got a good glimpse of the girl as she did this, and caught her breath. Maybe ten years old, with a dishevelled crop of messy brown hair sticking out from under the shawl, the girl was stunningly beautiful, with eyes wide and knowing, deep blue pupils surrounded by the whitest white.

The girl looked up at her, returning the stare. "Don't go," she said in English with absolutely no trace of an accent.

"Why not?" Eva replied without knowing why. "I have to go. They are relying on me. I have been chosen and many will perish if I give up."

The child's face was full of sympathy. "It is better for all hope to end here, quickly, than be drawn out in the terrors that wait beyond it."

"Beyond what?"

"Beyond your child." The girl stood, staring without further comment as she backed off from the rock.

"Wait," Eva called, "what do you mean?"

A hand touched her shoulder, and Eva span, the obsidian blade in her hand thrusting for a target.

Sajhid jumped back, his face a mask of fear.

"I'm sorry. You startled me."

"No, the apology is mine. Papers are confirmed. We are ready to go."

Eva looked back to the girl to find nothing. Not even any footprints in the dirt. "Did you see a child?"

"I cannot say I did. Should I have?"

Eva began to doubt her own eyes. "No, perhaps not."

"Do not worry yourself about it," Sajhid said in apparent consolation. "I'm sure it was nothing. Come, let us get on our way. We have a lot of road yet."

His blasé attitude towards what would have had Swanson and Gila drilling her with questions left Eva somewhat concerned. Not for the first time, she wished they were there with her already.

The road to Jalalabad wound its way up through the mountains. The route was slow, busy, and dogged with delays where decrepit trucks had broken down. Eva made the best of it by wrapping her shawl about her and attempting to sleep. There wasn't much to see beyond the range of headlights.

Eva woke once to find Sajhid watching her in the rear view mirror.

"Are we there yet?"

"The road is only just beginning to clear. We travel not much faster than the camel trains that would once have traversed the Khyber Pass."

They crawled past the skeleton of a burned out lorry, abandoned at the side of the road. It was one of many Eva had seen looming out of the dark.

As if sensing her mood, Sajhid continued. "This has always been a place of conflict, this country. It has the misfortune to be on the edge of very many empires throughout history. Medians, Persians, great Alexander and his Macedonians, Mauryans, Parthians, the Huns; the list of rulers is endless. It is the first place they invade, the last place they care about."

"What about now? Is the problem not being solved by all the international attention?"

Sajhid barked out a laugh full of derision. "The mighty Western alliance? They are as transient as the Taliban who would be the next empire. You think they will be here in a hundred years? You think they will be here next year?"

Eva had no answer, and as the speed picked up, they drove the rest of the way in silence.

The stop in Jalalabad was brief, and without comment. There was a strange smell in the car, so while Sajhid was out refuelling the car, Eva took her time stretching her legs. By the color of the sky, dawn was not far off. They had been all night in the pass, and Sajhid had not slept.

Even at this early hour, there were people about. A young woman shepherded a gang of even younger children nearby, and, as one, they saw her and surrounded her, babbling in what must have been Pashtu. Eva was momentarily overcome, reaching to protect her stomach. The woman admonished the children and they quietened. She then said something to Eva and pointed at her stomach.

Eva nodded, and from a sling on her front, the woman produced a baby, apparently her own, and passed it over to her.

The baby was a girl, and watched her with unblinking eyes. Eva felt the warmth of the child through her wrappings, and sought to maintain it, turning away from the biting wind. Instinctively, Eva began to rock on the balls of her feet, and the young woman beamed a smile.

Sajhid appeared from around a corner, and in an instant, the young woman took her baby back, starting to usher the other children away. Some looked in fear at him. The young woman uttered a phrase in her direction and then hurried off.

"What did she say?"

Sajhid looked her over, making Eva feel very uncomfortable. "Warkhataa. Ao neshay shetana der khod. She said you have the mark of the Devil in you. Come, I have secured us a new car. One with windows. We have a long way to go."

Again the facetious observation. Eva's stomach had clenched at the words, and in her numb state, she followed along obediently. She no longer felt at peace.

The journey became a series of stages for Eva. In between towns, she attempted to question Sajhid, who either evaded her questions or ignored them entirely. He glanced at her in the rear view mirror when he thought she wasn't watching, gazing at her for longer and longer periods. She always knew.

Other than his lack of conversation, and when he did speak, in inappropriate tones, Eva could not pinpoint what was wrong. The flutter in her stomach continued; the baby in its fetal state was certainly energetic. It was the only real company Eva had and she took solace in that fact.

Towns slipped by and the names were fleeting memories. Tirgari, Nengarach, Sakopacha, Mangshar. All were faceless and full of people who probably suspected but in reality had no idea what was about to happen. They lived in innocence of the horrific truth Eva was burdened with. Children denied their future, parents their heritage. In an instant, it could all end.

At length they began to head west into a valley nestled against the mountains to the north. Ruins appeared to their left, remnants of recent conflict. A few concrete buildings appeared in the distance, squat and ugly against the majesty of the mountains.

"Kheyrabad," was all Sajhid would say. His face was haggard, but he would not hear any of it when it came to taking rest. He had driven them for a whole day. One day closer to Madden. One day closer to the apocalypse.

Sajhid spoke briefly to some locals, who directed him to

the local refuelling point. They had been running close to empty for a while. He saw to the petrol, and waved his hand in an indication he was getting a drink. From where Eva could not fathom.

She was left alone in the car. It was night and there was nobody about. The sense of unease had not lessened, and the same strange smell of iron permeated this car as it had the other.

Eva got out, looking for Sajhid. Nothing. She was completely alone. Presuming the answer to lie in the trunk of the car, she walked to the back and popped the catch. The lid sprang up and a waft of carrion assaulted her nose. A large object in the rear of the car was the cause of the stench. Flicking on her torch revealed dark stains everywhere, and the size of the object caused her to pause. It was about six feet in length, curled up. A man.

Leaning over to examine the body, Eva was careful not to touch it. He looked as though he had been torn apart from the tears and gashes in his middle. His head was at an irregular angle, his face fixed in a silent scream of horror. The blood was everywhere.

This confirmed what Eva had begun to suspect. Sajhid was not the driver. This man was. As she flicked the torch off, and closed the trunk, she thought back over the conversations they had had. He didn't really know anything about her and the others until she had supplied the information. His views on the attacks, the strange happenings. They were far too whimsical for somebody set against the evil that threatened to overwhelm them all.

She was still alone by the car, and for that, she was thankful. Now she only had one thought. Escape. This Sajhid was driving her where she wanted to go, but for a completely different reason.

Getting back in, the interior light showed her to have blood all over her hands. Taking a bottle of water, she rinsed them and wiped them off with some tissue. She cracked the door open to dispose of the evidence, and Sajhid was stood just outside. Eva screamed.

"Are you well?"

"I was freshening up. You startled me."

Eva wrapped the tissues in a bundle and tossed them nonchalantly to the foot well. "There's so much mess here I don't really think a couple of tissues will matter."

"Indeed. We shall sort out the mess soon enough." Sajhid got back into the driver seat and started the engine.

The journey from that point onwards for Eva was one of confinement. Sajhid drove too fast to allow her to jump out without serious injury, and as night faded and the sun began to rise, the early morning seemed that much colder for her predicament. She had no idea where they were driving, except Madden and her only hope of salvation were ahead.

The air inside the car was stifling, and as the day began to warm, Eva moved to open the window.

"I would not do that," Sajhid warned. "Accidents can happen when windows are open too wide. You should just leave it shut." He kept his eye on her, barely looking at the road.

At first, she stared back, but the whites of his eyes widened a little too much; it was clear now exactly what he was. Trapped, Eva began to lose hope. She would go where he wanted.

The road took them straight through several towns, and at each, Eva prayed for something to make them slow. There was nothing. Locals peeled off to one side of the road as soon as they heard the car approach, watching with uncaring eyes as they passed.

It was only when they reached the town of Feyzabad that an opportunity presented itself. An army checkpoint was placed square in the middle of the road, and Sajhid was forced to slow. Eva kept silent, slowly reaching for the obsidian dagger on the seat next to her. Once she had hold of it, she reversed the blade, hiding it under her arm, drawing it closer. Acutely aware of what would happen should she stab him, she saved that action for a last resort. If she could not get free, then everything was lost anyway.

Sajhid edged into the queue of traffic, his eyes not leaving Eva, searching for a sign of flight. Eva watched him back, and crossed her eyes. Sajhid blinked, and Eva was off.She threw the door open and jumped out. In an instant Sajhid was out following her.

"Help, I'm being kidnapped!" Eva screamed at the top of her voice. The soldiers from the checkpoint looked up and began to approach. Eva ran as though her heart would burst, but Sajhid was faster. Bounding after her, he tripped her and she went sprawling in the dust of the road, landing on her back as she sought to protect her baby.

It all happened in an instant. Sajhid dived to grab her, the soldiers raised their rifles, and Eva tightened her grip on the dagger. As Sajhid clambered above her, one of the soldiers fired a round, hitting Sajhid in the shoulder. He began to swell as the demon sought escape, above her the air chilled as a portal began to coalesce, and Eva thrust with the knife. As she did so, she heard Gila's scream from the checkpoint.

"Eva, No!"

CHAPTER FORTY

THE FIGHT ERUPTED ABOVE EVA, HER POSITION SPARING her from the worst of it. The dagger was embedded in the road, surrounded by ice. Of Sajhid or the portal there was no sign.

Gila knelt beside her. "Are you well? Can you move?"

Eva wriggled a bit. "Surprisingly so. I think most of the blast went over my head."

"Lucky you," commented Swanson, who had joined them. "Now you get to witness the after-blast party."

Eva sat up, her back stiff from the fall. "I don't get your meaning."

Gila helped her to her feet. "We learned a few facts about the dagger during our time apart..."

"LOOK!" Swanson pointed to a distant field to their right.

Everybody who could understand him turned. There was a shimmering above the ground, and the sound of marching. Bodies materialised, at first indistinct and as more and more appeared, with greater clarity.

"Gila?" Swanson asked.

Stepping away from Eva, Gila raised a small pair of binoculars. "Simple robes and a strange, almost conical helmet. Hoplite... Scaled armour with crested helmets. Peltast..." She dropped the binoculars to her chest and turned to them. "It is as we feared. That is part of Alexander the Great's Macedonian army, and there are many. We need to get out of here. Now."

In the distance, the ancient army milled as more and more appeared. The confusion was wearing off for some, and those dressed for command began to bark orders. The army began to take note of its surroundings. They became aware of the checkpoint.

"Come, we have a helicopter waiting at the airport." Swanson put his hand on Eva's shoulder, ready to lead her away. The army had begun to close the distance, the demonic element within each soldier ignoring all caution.

Eva didn't move.

"Eva, come," Gila urged.

"We can't go. We need the dagger."

"We will find another way. The dagger. It is what lets them through. There are portals opening up all over the region. This is the vanguard. This is Leviathan's army given a head start."

"No!" Eva threw herself forwards and took a rock to the ice around the knife. The ice was thick, grasping around the knife like a fist. Eva bashed until her arm ached and found she had hardly scratched it. The army began to run at them.

"Eva, back." Swanson used the tone of voice that brooked no argument.

She moved away, defeated. A single shot rang out and the ice shattered. She darted in and retrieved the dagger. There was hope yet, it seemed. The shot had the unfortunate side effect of acting as a clarion all for the army, who roared in response.

"Deal with this," Swanson ordered the soldiers at the checkpoint, who pulled out automatic weapons and took point ahead of them. "Come," he said to Eva. "You will be safer elsewhere."

Eva still did not move, staring into the myriad faces of death.

"Eva, you have seen enough. We need to be elsewhere."

Gila brought a Jeep beside them, and coming to her senses, Eva climbed in. They hurtled through the checkpoint and behind the soldiers fired into the army. Eva did not look back, but already she could feel the chill.

"We aren't preventing anything. Just moving soldiers from one army to another." Eva closed her eyes, trying to calm herself. From behind she felt a compulsion, one she had felt and resisted once before.

"Swanson, stop. We are out of danger. There is something more here. Something you should see."

The jeep slowed to a halt atop a rise in the road. Eva wordlessly held out her hand for the binoculars, and Gila handed them over.

Eva scanned the now-distant army. As she focussed the sighting, she could already smell the wafts of archaic dust overlaid with death. Then she spotted what she was after. There was no mistaking it. She handed the binoculars to Swanson.

"Off to the right of them," Eva advised.

"There's a blonde woman walking among them," He wondered aloud.

"Do you not feel it?" Eva urged them. "That hunger, that longing for fulfilment, that overriding obsession?"

"Surely you don't think..."

"You are right. I don't think. I know. I was there when a mob ripped apart a small child. She was there too. She carried the child to them. Swanson, you are looking at Belphegor, principal demon of lust, and she is leading the army. Evacuate whomever you can. These people will all soon be under her spell."

Swanson reached for his radio and left it hanging. Hells army had begun to engage with the soldiers, the staccato echo of gunfire bouncing off the mountainside. The army tore into them, devouring anybody in their path. Even from this distance, one could hear the screams.

Out of the corner of her eye, Eva sensed a distraction and turned. Another shimmering portal had appeared right beside them. Disoriented soldiers poured out, their eyes settling on the jeep alone on the road. In an instant, they charged.

"Go!" Gila screamed, and Swanson hit the gas.

Eva was thrown back into her seat, and grabbed hold of the cold metal frame of the car. Several of the forerunners made it as far as the car before it could accelerate away. Swanson knocked them down, the car jumping as it ran over one of the soldiers. Such was the will of Belphegor that their fellows began to rip into them even as the portals opened and tentacles reached through. By the time the demons had reached the chaos, they were out of harm's way and did not stop.

Swanson kept the speed up, paying no attention to comfort. They hurtled along the valley road towards a collection of buildings to the distant north. All around them, the sounds of battle rang out. Ancient versus modern.

"What's there?" Eva shouted, the wind muting her voice somewhat.

"Airport," Gila shouted back. "It's how we got ahead. Everybody knows about the apocalypse. Everybody knows it's in Afghanistan. A demon got on television. Revealed everything. The whole world is in chaos and it's all centered here!"

"But how..."

"Not here Eva." Swanson shouted over their conversation. "On the helicopter."

The distant buildings edged closer and for every minute they travelled, Eva felt the crescendo of chaos increasing. The only noise was the engine of the car being strained to its limits, but she imagined the clash of demons, the carnage they would be causing amongst the innocent Afghans.

When they reached the airport, it was surrounded by armed forces. Normal military spread in every direction, ARC commandos dotted amongst them. One approached the road and saluted.

"Ring of steel achieved, sir. There are reports of the enemy all over the countryside, including your destination."

The helicopter was already alive, rotors spinning as the pilot waited for passengers. Swanson drove the jeep right alongside and in the downdraft of the blades silently thumbed at the door to Eva.

She nodded, grabbed the dagger and climbed aboard. It was an old army helicopter, and the furnishings were Spartan at best. Still, Eva was thankful for the chance to escape and strapped herself in with green, frayed belts. Gila and Swanson were close behind, and the door was shut as soon as they were on board.

The engines whined and the rotors increased. At a signal from Swanson, Eva donned a large set of headphones.

"This will keep the noise out and allow us to talk," he shouted above the din.

Eva nodded and looked out of the window. They were only a few hundred feet above ground but already the Macedonians had begun to swarm. The ring of protection around the airport contracted and gunfire pierced the sound of the helicopter. Many demons were released as the hell spawn realised they were ineffective and they started bounding over fences and ripping the army to shreds. Many jumped up; trying to catch hold of the helicopter, but it was already too high. The battle grew smaller, and at great length, Eva turned away.

"Such a waste," she said into the microphone on the side of her headset.

"They knew what they signed up for," Swanson replied. "They know there is a bigger picture."

"What about the innocent? There are villages down there getting torn to shreds."

"That's why we tried to stop you using the dagger," Gila said, her eyes full of sympathy. "We learned from the Codex that it is a key. It uses blood to open a gate. The wrong blood and it causes annihilation and a random portal. The right blood, and it will open to wherever the wielder desires. This knife is the key to the Book of Revelations."

Eva looked down at the knife in her hands, as if it were an alien object.

"It's my fault," she said, devastated. "I stabbed the driver, and caused the army to appear.

"It gets worse, unfortunately." Gila placed her hand on

Eva's arm. "The correct blood is required to open the seals on the scroll. Somebody is going to die."

"And yet we still head toward the end?"

"What choice do we have? The only way to stop this for good is to open the portal and then close it, trapping hell spawn on the other side. We have forces in place all over this region. Once they are unleashed in a concentrated effort at the point of the portal, we believe we can push them back."

Eva stared at Swanson, trying hard to make sense of this mad plan. "That's it?"

He nodded his head. "It's the best we can do. The apocalypse isn't coming. It's already here. The portal is a formality. We were stuck trying to formulate a plan of attack when you took off for Doha. This is all over the world."

Gila handed her computer over and Eva watched scene after sickening scene as demon kind fought mankind's armies all over the world.

"This is the nexus. This is the place where the battle will be won or lost. We just need to get you there and safely, and right now, even that is a remote possibility. What is going on out there started thousands of years ago when Alexander The Great led his armies to conquer this region. The Codex says he was driven to do this by an unnatural desire for conquest. An unnatural desire? Does that seem like anything you have witnessed lately?"

"Belphegor."

"Your demon has been around a lot longer than you think, and has been sowing the seeds of chaos for millennia. She knew this was the place, and the slaughter that happened in this region was designed exactly because this is the place, and now is the time. We have a sanctuary that will keep us safe, but we need to get there."

"Why do I have the feeling we will not be alone when we do," Eva replied. Nobody could answer her.

They had been in the air for approximately an hour when the helicopter began to descend. Mountains rose around them in all directions, the valley into which they dropped being relatively flat and protected.

Eva was first to get out of the helicopter, being helped down by an ARC commando.

"Doctor Ross. In the Hummer, if you please," he instructed in a tone more of command than a polite request.

Eva climbed in, finding a seat amidst all manner of military equipment and all manner of weapons. Swanson and Gila followed, along with two more ARC commandoes.

"Is it that bad?" She asked one of the newcomers.

He looked at Swanson and received a nod of approval. "Worse, ma'am. What you saw in Fayzabad was a skirmish. There have been pitched battles in every valley from Kabul to the border with Tajikistan. The only advantage we have over their numbers is the fact that whenever we hit them, they get sucked through these freezing portals."

"We are so close to the event they are leaking through everywhere," Swanson confirmed.

Eva gripped the door hard as the huge vehicle surged forward. "And if the portal opens and we don't stop them, our only advantage will disappear. Can you hold on? We have a week until the eclipse. It's only going to get worse."

"We will have to." The commando tapped one of the rifles, a monstrous gadget with a grenade launcher under the barrel. "We have enough firepower to level these mountains, but can we last? The onslaught is becoming endless. If it is as Dr Guyomard has described and the forces arrayed against us are without limit, we may just run out of bullets. Still, we may last that long in the refuge."

Eva looked from the commando to Swanson. "Even now, keeping your cards close to your chest."

"Well if you consider your recent travelling companion, would you be surprised? Don't get me wrong, we are overjoyed you are still with us, but if we had laid it all out for you at the start..."

"Don't. We aren't there yet, wherever 'there' is."

"Good choice," approved their driver. "Hold on, please."

The reason for the cryptic comment soon became evident as the driver began to swerve the Hummer in both directions across the road. They were close to a river in full flow, and at times, it seemed to Eva she could almost reach out and touch the torrent. On the road ahead a ragged column of yet more Macedonians attempted to slow them. Swanson loaded one of the guns and began to take shots. It became clear the assault was headed in the other direction.

"Where are they going?" Eva shouted above the noise of engine and gunfire.

"Same place as us," Swanson replied before he fired another volley. "It appears our secret is out."

"What secret? There's nothing but mountains here."

They emerged from the road into a wide, shallow valley at the foot of the nearest ridge. The snow-capped mountains thrust imperiously into the sky, oblivious to all that was occurring on their flanks.

In front of them, Eva beheld an army of what could have easily been a thousand demons, spread randomly.

"Dear God. What are they all doing there?"

"Don't worry. They don't react quickly. Technology is beyond them." Swanson dialled a code into a walkie-talkie. "We have them. Open her up."

CHAPTER FORTY-ONE

THE HUMMER SHOT THROUGH THE ARMY, BATTERING several individuals to the ground as it did so. A dark hole opened up in front of them and the driver aimed the car straight for it, increasing the speed of the vehicle yet more. In an instant they were through, the darkness around them absolute but for a row of guiding lights in the roof ahead of them.

Eva turned to see doors sliding shut in the distance behind them, the army attempting to fight through but being denied by concentrated bursts of gunfire. The light from behind was replaced by an eerie glow Eva thought to be a portal at first. It turned out to be a spotlight from the Hummer. It highlighted the fact that the tunnel was not new. The walls were roughly-hewn, but the road was smooth tarmac. There was barely a vibration coming from the vehicle beneath her.

"You knew this was coming a lot earlier than recently," she accused Swanson.

He inclined his head in acceptance of that fact. "We had to

be prepared. This isn't the only focus in the world for demonic activity, as you have seen. Wherever there is the potential for portals to open, and that is many different places, hellbounces are spawning. If just one portal opens, a random spawning will become a flood to the current trickle. You hold in your hands the key to it all. As you demonstrated so effectively, that blade allows them to come into this world at will. If the wrong person gets hold of the knife, it will signal the end for us all.

Eva hefted the knife. "But this is the only bargaining tool we have to save Madden."

"You have to look past your feelings for him. View the facts dispassionately. Are you not a psychologist? Look at this through those eyes. He is a hellbounce. By all rights he should not be saved. He has committed sin. He is a demon. He should be sent back to where he belongs. If you give them the one bargaining chip we have that could end all of this, how then do we prevent the apocalypse?"

"He was sent back to where he belongs. With us. You cannot see that. He went with them to stop our slaughter, or do you not remember that small fact?"

"Eva, I'm very grateful for it. Now, either they were going to let us live because they wanted us to find the dagger, or they have something else in store for you. It is the latter that has me worried."

Eva let the conversation lapse to silence. Swanson was right. No matter how she looked at it, there was no other reality. But he was important, to them as much as her. The fact Swanson and Gila still remembered him was proof. He had touched all of their lives in one way or another. Hers with love, and theirs perhaps with guilt. By her estimation, they had six days to find an answer. If the scriptures were to be believed, God created the earth in such a time. If no solution presented itself, all his good work would be undone in the same amount of time.

The Hummer roared on for a good twenty minutes or so, with Eva estimating they must have driven a good ten or more miles under what she presumed was solid rock. Once they were away from the door, there was no immediate need for urgency. The tunnel began to widen and in places, there were small recesses manned by guards wielding all manner of unsavory weaponry.

Eventually it became impossible to see the walls of the tunnel beyond the limit of the Hummers lights. Eva looked down, and caught sight of lights below them.

"Where are we?" she breathed in wonder.

Swanson chuckled. "Somewhere mere mortals would fear to tread. When construction began in the eighties it was given the nickname 'Grail', for it would contain the ability to destroy or to preserve. The authority calls it 'Location AF three'. Lately, it has just been known as 'Tartaros'. Lights!"

Around them lights burst on. Eva stood, awestruck in silence. The cavern was huge. Across it, pillars of rock were encircled by manmade structures and walkways stretched between them. A group of buildings nested in one corner, and Eva realised what she beheld was at least ten stories high. Above it, the lights stretched off into infinity, small lifts moving in both directions. Eva began to notice people everywhere going about their business. The cavern carried an ancient smell, one that implied she had a long way to go to reach the surface.

She turned and saw the road they had come along retracting from the tunnel behind them. More gun turrets faced outwards but by all accounts, the chasm below would prevent anybody coming across.

"I think the word you are reaching for is 'wow'", Gila said from next to her.

"Have you seen this before?"

"No, but I was aware it existed. Tartaros, in case you were wondering, is a mythological abyss, a prison below the underworld. It is where the wicked were sent for torment."

Eva turned to Swanson. "Not without a sense of the dramatic, are you? The question that really bugs me is 'why?'"

Swanson waved the driver on, and in a moment, the Hummer had disappeared down another tunnel leaving only a lingering stench of diesel and the echoes of its growling engine.

"Preparation against the end. A secure facility with no chance of demon spawn entering. People have a habit of dying everywhere, especially those who live south of the acceptable moral and social standards. Here, we have created a place nobody could possibly enter by that means. No army of ancients, no demon foreman. It is secure. But beyond that, it is a weapon. This chamber has been hollowed out for one specific purpose. Containment. The entire ceiling is lined with explosives. If the assault fails outside, we shall blow the roof, and all any demon entering through a portal will see is empty air. They will fall until they hit the very roots of the mountain, at least ten thousand feet. If we do not succeed, you will not have to worry about being around to witness the end of man."

"A last strike," Eva wondered aloud. The majestic structure she stood under no longer seemed like a sanctuary to Eva, but rather a tomb. Dark, cold and eternal.

Gila took her arm. "Come. Let us get some rest. There is comfort to be found, even here."

Eva was led to the building, and though the concrete walls outside were cold, they reached a room following a short lift ride that at least looked comfortable. To Eva's pleasant surprise there was a window.

"What a view," she said as she looked out over the mountain range, down the flanks of the mountain where a river rushed with joyous abandon to join the watercourse below. Shadows clawed around them as the sun began to dip beyond the peaks above.

"Projected," Swanson advised. "We really are in the base of it all at the moment, and that particular window is a couple of thousand feet up. It helps maintain the illusion though, especially with the chill. The picture at least is live. It is early evening now. Come take some food and then you can get some rest. No demons here, Eva. Not for now."

After a meal that reminded Eva she was most certainly eating for two now, she took to her bed, leaving the dagger on a table across the room. Nobody was willing to speak to her regarding the upcoming events, so turning her back on the outside world as she saw it; she stared at the window on the mountain valley until it too grew dark.

Her sleep was fitful, and several times, she awoke in a sweat, recalling dreams of demon armies, and corpses reaching for her. Even her subconscious would not let her escape. The only relief was the being inside of her, bouncing happily against the confines of her womb.

When she did at last wake, feeling much better for the

rest in an immensely comfortable bed, she sensed something was wrong. Her first thought was to reach for her swelling abdomen, but a quick check showed everything was fine within. The only thing keeping her sane was the sense of calm exuded by her child from within.

The screen showing the mountains had switched off during the night, and as Eva sat up both it and the lights flicked on. At least the lights did. The screen showed the same valley, but everything had dimmed.

She checked the clock beside her bed, certain she had slept more than a few hours. The red digital numbers read '11:38 a.m.'.

"What the hell?"

Throwing on her clothes, Eva exited her room and was met by a scene of utter chaos. ARC operatives ran past her in both directions, many in various states of undress. Up and down the hallway red lights blinked in warning.

A large group of commandoes rushed past, and Eva thought she spied a familiar face.

"Janus? Janus!"

If it was him, her guide and protector through much of her journey stateside did not hear her or could not stop. Eva followed the group, hoping they would lead her to someone she knew. It worked. Everybody was mustering in a large room that appeared hewn from the bedrock of the mountain.

Eva began to circulate, seeking the face she was sure she had seen. The soldiers waited with admirable patience.

A hand touched her shoulder and she turned. It was Gila.

"You weren't in your room. You forgot this."

Gila handed her the dagger, the obsidian blade

reflecting the red warning lights as if drops of blood had already been spilled.

"What's going on?"

Before Gila could answer, the force around them came to attention with the sharp crack of heels on stone. Swanson and two other men walked onto a platform ahead of them. Swanson moved to the front.

"Brave soldiers of Tartaros, it appears we have miscalculated in our predictions. Our enemy has found a way to bring forward the celestial event and the time for action is now."

Despite their discipline, Eva sensed this was unsettling news. There was a slight shifting, an exhalation by all in the room. Gila's face was ashen.

"I will be blunt. We are undermanned. Only a thousand or so populate the sanctuary, where we hoped to bring in twenty times that number. Therefore, it is down to you, brave soldiers of 'Legion' to see this through. Up above, you know the enemy. You have all fought them over the past two weeks. If the portal is opened completely, their weakness disappears. Our goal is containment. They will not be allowed to leave this mountain, even if we have to blow it sky high.

Behind me, you see a map. It shows the demons atop this refuge. The concentrated red pulse indicates they are in one place, and there are a great many. At least as many as are here. Our strategy? Draw off the majority to the west while fifty of you accompany doctors Ciranoush, Ross, and myself to the portal where we shall attempt to close it. They will expect attack. You can only damage them before the portal opens fully. So make every shot count. It has been my honour to serve with you all. Every one of you makes me proud to die this day if that is what it takes. Anges de la

Résurection des Chevaliers never had a finer bunch of miscreants. May God guide your arm."

It began from the back, but within moments, every soldier was chanting the word 'ARC' over and over. The noise shook the very stone, vibrating into Eva's shoulder where she leaned against the wall.

"Time to go," Swanson said, as he reached them through the crowd of dispersing soldiers. "Follow me, please."

Eva fell in line alongside Gila, a column of the deadly looking commandoes in front and behind. It felt as though they were being herded to an execution. Nobody spoke. It was all happening too fast.

At the end of the hallway, Swanson held a caged door open for them, and they were squashed into a small room. The floor lurched and Eva realised they were in a lift. The cage slid noiselessly up through the building and out onto the roof where it did not stop, but continued up a scaffold structure attached to the wall of the cavern. Eva's legs began to turn to jelly as she saw the solid ground drop away beneath them. Except for the buffering of humanity about her, she knew she would have dropped to the floor.

After a tortuously long time in the darkness, the cage lurched to a halt, and with an immense relief, Eva found she was one of the first to exit the lift. The party moved down a narrow passageway lined with bricks, narrow lights dangling from the surface. Eva took a look around her and laughed.

"What is it?" Swanson asked.

"Déjà vu. I walked down a tunnel like this once before. If we get out of this with our lives, remind me to take you on a tour of a furnace in Alabama."

"Would that you could," Swanson replied with a

knowing smile. "Sloss was razed to the ground following your encounter there. It seems Iuvart was not pleased."

"What's he going to make of this then?"

Swanson did not answer, but walked in front, lost in his thoughts.

The air grew cold very quickly as the brickwork gave way to natural rock formations. Stalactites threw fanged shadows across the walls, giving Eva the impression she was walking into an enormous maw, gaping and hungry. The ceiling lowered, and stalagmites accentuated this impression.

As leaden as her feet were becoming, Eva plodded forward. Ice began to form on the walls, giving them a gleaming sheen, and making the footing treacherous.

Swanson stopped the party at a series of doors. Opening one to the right, he ushered them all in. A mound of thick parkas awaited them, thick lined and snug looking, and the outer layer of purest white. Across the room stood neat racks of weapons and ammunition.

The commandoes went straight for the guns. Eva picked out a coat and shrugged herself into it. The coat was so thick she could barely move, but she was warm. There were matching trousers and snow boots with grips. All went on.

"You look like a snowman," Gila chuckled.

"That makes two of us."

The commandoes had mostly donned thin suits of armoured white, but some also chose the parkas. Swanson had gone for the thin costume, looking somewhat out of place among the heavily armed contingent.

"When we get out of the cave ahead, we have perhaps a few hundred yards before they see us. If luck is with us, most of the forces will have been drawn off."

"And what do we do then?" Eva asked, clueless as to her role in all of this.

"One way or another, we end this. Are you ready?"

"I'm a pregnant woman on a mountainside trying to kill a Prince of demons with a knife..." Eva said no more and led the way out into the cave.

CHAPTER FORTY-TWO

DESPITE THE ONCOMING ECLIPSE, STILL THE OPENING to the mountaintop shone as bright as day, in itself a portal to an icy hell. Eva waited until the last possible moment, when all of the squad were in the cave, before stepping forward.

"Strength, Eva." Gila whispered in her ear. "For your child."

Eva nodded and took the first fatal step towards a perceived oblivion. Keeping the dagger tucked up her sleeve, the hilt reversed and resting in her palm inside thick white fur, she crossed the threshold.

Outside, the morning was already dim. The wind howled about them, numbing what skin Eva had exposed in an instant. The sky was clear, yet the perceived eclipse had only just begun. Making room for the troops behind her, Eva just stared.

In the distance, the entire horizon had the pearlescent sheen of a sheet of ice.

"You see that?" She asked of Swanson. "What is it?"

He stood for a moment, dumbstruck by the enormity of

the vision. "I have no idea. But it looks like Iuvart isn't the only one planning to open a portal. One problem at a time."

Their path took them south, just below the peak of the ridge. From here, in stark contrast to the horror in the sky, the Hindu Kush mountain range stood out in beautiful and obdurate defiance.

Above them to their right, sounds of gunfire began to shatter the morning light. Roars of rage met the guns and the battle upon them. The occasional breath of piercing cold air showed the demons were still vulnerable as the portals sprang into life. And the sky darkened.

As the party followed the trail, the sounds of battle moved off to the west.

"Well that worked," Swanson said in a low tone. "Let's push on." He held his hand out to one side, clenching his fist. At the prearranged signal, the commandoes readied their weapons with a series of muffled clicks.

"It gets easy now," he whispered to her. "Altars, inter dimensional portals, horrors you have never before seen. Courage. Courage to us all."

They rounded a small rise to be confronted with what Eva could only perceive to be a void in the air at the end of the ridge.

"That is enormous," she breathed, mesmerised. "That's got to be at least a hundred feet across."

The portal swirled lazily, as if a slow whirlpool had been tipped onto its side. The scenery behind was distorted as it rotated. In front, a stone altar had been erected, and on it, a figure knelt within arm's length of the threshold. Behind it, perhaps two dozen others knelt in a series of rows. All were chanting.

There was only one object of Eva's search. She scanned the scene, ignoring the threshold to oblivion. There was a body slumped to one side of the altar. And the sky darkened.

"Madden!" Eva called without thinking, and the chanting stopped.

Madden raised his head, peering at her through blood-encrusted eyes. "Eva?"

The figure on the altar stood and turned. "Yes, my pet. Doctor Eva Ross. Come to this sacred place at the appointed time exactly as was foretold."

"Gideon?"

There was a low chuckle, emanating from the dark creature on the altar. "Come now, you know that name was never me. Gideon was a dream, a fantasy. My true name is Iuvart. You may call me death."

Iuvart stood to his full height, somewhere between six and seven feet tall, unfurling scabrous leather wings from his back, which stretched either side of him, the skin creasing as it caught on knuckles of bone within. He raised his arms, and as before, in the wadi, the mountain ridge was covered in dark shadows, semblances of a tortured and corrupted humanity.

Swanson turned to the commandoes, who had already prepared to fire. "Lower your weapons. We can't win this way."

"You can't win any way, little mortal. It is too late. The portal began to open the instant you brought her onto the mountain. Now all you have left before an eternity of torment is to witness the end of days."

Iuvart moved towards Eva, his eyes glowing red in the gloom. Above her, the moon blocked more of the sun's rays, and the temperature dropped. He reached out, and ran his hand over the front of her parka, pausing over her abdomen.

"Ahh. The seed of the demon is in your loins. This one will be powerful."

The phrase sent chills down Eva's spine. "I will die before I lose anything on the world that sides with you."

Iuvart moved his hand, black skin tipped with red nails, away from her stomach and down her arm. Gripping the end of her sleeve, he ripped the dagger from her grip, the blade slicing clean through the arm of her coat. He held it aloft, blade reversed in his hand, tip pointing down towards his head, and the demon minions roared.

"You are correct in one way. You will die, but only when I am done with you. Only when I am done with you both." He turned to Madden, still crumpled in a heap behind him. "Rise, my pet. Come stand with your beloved."

The shadowed masses of the twelve damned tribes herded the ARC army into place in front of the altar. Madden, as if strung up like a marionette, rose and approached. His face was screwed up in agony. He still held the case with the scroll, and his hands were blistered and weeping. His face appeared distended, but the demon within could not escape.

Iuvart ran one finger under his jaw, tipping Madden's face up towards him. "No, tiny demon. Not until it is done."

He turned to the portal, and began to shout in victory.

"As foretold, the Lamb, the child of David, has brought the sacred blade to us in this place, that we may summon you, our brethren, into this realm. And with this scroll, will the Lamb bring forth an eternity of night, a degenerate sanctuary for us all."

Behind them, the demons roared in anticipation. Eva turned her head to see the shadowed masses departing over the ridge to join the hunt for the ARC army. Iuvart was certain of his victory, and she had no idea what to do.

Two of the demons grabbed her from behind, lifting her to the altar and holding her in place, her arms stretched to either side. She tried to wriggle free, but their strength far outshone her own. Muscular and slobbery, with grimaces of massive disproportion, they eyed her as a cat would a mouse. There was no mistaking the future in store for her when she looked one in the eyes.

"Place the scroll on the altar," Iuvart commanded Madden.

Weeping, he put the bag down and opened it. As he reached in he began to scream, a sound of such agony it made his throat hoarse, but still he did not cease. The scroll made his fingers burn, and they began to go black by the time he had placed the scroll in a groove beneath her right arm. Hands ruined and clawed with tight skin, Madden stepped back, his head hanging in defeat. Despite everything, they faced the end.

Iuvart waived the knife in front of her, threatening her. He then proceeded to cut her coat from her body. Saying nothing more, he pressed the tip of the blade into the flesh of her arm, just below the elbow. Eva screamed in pain, but Iuvart ignored her and carved a symbol.

Quickly he was finished, and stood back to admire his handiwork.

"A Star of David. Significant I think a descendent of the tribe that saved the world so long ago should now be used to destroy it. Watch. Watch your world's end unfold Eva. Watch as terrors beyond the deepest depravity of your twisted dreams appear before your eyes, longing to feast on your flesh. But they won't. You belong to my master, and with his ascension to this realm, you and your child become his playthings. Leviathan, Demon King of the earth!"

Iuvart began to giggle, and Eva turned her head away.

The moon was almost completely across the sun now, giving the diamond ring effect. The frigid air washed over her. She tried to get Madden's attention, but her throbbing arm brought her gaze back to the altar.

The blood was flowing freely, running down channels in the stone, forming complex symbols as it made its way to the scroll. Eva watched in silence, willing the blood to clot. It did not. Eva tried to remember the Book of Revelations. There were horsemen.

The blood reached the scroll, which began to glow. After a few seconds, it shot a beam of deepest red straight at the center of the portal, which changed colour to match. Flames licked the outer edge of the threshold. Up above, the distant sheen of ice had begun to coalesce, stretching forth as a tornado would when it sought the ground.

"You aren't alone," she taunted, willing Iuvart to do something unplanned. "Your plans are about to come to fruition and yet you will fail anyway."

Iuvart stepped away, looked at the descending ice, and grinned. "Unholy rapture. It needs a few more participants."

The blood reached the first seal, which melted away. The portal boomed, and from the darkness within emerged a creature of nightmare which must have been three times as high as Iuvart. Of purest white was the beast, with the head and body of a horse, but from the back emerged the upper half of a heavily muscled humanoid. Both roared.

Eva turned her head, screwing her eyes shut as tight as she possibly could. Iuvart grabbed her hair in a clenched fist and forced her back.

"Behold the first of the four sentinels, Eva. As much as the damned creature in your womb, these are your children made flesh by your own blood. Watch as your life becomes theirs."

Her blood touched the second seal and it too melted away. The portal pulsed, and a red horror much akin to the first stepped through. It too roared, reaching out with an enormous sword to touch the wound on her arm, causing red-hot pain as it pressed the blade home. The humanoid part of the beast ran its tongue along the blade, shuddering with apparent pleasure, as it tasted her blood.

Two more seals melted away, and the portal's activity increased. The vortex wound faster, flickers of red and yellow replacing the view of the distant horizon behind. Two more beasts appeared, black and a pale yellow. All four stood on the altar, rearing with impatience, stamping hooves on the stone beneath.

"Sentinels, guardians of the gate," Iuvart announced. All four regarded him. "Our ancient enemy seeks to use our triumph to enter this realm. Go forth and do war upon him!"

The hell beasts roared, and leapt into the sky, brandishing weapons. They headed straight for the funnel of ice, swarming about it as they attacked. There was a hiss from the funnel, a noise filled with hunger and ancient malice. The ice stopped growing.

The blood touched the fifth seal of the scroll. Wisps of white began to emerge from the portal floating whimsically through the air until they touched the shadows. Where they did this shadows no longer remained, but instead demons, pure and evil, not agonised and bound to mortality, stood. And they hungered.

"Eva!" Swanson yelled from behind her. "Do you see what he is doing? Can you see what is happening? The twelve tribes! THEY are the vanguard of Hells army! They are here now! You have to stop them or we all die!"

Strung out between the demons, Eva could do nothing more than turn her head, trying not to distract Iuvart who paced ahead of her; she was desperate to plead with Madden to move.

The blood reached the sixth seal, and it vanished. The scroll pulsed, and the portal responded, swirling faster and faster, the motion pulling at Eva as air was sucked into the abyss. The sky plunged into darkness as the eclipse reached totality. The whole mountain began to shake as the vibration from the portal increased.

"Holy day!" Iuvart crowed. "Now you will witness my triumph!"

The portal span at a frenzied pace, and a beam of light shot from it, reaching heavenward, turning the moon red. As the noise increased and Eva felt herself screaming unheard, the portal changed. The spinning stilled, and became a window.

Beyond, the horizon reached off into infinity. There were distant mountains beneath a sky of flame. The foreground could have been a grassy field except for the fact everything was a sinister bloody red. In the distance waited an army, the numbers limitless. It began to move forward, and with every step, the mountain shook. Heat from the portal began to sear her face.

Iuvart turned towards her, almost a silhouette in front of the oncoming nightmare. "A little gift for you, Eva. You get to see your lover's end."

Iuvart picked up Madden with one hand and plunged the obsidian blade into his shoulder. "Behemoth, I summon thee!"

There was a roar from the portal. In the distance, the

army had stopped. As Eva watched, the portal was filled from within by an enormous head. Two enormous horns rose like a crown atop baleful red eyes, a mouth full of fangs as long as Eva's arm. Shoulders hulked behind, covered in black fur. Muscles strained as the creature climbed through the portal, standing nearly the entire height of the aperture. It raised clawed hands to the sky and bellowed in triumph.

The demons flesh began to cower. The shadowed masses scattered. This released the ARC soldiers, who stood their ground.

"Containment!" Swanson ordered. "Defensive formation. Eva, I'm sorry." He pulled out a transmitter and pressed a button. For a moment, he appeared confused.

"It won't work, mortal," Iuvart gloated. "We have planned this far too long for your technology to interrupt us now." He turned to look up at the beast, who watched Eva, slathering, and trembling with repressed hunger. "They are yours, great one. Feast on their flesh!"

Behemoth bounded off the altar, and in an instant, the soldiers were on the attack. She closed her eyes as screams filled the darkness, the monster being drawn off in the same direction as the rest of the army as it sought to feed.

The demons holding her had fled with Behemoth, either terrified for their own existence, or joining in the slaughter. In the distance, Eva heard the roars, and they were of pain and frustration as much as they were triumph. At the altar Madden slumped, the dagger protruding from his shoulder. Iuvart watched the approaching army, transfixed.

"All my plans came to fruition. Can you see, master? Everything your brother could not do, I could. That is worthy of a place at your side as a brother is it not? When the blood touches the final seal, the sacrifice is yours. The

Earth is yours. Sanctuary is yours."

Iuvart turned to watch the blood seeping along the scroll. On the other side of the portal, the armies awaited the breaking of the final chain. The host began to part as a solitary figure strode forward.

"Behold my Lord, Leviathan," Iuvart shouted above the noises of battle from one side and anticipation from the other. "All your hope is lost."

The blood reached the seventh and final seal. Eva closed her eyes, awaiting the inevitable and nothing happened.

Iuvart regarded the scroll. The blood was touching the seal, and just flowing past. "That cannot be!"

Madden stood, and with his free arm, pulled the dagger from his shoulder. He flung the dagger past the portal, where it scraped and skittered over the stone until it came to rest on the far side. In the darkness, the red glow showed a figure picking up the blade.

Iuvart's face was one of utter disbelief. He looked at her "You have denied me. What have you done?" Iuvart reached over and yanked the burned remains of Eva's tattered shirt down over her shoulder. The incomplete birthmark glowed red in the sooty light. "Where is it? Where is the sixth point?"

"Always do your research thoroughly, Gideon. Is that not what you used to say?"

Comprehension dawned rapidly. He had made a mistake. "You are not the one. Your child. I shall rip it from your womb. There be no stopping me! Blood is blood!"

Iuvart reached towards her, and a confused look spread across his face. A glint of light reflected across his chest, and Eva realised it was the obsidian blade protruding through.

He turned to his left and Eva saw a figure behind had him in a death grip.

"Iron he treats like straw and bronze like rotten wood. What about glass?" The figure twisted his arm and the dagger cut deeper. Iuvart screamed in pain.

"Eva, take the scroll and throw it to me," the shadowed man commanded.

Eva did as she was told, and the scroll, light still shining from it, was caught midair and pocketed. The light showed the face of her one-time companion.

"Janus?"

Iuvart turned his head, catching a glimpse of his killer. "You. It cannot be."

Janus smiled, and yanked Iuvart's head down. "Let's take you home."

Janus pushed Iuvart to the threshold of the portal. Madden had come to stand by Eva, his left arm hanging useless at his side. "Janus, throw him through. You don't have to do this. There must be another way."

Janus regarded them both for a second. "There is no other way. There is only fate. Remember me, my friends."

Throwing Iuvart's dying body ahead of him, Janus jumped into the portal, and the world went dark.

CHAPTER FORTY-THREE

THE DARKNESS WAS ABSOLUTE FOR JUST A MOMENT. Long enough for Eva to lose her bearings. A keening began, just a whisper at first, growing to a high-pitched wail. Impressions of form began to intrude upon the blackness, and with each that passed her, a sense of pulling. At first, it was only from the disturbances, but gradually there was a sucking from in front of her.

"Madden, the portal. It's collapsing. We did it!"

There was no answer from beside her where Madden had stood. The motion increased, the wail becoming a roar. Eva had no choice; if Madden was within hearing distance she could only hope he had made it safely away. But his wound was severe.

"Madden!" Eva screamed until her throat went hoarse. There was no reply, and she was now getting bumped. More light appeared as the eclipse ended, and in the second dawn that day she made her way off the ridge, heading south away from the portal.

Out of the path of the debris, Eva felt the cold intrude

on her being, her burned face raw in the wind. She would not last long in this frigid air. Despite this fact, she turned to watch.

A funnel had formed at the entrance of the portal, and was sucking everything in. Behind, the funnel began to extend out as the volume of matter increased in intensity. The four sentinels, still at war with the ice, faltered, getting dragged back. But there was more. Shapes not unlike the spirit forms of the twelve tribes started appearing from every direction. Hellbounces, demons, all were sucked in. Some were dashed on the mountainside and the resulting ice portals were absorbed by the energy of the collapsing rift.

The howling continued and the portal grew smaller. A roar equal in measure to that of the wind announced the recall of Behemoth to Hell, but the monster was torn apart in the contracting rift. The bodies continued to be sucked in at an alarming rate, and Eva forgot her discomfort as she wondered at just how many demons were already on earth.

At length the portal was reduced to the size of the ice portals, and the noise abated. Mere moments later it flickered out. Daylight returned, bathing the mountain in the sun's bright glow. The ice in the distant sky had disappeared.

Not wasting any time, Eva stumbled up the rocks to try to find shelter. A bloodstained parka was the first thing she found, and, ignoring the blood, she put it on.

She climbed back up to the site of the altar to find it was all gone. The ridge was clear, scoured clean of altar, demons, even snow. There was one bundle in a heap near where the portal had been. Eva hurried to it, desperation in every fiber of her being. There was a mop of brown hair and blood pooling off to one side.

"Madden!"

She rolled him over and checked his vitals. There was a pulse. Slow, but steady. He was in the early stages of hypothermia. Eva began to take her coat off to cover him, but a hand on her shoulder prevented her.

"Don't," said Swanson from behind. "We have this covered. You have to keep the child warm."

Eva allowed herself to be helped up, and hugged Swanson once she was standing. She kissed him on the cheek. "You were so brave. All of you."

The ARC soldiers who had avoided Behemoth and had accompanied Swanson back, smiled or nodded. She did not know them, but felt a connection, a sense of kinship, with each of them.

"I think I speak for everyone here when I say running from a monster and firing a gun pales into insignificance compared to staring into the face of hell and retaining ones wits."

"No, there was one braver. Janus sacrificed himself to see the scroll taken to a place where it was rendered useless. In the end, contrary to your beliefs, I was not the one, well not quite. The seventh seal did not open and the portal collapsed."

Swanson took a moment to absorb this information, then looked at her, confused. One of the soldiers thrust a steaming cup of hot coffee into his hands, and then did the same for Eva.

"Janus? I don't remember any of our operatives having that name."

"But he was a test subject in the States. He followed us. He saved me. He saved Madden. But for him we would never have made it out of Sloss. He was here in the sanctuary. He stabbed Iuvart with the knife and took it, the scroll and Iuvart through the portal. More than that, Iuvart knew him."

"Strange. I have never come across that name. I will look into it, but he sounds like your guardian angel."

"An angel wrote the codex..." Eva mused aloud.

Gila appeared in the distance, being helped by one of the soldiers. Eva ran to her, and the two hugged.

"I am so relieved you made it." Gila said. "Madden. Is he alive?"

"Over there," Eva pointed in the direction of the knot of soldiers. "He's unconscious, but he lives."

There was a ripple of commotion from the soldiers, and one stood up.

"Doctor Ross, you had better come here."

"Oh no," Eva said, fearing the worst. She approached her lover every bit as hesitantly as she had traversed the ridge. When she squeezed past the wall of operatives, Madden lay on a stretcher, his eyes open.

Eva knelt beside him, stroking his face. "How do you feel?"

"Like I've been to Hell and back. Eva, my shoulder throbs like you wouldn't believe, and my hands are all but useless, yet I feel different. The demon. It's gone. I can't feel the pain, the torture of being here. Everything is normal."

"Maybe it got sucked out of you when the portal closed."

Swanson's supposition got them all thinking.

"Every demon we met commented on how weak it was," Eva agreed. "But that is for another day. What say we get off this mountain before we all freeze?"

Madden tried to get up but Eva pressed him back onto the stretcher. "Not a chance, loverboy. You are staying right there. Let somebody carry you. I will be right beside you."

The party moved off, heading back towards the doorway they had used. As Eva walked past the ARC soldiers, each saluted, or offered words of congratulations.

"They know true courage when they see it." Swanson said as Eva gave him a questioning glance. "A lot of good men and women died on this mountain to ensure you had a chance at saving the world, and you did not disappoint. News spreads quickly, and the news is victory. If they weren't ARC operatives, I swear you would have your own private army right now if you so decided."

Eva laughed. "Too many mouths to feed. I only intend to worry about one extra." Madden took her hand as she walked. "Well, maybe two."

Swanson reached across and shook Madden's free hand. "You have been granted a second chance at life. Use it wisely. Treasure her and your child when it comes."

"I intend to," Madden said, wincing as the muscles in his shoulder pulled. "But where do we go?"

"Somewhere quiet. Somewhere safe." Eva said.

"I have the ideal place," Swanson offered. "I know a lovely little cottage in Sweden. It's off the beaten track. You will love it. When the time comes, there is a very good hospital only a few miles away."

Eva eyed Swanson with suspicion, her smile giving away the mockery in her voice. "Knowing you lot, the hospital will be right under my feet." She turned again to Madden. "If you aren't going to be a demon any more, you can help put things to right by being a father."

"Only if you will aid my recuperation by becoming my wife."

"We'll see," Eva said in response. She smiled, but could not speak any more, so overcome with love for Madden. She was the warrior who had faced the demons and won. She had stared into the abyss, and seen what was really down there. It was too soon to tell them. Eva swore to enjoy every minute of life she could.

EPILOGUE

THE MOUNTAINSIDE WAS STILL. IT WAS ONLY A DAY after the titanic events that had threatened to turn the earth into a paradise, a haven for his kind. They had come so close, but the instrument had miscalculated. Now they faced battle without reprieve.

Asmodeus stood in the howling wind, his blonde hair whipping about his face. Above him, the rift to Hell had opened, and would never do so again, not in this place. He thrust his hand into the new-fallen snow and retrieved a knife, the conchoidal fractures of the glassy blade glinting in the daylight.

His raptor gaze scanned the horizon, and he tightened his grip on the hilt. "One day."

Dear reader,

We hope you enjoyed reading *Hellbounce*. Please take a moment to leave a review in Amazon, even if it's a short one. Your opinion is important to us.

https://www.nextchapter.pub/authors/matthew-harrill-horror-author-bristol-uk

Want to know when one of our books is free or discounted for Kindle? Join the newsletter at

http://eepurl.com/bqqB3H

Best regards,

Matthew W. Harrill and the Next Chapter Team

ABOUT THE AUTHOR

Matthew W. Harrill lives in the idyllic South-West of England, nestled snugly in a village in the foothills of the Cotswolds. Born in 1976, he attended school in Bristol and received a degree in Geology from Southampton University. By day he plies his trade implementing share plans for Xerox. By night he spends his time with his wife and four children.

http://www.matthewharrill.com/

BOOKS BY THE AUTHOR

The Arc Chronicles

Hellbounce, Book 1

Hellborne, Book 2

Hellbeast, Book 3

The Eyes Have No Soul

Lightning Source UK Ltd.
Milton Keynes UK
UKHW020646040221
378234UK00014B/1300